KAI

IN HARM'S
WAY

by HUGH RUSSEL

Cover design: Hugh Russel
Hugh Russel's portrait by Denni Russel Photography

Published February 25, 2020
Library and Archives Canada
Paperback ISBN: 978-0-9916766-5-1
e-Book ISBN: 978-0-9916766-6-8

For information about this and other books by Hugh Russel Contact Negative Space Publishing:
email: negative.space.publishing@gmail.com

for Cheryl, Denni and Nicole

Acknowledgements

Family first, I must thank Cheryl my wife, and partner of over 50 years, who has worked with me from the beginning of my stop-gap career in radio, throughout my long career as a sculptor, and now as I concentrate on my writing. Cheryl reads and comments (with brutal honesty) on everything I write and much of what I say. She does the initial read through and finds all (or almost all) of my spelling mistakes and counters my rants with reality. She also has a thing against inappropriate commas. I like 'em by the way ... but she deletes them anyway.

My parents read almost every draft, of every story I ever wrote, and I've written a bunch of them over the years. They always commented and critiqued (unbiasedly of course) and never complained. Thanks also to my son Denni, a fantastic photographer, teacher, and writer who is always ready to discuss books, writing, and art with me and my amazing daughter Nicole, her encouragement, curiosity, boundless energy and creativity are inspirational.

Editors Martha Sharp, and Nathanial G. Moore worked with me as I began developing the character Kat Fernando and brought me closer to my goal.

Tony Hillman, my old school chum and his wife Di, have been a source of inspiration for years and Tony's support, advice, and humor have been tremendously entertaining. After he read a very early draft, I asked him if he thought my writing was any good. He quipped, "I've read worse books." At the time I thought that was high praise. Then after reading endless versions of this and other stories over the years eventually begged me to ... "Stop! I can't take it anymore." He hasn't read this manuscript though, so he'll have to buy the book like everybody else. Despite his objections, I will be sending him drafts of my new work soon.

Nancy Frater, a dear friend is the owner of Booklore an award-winning independent book seller in Orangeville, Ontario, my all-time favorite bookstore. Her help and encouragement as I wrote this series has been awesome. She does it purely for the love of books, writers, and readers. Nancy is truly a national treasure.

Thanks to my test readers, Susan Brown, Knut Holmsen and Frances MacFarlane, for their comments. And to my favorite pub master, Anna Alonzo, who some years ago asked if I would give her a copy of my first book the moment it was published. She'll get one for sure.

And a very special thanks to our Thai Che coach and dear friend Evelyn Fotheringham, who volunteered to proof read and did such a careful job detailing my errors on the back of a book mark and several scraps of paper. And to Tony Reynolds for questioning me on my abbreviations and spotting all the punctuation errors (including commas - Cheryl) I made after I thought I was done. Tony is a very understanding friend who has been putting up with me since the beginning of my radio days in Toronto almost 50 years ago. He was a copy writer then with CFRB/CKFM writing the commercials and patiently (?) listened to me mess them up as I read them in the recording studio. He has taken on the task of being my punctuation guru and so far, has read almost everything I've written. He and Evelyn were pressed into service at the last minute and really came through for me. Thank you both.

KAT

IN HARM'S WAY

Forward

The other day, Cheryl was entertaining her book club out on the veranda and, as luck would have it, one of her friends brought her husband David along. He and I passed the time talking about politics and art. Eventually our conversation got around to the subject of writing. When I'm writing, in my mind I see the story playing out like a movie. We can all visualize familiar things. But if we had never seen the thing or the person, it's not easy and perhaps impossible to form a mental picture. I have a slight case of OCD, so when I'm thinking about something that doesn't exist, I often spend a great deal of time drawing it. That way I will be able to maintain some consistency when describing it in the story. Currently, I'm writing a story set in the near future with a strong SiFi element. There are next-gen aircraft, space vehicles and architectural elements that need to be fully developed in order to write about them accurately. Eventually I come up with interesting 3-D designs and I like to show them to people.

David came down to my office to see some of the CGI, aka Computer-Generated Images, I'm creating using an architectural design program and Photoshop. As we talked about them, he asked if I would include the drawings in the book. "No," I said, "it's not going to be a graphic novel." Undaunted, he went on to say, "It would be interesting to see how others perceive the people and things you write about." On that point I had to agree.

Then, really getting into it, he said, "It would be an interesting experiment, don't you think?" "Uh huh," I said. He pushed on, "So, why don't you ask them?" At first it sounded a bit like, 'What I did last summer,' that make-work project the grade (3-8) teachers asked us to write or draw. It took me a while (days) to process it but then I thought why not? It would be fascinating to find out how you see Kat's world and the cast of characters.

Fiction is all about playing the story back in your imagination. OK, allow me to emphasize that this was David's idea. If you enjoy Kat In Harm's Way and I'm sure you will, and if you are going to play along, imagine that you are going back to school and have some fun with it. Show me what you picture when you are reading the book and send it to me. Pick anyone from the book, the protagonist or the villain, or if you prefer, show me some characters taking part in any action scene. This is just for fun, so if you're not an artist don't worry about it. You could even send me a photo of someone who comes close to how you see the character. A pencil drawing would be great, ink would do too, I used to draw with a ballpoint pen in art school. Do it in color if you've got nothing else to do during COVID. But I'll leave the method and medium up to you. Scan it, and save it as a .jpg, .tiff, or .pdf. and paste it to your email. Sorry, because of possibility of spreading a computer virus the publisher says they will not open attachments (and yes, there are other viruses out there apart from COVID)

It is not a contest, there is no entry fee, no entry form, no panel of judges, no pressure, and, especially, no prize. I ask that you give me written permission to use the images in the event that I decide to turn the responses into a book. Also, I am not eliciting, nor do I want pornographic depictions of any sort. It will be interesting to see what you see. Email your picture to my publisher, and they will forward it to me. Send it to:

negative.space.publishing@gmail.com
Coming up next in the Katrina Fernando Series

To Kill Kat
The House Kat
The Kat Came Back

Prologue

Inglewood, Los Angeles County, July 9, 1975

Katrina hadn't had time to deal with the shock of losing her father before she began living with her uncle. She was a happy child, loving and loved. It was always fun to do things with her father, helping with the housework had been a game. That first moment with his brother Ernesto made her realize that the games were over and the tragedy of being orphaned wasn't the end of the hardships coming her way. With him she lost her childhood, her freedom, and eventually her innocence as well.

Part 1

1

HIGHWAY OF DEATH

February 25, 1991, Highway 80, North of Safwan, Iraq

Cpl. Katrina Fernando had no choice, the great plumes of smoke blotted out the sun and now visibility was down to less than twenty-five meters. They'd been on the road for hours and if it wasn't for her wristwatch she couldn't say for sure if it was day or night. She had to stop the convoy and dig in. Not only was she nearly blinded by the smoke, it burned, and the toxic air felt like she was inhaling granular tar. With every painful breath she took, her gut told her that this was not going to end well.

Alone and sweating in her foxhole, she wondered why she was here. Yesterday she'd been a translator for Desert Storm's Multinational Coalition in Dhahran. Now, she was armed to the teeth in full battledress, leading a convoy of trucks carrying jet fuel up to the front.

She was the corporal, the only NCO on this detail, so these five male recruits had become her squad, a squad of mystery-trolls spread out in foxholes behind her.

She had their names, but she'd never seen them before and didn't know anything about them. She sure as hell didn't know if she could trust them and that made her nervous.

Especially that Redmond guy she thought. She peered over her shoulder as if she could see him but he was on the far side behind the back of the convoy.

As if Redmond wasn't bad enough, there were Iraqis lurking out there in the inky black, like the Zombie Army of the Apocalypse. She was surrounded by men and as far as she knew most of them wanted to kill her.

They called this the Highway of Death, and Kat couldn't argue with that. She was heading north to feed the hunter-killers, the Apaches helicopters and A-10 Thunderbolt Warthogs and from what she'd seen on the road behind her, calling them hunter-killers nailed it.

The Iraqi soldiers stole everything they could get their hands on when they ran from Kuwait City. They loaded their loot into tanks and battle buggies, stolen trucks, buses and cars and headed for Basra. Then, to add to their sins, they tried to cover their escape by setting the Kuwaiti wells and oil lakes ablaze. Hundreds of them. They thought it would blind their pursuers. It was nasty, totally ridiculous, and completely goddamn pointless.

She looked up at the smoke that rose over a hundred meters into the sky. Toxic ash fell like black snow, and those poor bastards couldn't see those hunter-killers bearing down on them. But that wasn't a problem for the American pilots. They were kids who grew up playing video games and treated this war as if it was a life-size version of River Raid. Down there the Iraqis were just images, avatars they picked up on their targeting systems. Now Iraqi bodies littered the highway, stacked like cordwood behind the burned-out vehicles.

For all Kat knew this wasn't Iraq anymore. Somewhere back there she'd crossed over from the Twilight Zone into Hell.

The first watch was hers. Pilgrim, her co-driver, was sleeping in his hole twenty meters away. When she pointed her flashlight at him all she could see was the crown of his sand colored helmet.

After a couple of hours with Pilgrim she counted him as a dead loss. As far as she could tell Lee and Harding weren't much better but Dempsey was different. He was quiet and he was the only one who seemed to know what he was doing.

She looked out into the black for any signs of movement, but it was no use, she couldn't see a thing.

She remembered what Pilgrim had said when she asked him about Redmond. Steer clear of that bastard he told her. Redmond had said he wasn't takin' no orders from no wetback Mexican whore.

She shook her head and sighed.

Whore, always their fallback. Why are guys always such assholes?

A breeze carried the toxic gunk right into her face and made her lose her train of thought, her eyes stung like they were on fire. Desperate for some relief, she started looking for the tiny bottle of eye drops. She was getting angry pulling things out of every pocket. "Jezzus, where did I put the goddamn thing?"

Then a fingertip touched the tiny bottle in her knee pocket. "Finally, there you are," she said aloud, as her hand wrapped around the familiar container. She had a quick look around, then leaned back, and squeezed in some drops. Letting the cool liquid dribble down her cheeks she shut her eyes for a moment enjoying the relief.

I'm going to go crazy out here.

With the barrel of her rifle resting on the foxhole's berm and the stock pressed into her shoulder, she draped her arm over the rail, took a deep breath and rested her chin on her arm. She looked across at Pilgrim again.

Shit, he's still asleep. How long have I got till I get some shut eye? She looked down at her watch, 0130. Aw Jezzus Key-ryst, another half hour. I swear to god I'm going to fucking die out here.

The next fifteen minutes passed in slow motion. She looked at her watch again. She tapped it as if that would make the time go faster. She sagged back onto her arm.

Kat heard a faint sound behind her, the crunch of a boot on gravel.

She spun around to face it.

A huge black shape was coming toward her. "Hold!" she snapped, projecting more confidence than she felt. She had her rifle pointed at his chest, her finger just a twitch away from squeezing off a round.

The troll's hands shot up. "Whoa-o-ho-ho!" the voice laughed. The ponderous Georgia accent oozed out like thick molasses on flapjacks, "I come in peace, Chica."

"Redmond?" She let out a sigh of relief. "Jesus!" she said angrily. "You asshole! What are you doing out here?"

"Come on, put the gun down, Chica."

"Someone should put a fucking bell round your neck."

He was less than a couple of meters away now and still closing.

"Nobody's puttin' no bell on me, Chica," he snarled, then paused to soften his voice. "Hey, lower the gun, I'm on your side, remember?"

"I told you to stop but you're still moving, so I haven't seen any evidence of that so far. And don't you ever ... call me Chica again." She held the gun steady. "What the hell are you

4

doing sneaking around in the dark? And where the fuck is your weapon? You should know that you don't go anywhere without your weapon."

"Don't worry your pretty little head about that, I've got my side arm." He lifted it out of the holster and waved it at her. "See?"

"Jesus, you're such an asshole. What do you want?"

He holstered the Beretta. "Relax, I got lonely, 's all."

"What?" she said, in disbelief.

"What say you and me get it on, Chica."

"Say WHAT?" She stood up and the barrel of her gun almost touched his chest. "Get the hell away from me before I do something you won't live to regret."

His hand swung out and snatched the rifle away from her. She staggered back but Redmond's hand shot out and seized the collar of her vest. He tossed the rifle aside then began to pull at the Velcro straps on her chest. "Let's see them big tits everybody's bin talkin' about."

Frantic, she clawed at his hands, drawing blood. Redmond released her. "So ..." he said. "You like it rough? Alright." He punched her in the chest. Kat stumbled back into the foxhole and her helmet tumbled to the ground. He reached for her. She swatted the blood-soaked hand away and backed up until she was pressed against a wall of dirt.

Redmond drew his Beretta and pointed it at her head. "Enough!" he snapped, and she stopped with one arm extended ready to fend him off.

"On your knees and open up for poppa," he said, pulling down his fly. "And if I feel teeth, I'll put a bullet in that tiny Mexican brain of yours."

"So-help-me-god, if you don't stop, I'm going to kick you so hard your balls will be coming out of your nose."

He started to laugh as he struggled to get his junk out. "You ain't gonna ...." And that was as far as he got.

Kat had long strong legs and Redmond was well within striking distance. She fired off a toe kick putting everything she had into it.

Redmond retched as he fell to his knees and let out a loud guttural scream. He would have landed on her, but she rolled away, got to her feet, and ran to retrieve her weapon.

He groaned, making miserable noises as he clutched his mashed genitals, "You-fucking-bitch!" She wasn't going to stop until she was safely locked in the Oshkosh.

Pilgrim woke up. "What the hell's going on over there?"

"You shut your fucking mouth!" Redmond yelled back. Holding his nuts, he stood up and aimed his pistol at her. "You're fucking dead, bitch!"

She was reaching up for the door handle just as he fired. His bullet slammed into her back with crushing force.

The Beretta M9 fired a hard pointed 9 mm round with sufficient velocity to penetrate the material of her bullet 'resistant' vest. It entered at the shoulder, hitting her right scapula. There was no exit wound because the bullet made a left turn and kept on going into her neck.

Twisting with the impact, she bounced off the huge front tire and fell on her back. I can't move. Dazed, her mind raced, trying to figure out why she was on the ground.

Oh Jesus, what happened?

Then it struck her.

Shit! The bastard shot me! She shouted; Somebody help ... help me!

But the words didn't reach her lips.

Kat tried to catch her breath but choked on the blood in her throat. She was conscious, but all she could see was the endless black sky above her. She began to feel cold and it was spreading through her body as death pulled at her. Then there he was again staring down at her, filling that void with his grotesque body. With his left hand clamped on his crotch he pointed the Beretta at Kat's face. "You're going to die, you little wetback-fuck."

She couldn't make a sound, let alone scream. The barrel was all she could see before everything went out of focus. A shot rang out, but she didn't hear it.

2

THE HUNTING TRIP

Off Highway 80

The four men had been threading through the instant junkyard along Highway 80 in an armored Humvee. Three of them were Rangers from the 1st Battalion Rangers, 75th Infantry. The fourth man was a Special Agent with Army Counterintelligence.

"I was wondering if we'd be seeing you again, Major," the captain said without any obvious enthusiasm.

"Always a pleasure to see you too, Grafton. You know, I haven't been hunting in a while; this is going to be great," Devlyn said calmly.

"Yeah, great. Who are we going after?"

Devlyn had the most recent satellite photos and maps, so he knew where the enemy game was hiding. "Our intel suggests that there are several groups of radical Iraqis slipping behind the lines and heading toward Kuwait."

Devlyn unfolded a copy of recon the artillery had been using. "They're spread out through this area. The flyboys were moving too fast to clear them all out, so we've got Republican Guard snipers up and down the highway," he said, pointing to locations marked in red. "Our supply convoys are going to get hit unless we deal with them.

"Which means we're cleaning up someone else's mess," Grafton grouched.

"You got something else to do?" Devlyn said. His cell phone rang. He pulled it out of his pocket and looked at the readout. "Fuck, that's my office. Hold up, I've gotta get this."

The Humvee stopped, and the Counterintelligence officer got out and walked away from the vehicle. The men inside did their best to ignore him. When he returned the captain grinned and asked, "Is your mommy happy now?"

"What can I say? You bring out the best in me." Devlyn said, as he sat beside him unsmiling.

Shit, if he only knew. Okay Fernando, I'm counting on you so do your best.

"They had nothing, so let's go."

"You don't know how happy that makes me, Sir," Grafton said.

"Yeah, I get that."

"Expecting anymore phone calls from home?"

Devlyn looked the captain in the eye without a hint of a smile. "Now how would it look if my phone rang when we

8

were sneaking up on some stupid-mother-fucker?" He patted his pocket and said, "It's off now, so Portland, are we going, or what?"

"You heard the Special Agent, Bobby, move out."

They teased him, but Maj. Devlyn was a good fit with the specialists; he'd gone through Ranger school, so he could tag along on little larks like this. His fellow hunters were Sgt. Bobby Portland at the wheel, Mast. Sgt. Pete Becker manning the 60 K on the roof and Capt. Ted Grafton.

Sitting in the back with a flashlight, Grafton and Devlyn went over the map and aerial recon photos. "Look at the building here." Then pointing out to the right Devlyn said, "that's just up that way. There's a building about five clicks up the road from here. The photo shows people on the rooftop by a tower. Maybe they're still there."

"Go dark Bobby and get off the road. We're going to head up that hill on the right," said Grafton. In seconds they were rolling over bone-jarring terrain.

"We haven't talked about the ROEs (rules of engagement), are we taking prisoners?" Grafton asked.

"Hey, I'm an intel officer, I speak the lingo and everything, so I'm usually up for a good old chinwag if someone wants to talk. But I'm not feeling chatty today. You?"

"So, that's a no?" asked Grafton. Devlyn simply raised an eyebrow. "Copy that."

A few minutes later Portland said, "There," pointing at Devlyn's landmark.

"Okay Bobby, stop here. We'll go the rest of the way on foot," Grafton said.

Moving slowly and crouching low they trekked up a rise that overlooked the rear of the building. Earlier that day it had been a large, fully functional house that the Iraqis converted into a fortification. Its strategic importance was that it was about five hundred meters from the highway.

Then US artillery sent in some ordinance late in afternoon. The structure was somewhat less than intact now. Bodies were scattered about in the rubble and in the burned-out vehicles nearby. But there was enough of a tower still standing to provide cover for a possible two-man sniper team.

The Rangers lay on their bellies and studied the crumbling remains through their NVGs, (night vision goggles) looking for movement.

"They may have bugged out already," Grafton said.

"That's certainly a possibility, but let's give it another fifteen," Devlyn advised.

Thirteen minutes later they spotted movement in the window of the tower. There were two men both looking toward the west. Grafton leaned over to Becker and asked, "Can you get a shot from here, Pete?"

"Affirmative," Becker said, patting his 'Light Fifty' with a night vision scope, "I'd only be able to take one of them out." Even though the Barrett M82 sniper's rifle used .50 caliber ammunition capable of going through bricks and concrete he couldn't hit what he couldn't see.

"Alright," said the captain, looking over the target area for a way in. It was his command, Devlyn was just along for the ride. Seeing an opening on the east end Grafton pointed to the right and said, "Then it's plan 'B'."

"Uh huh," Devlyn agreed.

"We'll move in fast and silent. Bobby, you take point, Pete you're behind me, Devlyn you watch our six and keep it tight." The men acknowledged.

"Okay, move out."

Like ghostly shadows, they sprinted in line down the slope to the flat where the charred vehicles provided some cover.

Looking for IEDs and taking care not to disturb the debris as they went, they arrived at the breach in the wall.

Certain they hadn't been spotted, Grafton patted Portland on the shoulder and they moved forward entering the compound one at a time. Porter spotted what remained of the concrete staircase signaled them to halt and took a knee. He studied the condition of the crumbling steps leading up to the second floor and from there to the roof and tower.

If the Iraqis could get up there, then so could he. He nodded to his commander and on Grafton's signal, Becker and Devlyn moved ahead across the compound to the stairway. Becker went up first, his right shoulder to the wall. Devlyn moved in perfect sync, his left hand on Becker's shoulder with his M14 Bullpup held up, resting in the crook of his arm.

They positioned themselves so that Becker could see the back of the tower room that had been cracked open by the bombardment. Devlyn watched for movement in the large roofless chamber.

Just as Becker reached the top step an Iraqi soldier appeared in a doorway down on the main level. He had no idea that his fortification had been breached and stopped to light a cigarette. He casually tossed the match away and moved out of the shadows.

A movement caught his eye and he looked up and saw Devlyn's back. He heard the man shuffling about and froze on the steps, his gun held across his chest. All he had to do was swing around and fire, but would he be fast enough?

The Iraqi threw down the cigarette and reaching for his side arm he ran back toward the door shouting, "Alarm! Ala ..."

Portland fired from the hole in the wall taking him down with a shot to the head.

The Iraqi sniper's spotter stepped into the open. Becker fired a single round and blew a hole in him you could drive a truck through and he flew over the edge. Then Becker charged forward, Devlyn followed taking the rest of the stairs at the run. As Becker went around the corner he practically stepped on the sniper. "Holy shit!" he gasped.

The Iraqi was pressed up against the wall like a roach and swung his long rifle around to fire. Becker kicked out with his foot, but the Iraqi got off a round which zipped passed his ear. Becker fired one round into the sniper from about three inches away which nearly cut him in half before it went through the concrete floor beneath him.

Devlyn arrived at Becker's side, looked around and shouted, "Clear!" Then he asked, "Are you good, Pete?"

"Yeah. You Paul?"

"Yeah," Devlyn said, "Okay, let's move back down."

Grafton and Portland had moved into the open in front of the door where the first hostile had fallen just as three more Iraqis appeared. Firing together Grafton and Portland dropped them like bottles on a rail. Devlyn and Becker hurried down to back them up.

Looking down into the hole Grafton said in surprise, "It's a stairway ... they've dug out a bunker down there. Bobby why don't you send them a little moving out present."

Portland tossed a grenade down the stairwell shouting, "Fire in the hole!" He ducked back behind the wall. The explosion sent debris and smoke up but when the smoke cleared there was still a light down below. They lifted their NVGs and went in slowly with Portland taking point again.

Devlyn was right behind them wondering if anyone could be still alive. Portland reached the first landing. All was quiet for the moment. The staircase turned to the right and he was about to step into the light when suddenly the facing wall disintegrated in a storm of bullets.

He waited for the shooting to stop and reload, then lobbed a second grenade around the corner. There were screams an instant before the explosion.

When the smoke cleared, they went down and found the bodies of the last three hold outs. Grafton checked the other room and shouted, "Clear!"

Satisfied that the horde of Praetorian zealots had been reduced by seven they hiked back to the Humvee to move on to their next target.

"I guess nobody wanted to chat with you either," Grafton said.

"Yeah, and I'd changed my mind about talking to someone too. You have no idea how disappointing that was for me," said Devlyn.

3

HARM TOUCKSBERRY

Logistical Command, Dhahran, Saudi Arabia

Nobody was getting ANY sleep and nerves were frayed as command worked to deal with Dhahran's overcrowding. It was going to destroy Col. Harmon Toucksberry too, if he didn't stop.

Throughout his career, Harm believed he'd been giving a hundred percent. At least until this strange little war came along. Feeling completely exhausted and experiencing some chest pain, he went to see the base physician. The results of the examination were not all that surprising and the report had to be sent to his CO.

He had participated in the Cold War's Return of Forces to Germany, called the Reforger exercises. Based on the work his team did on that they were asked to join Maj. Gen. William G. Pagonis' expanding staff to draft a logistics plan for Desert Shield.

Harm suddenly found himself in a logistical nightmare as combat troops arrived by the thousands and quickly overwhelmed the local resources in Dhahran. When they had finally worked it out, the officers on staff all looked like zombies.

Before he became a staff officer, Harmon had served with 75th Rangers in Vietnam and then in every conflict that followed. He'd engaged with Cuban soldiers in Grenada for Ronald Reagan in '83 when the President was wounded in an assassination attempt. Harm was wounded too and after that he was off the battlefield. When he recovered, he was reassigned to strategic planning.

Now after years of service he was sitting at his desk drafting his letter of resignation. It was something he'd never imagined doing till now.

He picked up his medical discharge form, filled it out and delivered it by hand to his old friend MGen Ramsey Hershoff.

Hershoff had already received the doctor's report, so getting Harm's DD Form 214 and his resignation from the Army was no surprise. Even so, the General sank into his chair. They'd known each other since Nam. Despite the difference in ranks and ages they'd become close friends and relied on each other. So, it was hard to deal with the idea of losing him forever. "Look Harm ..., I don't want to accept this ... you know that," he said, pushing the envelope back. "Is it what you really want?"

Harm returned it like they were playing ping-pong. "You know I don't have any choice Ramsey."

"Damnit son, they're treating you like you've got something fucking terminal. What are you now, forty-one? You've got decades ahead of you, decades! Look at me, I'm sixty-three and you don't see me putting in my papers do you."

"There's not a whole lot I can do about it, Ramsey. They said the stress on my heart was serious enough that if I don't stop, it'll kill me."

"Shit." Ramsey rubbed his forehead. "I don't want to list you as KIA, but what the fuck am I going to do without you?"

"You'll do just fine, Ramsey."

Hershoff shook his head. "It's just not going to be the same without you. I am truly sorry to lose you."

"It's been an honor, Sir."

Hershoff looked Harm in the eye. "Listen to me, after you get stateside, don 't you fucking forget me! You'd better stay in touch or so help me I'll fucking haunt you till the day you die. You hear me?"

"I hear you five by five General," he replied, with a tired smile.

"Alright, until your papers come through, I'm handing you over for a TDY with PR for light duty. That should take the stress off."

"You're kidding right, PR?"

"That's the deal. You can pick your own assignment or hide out on your bunk, it's up to you."

"I'll take it."

"Good. We'll get a drink together before you get your Dust Off." He stood up and they shook hands. "I'll save the goodbyes until then."

FRIENDLY FIRE

King Fahd Hospital Al Khobar

The scud missile hit the warehouse at Aujan compound at 20:45, that was at about the same time on the same night that Redmond's bullet pierced Kat's vest. When the Blackhawk set down on the helipad at the 207th U.S. Army Evacuation Hospital in Al Khobar, the regional Saudi trauma center, they were still doing triage on the sixty-one victims. Exhausted, the triage nurse looked up and with faint hope that it was bringing in someone who could be treated and released.

When the door slid open, she saw the three troopers from the convoy, one on the chopper's bench in handcuffs, under guard and looking terrified, one on a stretcher, and one in a body bag.

Lt. Hillary Tang looked up to heaven and asked "Jesus, what now?" She rushed her team out to receive the soldier on the stretcher. "What have we got?"

"Friendly fire."

"Aw shit, are you kidding me?" All she got in return was a shrug. "Okay fill me in."

"Victim's female, approximately 20 years of age," the medic said. He read from her dog tags. "Name, Cpl. Fernando, Katrina, blood type O positive, no allergies. GSW to posterior right shoulder, no exit wound, substantial blood loss, unconscious, and her vital signs are weak."

"How long ago?"

"It's a guess, we picked her up ..., 53 minutes ago. I don't know how long it was before we got the call. She's all yours now, Lieutenant."

Tang looked over at the chopper. "Wait a second. What about that guy?"

"He's not your problem. He was the one who put the shooter in that body bag. We're turning him over to the MPs."

"Terrific," she said sarcastically, then shouted, "Okay people, trauma bay. Come on, come on let's move it!"

Dr. Grey was examining Kat as Lt. Tang relayed the information from the paramedic. "Anything else?"

"There's no exit wound so we're going to have to go in to extract some metal fragments. Apart from the GSW, she had blood in her mouth possibly related to a minor tongue laceration."

"She bit her tongue?"

"Yeah, I'm guessing it was after she was shot."

"Okay, we're going to transfer her to the table on three." Grey, Tang and two other nurses grabbed corners of the mat. "One, two, three, lift." Kat was smoothly shifted from the gurney and placed on her side so Grey could study the entry wound. "I'm going to need pictures. I want to find that bullet. Get me chest and abdominal radiographs, stat."

While she waited, she tried to trace the course of the bullet with her fingertips. "Shit, I think it may be in her neck."

"That would explain the blood in her mouth," Tang said.

"And it looks like it's really close to the spine."

She looked up at the monitors then back at Kat. If she was right and if the corporal lived, she could have some serious problems to look forward to. She waited for the films to come back.

"I've got the pictures Doctor," the radiologist said.

"About time. Pin 'em up and let's have a look." The radiologist slid the films up on the backlit screen and stood back. Dr. Grey moved up close and followed the pattern left by the bullet. She was right, it looked like the wake left by a finger in the sand.

"Well, I'll be damned," Grey said. "Will you look at that. It tracked right across the shoulder. It must have slowed right down by the time it hit the esophagus. See there? A tiny hole and then nothing. So, where the hell did it go?"

"Jesus. I think I've found it, Dr. Grey," said the radiologist.

"Where?"

She looked and her mouth dropped open. "Oh my god," It was all she could do to resist the impulse to put her hands on her hips. The other doctor and nurses gathered around to look.

"Wow, if you'd told me about this, I wouldn't have believed you." She looked closer. "That is the damndest thing I've ever seen."

The bullet had done a 90° right turn and ended up in her stomach. "Can you get me another picture? I'd like to be able to pinpoint that thing."

She turned back to her patient as the radiologist placed another plate under Kat's body and said, "Soldier girl you are one lucky woman."

The x-ray machine clicked, the plate was removed, the shields came off and Grey moved back to the table. "Alright, she's a pretty girl so I want to make this as neat as possible."

A new tray of surgical tools was placed on a stand beside the patient. "Here you are Doctor."

"Thank you." She did the necessary repair work on the shoulder then said, "Okay team let's stich her up."

The radiologist returned with the new image and slapped it up on the screen next to the others. Grey had a look and then said, "Yeah, that's what I was expecting."

She pointed to the dark spot in the abdomen. "It's sitting in her stomach just like yesterday's lunch. We'll repair the hole in the esophagus first then remove the bullet."

She closed the hole and incisions with dissolving sutures and then with fine sutures.

"Only your lover will notice that one kiddo, you're welcome. Okay let's get her on her back and have a peek in her abdomen."

When Dr. Grey closed the last incision, she took off her mask and wiped the sweat off her face. "Some angels must be looking after you tonight Corporal Katrina Fernando, because that bullet should have killed you. I hope it's the last one anyone ever has to pull out of you."

She stepped away from the table, removed her gloves and pulled her mask down to her neck. "Okay, good job everybody. You can wheel her off to recovery now."

HIS FIRST P.R. MISSION

Al Khobar, Hospital

A staff officer from the Army PR office was standing outside the OR waiting for word on her condition when Dr. Grey came out. She looked at him and thought, now there's a guy who could use a little R&R himself right about now. "Yes Colonel, what can I do for you?" she asked, while she dragged the cap from her head.

"Were you just operating on Cpl. Fernando?"

"Yes." She pulled her arms out of the bloodied gown then looked back at him. "Not a friend of yours I gather." She could tell he was just there for the verdict, there was no emotional attachment to her patient at all.

"I just have a few questions for her about the incident."

"Incident? One of her buddies shot her in the back, Colonel! I'd call that attempted murder, wouldn't you?

"I'd have to agree with that, yes. How is she?"

"The operation went well and I expect a full recovery."

"That's good news. Uh ... so, when will I be able to talk to her?"

"You've gotta give her some time to rest. By the way Colonel, it looks like you could use some rest yourself. I recommend you use the time to get some shut eye in the doctors' lounge. Now if you'll excuse me Sir, I have another surgery."

He took her up on that suggestion, found a cot and fell asleep.

He needed Fernando's statement about the shooting to see if her story corroborated the one given by Pvt. Bill Dempsey. If it did, then he could report that the homicide of Pvt. Redmond was justifiable, and Dempsey could return to duty. Once that was done, he could brief the press, tell them that the patient was going to recover and that would be the end of it.

He woke up and returned to the corporal's room and took a seat beside her bed to wait until she woke up. He was thinking about what he'd tell them. It would be a short bad news/good news story: bad guy shot the girl, the good guy shot him and the girl will recover. End of story and he'd be done.

He had zero expectation of any prolonged involvement here and had already booked a seat on the next transport back to the US of A. He expected to reach Washington sometime in the next 48 hours, get discharged, head to the West Coast and start his retirement forthwith.

That was the plan anyway, but then she woke up.

DUST OFF

North on Highway 80

The Rangers and their Special Agent had several more stops and 37 more Praetorians died.

Devlyn checked the time, it was 20:40 which meant it was 14:40 hours in Maryland.

"Pull over Becker, I've gotta check in with the office again." Devlyn had been out of contact since they hit that first sniper's nest and during that time several terrible things had happened.

He got out of the truck and walked off about fifty yards to make the call. The Duty Officer answered, Devlyn asked for a rundown of the week's news.

Among the items that were related to him was the news of an incident on Highway 80 that caused him to stop and take a deep breath. Wishing he had a seat to sit down on he asked, "Wait a fucking second there. Are you certain it's her?"

"A positive ID, Special Agent. Cpl. Katrina Fernando, WIA."

"Jesus Christ. Tell me what happened."

"No details Devlyn, all I've got here is that she was shot."

"What?"

"She was ..."

"Yeah, yeah I heard you," he said, feeling like he'd just been hit in the gut. "She was shot. Holy fucking hell. Enemy fire?"

"Afraid not. A friendly shot her."

"She was shot by one of her men?"

"That's what the report says."

Devlyn's arm fell to his side, but he managed to hang onto the phone.

The thought of having to start again was depressing. He'd miscalculated and wasted three goddamn years. He lifted the phone back to his ear and asked the question he dreaded. "Dead?"

"No sir, they say she'll be OK."

"Thank fucking-Christ ... wait, what do you mean by OK?"

"That's all I've got, Devlyn."

"Fuck!" He rubbed his forehead, there's no way this was her fault. "Yeah okay, is there anything else?"

"No, that's it.

"Alright, I'm pulling out, I'll be heading for Dhahran. Oh, where is she?"

"In Al Khobar, King Fahd Hospital."

"Okay." Devlyn made a second quick call then went back to the Humvee. "You're going to have to finish this trip without me, ladies. I've called for a dust off, so you can hit the road."

"Something serious?" the captain asked.

"I have to assess the situation before I know how to proceed."

"A guy's gotta do ... Okay Bobby, move out. It's been a slice, Major." He shut the door and the Humvee pulled away.

Twenty minutes later the Blackhawk to pick him up. "Where to, Sir?"

"Dhahran."

"You got it, Major."

4

INTRODUCTIONS

Kat's Hospital Room

Harm had spent nearly eight hours with scattered thoughts banging through his head while he waited for her to open her eyes. Eventually she saw him sitting there and watched him quietly for a while, wondering who he was and why he was there. He looked like a nice man, so she started off with a very quiet and raspy. "Hello." Harm had no idea she was conscious until she spoke. It was so faint he nearly missed it, but he looked up.

She attempted a smile that only just made it to her eyes.

"Oh," he said, and stood up to move his chair closer. "Hello."

"A man was here yesterday, was that you?"

"Uh huh."

"Are ... are you ...," she was having trouble swallowing and

talking was painful, "a chaplain or ...?"

"Uh ..., no, I'm not. Did you want to speak to a chaplain?"

"No," she whispered.

"Okay. Um ..." Now that she was looking at him, he felt unsure, everything seemed to have changed and he had to re-think where to start.

"If you don't mind me asking, why are you here?"

24

KAT IN HARM'S WAY

"Okay, Cpl. Fernando, I'm Col. Toucksberry, I'm from ...," he began, "Uh ... how are you feeling?"

"Sore ..." Her voice was barely audible. She winced and put her hand to her throat and said, "Sorry."

"No, I'm sorry, I can see you're in a lot of pain, so I shouldn't be trying to get you to talk now. I'll come back tomorrow and see how you're doing. Okay?"

She nodded and shut her eyes.

Yes, he was a nice man.

INTERVIEWING THE SHOOTER

Military Stockade, Dhahran

The following day, Harm realized that he'd have to cancel his flight and reschedule when he knew he'd finished the job.

He decided he should head over to the brig to interview Dempsey. Seated across a table from him Harm started the questioning.

"This won't take long Private; I just want to clarify a couple of points."

"Are you from JAG, Sir?"

"No." He paused. "Wait a second, haven't you seen a lawyer yet?"

"Yes, Sir, he came by earlier."

"Okay, good." He opened his file folder and read the brief description of the event. "I'm looking into what happened for Central Command. I'm not a lawyer, so what you say to me is not privileged information. You don't have to talk to me if you don't want to. Do you understand?"

"Yes Sir."

He took out a small pocket recorder. "I'm going to record the conversation. If you don't like a question don't answer. Okay?"

"Yes Sir. Do you think they are gonna charge me with murder?"

"I'm sorry, I don't know what they intend to do."

The young man told his part of the story without embellishment. He had no idea why Redmond had tried to kill her.

"He was a bad man, Colonel Sir. I didn't mind puttin' a bullet to him one single bit."

"I met Cpl. Fernando briefly yesterday. You saved her life; you did good soldier."

"Thanks Sir."

As he left the room Harm said, "I'm betting that you'll probably be released and sent back to duty." Harm left and headed over to the hospital to see if Katrina was able to talk.

NEED TO KNOW

Dhahran, Saudi Arabia

Devlyn requisitioned a vehicle and drove up to Al Khobar. He needed to see her to assure himself that she was still viable. Though he had no intention of telling Fernando who he was, or why he was interested in her.

All the way up there he replayed what he had gone through over the last three years to put her in play. The irony wasn't lost on him, after all his planning and command manipulations, the first time he sends her out some Cracker

26

screws it up. It was a good thing that Redmond was already dead otherwise Devlyn would have done it himself.

If she had died, and at this point he still didn't know if she would survive, it would have put him right back to square one. He'd been watching over her for three years, keeping her out of trouble as much as he could.

It wasn't so much what she did, the glitch was what people did to her. It never occurred to him that he was a major part of that problem. He'd intervened before, slipping in and out of her life like a ghost and Kat was completely unaware that he existed. He was going to keep it that way until she was ready for him.

He didn't know what her life was like before she joined the Army, but he had a pretty good idea that it couldn't have been good. He gathered she'd joined the Army to get away some sort of domestic abuse. He was struck by the irony of that as well. She'd escaped whatever little hell and landed herself in this mess.

The file the recruiting sergeant sent him told him the basics. Top of her class all the way through school, loved sports. Was first team material for every sport they had, but for some reason she never tried out for anything other than track and field and never participated in away events.

Her native language was Spanish, but she could speak English and three others, French, German and Italian fluently and her accent made her sound like she was born to it. She also started studying Russian before she graduated. So yes, she was the perfect candidate for his purposes.

The rest of her details were filled in when she showed up for her physical. She was slightly undernourished which may have been part of the domestic abuse.

The Army dealt with the nutrition issue. At six feet tall in bare feet, 142 lbs., and not an ounce of fat on her, she had the potential to be a hell of a warrior.

Now that she was in perfect health Fernando was an intimidating figure.

But that wasn't what she signed up for. She had language skills and she wanted to use them. Her attitude was something he had to work on, to show her what her real potential could be and make a soldier out of her.

One of her assets was she wasn't a talker. When people in her platoon tried to get her to open up, all she would say about herself was how much she loved school.

It was the only place where she felt safe and happy, she said. He guessed that was one reason that she didn't make friends, for the job Devlyn had in mind that was a plus.

Her problems started in the women's barracks as soon as they realized that she had a lot more going for her than her looks. She was smart, well read, quick witted, agile, and athletic.

Boot Camp was easy for her. While the women in her platoon had difficulty keeping up with the men, she seemed to breeze through. She was everything they weren't and because of that they resented her.

Their major issue was that the men they wanted, all wanted her. She wasn't interested in any of them.

Devlyn was aware that people would begin talking about her the moment she showed up with the new crop of recruits. He expected that, but not the rumors.

A few guys who'd been given the cold shoulder began spreading it around that she was gay. For most of the men that was hard to believe. All she had to do was walk by and their fertile imaginations took over.

She became the subject of creative storytelling and those stories evolved into the stuff of legend. According to the men who said they'd slept with her, she was flawless. That was true, she was a beautiful, exotic creature. Her eyes were almond shaped and the color of dark amber and her light caramel skin was silky smooth to the touch.

The description of her gravity defying tits was the high point of the stories and always presented while pretending to be gripping big, ripe, melons. For the sex-hungry recruits she was the perfect sex toy, the ultimate wet dream.

Some lied about paying to sleep with her. Most expanded on the lies with details about how wild she in bed. There was nothing Devlyn could do about that.

After seeing her out on the field in her regulation Ts and shorts no one disputed their stories. Just watching her doing push-ups and squats was all the proof they needed. A woman like that had to be making a fortune putting put.

Kat was undeniably a sensual and highly desirable woman, but the truth was that she never dated, let alone slept with any man in the Army. Even if she wanted to, which she didn't, all the men were secretly intimidated by her and afraid of rejection, so they kept their distance.

Because the stories persisted, the Drill Sergeant looked into the problem. He found no evidence of inappropriate behavior. If there had been, he would have recommended a dishonorable discharge. She'd be out on her ass for bad conduct and there was nothing Devlyn could do about that.

Based on the DS's report, the Company Commander chose to ignore the gossip. "Let the men have their fun as long as nobody gets hurt." He was only referring to the men when he said that.

With the brass turning a blind eye to the abuse it ensured that the stories would follow her everywhere she went.

Once she got the posting as an Army translator Devlyn had to wait until there was an opportunity to get his agenda underway.

That day came closer when Iraq invaded Kuwait and the Coalition moved in on the 2nd of August 1990. He had yet to confirm whether she was still a viable candidate.

On the 24th of February he got his chance and managed to get her a TDY to Logistics driving a fuel truck into the combat zone. There was a good chance that she'd meet with some opposition, then he could see how she handled herself.

If it hadn't been for that fat-fuck Redmond, it might have been a very successful test and he'd be able to move her on to other more demanding missions.

Hell, if she didn't fully recover, he'd still have to start again. The thought of having to do that made him contemplate scrapping the whole idea. It was his own damned fault for sending her out there cold. If she was still viable, he wouldn't make that mistake again. He'd get her into a serious combat training program.

DR. GREY'S CHALLENGE

Nursing Station

Harm arrived for a scheduled meeting with Katrina's doctor prior to visiting her. Dr. Grey was waiting for him.

She was a slender, reasonably attractive, woman in her forties and wore the green scrubs and lab coat as if they were fashions from Saks. Her prematurely grey hair was twisted into a bun at the back of her head and held there with a pair of black lacquer chop sticks. She carried her patient charts folded in her arms across her chest like a shield.

From the directness of her comments at their first encounter, Harmon sensed she was a strong, no-nonsense, capable surgeon. With a cocked eyebrow she watched him approach. Peering at him over her half glasses, her steel grey eyes said, not you again loud and clear. He felt obliged to begin with an apology. "I'm sorry Dr. Grey, I know you're busy ..."

"I'm sure you are too Colonel so let's save time, shall we? You're here about Cpl. Fernando. I expect that she'll be up and around quickly."

"So, she's going to be okay?"

"Physically she'll be fine with physio to get her arm function and strength back. She was very lucky that the bullet didn't do more damage than it did. But this began with sexual assault Colonel and we both know how this works. I hope that if she is having problems, she'll seek help. My concern is will she be able to get the help she needs, and if so, who is going to pay for it?"

"I wish I knew."

31

"Colonel, I've seen her history, so I'm going to be frank with you. That girl is extremely bright, she's got no family and no support structure at all. The bright girls figure things out really fast which means she is a high risk for problems down the road. She is going to need that help if she's going to survive. I have no doubt about that. So, someone is going to have to be there for her." Harm was speechless. "Think about it," she said.

"But I'm not her ..." She turned and walked away. "What, I don't think you understand. I'm just doing the press statement I'm not a social ... worker." She was gone and didn't hear any of that.

He was trying to get his head around what she said as he reached her room. Pausing at the overwide door he thought Kat was asleep and decided to look around the room.

There were three unhappy looking beds against the pale green wall. Above each bed was a panel with different colored outlets for electrical hookups and a nozzle for oxygen.

The room was just long enough to fit a chair between each bed but wide enough to allow a bed to pass the others during a patient transfer. The thin privacy curtains that hung from tracks in the ceiling around each small area were open.

She was the only one there. He studied the young woman as she lay there, the head of her bed raised slightly.

Lost in thought he watched her breathing, the slow rhythmical rise and fall of her chest. She seemed to be at peace. Where was the stress the doctor was so concerned about? Once again, he wondered why he was there. He had problems of his own to deal with.

He was about to walk away when she opened her eyes.

"Hello, are you here to see me, Sir?" she said.

"Oh, uh yeah, hi. I thought you were asleep. Do you remember me?"

"No, I'm sorry."

"That's okay. May I come in?" She nodded carefully. He entered the room and aimed for the chair beside her bed. "My name is Col. Toucksberry, I was in to see you yesterday." She didn't react, but he figured she probably understood what he'd said and continued. "I was hoping I could talk to you." Kat nodded. "How are you feeling corporal?" he asked.

"I'm going to live I guess, Sir, but my throat is really sore, I must sound like a bullfrog." She had a cup of ice chips on the table beside her. She took one and eased it into her mouth.

"You sound okay to me," said Harm, as he sat down. "I just have a few questions about the incident, if you don't mind."

"No, I don't mind." She told him how Redmond approached her in the dark, grabbed her rifle from her hands and threw it away. Then he pulled out his gun, told her what he wanted and began to expose himself.

"I have no idea what happened after that."

"It was lucky that you had a friend nearby."

"A friend? Who are you talking about?"

Harm filled in the blanks based on what Pvt. Dempsey told him. "Dempsey was in his foxhole on the other side of the convoy when he heard the shot and ran to see what had happened. He saw Redmond standing over you with his gun aimed at your head. He said he had no time to think, he fired his carbine, and killed Redmond."

"Oh. Wow," she said, "That's almost funny, he'd be the last one I'd expect to stand up to Redmond. I can't believe how wrong I was about him." She looked out the window. "I wish I could thank him."

"Yeah, about that."

He paused to consider what he was about to say. This young woman would need some guidance to work through the process but he wasn't the man for the job. Yet after thinking about it he knew that he couldn't turn his back on her.

"Sir," she said, "you were going to tell me something."

"Yes sorry, I sort of drifted off there. Anyway, I'm going to have to dump on the Army, but damn it, this isn't a secret. Or it shouldn't be anyway. Right or wrong, the Army doesn't play fair when it comes to these sorts of male vs female issues." She seemed puzzled. "Okay, to be honest here, women are treated like door crashers in a men's club. If there's a problem between a man and a woman, the woman is always to blame. Do you understand what I'm saying?"

"I do, yes."

"Women are labelled as troublemakers and they're punished, sometimes they get booted out of the Army with a dishonorable discharge. You'd lose your pension, it would make it difficult to get a job, it's a big deal."

"I know."

"It's got to stop, but it's not going to until ... what?"

"I know ..." she swallowed with difficulty. She tried to speak up but it was hard and she reached for the cup of ice.

"Here, let me get that for you."

After placing an ice chip in her mouth, she said, "They'd say it was my fault, that I led him on and so on."

"Yes, they would."

"I get it." She closed her eyes and took a moment before she finished what she was going to say. He waited patiently. "Redmond is dead. I don't want to stretch it out any further. This isn't my first time around this particular block."

"Were you assaulted by a soldier before?"

"Not by a soldier. But yeah, I've been 'assaulted' before. It's no biggie, Sir."

"Jesus ... I ..."

"Sir, I've been fending for myself forever. I joined the Army thinking it would be different here, but it isn't. I haven't made a single friend since I signed up. People have been avoiding contact with me like I had the plague or something and I really haven't any idea why. But it doesn't matter, I'm just going to say that Redmond went nuts, said he was going to kill all of us and started with me. That's my story and I'm sticking with it."

"That's it?" he asked.

"That's it."

"You are a remarkable woman, Cpl. Fernando." Embarrassed, she lowered her eyes. He changed the subject. "Your doctor said you're going to recover physically, but she's worried about your emotional recovery. The fact is that the Army probably won't offer you the help you'll need."

"Trust me, Sir, after what I've been through growing up, I can handle this."

"Are you sure? I'm not presuming to know what you've gone through, but ..."

"I've got this, Sir," She studied him for a moment then said, "Colonel, are you feeling alright?"

"I just need some rest," he said, but he could tell that she thought it was more serious. It was a strange twist but he thought he had to say something to reassure her. "It's been non-stop stress since we got here. Odd isn't it? After what you went through, here you are worried about me coping with a little stress." He stood up and prepared to leave.

"What are you going to do, Sir?"

"Do?" he asked. He felt exhausted and sat down again. "I don't know why I'm telling you this, but you're right, I'm not doing very well. I've put in for a medical discharge. As soon as this incident is resolved, I'm heading back to the States. Maybe they should have assigned this detail to someone else."

There it was, she gave him an out and he took it. "You could be right."

Figuratively speaking she was helping him to the door. "As far as I'm concerned, it's over now, Sir. I'm going to be fine so ..."

"Yeah," he agreed. She said it herself it's over. But he hesitated. "Um ..., is there anything I can do for you before I go?"

"Thanks Sir, but I'll be fine. I just need to get back to work."

"Really?" That surprised him. "Is that what you really want?"

"Yes Sir. I just wish I was doing something that was more interesting than being a truck driver."

"Are you thinking of a transfer?"

"Yes Sir, I was hoping I could do some undergrad studies, I don't know, maybe go to OT (Officer Training), but that seems to have gone up in smoke."

I can't believe I'm going to say this. "Maybe I could help you with that."

"I can't ask you to do that, Sir."

"Actually," he began, realizing that for some reason he didn't yet understand, he was prepared to make a commitment now. "I'd like to help if I can."

He'd have to reschedule his departure again but he felt like he didn't have a choice. "I'll be here for a couple of days, so maybe we can talk about what you'd like to do."

"I would like that, thanks."

"Okay." He stood up again, "I'll let you rest now and come back tomorrow. Is that alright?"

She smiled.

Damn, he thought as he walked out the door, I must be losing my mind.

A MODIFIED PLAN

Nursing Station

Devlyn tapped on the desk at the nurses' station. "Excuse me, nurse?"

"Oh, yes Sir, how can I help you?"

"I understand you have a patient, Cpl. Katrina Fernando?"

"Yes, Major. Is she one of yours?"

"A person of interest. How's she doing?"

"Amazingly well, considering that that bullet should have killed her. She's a lucky girl." She noticed that that didn't seem to reassure him. "Sir, she's going to be fine."

"Is that official? She is going to have a full recovery?"

"Uh huh. Her doctor said she'll be able to walk out of here in a few days."

"I want to see her."

"I'm sorry, Sir, there's a Colonel with her now. You can wait over there if you like."

"No, I'll come back another time."

"I can tell her you were asking about her." Devlyn wore no name badge or company insignia, that she could see, so she asked him for his name. Devlyn had the answer he needed, seeing her now wouldn't serve any purpose, so he left ignoring her request.

If Fernando failed at any stage, he'd have to walk away. But for the moment, he saw no reason to change his game plan. His new problem was how to fit her recovery into his schedule. He had a little time to make adjustments. But how long would it take?

As he left the hospital it occurred to him that perhaps there was a silver lining to this. She was strong, the next task would be to test her resilience. You don't get out of this without getting a few scars. But how long would it take for her to recover? Would she be able to handle the pressure of a really challenging TDY?

He was going to be placing her in harm's way again and he'd keep doing it, upping the risk level each time, until he was sure that she was ready for him.

This miserable excuse for a mission hadn't been a real test. Being taken out on the first day by a psycho on her own team told him nothing about how well she'd do under pressure. The next test, whatever it was, would have to tell him if he could depend on her. It would mean pulling strings and collecting on a few favors. He hoped she was fucking worth it.

RETURN VISIT

Kat's Room

At eleven-twenty the next day Harm showed up at Kat's door and found her with her nose in a book.

"Good Morning," he said, as he removed his lid.

"Hey." She smiled putting the book down on her chest. "You came back, I'm glad. Oh, I'm sorry Colonel. Please, come in and have a seat."

"Thanks. I didn't know you had company."

Her new roommate was sleeping in the bed closest to the door. A young woman about Kat's age with both arms encased in plaster up to her shoulders and a leg in a cast suspended from a frame.

Kat could see that Harm was uncomfortable, so she said, "Don't worry about her, Sir. They told me she practically slept through that scud disaster. She was still in her bed when the medics found her. Apparently, it was upside down at the time."

"Oh." He tried not to laugh without much success. "Okay. How are you feeling?"

"My throat still feels awful, and my shoulder feels like it belongs to someone else, but other than that I am doing okay, thanks."

"Your voice is sounding a little stronger."

"Yup, I'm healing quickly but they want to keep me in here for a couple of days."

He looked down at his hands. "So, you mentioned taking some college courses." Then reached for his briefcase and took out a sheet of paper. "I put a list together. Some

39

courses you could take at the University of North Carolina at Chapel Hill, to help you on your way. But it'll involve more training if you want to go to OT at Bragg."

"That's SOP, Sir," Kat said, placing a bookmark between the pages. She set her book down beside her bed on the small table.

It was difficult but he made an effort to focus his attention on her eyes. "Right. I started looking at different things then I realized that I didn't know anything about you. So, tell me, what sort of things did you do before you joined up?"

"High school, Sir, that was it. Oh, and I was a cashier at a food market."

From her expression he got the feeling that she was leaving out a lot of detail. "Just school and a part time job. That's it?"

"I was totally focused on school. I got straight 'A's all the way through."

"What was your favorite subject?"

"I loved languages and I was good at math too. I went out for sports whenever I could."

"Oh, what sports?"

"Track and field. I had to work a lot, so I didn't get to compete, but I trained hard."

"You didn't like your job at the market?"

"I hated it," she said quickly. "Let's change the subject, okay?"

"Okay. How was home life? You lived with your uncle I understand?" he said, and immediately realized that he'd hit on another painful subject.

"I'd rather not talk about him, if that's alright Sir."

"Sure, no problem."

"I have this image of my dad though," she said, "He was a wonderful man, really smart, you know. He could do anything. I hold on to that, it gives me some sort of ... I don't know, a sense of home, I guess. He moved up from Mexico to LA a long time before I was born and started his own business in construction." Her voice faded, "He died when I was four."

"I'm so sorry."

"He was everything to me. It was like he was there with me all the time no matter what. Having his memory helped me through some really bad stuff."

"What about your mother?

"She left us when I was three. I don't remember her at all."

"You've had it rough for a long time then."

"A long time," she echoed.

"Tell me about the languages, how many do you speak?"

That perked her up a bit. "We spoke Spanish and English at home. I picked up French, then Italian, and by the time I graduated high school I'd learned German too."

"You speak five languages?"

"Six now. I've been studying Russian since I joined up and I'm learning Portuguese."

"God, I can see why you're feeling unfulfilled driving a truck. Why did you join the Army instead of going to college?"

Again, her mood darkened. "Yeah, I wanted that, but without a full scholarship it was impossible."

"I would have thought that would be automatic."

"I didn't qualify."

"With your grades, colleges should have been lining up to get you."

"Because I was basically a street kid, I needed the guidance counselor to put in my application for me."

"And he didn't do that?"

"No, she wouldn't do it."

"Why?"

She could have answered that. She could have told him that the counselor said she was Hispanic trash and was not worth the bother, that's why. But instead she said, "I'd like to stop now, if you don't mind, Sir."

She was angry with herself for letting it get this far. She had revealed more to him in this short exchange than she had to anyone, ever.

"I'm sorry, I didn't mean to upset you, Katrina. What can I do?"

It was humiliating and she felt profound shame. "Nothing, Sir. I'm okay. Please, I'm not feeling well now. I'm tired."

"Oh ..., uh ... should I get the nurse?"

"No, Sir. Thank you for coming to visit me, but maybe this wasn't such a good idea. I'm sorry I've wasted your time."

"I don't understand. Did something happen to you? Is that why the guidance counselor wouldn't help you?"

Something happened to me, and it happened almost every fucking day of my goddamn stupid life! "Honestly, Sir, I can't talk about it anymore."

"I ..."

"Please Sir."

"Okay," he said, but after committing himself he wasn't prepared to just give up. "Katrina listen, I'll be heading back to the States soon."

He turned over that sheet of paper, tore a strip off and quickly wrote down an address and phone number. "This is my cell and the address of a place I've rented in Venice Beach."

"Jesus," she said, on the verge of total a meltdown. "Why are you doing this?"

"Look, I'm sorry I've upset you. It wasn't my intention to hurt you, honestly. I have no idea what just happened."

"It really doesn't matter anymore."

"No, I think it does. Whatever it is, I don't think it's something you can deal with on your own and I really want to help you if I can."

She studied his face looking for some sort of recognizable sign that told her he was full of shit. She'd spotted that expression before on the faces of so many men it was easy to see. Though it didn't appear that he was full of it, she was still leery.

Sure. I mean come on, that's what he says he wants. He seems like a really nice guy, but ...

She looked over at the window then down at her hands.

He understood the meaning behind the pause, but he wasn't going to give up. "Write to me, or call me, call me collect if you need to. Will you do that?"

She shrugged without looking at him. Why do I feel like I should trust him? Is that stupid? Yeah, it's probably stupid. "I don't know."

He put the paper on her bedside table. "I hope you will, Katrina."

5

DEVLYN'S REQUEST

Fort Irwin, California

Two days before Kat was released from hospital Devlyn had set up an R&R program with a physiotherapist for her in LA.

He called the CO of Fort Irwin to make arrangements for the next stage of her training. The general questioned the wisdom of his request.

"I have her jacket right here. After looking it over Major, I've got to ask you why you think this bimbo is going to be an asset to my regiment?"

"Sir don't let her looks fool you, this woman is no bimbo. She's tough, smart, and works hard. My instincts tell me that she'll be an asset."

"Really. You don't think she'll be a distraction?"

"Sir, your people can assess her capabilities while she's training with the 11th. If she doesn't meet your standards, then she won't meet ours either, and I'll arrange her transfer to Bragg or Benning before you deploy."

"It's just as simple as that?"

"Yes, Sir. I want to see how she performs before I commit her to training at Huachuca."

"Alright, since it's for CI, I'll give her a shot, but frankly Maj. Devlyn, I don't hold out much hope for her. How will my people contact this woman?"

"She's in the Duty Officer's office right now."

"How the hell do you know that? Never mind. I bet you think you run this goddamn Army, don't you, Devlyn? Alright, you've got your placement. But hear this. If your protégé flames out, then I'll see to it that you burn right along with her. I hope she's worth it."

"Sir, believe me, so do I."

THE TRANSFER

Fort Irwin, California

Kat arrived at Fort Irwin and was taken directly from the transport to the Command Office. Once again, she had been transferred with no idea how or why.

Perhaps Colonel Toucksberry had done it without checking with her first, she thought.

Devlyn timed it so that she entered the Duty Officer while he was on the phone with the general. Her orders were to report in, then go to LA for rehab with Army vouchers for physiotherapy at a clinic in Santa Monica. When the therapist declared her ready, she was to report back to Fort Irwin.

She entered Maj. Brian Westlake's office to present her orders with her arm in a sling and looking like she'd been dragged all the way from Dhahran. After he read the TDY (temporary duty transfer) he sat stone faced not knowing what to think.

"Sir, did Colonel Toucksberry send me here?"

"I don't know who Col. Toucksberry is, but these orders didn't ..." Just then the commandant called. "Ah, yes General, she is here with me now." He paused looking at her and said, "Yes, Sir. I'll take care of it."

"Okay Fernando, you're a gift from the DoD, so you're our problem now. You've got one chance at this, so don't fuck it up."

"Yes, Sir."

"Alright, it's 14:36 now, you've got another six-hour drive to the city and you already look like shit. Get cleaned up, get some food at the canteen, then report back here in uniform." He opened a file drawer and took out a folder.

"Here's a list of billets in Santa Monica. LA is expensive, so take my advice and stick to the list. That's Sgt. English in the outer office, he's heading to LA at 16:00 hrs. He's you're transport, ask him to show you where to leave your gear. Be back here at 15:45, don't be late."

"Thank you, Sir."

"Don't thank me, Fernando. Dismissed."

It was after 21:00 hrs. when they arrived at the Santa Monica Motel. Kat took one look at the place and asked him to wait until she found out if they had a room.

"Well step on it, I've got places to go." English was not thrilled with the idea of letting women into the Army, let alone this bimbo into his unit.

It took her under two minutes to go in and out. She got back into the car as if she was being chased. "Are you kidding me Sarge? Is this really the place they suggested?"

"What's the matter, not good enough for you, princess?"

"But Sarge, they want a hundred and forty-three dollars a night. I can't afford that."

"Look Corporal, this is Santa Monica, they don't fucking come any cheaper than that in this goddamn town. This is it. I got things to do, so quit wasting my fucking time."

"Perfect."

"No more lip from you girl," he said, pointing a bony finger at her, "just get out of my car!"

"Okay."

"I said move it."

"Alright, I'm out, okay?"

The second the door closed he was gone.

INEVITABLE ENCOUNTER

Santa Monica, LA County

There was a diner nearby but the thought of eating made her queasy. She'd spent more than twenty-six hours on a bench in a C-130 from Dhahran and was bone tired.

By the time it touched down at Fort Irwin she was in agony. Now, thirty-three hours later when the man at the front desk asked her name, she was hard pressed to remember. She took the cheapest room with a single bed.

As soon as she opened the door, she dropped her gunnysack. She kicked the door shut with her heel then went into the bathroom for a glass forgetting how bad LA's water tasted. Braced against the wall she popped one of the Tylenol-3s Dr. Grey had given her, then she stripped, hung up her uniform, flopped naked on the bed. Sleep came immediately.

At 08:00 Kat began her search for a billet with another Tylenol-3 and some bottled water for breakfast.

Taking a cab, she went to the first place on the list owned by a Korean War vet. It didn't look right, so she asked the driver to wait.

When the man opened the door, he reminded her of all the men from her past "Sorry, my mistake," she said, and hurried back to the cab. "Let's try the next address, please."

Suggestion number two was pretty much the same story. So was the next, and the next one after that. How old was this list, she wondered? She got to the end of the list with nothing to show for it except a $193.00 cab fare.

The cab left her at the motel and she walked to the diner for a Cobb salad, another Tylenol-3, and a copy of the L.A. Times. Her pain was easing, but her mood hadn't improved. She circled the rental possibilities in the want ads and the following day continued her search by bus.

It was nearly four when she got off the bus at Market St. to look at an apartment in a small building up the block. She was exhausted and frustrated. Her spirits lifted a bit when she saw it. The apartment was a clean, furnished bachelor suite with a kitchenette at one end and a bed at the other. It seemed perfect, but then the woman told her the rent had doubled.

"Holy Jesus," she said. "The ad said six hundred a month."

"What can I tell ya."

"I'd like to think about it for a while. Would you mind holding it for me while I get a cup of coffee?"

"Well, I got other people lookin' here, so don't take too long."

Walking away she plunked her hand into her purse for another hit of codeine and touched on the piece of paper Harm had given her. She hadn't intended to keep it but had forgotten about it. Making a snap decision she hoped she wouldn't regret, she turned around quickly and said, "Excuse me, Ma'am."

The woman stopped in the doorway. "Yeah what?"

"Can tell me how close we are to Venice?"

"About as close as you can get without falling in a canal. It's that way," she said, pointing south. "I'll give you half-an-hour soldier-girl, that's it."

Until that moment, Kat had no intention of contacting Harm, but she was desperate. She took out her cell phone and entered his number. She was just about to hit the end button when he picked up, "Hello."

"Hello, is this Colonel Toucksberry?"

"Speaking," he said, then a beat later he placed the voice. "Hang on, is that you Cpl. Fernando?"

"Ah ... yes, Sir. Hi."

"Hi," he said, warmly. "I'm glad you called, what can I do for you?"

"Sir, I know this is sort of weird, but I need some advice."

"That's why I gave you the number."

"I know, but I was wondering ..., are you free ..., like right now?"

"Sure, do you want to talk?"

"Yeah, do you think you could meet me for coffee?"

"Hold on! Are you here in LA?"

"Yes, Sir. I probably shouldn't have called you, but I ..."

"No, no, no it's okay, I'm glad you did. Where are you? I'll come and pick you up."

"Thanks, I'm at ..., ah ..., let me look. I'm at the corner of Market St. and Main."

"I'm on my way."

Five minutes later a Camry pulled up beside her and Harm leaned over to open the door. Just seeing him somehow made Kat feel safe. She had never felt that way with a man before.

There had to be a first time for everything, she thought. He took her to his house and they talked over coffee. The more they talked the more relaxed she felt. She was telling him about her trip to California and the hell she was going through trying to find a place.

Harm looked at Kat's cup and said, "Hold that thought while I'll get us some more coffee. Say are you hungry?"

"Yeah, I guess I am."

"Peanut butter okay?" She nodded appreciatively. "Are you a purist, or do you like jam with that?" She shrugged and smiled. He made some PB&J sandwiches and the conversation continued. Harm was so easy to be with that the time flew by and so did the deadline for the apartment. She glanced at her watch and practically deflated in her chair.

"What is it?"

"I've missed my deadline to decide on an apartment. She only gave me a half hour. I have to call her. Do you mind?"

"No, go ahead."

She made the call. "Hello, Mrs. ..., oh, it has? Okay is there another ... ah, hello?" Looking totally lost Kat put the phone back in her purse. "She just hung up on me. I guess it's not my lucky day."

"Maybe your luck is better than you thought. I know of a room with a view, and a four-piece en-suite that's available right now."

"Really, is it far?"

"Not far at all." He pointed behind her. "It's just up those stairs."

She put her bag on her lap thinking she should have seen that coming. "That's a very kind offer, Sir, but I couldn't accept."

"Why not? It's a big house and you can have the room rent free."

More warning bells went off in her head. She thought she knew the answer, but she asked anyway. "Why would you do that?"

He'd looked at her boobs a few times, but she hadn't known a man who hadn't since she was thirteen. Oddly though, her creep-detector wasn't making a sound. He seemed to be a genuinely decent guy. She decided that she would trust him and gratefully accepted.

"Great. There's one condition."

"Okay here it comes," she whispered into her coffee cup.

"I'm retired now, so call me Harm, okay?"

"Oh. Okay, I'm Kat."

Her first physio appointment was the following day. Harm drove her to Santa Monica that morning and every morning after that. They quickly fell into a rhythm of peaceful, and pleasantly platonic, coexistence.

HIS ROOMMIE MOVES OUT

Venice Beach, LA

They'd been sharing the house for seven comfortable weeks and part of their routine was sitting on the rooftop deck to watch the sunset together.

They would meet at five-thirty in shorts and T-shirts with a couple of cold ones and talk about anything that interested them. This evening would be different though, it was a hot one and the brown haze rippled over the city like the sizzle over a fry pan full of bacon. Kat had that dreadful woody feeling in the pit of her stomach that always came when something bad or sad was coming.

This thing was big, possibly life changing, and Harm had an uncanny ability to sense her moods immediately, so there was no way to hide it from him. Not that she'd want to or could.

She was ambivalent and anxious, so she went up to the deck early, taking her Beretta and the cleaning kit with her so she'd have something to do while she waited for him. She stripped it down and did a meticulous job cleaning and oiling every part. She finished the chore just as her roomie appeared with two beers right on the dot of 5:30.

Her physiotherapist had called Maj. Westlake to report that she was finished with physio and ready to start training. Westlake ordered her to be on the next bus to Fort Irwin and she was ready to get to work, that was fine. Telling Harm that she was leaving in the morning was going to be hard.

Even with his mirrored aviator glasses she could tell he noticed the weapon the moment he reached the deck.

He knew something was coming that he didn't want to hear. Their chairs were close together so, without comment, he went to his, slouched down into it and put his feet up on the rail.

"Hi," he said, and handed her a beer.

She took it and put her feet up too saying, "Thanks."

"So, anything new today?" he asked.

"Stuff ..., you know. How about you?"

"Yeah ..., same," he said, closing his eyes.

She nudged him with her sweating beer bottle, "Harm?"

He wiped the moisture off his arm without opening his eyes. "Talk to me."

"I just wanted you to know how grateful I am to you for letting me stay here with you. I can't imagine that it's been easy for you to have a kid around all the time."

"Have I ever complained?" He lifted the glasses to his forehead and turned his head slightly. She was right, it hadn't been easy for him, but it sure as hell wasn't because she was a kid. But he never complained.

He turned his head away, put the glasses back down then got right to it. "When are you leaving?"

"Tomorrow."

"Oh. ... That soon?"

"Uh huh, I'm on duty at 07:00 Monday."

"Oh," he said, again. The silence stretched on for a couple of minutes. It was unhappy news and she knew he'd need time to process it, so she waited. After a long pause he said, "Don't you think you're pushing it a little?"

"Hank made the call. He says I'm ready."

"Shit," he whispered, under his breath. "Well he oughtta know I suppose."

Her chin sank down on her chest and she used her thumb to pick away at the label on her bottle.

Harm rolled his head to the side and lifted the sunglasses to his forehead again so he could really look at her something he generally tried not to do. It was easier not looking at her.

"It's time, Harm."

"Shit," he said, once more. He may have whispered it, but, to her, it sounded like shouting. It was sadness talking, not anger. Kat knew that he'd fallen for her. "This place isn't going to be any fun without you."

She'd never had the experience of being loved before, at least not since her father died. Being an object that someone obsessed over, for sure ..., ever since her buds turned into boobs that was the norm, but no one ever loved her. "I'm really going to miss this."

"You've been a great roommate, Kat."

"You too Harm. But as nice as it's been, I can't sit out here any longer watching the canal get all choked up with weeds. Besides," and there was a lot of truth in what she was going to say, "I've been distracting you from finding something to do."

"I hope that's not why you're leaving."

She shook her head, "It wasn't my idea to leave, but it's true, isn't it? I've been holding you back."

"That's not true at all," he lied.

"Isn't it?"

A man in a rowboat was drifting down the canal and Harm couldn't help drawing a parallel to his own life. They were both heading for the seaweed. "Yeah ..., maybe a little," he said reluctantly. This was an admission to himself as much as to her. He'd been in denial about his feelings for Kat since Saudi Arabia.

But he was twenty-one years her senior and dragging her into a spring/fall romance would be stupid and unfair, so he kept it to himself.

At least he thought he did. "Why don't you reassemble your damn weapon before that gull craps on it?" He rolled his head back, lowered the glasses, and closed his eyes again.

Kat hadn't expected to become so attached to him, either; he made it so easy though, Harm was the most generous and decent person she'd ever known and her feelings for him just grew stronger.

She just wasn't able to recognize what she was feeling because she had never felt connected in that way to anyone before.

She put her bottle down and quickly reassembled the gun without looking at it. Since that night on the highway she'd become very serious about how to handle guns. Nobody was ever going to take a weapon away from her like that again. She checked the action, put on the safety, and then set it down on the clean rag. "All done." She picked up her beer and sat back down.

"From what I hear you'll be over there to sustain a presence, so the Kuwaitis can begin to rebuild. Is that right?"

"I'm not doing it alone," Kat added.

The guy's boat drifted into the weedy little Sargasso Sea and stopped without waking him up.

How fitting Harm thought. "I just want you to take care."

"I will," she promised. "Will you stay in touch with me?"

"Do you want me to?" he asked.

Kat's head snapped around. "Jesus Christ, Harm ..., yeah! I want letters from home."

"I'll keep in touch." The guy in the boat hadn't stirred and as Harm looked over the rooftops of the neighborhood it seem like all of Venice Beach was taking a siesta. Even the Pacific was calm. But not Harm, not with his gut twisted into a knot.

6

A RELUCTANT BLACKHORSE

Camp Doha, Kuwait

The 11th armored cavalry deployed to Kuwait on June 13.

Two weeks after the first Blackhorse soldiers arrived at Camp Doha, the Regiment took over the responsibility from the 1st Brigade, 3rd Armored Division for the defense of Kuwait. Kat's new posting was a sprawling complex surrounded by an eight-foot high wall.

There was no significant threat of front-line combat, so she was assigned to one of the three line-squadrons.

They took turns pulling "Z Cycle," a designation that included responsibility for security.

Intel suggested that the Iraqis were itching to get at it again. The 11th ACR wanted to reduce their response time by keeping its combat vehicles 'combat loaded', even in the garrison. It was a dangerous practice, but they were careful.

Kat wrote to Harm about it.

"Dear Harm,

I'm doing okay, working hard. They put me with a special team doing security sweeps through town. It gets a little hairy sometimes. Our biggest fear is having someone ambush us from the roof tops. So far so good.

"I'd forgotten about the heat; I mean it was 50 degrees today and I'm practically dressed for winter. I'd also forgotten how sad and boring this place is most of the time. Almost everything around me is the color of sand, except for the women dressed in black from head to toe.

The desert sand goes on for a gazillion miles, the houses are all bland, the streets are sand and the men, well I don't want to talk about the men.

"I've made a couple of friends from the British unit here on the base. They're good guys. Seems like all of them are married with kids. That's all they talk about, constantly. It's funny because half the time it's hard to understand what they're saying, but nobody seems to care.

"Unless we're out on patrol my guys leave me alone. I think they've got orders to keep their distance. There are a few other women here, office workers. We bunk together, but we've got nothing in common, so it gets a bit lonely.

"I miss our talks up on the deck. Do you remember that guy in the boat? I could use a little time in a rowboat about now.

Speaking of talks on the deck, where are the cookies you promised me, Harm? Seriously, I hope you're doing well. I keep wondering how you're making out with ideas for that new career you talked about. Truth is I think about you all the time. Sorry to sound so needy. I'm not really, I'm just venting. Please write to me soon.

"Well that's it for now.

"All my best,

"Kat."

She mailed the letter at the end of her first week in country.

THE OLD FAMILY HOME

Durham N. C.

Harm received that first letter with great excitement. It wasn't a very happy letter, but it made him feel like a part of a family again.

From that moment it was all he could think about. He realized that he needed Kat's letters as much as she needed his.

Suddenly he couldn't stand being alone in California anymore. He needed a place to call home. He went online to look for a house back in his hometown, Durham, North Carolina and was stunned to read that the house he'd grown up in was listed for sale.

He thought it was exactly what he needed and he bought it, packed up and left L.A. for Durham.

He wrote to Kat about how happy he was with the house and the renovations he was doing. He included before pictures along with a box of cookies. She wrote back saying she was so excited for him.

Kat's letters arrived every few days and he continued to send progress photos with his letters along with boxes of cookies. She got a thrill every time her name was called out at mail call. Getting the photos was beyond exciting. She wrote back right away to thank him and said she couldn't wait to see it in person. She filled him in on the minutia of the routine around the Base Camp, talking about the stress of being combat ready 24/7, experiencing long periods of boredom and one or two quick bursts of terror.

Harm knew all about that. In war, a soldier's time had always been broken down into those two basic units, 95% boredom 5% terror. He'd lived that most of his adult life. But now that he was retired his reality was quite different.

For some reason this last letter seemed to make him more conscious of that difference. He put it down for a moment. Being alone had given him a lot of time to think too, perhaps too much time.

His thoughts tended to dwell on that one thing that was missing from his life.

It was the same thing that Kat had always said she wanted. He wanted a family.

He thought they'd have it all there, but without her it was just a house. Home was becoming an ideal that was slipping away from him, and with it went the initiative to start that second career he'd promised himself.

He began feeling resentful of Kat. It wasn't rational, he knew that but he couldn't control it. She was a young soldier on deployment so it wasn't her fault, yet he resented it all the same. It didn't affect how he felt about her, he loved her more than he could have imagined, but he resented how it affected his life.

He realized he'd bought the house and done all that renovation for her. He wondered if she would ever come back to him. He lifted the letter and continued to read. The letter ended; "With all my love, Kat." It was the last letter from Kuwait that he would read.

AMO INFERNO

Camp Doha, Kuwait

On July 11, her unit deployed two of its three combat formations into the field.

That left a single squadron to guard Camp Doha and they had all their equipment parked in the North Compound, loaded and ready for combat.

Kat's line-squadron was maintaining security. The place was huge with several motor pool pads, each one about the size of two or three football fields. It had administration buildings and barracks housing two-hundred and sixty British soldiers and was surrounded by a tall fence.

At about 10:20, a defective heater in an M992 ammunition carrier loaded with artillery shells caught fire. No one knew how long it had been burning before the smoke had been spotted, but it was quickly apparent that the fire extinguishers were useless.

The blaze was out of control and the order was given to evacuate.

It took a while to move the troops out and as they were heading for the gate the ground shook as the ammunition carrier exploded. Artillery submunitions scattered over the rest of the combat-loaded vehicles causing more explosions and it quickly became a horrific inferno.

Great plumes of black and white smoke rose hundreds of meters into the sky. It was like an invitation for the Iraqis to attack. The cloud drifted east-southeast, to Kuwait City, taking Kat right back to Highway 80, the burning oil fields, and Redmond. Pushing that nightmare aside she concentrated on getting her people out of there. For the next hour Kat helped with the evacuation as explosions and fires devastated the compound.

By mid-afternoon there wasn't much left to burn, and the fires died down enough to allow the line-squadron to go in to assess the damage. Kat couldn't believe what she was seeing; the destruction was simply overwhelming.

The fires had been so intense that even the big equipment like howitzers had melted. The stench was unbearable. The compound was a minefield of unexploded ordnance.

Debris was scattered everywhere, depleted uranium rounds, oxidized in the fires, added the risk of radiation poisoning. Forty-nine US soldiers and four British soldiers were injured, two seriously. The majority suffered fractures, sprains, cuts, and bruises from trying to escape over the four-and-a-half-meter high wall. Thankfully there were no deaths.

The risk that the Iraqis would take advantage of the situation had become very real and the pressure was on to restore the base's combat potential. Kat's line-squadron was sent out on patrol, under constant threat of sniper fire from everywhere. The enemy was close by, belligerent and dangerous, and could attack at any time.

Safe at home in Durham, Harm watched his mailbox every day, desperate to hear what happened, but for a long time there were no letters from Kat.

All he wanted was to hear that she was alright. As far as the Army was concerned Kat had no next of kin to inform in the event of death or injury. The significance of that for Harm was that he might not ever know what happened to her.

Without her, he began to see the world as a very dark and lonely place.

Following the disaster, Camp Doha's CO wrote in his dispatch, 'Had it not been for numerous individual acts of heroism and the Regiment's disciplined response to the emergency, things could have been much worse. Miraculously,' he wrote, 'there were no fatalities.'

He was surprised that he was adding Devlyn's bimbo Cpl. Katrina Fernando's name to the list of soldiers who made a significant contribution to ensuring the safety of the regiment in that dispatch. He called Maj. Devlyn to tell him that she received a commendation and he was giving her a Secondary Zone Promotion (field promotion) to Sergeant.

Kat was transferred to the Non-commissioned Officer Academy (NCOA) at Fort Benning, Georgia.

She started writing again to tell Harm all about her promotion and to wish him a happy New Year. He didn't open it.

Feeling vindicated, Devlyn's plan for her move to Army Intelligence was back on track.

NO RESPONSE

Fort Benning, Georgia

Harm refused to open anything that came from Kuwait, afraid it might tell him she wasn't coming home to him. That meant he didn't know she had returned from safely and it was her turn to wonder why he'd stopped writing. Devlyn had been paying attention to everything she did and was relieved that Harm seemed to be out of the picture at last.

Devlyn travelled to Fort Benning to meet with the CO and request that she stay on at Benning for the Airborne Course. After reading her jacket the CO was happy to agree.

With that taken care of he arranged to crossed paths with her in the mess hall. Wearing his Army fatigues, he appeared to be just another major vising the base.

She was sitting by herself so he took his tray over to her table. "Do you mind if I join you, Sergeant?"

"Not at all, Sir." Curious about why he'd chosen her table she waited for him to initiate the conversation.

"How's the Army treating you, Sergeant?"

"I'm doing okay, Sir."

"Are you signing up for Jump school?"

"I'm waiting for my orders. I see that you've been through the program. Are you still active, Sir?"

"I'm currently assigned to administration up at Fort Mead, have you heard of it?"

"Sure."

He smiled and folded his arms on the tabletop. Casually he pointed to her chest. "I was just looking at your service ribbons."

Yeah right, Kat said to herself.

"I see that you've been to Iraq and Kuwait. Did you see any action?"

"Not with the enemy, but I did get involved with some excitement while I was there. Were you in Iraq?"

"As I said, I'm more of a desk jockey. Any plans for the future?"

"After jump school you mean?" He looked at her expectantly. "At the moment I like what I'm doing, but I'm always looking for new challenges, Sir."

He looked at his watch. "Sergeant ...?"

"Fernando, Sir."

"Good to meet you Sgt Fernando. I've got to head out, but I hope we'll meet up again sometime."

"Looking forward to it, Sir," she said, but didn't mean a word of it.

"Good luck with Jump School."

He got up, leaving his tray but not his name. When she thought about it, she couldn't remember seeing his name badge. *Odd*, she thought.

Before Devlyn left Fort Benning he dropped into the commandant's office with a further request that Kat be assigned to the 507th after she finished the course.

He thought of it as putting her in storage until he was ready to invite her to the program at Fort Huachuca, Arizona. She was doing a commendable job, so the commandant was once again happy to have her stay on.

Kat graduated and received her US Military Parachutist Badge, then quickly settled into life on the base with the 507th infantry. Her enthusiasm, intelligence, agility and skill made her stand out and it wasn't long before she was recommended for another promotion.

After graduating from another course, she made Staff Sergeant and became an instructor. With all that was going on she continued to write to Harm with no response. She even tried to call his phone but he never picked it up. In the last letter she wrote, she asked him what had happened to him, why he had stopped writing.

When January 12th rolled around Kat celebrated her 21st birthday, and like every other birthday since she was four, she spent it alone. It was upsetting, but she told herself Harm was probably off somewhere busy establishing his new career. It made it a bit easier but it wasn't true.

Somehow Harm had lost his way and, blinded by depression, couldn't see any way to get back on track. He missed Kat and without her there was no future. Afraid of what it might tell him he simply added her last letter to the growing stack of unopened envelopes on the hall table.

7

REUNION

Fort Benning, Georgia

After another month of silence Kat had had enough. She wasn't about to write Harm off so she finally did something about it. She requisitioned an Army sedan and drove up to Durham. It was risky because he might have moved on but she had to try to connect with him again. She finally understood that feeling she couldn't identify earlier and he had to know before she gave up on him.

The small, freshly painted two-story house with two dormers and a front porch stood on a quiet street with huge old trees dripping with grey moss. It was a beautiful scene even though the garden needed some TLC.

She went up to the bright red door and knocked and waited for someone to open it.

Harm had seen her drive up and started for the door then froze. After all this time he just could not face her. Trying to ignore Kat's knock he hoped that she would give up and go away.

She didn't though, she simply knocked again. "Harm, I can hear you in there." She knocked again. "Harm come-on please, open the door."

"Hello Kat," he said, when he opened the door.

"Is that all you have to say?"

"I-I'm just surprised to see you." He paused reading the frustration in her eyes."

"But I'm guessing it's not a happy surprise."

"No, no I ... I'm sorry, come in," he said.

"Thank you." She crossed the threshold. He closed the door behind her. "What's going on Harm?"

"It's difficult to explain."

"Well I hope you will Harm, because I drove up from Benning and it's a long way for an unenthusiastic hello."

"Yeah, I'm sorry," he said. "Can I get you something, some tea perhaps?"

Looking around Kat spotted the letters piled up in a china salad bowl on the small hall table. "Coffee if you have it," she said.

"Sure, I'll make a fresh pot."

She followed him into the kitchen and as he started to scoop the coffee into the coffee maker she leaned against the counter and said, "Did you read any of them?"

"The letters? I did, yeah. But then … I don't know … after the fire I couldn't read the others. I stopped calling friends, I stopped writing to you, I… I just couldn't cope with anything anymore."

"Oh Harm, I'm so sorry. Is there anything I can do?"

"I see that you've been posted to Fort Benning. The 507th?"

"Yeah I was transferred there to attend the Sergeants' Training course."

"And you made Staff, congratulations. I'm not at all surprised that you're moving up Kat. You're going to do really well."

"OK Harm stop it. What's happening here?"

"I don't know."

"I think you do and we need to deal with it."

We?"

"Yes of course we! Come-on, give."

"Alright." He left the coffee maker and sat down at the kitchen table. She sat across from him and waited expectantly. With eyes down and folding his hands together he tried to think of how he should begin. She waited quietly. "Okay, the truth is … I got lost."

"What do you mean you got lost?" He had expected her to be angry but she wasn't at all. She was sympathetic and her question was delivered gently.

"I mean I thought I would have come up with an idea, you know, for what to do with the time I have left. But when

I finished the house renovation my mind was a total blank. I couldn't even think about what I wanted for dinner. I just vegetated in front of the TV. I couldn't even tell you what I watched.

"I wanted to make this place a home … and I failed. I'm sorry Kat."

"Awe, don't be Harm. Listen to me you've been through a lot and you need time to decompress. Nobody expects you to just come up with a brilliant idea right out of the gate."

"But it's been months now. I should have come up with something."

"Who says? Harm come-on, you've done a fantastic job with the house," she said. "I love it."

"You do?"

"As far as I'm concerned that's a win." Kat went to Harm and wrapped her arms around him. Closing his eyes, Harm hugged her arm and rested his head against her shoulder. Too soon the coffee maker beeped to tell them to break it up. "Oh right, I came all this way for a coffee, so are you going to get it for us or do I have to do it?"

"I'll get it," he said. They stood at the counter quietly sipping the brew from tall mugs. At last he put his arm around her shoulder and said, "How did such a pretty young thing get so wise and patient."

"I don't know about wise, but when I was growing up no matter how bad things got, I knew that I'd be free one day. Holding on to that allowed me to shut everything else out. I believed if I could survive that I can survive anything."

"It must have been really awful."

"It was. It left me with some baggage but I'll get over that too … eventually." She smiled, but she'd said that as much to reassure herself as it was to inform him.

"We're all dragging around some baggage Kat."

"No doubt." They were silent again, each dealing with their thoughts as the minutes passed by. Then she took his hand, gave it a little squeeze saying, "I love you Harm."

It wasn't said with exuberant emotion, it was a quiet statement of fact. Somewhere along the line she realized that she was truly and deeply in love.

"I love you too Kat. I suppose I have since the day I first saw you." That was all she needed to hear.

They had dinner out that night and over the next few weekends as winter persisted, they began to fall back into the same old routine of comfortable loving but platonic coexistence they'd developed in Venice Beach. She would drive every chance she got drove the seven plus hours up to be with Harm.

DINNER AT NANA'S

Durham, N. C.

It was unusual. The snow had been snowing all day and he was concerned about her driving up. Harm had his coat on, ready to leave for the restaurant when Kat called to say she was going to be late getting there.

"There's a snow squall blowing off the mountains so driving is a little treacherous down here. But don't worry," she said, "I am coming."

They'd arranged to meet at Nana's, a nice little restaurant out past Duke University. "But I am worried. Be extra careful, Kat. There's no rush, I can wait for as long as it takes."

She took the familiar exit off I-85 N to highway 40 then down to Chapel Hill Rd. and there was Harm's Camry parked out front and covered in snow.

It felt so good knowing he was inside. She saw him standing by the window and waved to him. He waved back, much relieved, and met her at the door. "Hey there! Are you okay?" It was a familiar spot. They'd dined there several times, always in the Wine Room, a warm wood paneled space with a stone hearth and crackling fire. The owner and her staff always seemed delighted when Kat and Harm came in.

"Hi, yeah I'm fine," she said, dusting the snow from her hood.

"Rough drive?"

"Oh boy, I-85 is a nightmare, especially around Charlotte. Cars and trucks off the road everywhere. I'm sorry I'm so late."

"I'm just glad you're here safe," he said, hugging her. "Can I take your coat?"

"I'll just keep it on, thanks. It's going to take me a while to warm up. Do we have our usual booth?" Harm nodded so she sat down and pretended to shiver.

He slid in put his arm around her protectively and held on to her. *Mmmm Nice.* "It looks like the storm followed me here."

"It's been like this all day. I ordered a glass of the house red for you. I hope it's okay."

"It's perfect, thanks." She had a sip then smoothed the red and white checkered tablecloth before she set the glass down. "Okay, I want to hear how you're doing."

"I'm doing great," He said, then paused and Kat waited patiently. Harm didn't want to talk about it so he went back to the weather. "The storm was much worse than they said it would be."

"Yeah," she said, rolling her eyes, "tell me about it." She sipped her wine and waited for him to say something relevant. He cleared his throat and put a little distance between them.

I'd imagined that this was going to be romantic. Okay Kat give the guy some time. He'll come around. He'd better come around.

She tried again. "It was much nicer in Atlanta; it was cold but they actually had sunshine."

"Did they?" he said, then let it fall.

"Yeah ..., it was nice." He was unusually quiet and it was bringing her down. She'd been looking forward to this evening so much and now it seemed to be going flat before it began.

Nope, I'm not going to let that happen. Trying to brighten the mood she asked, "So what have you been up to, it's feels like ages since we talked on the phone."

"Nothing much at all really. I've done some reading. That's about it."

"Oh. Um ... anything I should read?"

"Not really."

"Okay Harm, I can tell there's something bothering you. Do you want to talk about it?"

He was looking out the window watching the snowfall. "It's nothing, really. I was worried about you, that's all. Ever since I heard about that fire at Doha I ... Sorry about this, I'll get over it."

"I'm sorry I worried you."

"Well don't be," he said, putting a little more strength in his voice. "Everything's okay." He watched her sip her wine. "Are you warming up at all? I can take your coat and hang it up for you."

"Sure, thanks," she said, with that special smile. She slid out of the booth and stood in front of him with her arms folded across her chest.

"What are you hiding?"

"You'll see." She turned so that he could take her coat. Her bare shoulders excited him and then he saw red silk. "Is that a new dress?"

"Uh huh." She turned to face him giving him his first real glimpse of the dress.

He stared in awe. "Wowzers! Now that ..., that is a hell of a dress."

"I'm glad you like it."

He hung the coat over his on the post hook at the end of the booth. Standing in front of the large windows with the black sky and the snow falling gave her an excellent backdrop to show off the new frock. "You look ..., ah. It's not your birthday yet, is it?"

"No," she said, with a little pout, "that was in January."

"Right. I missed it, didn't I?" He rubbed her arms nervously, as if he were trying to warm her up. "I'm sorry."

"It's okay, it was just another day."

"But that means I've forgotten something else then." His brow furrowed and his eyes grew dark and heavy. He was fixating on the negative and she felt like she was losing him again.

"Just tell me again how much you like the dress."

"Like?" His eyes brightened and he seemed to stand a little taller. "That's an understatement." He brought her a little closer.

She put her arms around him feeling his warm, soft sweater against her skin. They'd never been so close before and he could sense the enormous power in her arms. She's a super woman, an Olympian a ...

He's drifting again, she thought. Kat tightened her grip pressing her breasts against his chest.

"Uh ... Kat," he said, nervously looking around.

She relaxed and stepped away from him so he could see her. "Hey, the dress, what do you think of the dress?"

"Wow," he whispered softly. "Without a word of a lie, Kat you look spectacular."

"Good. So, let's sit down."

He could hardly take his eyes off her as they slid into the corner. He raised his glass. "So, what's the occasion?"

She raised hers and said, "You."

"Me?"

The server came over "Hi guys, do you want to hear about the specials now?"

"Could we have another few minutes Rachel?"

After having a little peek at Kat's cleavage, Rachel smiled at him she said, "You got it, Harm, just give me a wave when you're ready."

"Thanks."

Kat picked up the conversation again. "On my way through Atlanta this morning I saw this in a shop window and I thought of you."

"That's really sweet, but why?"

She wrapped her arms around Harm's arm and snuggled in, so that her breasts made full contact and were nearly spilling out over the plunging neckline. "Okay, tell me something. I see how you're looking at me right now, what are you thinking?"

"That's classified."

"Good answer." The guy at the next table grinned at Harm. She let that thought germinate for a moment. "Did you know that you are the most important person in my life?"

"I did know that, and you are mine."

"I'm glad. Have I ever told you that I love ..., your house?" she asked, coyly.

He coughed. "You want to talk about the house now?"

"No, I wanted to talk about what we could do when we get there."

"Ah, Rachel! Cheque please."

Rachel looked over and nudged Nana in the ribs. Then picking up their bill from the counter said, "Told you so." Her reaction was echoed around the room. People had apparently been enjoying the show. She walked over and put it on the table by Harm. "There you are Honey. No rush," she said, as she walked away.

That brought a laugh from the woman at the next table, who quipped, "Yeah, like he's going to take his time."

Harm glanced at the cheque, dropped thirty dollars on the table and hurried to get their coats.

When they finally reached home, they rushed inside slamming the door behind them. Dropping their coats on the floor, they reached for each other clinging like a magnet to steel. He was trembling with excitement. "Did I mention how much I love this dress?"

She laughed. "I think you did." He froze momentarily. "It comes off you know," she said playfully.

"Oh, how?"

"It's under here." She raised her arm, so he could find the hidden zipper at the side.

"Clever." He slowly pulled the zipper down and the dress slipped a little. "I love the way it's coming off."

"Me too."

He gently peeled the top of the dress away. "Wow look at you," he said.

"I've seen them before thanks." Placing his hands on her he squeezed them gently and circled her nipples with his thumbs. "You are incredibly beautiful."

She kissed him hard. "Enough talk, just concentrate on what you're doing." He began to explore her body, feeling the softness of her breasts against his bare chest. "Yes," she purred

They left a trail of clothes behind as they hurried to the bedroom. This was far from her first sexual experience, but it was the first that hadn't been forced on her. Harm was so loving, and giving, and considerate. With Harm, Kat experienced something else for the first time. She'd heard about it, women were always bragging about them, dreaming about them, or complaining about never having one. But she really had no idea what they were talking about until now. Now she knew all about it and, somehow, he made it last until she nearly passed out. She began to cry quietly and when he saw the tears he was devastated and asked her what he had done.

"Nothing bad. It was just different that's all." She left the tears on her cheeks, but he gently brushed them away. "Harm?"

"Uh huh?"

"I love you." They lay on the bed with their eyes closed for a while resting. After a while she nudged him. "Harm?"

"Uh huh?"

"Could we do it again?"

It was nearly noon when Kat finally rolled out of bed. She went into the bathroom and shut the door. Harm lifted his head when he heard the shower running. The image of the water splashing over her body pulled at him until he couldn't keep still. "Do you need some company in there?" he said, from the door.

She looked at him over her shoulder. "Oh, alright, I'll let you this one time. But only if you promise to wash my back."

"I can do that too," he said, stepping under the shower.

He took the soap from her and began massaging her with it.

"Harm."

"Yeah."

"Harm ..., that is not my back."

Later, when Harm emerged from the bedroom dressed in jeans, a button-down shirt and a warm sweater he found Kat standing in the kitchen with a cup of coffee. She was looking very comfortable in his terry robe, tied loosely at the waist.

KAT IN HARM'S WAY

"Are you hungry?" she asked, smiling contentedly. All it took was one look at her glorious young face and the swell of her breasts, barely contained beneath the plush blue material to get him going again.

"Absolutely," he said. He moved in close and kissed her. She kissed back. While their lips touched, he pulled on the cord and with a sweep of his hands across her chest the robe fell away like theater curtains.

She stopped it in the crook of her arms. "Uh, uh, uh." She calmly put her coffee mug down and covered herself and retied the cord.

"I was talking about food, Harm."

"Oh, you were?" He slid his hands under the robe once more and let them rest on her hips.

"Yes," she said, and, gently but firmly, removed his hands and pulled the robe together again. "I think I've had enough of that for a while and so have you." This time she tied the knot firmly.

"I could argue with that."

"But you're not going to, are you?" she said, with an expression only a drill sergeant could manage.

"No, I suppose not. So, what should I cook for you?"

"Eggs, two of them ..., over easy, whole wheat toast and do we have any bacon?" she asked.

"We do ..., and what about some coffee?" he asked.

She picked up her empty cup and waved it in front of him. "I've already made the coffee but you can pour mine." He did and was about to put it back. "My turn now," she said, taking it from him. "Are you having yours black, or with milk and sugar?"

"You know I always have it black."

"I did, but last night you surprised me. I thought there might be more surprises coming my way."

He wrapped his arms around her he began kissing her neck. "Perhaps there are, but not about the coffee," he said, and kissed her again.

With a wry smile Kat shrugged out of his grip and gently pushed him away, "Down boy, we're talking about coffee here."

"Yes Sergeant," Harm said, reluctantly backing away. He reached for a mug from the cupboard and held it out for her.

"That's better." Kat filled it and then sat down. "Now, be a good boy and cook me some breakfast."

Later they were sitting at the kitchen table with nothing but bits of toast on their plates.

"OK, breakfast's out of the way, so are we going to start planning my career?" he asked.

She flashed a wicked grin. "Or, we could do something else for a while."

SHARED HAPPINESS

Their House, Durham

A few weeks later Kat woke up with the sun, his arm was stretched across her chest. "Are you alive?" Harm stirred, growled softly and then they made love.

After breakfast and a long walk, they ended up on the couch in the living room before lunch. It was a comfortable room, obviously decorated by a single man. Photos and mementos from his military career hung with pictures of his parents, a portrait of a young man who was a slightly less imposing version of Harm, and a recent one of Kat. There were also two folded flags in triangular box frames showing the stars on blue. One was presented to his mother at her son's funeral, the other to Harm at his father's.

"Tell me about this place, Harm."

"I've told you all about it before, haven't I?"

"Nope, tell me now."

Harm lead her towards a window. "Okay. It was Mom and Dad's first house and even though we were only here when I was a kid, it's always been a part of my life. The Army moved us around, but Dad always brought us back. The memories of this place, the happy unspoiled life we had here, it never leaves you, you know?"

"I wish I did. That's your dad's flag?"

"Yeah."

"What was your dad like?"

"He was great, when he was here, we'd play catch out on the lawn, he'd take us for walks in the bush, you know teach us about things. It was great. When Dad became the Exec at Fort Bragg, they sold it and we moved down to Fayetteville."

"It's funny, but I'd always pictured you as a Connecticut Yankee."

"Bite your tongue woman."

Kat burst out laughing, "Oh, now that expression is priceless." His face split into a wide grin. "But I like that one much better. Harm, after all this time I know next to nothing about you."

"I could say the same thing about you."

"Me? I'm an open book."

"That is absolutely untrue. But I'm a gentleman, so I'll let it pass for the moment."

He looked around the room as if he could see his family as they were. "My brother and I were typical Army brats. I did well in school, but John always did better. I was the jock, the QB, the sprinter, all of that stuff."

"You must have been quite something."

"I thought I was at the time. John was an academic, the class president, the valedictorian. He wanted to be a teacher, but Dad was a West Pointer. He insisted that we had to go too."

"Are all fathers like that?"

"I keep forgetting that you didn't know yours."

"There wasn't time."

"I'm sorry. Anyway, John didn't want to, but Dad said it would make a man of him. I was two years behind him. When he graduated, John went right into the 1st. Air Cav, as a 2nd Lt. That surprised me because he had been talking about going into Intelligence as an analyst."

"What happened to him?"

"He went over in '69 and was killed the first time he stepped out of the Huey. That's his flag next to Dad's."

"Aw Jesus. I am so sorry."

"Yeah. That was the shock of my life. I was going to follow him into Air Cav. But because of him I chose Army Intelligence and was deployed to Vietnam in '71. Intelligence was not a good fit for me. M-I and the CIA were into some things that were just wrong as far as I was concerned. That's all I'm going to say about that. I asked for a transfer.

"I applied to the Ranger program and got in and made it through thankfully. As soon as I made it through, I was selected for a Rangers' LRRP team (Long Range Reconnaissance Patrol)."

"Which unit were you in?" Kat leaned into him, folding her arms around his then she reached for a picture of a squad of Rangers taken at a fire base in Vietnam.

"The 1st Battalion Rangers, 75th Infantry at Devlyn Army Airfield, down in Georgia."

"I spent a little time there."

"Yeah? That's me there," he pointed, "second from the end. I was the platoon leader. A good bunch of guys."

They lighted on the couch again. Kat folded her legs under her, leaned back and rested her arm over the back. He sat in the middle with his hip touching her knees. She twisted slightly to place the picture back on the end table. Then turning back to him she traced small, lazy circles on his shoulder with her fingers. "Where did you see action?"

"You name it, Laos, Cambodia, Nam. Then the war ended."

"What did you do after that?"

"Reagan's bunch came up with Operation Urgent Fury in '83, so off we went."

"You're kidding, you went to Grenada?"

"I did, and trust me, it was no trip to the beach. We were the Spearhead Force for the operation and they were going to send us in to secure the airfield the Cubans were building. There were three C-130s carrying us down there.

The first two planes had the lead assault company and we were to provide backup from the third ship, but then things got royally fucked up. They had to abort their drops." He casually placed his hand on her hip.

She put her hand on his. "What happened?"

81

"Both transports had failures in their inertial navigation system and radar. Like I said, I was in the third plane and its systems worked fine. Suddenly we were the lead assault element, the first ones in."

"Was there any opposition?"

"Some antiaircraft and small arms fire popping off as we came down, but there were some Air Force AC–130 Specter gunships circling above us and they gave us some assistance. We hit the ground and returned fire, then set up the command post.

"What a goddamn mess that operation was. I think we were the only ones who knew what we were doing most of the time. Anyway, I took a Cuban round that put me out of action. But they rescued a whole bunch of people, so it wasn't a complete screw up."

She squeezed his hand. "So that's where you got that crater in your chest."

"Speaking of chests ..." he said, with a raised eyebrow. "Do you know what I'm thinking about now?"

"I think I do, yes, but aren't you too tired for that?"

"No ma'am, I am not," he said resolutely, and his hand moved from her hip.

She beamed at him. "Okay Studly, hands off the boob and finish the story. You were going to tell me how it happened."

"I was not."

She kicked him and punched his arm. "Oh yes, you were. You can't leave me hanging like that."

"Speaking of leaving someone hanging, I'm sort of left hanging right now." He looked down at the tent growing in his pants.

She did too, then covering her chest with a pillow. "And who's fault is that?"

"Okay, now that was just unfriendly." She looked at him sternly. "Alright already, I'll finish the story. It happened after we started taking the high ground. We were busy cleaning out the snipers and started gathering in some Cuban prisoners. After that we could begin clearing the trucks and things off the strip. When the field was functional again the aircraft began delivering some gun jeeps.

"The whole point of the operation was to get the students out, so I picked a few guys from my platoon, took one of the jeeps and headed up to the True-Blue Medical School campus to rescue them."

"That wasn't really the name of the school was it?"

"Yup. Anyway, we came to a fork in the road, and like Yogi Berra said when you come to a fork in the road ..."

"Take it. I know."

"Of course you do," he said, rapping the pillow with the back of his hand. "It was a dirt road by the way, one that didn't show up on the map. I had the driver go left when we should have gone right. My fault entirely.

"We got lost and while we were trying to get back to the fork we were ambushed. Four of my guys were killed and I took one through the chest. My sergeant, Charley Packard, looked after me. I owe that guy my life. I'd like you to meet him some day."

"Me too, I like him already. What happened after that?"

"I was shipped home. They said I'd have a problem with my ticker, so when I got out of the hospital, I was transferred to a desk job. I joined Hershoff's staff and started doing work for NATO. He was a colonel then and when he got promoted, I got promoted and eventually we were assigned to Maj. Gen. H. Norman Schwarzkopf. And the rest is history."

"Can I ask another question?"

"Shoot."

"How did your parents die?"

"Cancer took them both when I was on deployment. Mom went first, I came back on compassionate leave. Then Dad passed." He paused, remembering. "Even in my thirties I felt like an orphan. It was strange, but that's how I felt after you left Venice Beach."

"How come you never said anything?"

"I don't know. Anyway, that's why I had to have this place. This was the last place where we were all together and things were good."

"And I love it here," she said.

"Me too. Now let's get back to the pressing issue of our day."

"And what, pray tell, is this pressing issue of which you speak?"

"Are you going to give me that pillow, or am I going to have to take it from you?"

"I'll give you the pillow alright!" She smacked him with it then tossed it on the floor.

DISILLUSIONED

Fort Benning, Georgia 1994

Kat was totally committed to her job. It was challenging, and she felt what she was doing was important. She'd earned the respect of those in her command. Her evals were excellent and she'd received commendations for initiative and leadership. Devlyn was pleased, but she didn't know that, nor would she have cared if she did. Her success made her intensely happy, though not as happy as her relationship with Harm.

They spent a special long weekend on Paradise Island in the Bahamas that January to celebrate her 23rd birthday. Despite the activities available they spent most of the weekend in bed and when they returned their routine continued. Fridays she'd leave the base right after work, drive up to Durham and arrive at his house around midnight. For Kat, weekends were wonderful, work was going well, and she thought Harm was doing okay too.

It was the middle of summer when she arrived to find all the lights out. Worried, she searched the main part of the house then quietly went upstairs to find him in bed asleep. She undressed and climbed in beside him and nuzzled up to his back, but he didn't respond.

She woke at dawn realizing that she was alone. He was sitting in the kitchen with the lights off. "What's going on?"

"Nothing. Couldn't sleep." She went for the light switch. "No, don't turn on the ..." he began, but she'd already flipped it on. He shielded his eyes.

Obviously, something was wrong. "Alright, what's bothering you. Do you want to talk about it?"

"No."

"Please, Harm," she said. His face was set in a horrible scowl and that old woody feeling in her gut came on with a vengeance. "What's going on?"

He banged on the table with his fists and raised his voice. "Fine! It's all turning to shit."

She was astonished by the violence. She'd never seen him like this before. "What?"

"I have no idea of what I'm doing anymore."

"What are you talking about?" She moved to the table and sat down.

"This ..., us ... I just sit around here waiting for you to come back. I'm useless. No ... it just ... it isn't working anymore." Harm buried his face in his hands.

"I have some leave coming, maybe we could take a ..."

He turned away from his hands and glared at her. "Kat, a fucking trip won't fix this! Okay?"

"Whoops." She stood up again and backed away from the table." Excuse me? Where did that come from?" she asked, but he didn't say anything. She leaned over the table her hands set on the surface her expression softened as she tried to calm him down. "Look, I just thought ..."

"You don't have a clue, do you?"

She backed off again and the sympathy was waning. Now she was getting angry too and her mood growing as dark as the pre-dawn sky outside the window. "I thought I did up until a second ago, but I guess I was wrong."

"You guessed right," he said, "Jesus Christ, Kat, what are you doing here, can you tell me that?"

"Harm, lower your voice and tell me what's going on." She moved away from him and was standing with her back against the stove, her body rigid and trembling slightly. "Have I done something wrong?"

"How could Wonder Woman do anything wrong?"

"Don't you lay that crap on me. I'm doing my job," she said, raising her voice to match his.

"Oh, no doubt about that, you're going places. It's me. I'm the fucking problem. I'm the has-been."

"I don't know what brought this on, but you've got so much to offer."

"I've got fuck-all to offer."

"Where the hell is this coming from?"

He scowled at her and turned his back. She couldn't deal with him anymore. She went up to the bedroom and got the suitcase she'd arrived with hours earlier.

He was standing at the foot of the stairs when she came down. "What are you going to do?" he asked, as if it wasn't completely obvious.

"I'm going back to Benning." She tossed her house key onto the hall table as she went to the door.

"So that's it, you're just going to leave me?"

"Isn't that what you want? Look, I have no idea what's happening to you, Harm," she snapped, then quickly forced herself to regain control. "Harm," she said, as her trembling voice involuntarily rose an octave, "I ..., shit!" she took a deep breath. "I love you Harm. I love you so fucking much. Right from the beginning it's been like a dream."

He banged the newel post with his fist "Some dream," he growled, and her reaction made him instantly regretted it.

Trying to keep a headache at bay, she rubbed her forehead and then slammed her fist against her thigh. "Now you're sounding like every other man I've known, so shut the fuck up!

"Clearly, I'm making you unhappy. I don't want that, so listen up, Lover." He started to say something, but her hand shot up to stop him. "No .... just listen. You're the only one who can figure out what to do now. You don't need me here to distract you. So yes, I'm going to leave. Don't think about me, don't call me. Just focus on you. Get something to do. Then, if you change your mind, write me a goddamn letter to apologize for this shit and maybe ... maybe I'll come back."

"Fine with me," he said, and walked back into the kitchen.

"Oh ..., oh," she fumed. "Well isn't that just fucking peachy! Thanks a bunch, Harm." She opened the door and left.

8

FIRST STEP

U of NC, Chapel Hill

Harm hadn't meant for any of that to happen. He needed to do something to get her back and it was painfully apparent that he couldn't do it without help. He needed someone he could talk to.

Sitting at the table it suddenly came to him that the person he needed was practically next door. Alan Bethel, a professor at the University of North Carolina, had been a diplomat at NATO HQ when Harm was there.

They'd become friends and Alan told him to call if he was ever in Chapel Hill. So, Harm called him, and Alan invited him to dinner.

As they were coming to the end of a perfectly cooked medium rare prime rib, Alan said, "You tell a hell of a story, Harm. Have you ever thought about teaching?"

"Teaching, what the hell would I teach?"

"Why not modern history, after serving in Vietnam, at NATO, and then the Gulf War you were a part of it."

Harm leaned back in his chair and took a sip of wine. "That's an interesting idea."

"You know what you could do? You could get started by coming to UNC to give a talk about Army life."

He raised his chin and scoffed, "It's been done."

Undaunted Alan countered, "That's true, but Harm almost everything's been done. The key is to bring a unique perspective. I think you could pull that off. You've been involved in so many things." He thought about it for a second.

"Why not give us a lecture on the modern history of war from a field officer's perspective, from Vietnam to Grenada to Desert Storm? Or, perhaps the politics of the Pentagon, or working in NATO?" As Alan spun out his ideas, Harm started to see possibilities.

"I've created presentations, but I've never taught. I wouldn't know where to begin."

"They're very similar. Begin with something simple and straightforward and prepare to ask and receive questions to open a discussion. At the very least the students would have a better understanding of what's been going on over the past 25 years."

"Okay, I'll write something and send it to you. You can tell me whether it's worth repeating."

"Perfect."

A couple of days later Alan read Harm's draft and phoned to say the material was great and arranged for the first of what would become many guest engagements.

DEVLYN'S TRIUMPH

Fort Benning, Georgia

Kat had been promoted to Sergeant First Class. As an instructor, she was tough, detail oriented, and quick to criticize poor performance.

When her students graduated, they may not have been as infatuated with her as they were at the beginning, but they came out really knowing what they were doing.

She had become a master in mixed martial arts, an expert marksman, and was still adding languages to her list. Devlyn heard that Command was considering her for the Officer Training program, so she was ready for M-CI now. The timing couldn't have been better.

Just after morning parade she got the message that Col. Gene Whitaker Jr. had requested her to come into the office for a chat.

She hurried over to McGinnis-Wickham Hall and was shown in by the Colonel's secretary. "Sergeant First Class Fernando, Sir," he announced at the door and stood aside so she could enter. She saluted and waited for the officer to respond. The colonel's desk was on the far side between the garrison's flag and Old Glory.

She let her eyes scan the room. It was a good-sized office with honey colored paneling, neatly decorated with company coats of arms and photos of troops training, troops jumping from WWII DC-3s over France, recent shots of troops jumping from C-130s over some desert.

In the center of the wall to her left was a large oil painting of "Old Rock" General Henry Lewis Benning a brigadier general in the Confederate States Army during the Civil War.

Whitaker stood and returned the salute. "Thank you, Sergeant Pindar." Pindar left the room, shutting the door behind him. "At ease Sergeant Fernando, thanks for coming in." With an open hand he indicated one of the two wooden chairs that had been placed in front of his desk. "Take a seat."

"Yes Sir. Thank you, Sir," she said, and after he was seated Kat picked the chair on the right. She sat ramrod straight on the edge of the seat an inch away from the backrest. Colonel Whitaker took a moment to review her service file.

She waited in silence until he pushed the jacket away and took off his glasses. "I've called you in because Lt-Gen Hockley and I have been reading a lot of good reports about you."

"Thank you, Sir."

"You're doing an outstanding a job here. Outstanding."

"Thank you, Sir."

"How are you feeling about things?"

"Fine Sir," she said, wondering if there was a point to all this flattery.

"Good. Okay." He paused to put on his glasses and looked at her jacket again. Then looked up at her. "There was a note in your jacket from the recruiting officer stating that your aptitude was more suited to Army Intelligence ... and frankly, I'd have to agree with that. Coincidentally I've just received a request from M-I to have you submit an application."

"I don't know what to say, Sir." Her eyes widened with excitement, but she stayed focused on the Colonel.

"As much as we'd like to keep you here, they want you at the USAICoE."

"Excuse me Sir, but what is the USAI ...?"

"It's the United States Army Intelligence Center of Excellence, the Army's school for professional training of military intelligence."

"Oh, thank you, Sir." Kat's excitement was almost impossible to contain.

"More specifically, it's the people at Counterintelligence who want you. Bottom line, Fernando, the choice is yours. Whether you stay here or move over to M-I, your career will advance, I can pretty much guarantee that."

"Thank you, Sir. Do I have to make my choice now?"

"You have a couple of days. The next course starts on the 29th. It's a twenty-two-week program and then, when you successfully complete the course, you'll be on a one-year probationary period.

"Now, considering the limited window of opportunity, if you want to get into this program, you should let me know ASAP."

"Yes, Sir."

"Fernando, a question came up in our meeting."

"Yes, Sir?"

KAT IN HARM'S WAY

"Just out of curiosity, how many languages do you speak?"

"Twelve Sir."

"Twelve! Christ. With everything else you've been doing when the hell did you have the time to ..., never mind. Alright, the course is at Fort Huachuca in Arizona. This is a big decision, so take a little time to think it over and get back to me. Your application should be in by end of week."

Without hesitation, she said, "I'd like to do it, Sir."

"Wow. That was quicker than I expected. Are you sure? You're not going to talk it over with ..."

"No Sir. This sounds like a wonderful opportunity."

"Yes, it is." He pushed the packet across his desk. "Okay, here's the application, fill it out, bring it back to me and I'll put it in the works." He stood up and shook her hand. Good luck Fernando and congratulations."

"Thank you, Sir."

Kat did some reading to find out more about what she had just agreed to do. The opening paragraph said that the program requires its members to be mature, intelligent, and personable.

To carry out the broad range of CI functions to detect, identify, exploit, and neutralize the Foreign Intelligence and Security Services (FISS), International Terrorist Organizations (ITO), and threats targeting U.S. forces. "Hell, I can do that," she said, filled out the forms and handed them in.

After she was accepted into the program a copy of her application was forwarded to Fort Mead, Maryland. The first order of business was to obtain her Top-Secret Security Clearance and she was amazed at how fast that was. Her background check had been done years ago and her TSSC had already been approved.

She called Harm who said, "I thought you weren't going to talk to me until I wrote you a letter."

"Is that a problem for you? Because if it is then ..."

"No! No, of course not. What's happening?"

"Something's come up and I'm going on a twenty-two-week course in Arizona. I just wanted you to know where I am if you ever wanted to talk to me again."

"Listen Kat, I'm sorry. I never meant for us to break up. Christ, I've made a mess of things. I am truly sorry."

"Really?"

"Honestly, I don't know what I'm doing half the time. I can't believe how much I've missed you. I want it to be like it was, if that's possible."

"We can't go back, Harm. But I believe we can start over, if you're willing to try."

"I want that more than anything. Can you come up and see me before you go? A lot has happened since you left, and I'd like to tell you about it in person."

"Of course." She drove up the following Friday and Harm told her about the help he got from Alan Bethel and that he'd started giving talks up and down the coast. "Things are going so well I have engagements booked from now until the end of December '95."

"That's wonderful, Harm." She threw her arms around him. "I'm really proud of you."

"Thanks, but the biggest news is that I've decided to open an academy. I've pitched my business plan to the Army and Navy and have already got the funding and the land for it."

"That's amazing. What would the academy teach?"

"Survival training. My students would be diplomats and corporate types deployed to the world's hot spots. The money comes with certain conditions with the DoD that I can't to get into at the moment, but they're manageable."

"Holy shit, That's fantastic. Where's it going to be?"

"The Navy is providing a section of a mountain top just outside Werner Springs, California. That's just east of San Diego. It's perfect for the kind of training I have in mind. I have an architect in San Diego working on the design right now. I tell ya, it's going to be incredible, Kat."

"I have no doubt about that. Have you got a name for it?"

"Not yet. I 've had some ideas but ..."

"Tell me about the mountain, what's it called?"

"Oh, sure. It's Hot Springs Mountain."

"No, that would make it sound like a resort. Maybe there's something else around there that has a name you could pick up." She thought about it for a while then said, "How do you get up there from Warner Springs?"

"There's a dirt road, Eagle's Nest Rd., that winds up to the top."

"Hey, I like that. You could call it Eagle's Nest Academy."

He let that settle for a moment. "Damn, why didn't I think of that? ENA, I like that. Okay then, Eagle's Nest Academy it is. I should have the finished drawings soon and the USACE crew is already breaking ground."

"I'd love to see the plans."

"What course are you taking in Arizona?"

"It's the USAI Course at Fort Huachuca."

"No kidding, you're going into Intelligence?"

"Counterintelligence."

"Whoa, well I wish you better luck than I had with them. I tell you what, I'll bring the plans up to you when you get a weekend pass."

After she left for Arizona Harm locked the house up and flew to San Francisco, gave his talk, then drove down to San Diego to spend a couple of days with the architect and an officer from the Army Corp of Engineers.

It was a dream he'd never have had if Kat hadn't given him a kick in the ass. Now in just a matter of months it would be a reality. He couldn't be happier; the design was incredible the ground had been broken and the foundations were in and he had Kat back.

PUPPET MASTER

Sierra Vista, Arizona

Two days before the course began Kat arrived at Fort Huachuca and was standing in her Class A uniform on the tarmac in the blistering heat with the other passengers, waited for the pilots to unload their luggage. Picking up her heavy gunny sack she walked smartly to the small terminal building. Her blouse was wet with perspiration and felt a sudden chilly when she got inside with the air conditioning.

She wasn't surprised to have a rugged, no-nonsense cowboy type zero in on her but certainly didn't expect him to greet her. "SFC Fernando?" he said.

"Yes?"

"Good to meet you." His deep, honey-colored voice had a touch of a western twang that seemed to complete the image. He reached out to her with a large leather-hard hand. His grip was firm, without trying to prove anything.

There was something familiar about that voice but she couldn't quite place it. His eyes were hidden behind a pair of no-glare Aviator sunglasses, so she couldn't see what color they were. She guessed they'd be blue.

"And you are ...?" she said.

"I'm Paul Devlyn."

"Hello Mr. Devlyn." He released her hand and gave her a complete once over. With her two-inch heels, Kat stood six-two and he was an inch or two taller. Slim, and reasonably good looking he was brimming with self-confidence. She wondered why she was being met by some friendly cowboy instead of someone from the base.

"That's Maj Devlyn, Senior Special Agent, Army Counterintelligence, and your official reception committee."

"Sir," she said, dropping her kit. She stood at attention and snapped off a smart salute.

"Jesus, relax Fernando, and welcome to Sierra Vista. I was the one who requested your participation in this training course."

"Oh! Well uh ... thank you, Sir," He looked decidedly unmilitary, His gray flecked dark hair was a little long and combed back over his ears. His sideburns were touched with a bit of red and flowed into his short dark beard.

It must have been 102° in the shade, but he seemed unaffected by the heat.

"Uh, I'm curious, Sir." she said, "Would this be casual Friday at Fort Huachuca?"

"No. Why do you ask?"

"I'm feeling a bit over dressed."

"Right, well as it happens the M-CI Agents generally don't wear the uniform. We wear business attire, although there's discretion depending on whatever is appropriate for any given assignment. But I like the casual Friday thing, so let's go with that."

"I'll have to keep that in mind, thank you, Sir. Ah ..., Sir, I am honored to be invited to the course, but why did you ask for me?"

He removed the sunglasses for a moment to lock eyes with her and she was right, they were blue. "We're going to file that question away for another time.

It was a useless answer but she had to accept it. "Yes, Sir."

"Okay, grab your kit and let's move out."

He talked as they walked. "I've taken the liberty of arranging for a short-term lease on an apartment for you.

"Uh, I wasn't expecting that but thank you very much, Sir."

"Pleasure, my car's out this way." They walked to the front of the building and stepped out into the harsh Arizona sun, he asked, "Have you got shades with you?"

"I do, yes Sir."

"Well now's the time for 'em. I've got the top down." *Of course,* he was heading for the cherry red Mustang parked at the end of the path. Somehow, she knew it had to be a Mustang. He opened his door. "Just toss the bag in the back and mind your butt, the seat's a trifle hot."

He wasn't kidding. She pretended it didn't bother her, but she wished she'd worn pants.

Devlyn tore out of the parking lot like a teenager. Once again, she tried to look as if she was okay with that, but it was impossible not to hang on like her life depended on it.

He pulled on to Brainard Rd. heading west and then performed a slick drift onto Arizona St.

"Oh! ah ..., yahoo," she said, with mock excitement mixed with terror. "Is this fun, or what?" He grinned as if he was just doing this to tease her.

A field stone entrance marker announced Fort Huachuca 1877 "That," he said, pointing over the dashboard, "is Fort Huachuca." The barrier opened just in time as he sped by. He zipped by the security station with a little nod to the guards inside.

"We'll do a little drive through so I can point out a few things that you'll need to remember. Don't mind the boys on horses. They are our version of 'F Troop'."

"Is 'F' Troop based here at Huachuca?"

"No, those are some of our instructors on the horses," he laughed, "F Troop was a western on TV back in the early '60s, a comedy," he said, but she didn't get it. "Yeah, it was before my time too."

"You were going to tell me why you picked me, Sir."

"Nice try, but no, I definitely wasn't going to do that."

"With respect Sir, I need to know why you asked for me. If I'm to succeed in the course I need to know what you expect from me."

"Look, Fernando, you were recommended to me some time ago and I've read your jacket cover to cover. You're going to find out soon enough that this is a tough program. I picked you because I believed you could handle it. I'm counting on you to do well. Prove me right."

"Sir, I have always done my best."

"That's all I ask." He let the road rush by in silence for a moment. "Fernando, listen to me. This is where you belong. There aren't many women who come to CI as well equipped as you." She wondered what equipment he was referring to, exactly. "Anything other than excellence is unacceptable."

"Yes, Sir."

He pulled into a nice-looking apartment complex and stopped the car under the shade of a huge Arizona ash. "You're up there, apartment 207. Orientation is Monday at zero-eight-hundred, in that big building I pointed out."

He got out and reached over the back for her gunnysack, tossed it to her as she got out. "Next time I see you will be at your graduation. Get yourself settled in. Study hard, make me proud." He tossed the apartment key to her.

"Yes, Sir. I'll do my best."

"I know you will, Fernando." He took a moment to ogle her and with a lopsided grin left, saying, "Damn, you are one fine lookin' woman. Okay, end of the tour, you're on your own,".

Kat just stood there for a minute wondering what the hell had just happened.

BACK TO SCHOOL

Fort Huachuca, Arizona

The work was challenging but she did very well in her courses on domestic and international law, law enforcement and counterintelligence. Initially, classes focused on the investigation of national security crimes; treason, spying, espionage, sedition, subversion, sabotage.

Then those lessons moved out into the field with simulated real-world scenarios. Working with strangers she found out the different methods she could use to turn enemy agents into double agents. How to take out bad guys with instructors taking on the role of terrorists. And situations that pitted student against student. There was advanced weapons training and live fire exercise.

Working from behind the scene Devlyn saw to it that everything she was doing was preparing her for his specialty. He wanted her in the field as an investigator and as an operative, working undercover when necessary. He wanted to test her in as many situations as he could in order to find how best to use his new asset.

A VISITOR

Sierra Vista Airport

There wasn't anything that resembled free time, but sixteen weeks into the twenty-two-week program Kat was finally able to enjoy her much anticipated night off.

She'd made Harm put the date on his calendar and Harm made sure that he was able to fly in from San Diego. It was a brief overnight visit. A tiny window of opportunity and they weren't going to waste a second of it. She'd rented a car and the instant she was dismissed she drove to the airport to pick him up.

He was as excited as she was. He knew that she couldn't say a word about what she was doing but that was fine with him, because he had so much to tell her. Harm brought along a briefcase full of material to show her. Photos and copies of the plans for his academy and he was going to tell her all about how the project was taking shape.

But as soon as they saw each other, there was only one thing on their minds. It seemed unlikely that they'd be getting into the details of the academy any time soon.

Kat pulled into the parking lot under the big old shade tree. "This looks like a nice place," he said.

Taking his hand, she said, "Yeah it's OK, but the neighbors tend to be nosy. They're all practicing the art of being a secret agent." And she led him up to her apartment.

"Are they?" he asked.

"Are they what?" she countered.

"Secret Agents?"

"Just Wannabes right now." She unlocked the door and pushed it open. "Come on in." Kat closed the door behind him. "Take your jacket off," she said.

"I'd like you to do it."

"Would you now?"

Once the curtains were drawn Kat stood very close Harm with her hands on the lapels of his jacket. He didn't have time to look around the place and he didn't care. He just looked into her dark amber eyes. "Kat."

She smiled at him, her expression exposed everything she was thinking, everything she was feeling, her anticipation and her hunger for him. She pulled him closer. "God, I missed you."

"Me too, it's been too long."

"It certainly has."

THE BREAK IS OVER

Fort Huachuca

Kat studied special investigation techniques, gathering intel, and putting together and delivering reports.

Like the FBI, the Special Agents would have the power to detain and arrest subjects, but it went further than that. In preparation for advanced field work, ten of the top students moved on to receive special ops training. They learned techniques for covert actions against a variety of enemy targets, as well as undercover and infiltration work.

Three didn't make the grade and were sent back to the main body of trainees.

But during that probationary period, they would continue their training in other disciplines to allow them to work in the field with teams from Special Forces, Army Rangers, and Navy Seals.

Kat had been selected to be part of that advanced class and with her language skills her specialty was infiltration and espionage.

She proved to be an excellent student and did well in all areas. By the end of the course she was the top of her class. She really didn't have time to think about anything other than her training.

Even though she never saw Devlyn at Huachuca, he was watching her progress very carefully. There were several reasons why he chose her back in 1988, and all of them were spelled out in a memo he'd sent out to recruiting officers all over the country. She had excellent academic scores, amazing scores on her ASVAB, the languages skills, the athleticism, and her looks.

Another one of those reasons was that she had no family, no friends, no attachments. That was until Toucksberry came along. Her deployment with the Black Horse outfit should have dealt with that. But it didn't take. Then news of her break-up with Harm quickly spread through Fort Benning and he thought that problem had been put to rest.

Then he got word that Kat had entertained a gentleman friend in her apartment. An agent in a relationship was a serios problem. It was a weak point the enemy could use against them, a distraction and a conflict with the duties of an agent in the field. He had to find a way to break them up again and this time make it stick. Providing she survived it, the perfect solution might have been a deployment in Honduras. He was going to send her there as soon as she graduated.

PART 2

9
THE UNUSUAL TDY

Fort Huachuca, Arizona

Senior special agents are the ones who assist U.S. Army Special Forces groups with liaison, source operations, and intelligence investigations (typically in support of force protection), but there were exceptions to that rule.

When Kat graduated from the course she had no idea that she would become one of the exceptions.

The graduation ceremony was on a Friday and Kat saw Devlyn's name on the program. He'd had flown in to give the commencement speech, but Kat didn't see him until the commandant finished his opening comments and introduced the guest speaker. He walked out onto the stage looking nothing like the man at the airport. Now that the beard was gone and his hair was neatly trimmed, he looked roughly the same age as Harm.

In his business suit and dress shoes, he could have been one those upper echelon executive types tall enough to have played round-ball in the big leagues.

Now revealed to her he certainly wasn't as good looking as Harm. His features were hard, almost cruel. His slightly downturned nose, the thin lips and those piercing blue eyes gave him an aggressive bird of prey look.

The face from Fort Benning that she remembered now. *Yup, that's the guy alright. He's a chameleon. Why did he keep who he was a secret? He said that someone had mentioned me to him. Who was talking to him about me and when was that? Jezzus, how long has he been watching me?*

Devlyn's speech raised some eyebrows when he addressed the issue of drug trafficking from Central and South America. He equated it with acts of terror against America's national security.

"In my opinion," he said, in conclusion, "CI should play an active role in the war against the drug cartels." It went over very well with the crowd. Following the ceremony, he singled out Kat for a private conversation.

"I've been hearing good things about you all the way through the course. You're a top student, congratulations. It's time to put you to work Fernando. You were assigned to the 66th Military Intelligence Brigade, for deployment in Europe."

"Yes, Sir."

"I've put that on hold for the moment."

"Oh?" she wasn't particularly disappointed, but ... "May I ask why, Sir?"

"My new priority is the South American drug problem, so I'm sending you down there."

"Really?" *Shit, it means more time away from Harm but I knew that coming in. No, what matters is what he does from this point on. Why is he so interested in me?*

"Thank you, Sir. What's my assignment?" She tried to make it sound enthusiastic. She hoped it worked.

"We need an agent to conduct liaison and operational coordination with our allied force in Honduras."

"Honduras?" *Whoops!* Suddenly she was reminded of the bullet in the back on the Highway of Death. *And how prophetic that name turned out to be? Was he involved in cutting my orders to send me out there? Jesus Christ! He must have been. How far back does this thing with him go?*

"But Sir, you said in your address that you expected that that would involve direct contact with the enemy and I ..."

"Yeah, I know, you're a probie and this is a Special Agent level assignment. Under normal circumstances women don't have direct contact with the enemy. But these aren't normal circumstances and you're my pick for this particular TDY."

Kat's assignment was to join the Joint Task Force Bravo (JTFB) in Honduras. Her posting was at the Enrique Soto Cano Air Base, located about ninety kilometers northwest of Tegucigalpa, near Comayagüela.

A contingent of 1,100 US troops rotated through the base. She was being sent down to monitor both Honduran and American activities and send back weekly reports.

Kat was going undercover as an observer with a newly trained platoon and once they were there they'd be pairing up with Honduran regulars.

Her covert assignment was to provide detailed reports on those Honduran soldiers and all action in which they were involved. Devlyn wanted to know what was happening inside the unit before the platoon was deployed on their away missions.

He told Kat that Agents from Human Intelligence had been doing controlled intel collection operations and interviews and knew there were cartel people planted in the Honduran Army. They just couldn't identify them.

Devlyn was putting her right in there with them, to train with them, gain their confidence, make friends with them. He wanted her to root out the rotten apples and eliminate them.

"You want me to arrest them, Sir?"

"I want you to eliminate them, by any means necessary. Do you have a problem with that, Fernando?"

"No sir." *With certain limitations of course,* she added silently.

Although he wanted her to leave immediately the timing was off. The platoon she was to join hadn't finished their training. That gave her a week's leave to spend with Harm in San Diego.

SIX DAYS LEAVE

Eagle's Nest Academy, Warner Springs, CA

After five days with Harm traveling up to Sulphur Mountain to visit the project by day and enjoying San Diego by night, the last thing Kat wanted to do was leave.

He made her feel like a woman again, like a whole person. And seeing the progress, his ideas coming together at last, just as he had imagined they would, that was incredibly exciting. Construction of Eagle's Nest Academy (ENA) was ahead of schedule and it was going to be spectacular.

The Hacienda and staff quarters were up and the classrooms were almost finished. The perimeter wall was rising from the mountainside like an ancient Spanish fortification and inside trees and gardens of cactus and aloe were being planted. Harm was really excited that the furniture was coming soon and it would begin looking like a grand hotel with special purpose.

Its official name was Eagle's Nest Academy School of Strategic Studies.

As promised, Kat finally met Harm's friend Charley Packard in the cinderblock shell of one of the future classrooms. "This is going to be the Dojo. Maybe you'll be doing some training in here in the future.

Spotting a tall man in army fatigues crossing the quad Harm called out to him. That stiff short brush of white hair crowning his head placed him in his late fifties but his physical conditioning suggested someone much younger. "Charley, come meet Kat."

"Hey it's a pleasure to finally meet you," she said, "Harm has told me so much about you. And by the way, thank you for saving his life."

"Well Katrina, it looks like you're real after all."

"My friends call me Kat."

"OK. Ya know Kat, he's been telling stories about some beautiful young woman for so long I was beginning to think Harm was just pulling my leg. To be honest, since he dreamed up this academy idea I've been wonderin' if saving his life was such a good idea after all."

"Come on Charley, you know you love me," said Harm.

"Ya see what I have to put up with here?"

"I do, and I feel so sorry for you. Honestly, I do."

"I like her Harm, she's a keeper." Charley said. Fixing a friendly grin on his rugged, wind burned face he gave her a one-armed hug.

She liked him too. Harm said Charley was going to be the backbone of the instruction staff, basically their regimental sergeant major and she could see why.

There were a few other men Harm had served with and they were coming in as instructors. Doug Laymen had been

110

the lieutenant of his Ranger unit in Grenada and a good man to have on his team.

What astonished Kat was that when Harm introduced her, he said he hoped she'd be acting lead instructor from time to time too. She wondered how that was going to work when she fully expected to be posted to the Six-Six Brigade in Germany.

At the end of her leave she turned to Harm and asked, "Harm you know I won't have the time to come back here to do any teaching. Why did you say that?"

"Okay, you got me. Kat, I want you here with me all the time."

"But you know I can't, right? I've made a commitment."

"I know. Trust me Kat, I can wait."

"Will you?"

"Count on it. This is going to be a lifetime career for both of us."

"I love you," she said, and that's how they left it.

HER SECOND TDY

Yuma Proving Grounds, Army Base, Arizona

Kat flew out of San Diego to Yuma Army Base to join a newly minted platoon of combat troops heading to Enrique Soto Cano.

Their leader was Cpt. Brian Pacini, twenty-nine, tall and quite handsome in a rugged sort of way. At 6'-2" and weighing in at 190 lbs., he wasn't huge, but he was a powerhouse.

His brown hair was short and he had intelligent, emerald green eyes He was an all American, the boy next door, polite, never swore, was quiet, and serious. *Where do they get guys like that?* she wondered and then she found out.

Pacini was the son of an Aspen, Colorado ski shop owner. He'd been the high school quarterback and a West Pointer scholar. To top it all off, he was a really sweet guy. To look at him she wouldn't have guessed that he was a veteran. But he certainly was, two grueling tours in Bosnia and Croatia.

THE ASSIGNMENT

Enrique Soto Cano Air Base, Honduras

She'd landed in the nerve center of intelligence gathering, communications, and logistical support for US military operations in Honduras.

A joint exercise involving US and Honduran troops and naval elements in various parts of the country under the code name Cabañas 93. They were testing the coastal patrolling, drug interdiction, parachuting, and psychological warfare capabilities of the two armies. Kat worked undercover, as far as everyone knew she was simply an observer with Red Platoon.

Prior to her deployment she was briefed on the Intelligence agents working there, but they didn't know anything about her and Kat kept a very low profile. During the first four months her platoon was limited to training mode, jump and deploy practice missions and recon. She observed and filed detailed reports on their activities, as ordered and during that time she was closing in on the cartel's network.

Kat identified two moles in her reports. The information was sent back from Fort Mead and the suspects disappeared. She asked about them and was told they had been arrested by the Honduran MPs and were not her problem anymore. She dug further and found no arrest reports and no one ever saw them again. She knew there was at least one other man in one of the platoons in her company, but still hadn't been able to identify him. She had to operate very carefully because the cartel made no secret about what they did to people snooping about. Headless bodies were often strung up in town for people to see.

She sent postcards to Harm almost every other day. He wrote back short letters about the progress on the mountain and kept asking when he could come down for a visit.

Six months into her temporary duty she was granted a few days leave and wrote him a quick come-hither card.

A week next Thursday. I've made reservations on the Gulf Coast. Meet me at the airport and bring a bathing suit. Love, Me.

Harm travelled down twice for long weekend visits. They flew east to La Ceiba on the Caribbean coast where there was a small hotel right on the beach. They were both ecstatically happy.

Harm was certain that ENA would be in the black by the end of the first year. Kat didn't care about that. For her, the best thing was being with him. The beach was beautiful, the water was warm, the beer was cold, and the sex was frequent.

THE MISSION BRIEFING

Command Ops

At 15:20 hours, two days after Harm left, Kat was in the mess hall nursing a bottle of water while munching on a small banana.

A Honduran trooper came over and said, "Pardon me Sergeant, the commander wishes to see you in his office." She finished the water and carried the banana outside where she met Cpt. Pacini on his way there too.

As they walked together, she munched on the fruit and asked, "Do you know what this is about?"

"I'm guessing that we've got a real mission tonight."

It was an oppressively hot and humid day with no breeze at all and Kat was looking forward to being inside with the air conditioning.

She was disappointed to find that there was no AC. The large shutters had been swung down shutting out the sunlight, but that didn't help. It was even hotter inside.

Commandant Hollis Denton, BGen Ortega of the Honduran contingent and three of his officers were waiting for them in the large ready room.

They'd been talking with Denton quietly and referring to some notes on the table in front of them. They stopped when they saw Kat and Pacini and two of the men stood up expectantly. Kat knew the younger men and had worked with them but she didn't know the Honduran General.

She dumped the remainder of the banana in the trash because the smell of the American general's cigar permeated everything. He was at the far end before a large, freestanding corkboard with maps and aerial photos pinned to it. Denton pointed at them with his willow switch and said, "Take a seat."

The Hondurans sat and Kat took a chair as far away from the smoke as she could hoping that that would spare her but it wasn't far enough.

Denton added, "Smoke 'em if you got 'em." The Hondurans immediately pulled out their cheroots and lit up.

Oh, perfect, lung cancer here I come.

Pacini reached for a bottle of water from the table and chose to remain standing beside her. Kat took some water too and waited for the briefing to start.

Denton began by swinging his long stick at an aerial surveillance photo through the curling smoke.

Circling a mountain top, he looked at Kat and Pacini and said, "This is why we haven't been able to find the bastard's lab before this," he said, speaking of the drug lord Caesar La Bibiru.

"It's on a goddamn mountain, out in the middle of butt-fuck-nowhere. A Navy surveillance plane spotted La Bibiru's helicopter heading north from Tegucigalpa." He picked up a printed sheet.

"I've just received actionable intel on the whereabouts of La Bibiru," he said, waving the paper at them before he tossed it back on to the table. "His pilot filed a flight plan to San Pedro Sula, but he set it down over here," he said, stabbing the aerial photo with the point of his stick. "On this plateau just south west of Los Murillos." Turning his attention to the map beside the photo "We have no idea how long he'll be there, so we have to move on this right now."

He swung the stick around and pointed at Pacini. "Captain, I'm sending your unit in. You'll go in light, two squads. SFC Fernando will be your 2IC."

Kat looked up in surprise, but he ignored her for the moment, "You'll be taking sixteen Honduran troopers from Major Guillea's command and the two US advisors."

"Excuse me Sir."

"Save your questions sergeant. Major Guillea, you're up."

One of Ortega's officers took over and provided the details using his cheroot as a pointer. "There's a river at the base on the east side, a cliff to the south and dense forest to the north." He swung the pointer over an area just above the plateau. "There are taller mountains here. As far as we can tell the only way to get in there is from the air. There's a clearing on that plateau," he went closer and pointed with his finger, "here. That's where they spotted the helicopter. It's hidden under a camo tarp but you can make out its shape in this blow up."

"Were there any photos showing his gang members, Sir?" Pacini asked.

"We saw no people on the ground. That doesn't mean they aren't there. They could be in the bush around the clearing."

"So, we don't know how many there are there."

"No," Guillea said.

"Okay, that's it," Denton said.

Major Guillea stepped out of the way and sat down.

"Alright Gentlemen," and as an afterthought he acknowledged Kat with a nod, "here it is." Then tapping the spot on the photo with the stick Denton said, "That's your LZ.

Elevation 3871 feet, at 15° 12.04' 59" North, 86° 36.20"40' West." Kat wrote it down on the pad taped to her knee. "If the Navy plane hadn't spotted them setting the chopper down, we never would have found him. Pacini, your code name is Red One. As senior NCO, Fernando you'll be Red 2." He pointed at her and said, "You had a question Fernando?"

To maintain her cover, she had to make it sound like she was afraid to go with them. "I haven't been cleared for combat Sir. I shouldn't be ..."

Glaring at her Denton cut her off. "Are you telling me that you're refusing to go on this mission?"

"No Sir, I'm just pointing out that women are restricted from front line contact with the enemy."

"Not anymore you aren't, you're exempt from that restriction and Maj. Devlyn assured me that you're qualified and mission ready."

Wait a second, he knows about Devlyn? That means he knows what I'm really doing here. Why didn't Devlyn tell me that in his briefing? Slow down Kat, he's the goddamn CO, he had to know about me. "I see, thank you Sir," she said, and glanced up at Pacini. He nodded to her reassuringly and then looked back to the general.

"That's better. There'll be a Sherpa on the runway to take you to the LZ." He stepped away from the board and hunched over the table looking at them through his eyebrows. "You'll be dropped from 10,000 feet. Now okay, we don't know who he has with him, it could be just our guy and the pilot."

"Then you're saying the max number is four?" Paccini asked

"Who knows?" the general said, "pick a number. The plan is that you go in dark and catch the bastards sleeping. It should be a simple matter of rounding them up and destroying their lab."

Paccini didn't look happy and neither did Kat.

"On your call, we'll send in Blackhawks to recover you and your prisoners. Questions?"

"General, if we don't have a count on the hostiles then we could be jumping into a hornet's nest. Shouldn't we wait until we have better intel?" Pacini asked.

"That intel is unavailable, Captain. But the only thing we could see on the ground was his chopper. It only has four seats, so you do the math. This is our window of opportunity and we can't miss it, you're going in."

Wanting to back the captain up Kat said. "But it is possible that we could encounter a much larger force. Sir, do we have any reinforcements on stand-by to back us up?"

"No can do, Fernando. For reasons of security, this is 'need to know' and you should know all about that. Am I right? We're limiting the personnel involved to your squads. You'll have the element of surprise on your side. You can radio in a count once you have them in custody, then we'll send in the Blackhawks to extract them. We've got a chance to get him this time."

"What are the ROEs?" (Rules of Engagement) Kat asked, looking at the general cautiously.

"These are the bad guys, Fernando. Need I say more?"

Well that's plain enough I suppose, she thought. "No Sir." *He's dropping us blindfolded into a shit storm.*

"Alright, get your people ready. You go at zero-dark-thirty. Again," the general said, "security is tight on this one.

Captain, pick your team and sequester them. No briefing until you board the plane. Sergeant, you'll draw your equipment You're going in black which means NVGs, infrared scopes, restraints for the prisoners." Kat finished writing her notes and the general ended by singling out Kat with a raised eyebrow, "Questions?" *We're going in dark with a full moon behind us, what questions could I possibly have?* She returned his gaze expressionless and silent. "Outstanding."

She stood with Pacini as Denton gave them an earnest, fatherly look and said, "Alright, dismissed and give 'em hell."

While Pacini selected his squads and put them in the ready room, Kat drafted a short report detailing the mission, command's low estimation of potential resistance, and the limited intel they were working with. She mentioned having reservations about the viability of the mission.

Nothing was ever as simple as what Denton had described. She sent it off to Devlyn before she headed off to the Quarter Master's shack, taking four trusted men along to carry the supplies.

ON THE TARMAC

Enrique Soto Cano

It was zero-dark-twenty, mission time, the C-23B Super Sherpa was standing on the apron ready for immediate take-off.

Kat was studying the expressions of the men, looking for some indication that a mole was looking for a way to make contact but was interrupted when the aircraft's crew chief entered.

"Are you guys ready to go?" he asked.

Pacini nodded and stood up, "Alright men let's mount up."

Kat hadn't seen anything suspicious so far. "You heard the man. Grab your gear and get on your feet! Let's go! Let's go!"

The twenty men crammed like sardines in the Sherpa's cabin with their chutes and weapons bulking them up and Kat was the last one on. They took their seats with their backs pressed tight against the fuselage on both sides, their knees almost touching in the middle. Pacini gave them the quick version, destination, potential opposition, mission goal.

Just as the gate was being lowered one of the Honduran troopers keeled over into the lap of the man across from him. Kat tapped the crew chief on the shoulder and pointed to the fallen soldier.

"We have a problem." Kat didn't believe that he was actually ill and that gave her another reason to get him off the plane.

I'm not going to give the bastard a chance to shoot us in the back.

The Master Sgt. stopped the gate and Kat radioed for a medic and MPs as the gate was raised. They would take precious minutes to get to the plane and the clock was ticking.

120

Four men had to dismount to allow the stricken trooper to be removed. The MPs surrounded the man as the Honduran medics checked him out. One of them said, "He's got a fever."

As they loaded him on a stretcher Kat took one of the MPs aside speaking over the noise of the airplane, "It's imperative that he doesn't make contact with anyone tonight. And keep an eye on the medics too, I'm not sure whose side they're on." He looked at her, wondering what the hell was going on, but he didn't question her orders. "I want you to maintain maximum security. Stay with him until we return."

"You got it, Sergeant."

"Very well, take him away." She turned back to her troopers and said, "Okay, mount up and let's get this bird rolling."

The ten-minute delay and the absent trooper put a strain on the operation. They had to make up the lost time. The pilot did his best to do that by taking off while the gate was being lowered.

OVER THE MOUNTAIN

Los Murillos

The LZ (landing zone) was a rough plateau that sloped off gently into the trees. Nothing about this was going to be easy down there in the dark. They had no idea who would be there to welcome them and the moon would backlight their silhouettes to whomever cared to look up.

The pilot pushed hard to make up the time and as they approached the LZ the crew chief raised the rear door. Cpt. Pacini gave the command to stand and lift the benches to clear the way for a quick exit. Each man checked the gear of the man in front and the last man turned to check the captain's harness. Kat stood at the opening gate as the icy wind poured in.

121

The amber light lit up. "Ready," Pacini shouted from the front of the plane.

"Ready," Kat repeated at the back.

"Ready!" they all shouted back. The green light flashed on.

"Go! Go! Go!" Pacini shouted.

Kat instantly dove into the black and the rest followed. In seconds, they were all in freefall. The sound of the plane faded quickly and for a few moments, the only sound was the air moving by her face at 180 feet per second.

She opened her chute at 5,671 ft., 1,800 ft. above the plateau giving her some time to maneuver so she'd hit the clearing.

The quiet was suddenly blown away as the forest around the clearing erupted with muzzle flashes and the roar of automatic weapons.

Bullets were zipping all around her, many close enough to feel their heat. *Holy shit!* She heard men grunt and die above her as the hail of bullets found them.

The cartel killers hadn't been sleeping at all, and there were more than four of them. They'd been warned and were lying in wait, listening for the jump plane. As soon as they spotted the movement of the chutes against the moonlight, they opened fire.

Her chute was being shredded and spilling air and she was picking up speed. Holy shit! With a twang her left control shroud snapped just above her head and she immediately began to spin out of control.

She missed the LZ entirely. Spinning down the side of the mountain like a doll on a string and watched the river valley rushing up to meet her nauseatingly fast.

I'm going to die and there's nothing I can do to save myself.

Fear froze the breath in her lungs and sent jolts of electricity through her body from her toes up to her head. She wanted to scream but couldn't.

Birds scattered from their nests as her boots crashed through the canopy, tearing leaves and snapping branches. She covered her face as she fell through clouds of insects, but a thought zipped through her mind.

What does it matter? I'll be dead in a second.

Down she plunged toward the ground like an anvil, large branches cracked and tore at her jumpsuit.

I'm making so much noise someone's bound to find me and then ...

The black streamer trailing behind her began to catch on the shattered limbs, repeatedly tugging at her harness, slowing her down.

But if she didn't stop now, she'd hit the rocks or the rapids, and it would be all over. She shut her eyes, imagining the pain as her body crushed in on itself ...

And she stopped.

When she opened her eyes, she saw that she was dangling less than a meter above the jagged edge of a slab of stone.

She swallowed hard and closed her eyes again.

Holy crap.

Monkeys who had scattered as she arrived were back now and complaining angrily above her. A sob of relief broke from her lips, and for a moment she just hung there trembling and cried.

Jesus! Will you get a fucking grip, Kat?!

She moved her hand to the release to snap out of the harness, then realized that even from a meter, landing on that sharp edge would probably kill her.

She found her knife and reached up to cut the shrouds away one by one. As each one let go with the twang like a broken guitar string, she gradually lowered herself until she could touch the stone with the toe of her boot. She tiptoed away from the edge, then cut the last shroud away. She took a swig from her water bottle and several quiet breaths. She was free and miraculously alive.

She bent over to ditch the harness and felt a sharp pain below her right breast. It just about made her pass out. "Christ," she hissed, "I think I've broken something in there. Perfect." She looked. The uniform had been torn open and was covered in blood. "That's going to leave a mark." *Okay I'm bleeding and it hurts like a son-of-a-bitch, but there's nothing I can do about that. I just won't look at it and I'll be fine.*

She took out her radio. "Red one, this is Red two." She waited for a reply. "Red One, this is Red Two, come back."

The silence stretched out and she was beginning to think that she was the only one who survived. Panic rose through her like a monster from the deep.

"Red One! Red Two calling. Come back!"

"Red Two, this is Red One, I thought you were dead for sure. Where are you? Over."

"I came down by the river. What's your status? Over."

"Five dead, one critical." There was a pause. She'd heard gunfire in the background as he spoke. There was a battle raging above her. "We are spread out in the bush. My guess is they outnumber us three to one, but we're doing our best to even it out. Are you injured?"

"I'm, okay," she lied, "I'm coming to you now."

"Kat ..., be careful. They're everywhere."

"Copy that. Two out." Kat looked up. She had two hits of morphine in her kit, but if she gave herself a shot now, she'd be out of it and they needed her up there.

The slope was treacherous, but she was practically running, hacking at the undergrowth with her machete to clear a path.

All she could think about was getting back to her people fast. She pushed through the vegetation, hoping that they were still alive because, good or bad, her fate lay with them. She began to climb.

Two gunmen had watched her precarious descent and cut away from the gang on their way down to make sure she was dead.

Kat was more than halfway up when a small cascade of dirt and stones tumbled down on her and she knew that someone was coming for her.

She had just been on a ledge about a yard wide and running across the cliff like a short path. She quickly descended to it and rolled under a broad-leafed plant, hoping it would be enough to hide her. She disturbed something, something large. Thankfully it slithered away.

The moonlight didn't reach her part of the shelf, so they wouldn't be able to find her unless they stepped on her. Crouching low, Kat prepared to fight.

The M4 carbine had been on her back for the climb and she wished she had it in her hands now. Very carefully she rolled onto her back and pulled out her Beretta, chambered a round and waited. She took a shallow breath and then another and another until ...

First one man dropped onto the ledge. Right behind him the second man slid into view. They were silhouettes against the moonlight.

"I heard a machete cutting down there, he's climbing up." There was no doubt that these men would spot her if they looked down. If that happened, she'd be dead.

She took aim and fired. The first shot went through the temple of the man closest to her and he toppled over the edge. His partner turned on her lifting his AK-47.

She fired again, hitting him in the gut. He dropped to his knees right in front of her. His eyes were wide open staring at her. She fired again, his head snapped back and he fell, following his partner over the edge.

Her first kills.

She sat up and vomited.

Wiping her mouth on her sleeve she thought, *Jesus Kat, you haven't got time for this.* Getting to her feet, she grunted in pain. *Aw Jezzus this is unbelievable!* She leaned against the rock and put pressure on the wound. *I can't quit, not now. Just shrug it off and keep moving Kat.* She continued to climb.

Minutes later, she came to another ledge that was just wide enough to take a knee. She stopped for a moment to catch her breath. After checking her weapons, she called her team leader to report in.

"Red One, this is Two, over." Ninety seconds later there were two clicks from the Captain's radio. She pressed send again and said, "I've taken out two and am following their trail to you now."

"What is your position?" asked Capt. Pacini.

"I am northeast of the LZ, downhill about twenty meters."

"Copy that. What's your condition?" he asked.

"I'm good," she lied again, everything hurt now. There was something sharp sticking out of the chest.

"Good. Try to move around to the southern slope otherwise you'll come up behind them."

Was it the rib or part of the tree? Did it matter? Whatever it was, she was still bleeding. "Copy that," she said. All she had to do was get there ... and not die.

"Quick as you can, Kat. We need you."

"Copy that. I'm on my way. Two out." She turned the radio down and continued her climb.

The firefight was very close now. The terrain south of her made circling impossible. She had to climb higher. At the top she heard someone running toward her and ducked down, then with her NVGs she recognized the wounded man. There were two gunmen right behind him. She swung her carbine up from her back and fired a quick burst and the men dropped. The trooper fell as well, just out of sight behind a large fallen tree.

Kat ran over to join him and took a knee beside him nearly frightening the soldier to death. "Easy, Lorenzo. It's me, Fernando."

"Sgt. Fernando?" Lorenzo said, his face wincing in agony.

"Where are you hit?" Kat asked, her eyes searching what she could see of him.

"My shoulder. They are all around us."

126

"I know, it's okay I'm going to get you out of here."
She put her hand on his shoulder to examine the wound. He
flinched, and her hand came away wet with his blood. "I have
something that will stop the bleeding."

"It hurts bad, sergeant."

"I know." She removed her small medic kit from her
pouch and applied some QuikClot. "Where's the captain?" she
asked, tending to the wound.

"I don't know."

"Can you still shoot?" Lorenzo shook his head. "Shit.
That's okay, just watch my back." Kat clicked on the radio
and turned up the volume.

"Red One? Two. I'm here with Lorenzo. He's taken a
round to the shoulder. What is your position?"

"I'll fire a shot in three ..., two ..." BANG.

Kat spotted the muzzle flash, "I see you. I'm coming
to you now."

"Copy that."

The moment she switched it off, two more men came
at them from the left, firing. Kat ducked behind the tree as
bullets thudded into the ground where she had just been. Their
next bursts tore chunks out of the tree near her head. They
were running straight at her. They were practically standing
on her when she fired up on full-automatic, killing them both.
Their bodies folded into each other and dropped out of sight
in the dark.

"Are you okay, Lorenzo?"

He grunted. She felt his forehead. He was hot,
sweating profusely, trembling. That's not good, she thought.

"You'll be okay," she said, but she had her doubts
now. There was nothing she could do for him if he went into
shock.

Bullets came at her from the right and they were so
close that she could feel the heat as they zipped by her face.
She returned fire into the charging figures until her mag was
empty.

They went down, she quickly released the empty magazine, replaced it, and chambered a round. Now she was out of breath. Her chest felt like it was on fire and her heart was pounding against her sternum so loudly she thought everyone could hear it.

The first time I take a life and now eight men are dead because of me. My god, eight people.

Kat turned back to Lorenzo and saw him lying motionless. "Oh shit, no, no, no." During the exchange, he had taken another hit. "Lorenzo!" she pressed two fingers against his neck. His pulse was faint, but he was alive. "Lorenzo?" He coughed. She dragged him back behind her tree and put pressure on the new wound. It was a through and through just above his hip.

She looked around. "We're shielded here." She had enough QuikClot left to pour onto the wounds. Then she took out the morphine syringe she didn't use on herself and injected him. He groaned.

"I know it hurts, but this should help some." She looked around. "I've got to get you to the captain. Do you hear me?" He nodded again.

She slung the rifle across her chest and carefully drew the small man onto her back in a fireman's lift, then headed toward the spot where she'd seen the captain's muzzle flash.

After covering about a hundred yards she had to rest. She took a knee but before she could set him down, they were spotted. A man ran at her with a machete raised over his head.

She drew her side arm and fired just as he came within striking distance. The shot hit him high up on his chest and stopped him in his tracks. He let go of the long knife, which flipped over behind him and plunged into the soft ground handle first. He fell back and was impaled by it.

"Nine," she said. Near exhaustion she gently placed Lorenzo on the ground. "How are you doing?"

"Don't leave me," he whispered groggily.

"I won't. Hold on I'll get you out of this. I just have to catch my breath." Even though she was in tremendous pain she only paused for a few seconds, then picked him up again and struggled on.

As she drew near the clearing all the shooting stopped. For the first time since her chute opened, the forest was quiet. Kat called out, "Cap!"

"Fernando?"

"We're over here."

"I see you," Pacini shouted, and ran to them. "Are you okay?"

Exhausted, but relieved she said, "I'm doing fine, Sir. Where've they gone?"

"Dead ..., most of them anyway. I think a few of them must have retreated," he said, and she thought that they were probably the ones that she'd just killed. "Lorenzo?"

"He's been hit twice. It's not good."

"Okay." He turned and shouted, "Corpsman!"

"A young Honduran trooper ran over. "Si, Capitan."

"Stay with him. The rest of you, with me." While the corpsman looked after Lorenzo, Kat opened her vest and had a look at her right side. It was soaked with blood and a piece of tree branch was stuck between her ribs.

"Fucking hell," said Pacini, "that's gotta come out."

"Yeah. Okay ..." She hesitated for a several seconds taking a few deep breaths then, suppressing the scream that begged for release she pulled it out.

"Jesus, Kat."

She could see his face clearly in the moonlight. He looked so worried she had to put his mind at ease. "No, I'm good." She put her back against a tree at the edge of the clearing. The men who were left standing gathered around, the silver light from the moon outlined their dark silhouettes. They were all Honduran. "Where are the advisors?"

"Dead." Pacini shook his head in wonder. "Jesus Kat. You're something else, you know that?"

She pulled the Velcro tight and pressed it back together and sat for a moment while the team went over the battlefield locating bodies, theirs, and those of the cartel. They were down to eight functioning soldiers. Seven men dead including the two American observers; three Honduran soldiers were wounded.

Cpt. Pacini had estimated that there were roughly fifty cartel members. They found fifty-three counting the nine kills Kat made. If anyone survived, they'd melted into the jungle and were long gone. She looked at her watch. "It's quarter of four, the sun will be coming up soon. If we're going to find their boss we'd better get going."

"How's that wound doing, Kat?" Pacini asked "Let me have a look."

She didn't want to release the pressure on it. "It's okay, Cap. I'm just a little ..."

"Shut up and let me see it." He pulled the Velcro open and moved the vest aside. "Oh shit." He had her lie down, took the QuikClot from his kit and applied it to her injury.

"I wish I could do more for you."

"It's okay, Cap. Thanks. We've got to get La Bibiru." she said, as she reached up for assistance.

"He wasn't here. The helicopter was gone." Pacini said, taking her arm and helping her to her feet. "Can you keep going?"

"Yeah, I think so."

"Okay let's blow up the lab and get the hell out of here."

They set some charges in the chem lab and blew it up then returned to the clearing. There were two Blackhawks waiting on the plateau, one being loaded with the wounded along with those KIA in body bags. The other was waiting for them.

The trooper who'd bailed on the mission was obviously the mole.

After interrogation he gave up the medic who told her he had a temp.

They found the cell phone the medic used to warn La Bibiru that they were on their way. He also told them where they could find his boss. Caesar La Bibiru was hiding in a tunnel under a house in Tegucigalpa. He was killed along with eleven of his men in a shootout.

How long it would take for someone else to fill the void was anyone's guess.

She gathered a great deal of actionable intel and three similar missions followed in quick succession before her year was done.

HOME TO THE NEST

ENA

After she flew out of Enrique Soto Cano Air Base to Maryland, she spent a few days in hospital dealing with a recurring infection from the wound.

Upon release she was given three weeks of R&R which were spent with Harm at ENA. She began referring to it as 'the Nest' and it caught on.

While she was recovering, she received orders to report to D.C., so she and Harm flew back to Maryland. She didn't hear what it was about until the day of the presentation at the White House.

Cpt. Pacini had put through a commendation; it went up the chain of command and it was decided that she would be awarded the medal for bravery.

WASHINGTON D. C.

The White House

President Clinton presented the award but before he placed it around her neck he read from the citation; "For a selfless act of courage. Wounded and under heavy enemy fire, First Sergeant Katrina Fernando with disregard for her own injuries and safety, carried a wounded comrade on her back over 200 meters through enemy lines to safety.

During the rescue, First Sergeant Fernando killed nine enemy combatants."

"It's quite an honor Fernando," said Devlyn, after the ceremony. "The only other woman to receive the Medal of Honor was Dr. Mary Edwards Walker."

"Who was she, Sir?"

"A volunteer with the Union Army at the outbreak of the Civil War. You should be very proud. You're a real American hero now."

"Thanks, but I only did what anybody else would have done."

"Don't believe that for a second. You've got what it takes, Katrina. There's a promotion coming your way, but we'll get to that later."

"Thank you, Sir."

"I understand you've been given another week's leave. Are you planning to spend it in Washington with your boyfriend?"

It was the way he said 'boyfriend' that made it sound adolescent and insulting. "With Harm, yes sir."

"Take a word of advice, Katrina. In our line of work, it's best not to make long term commitments. When things get hot those commitments tend to cloud our judgement."

Holding the medal, she said, "So far it hasn't been a problem, Sir."

He disregarded her response. "I understand that women have needs just like men. Feel free to go ahead and scratch it when you've got an itch. But keep your relationships casual. It'll be better for everyone that way."

"Sir, I hardly think that ..."

"It's your decision of course. I'm just saying relationships always cause problems down the road. Save yourself some grief, cut Toucksberry loose before it gets too serious."

"Not a chance, Sir."

"Like I said, the decision is yours. You'll begin your next assignment as soon as you're done here."

"Will I be joining the 66th?" she asked, anticipating a posting to Germany.

"The general and I have something else in mind."

10

BOTTOM LINE, MORE TRAINING

Fort Rucker, Alabama

Kat had spent a considerable amount of time avoiding the subject of Devlyn during her week in Washington with Harm, but that ended with a phone call. She saw the caller ID. "Oh crap, it's him. I've gotta take this. Hello." Harm looked concerned, afraid that he was going to take her away from him again.

Her heart sank when Devlyn said, "I'm here to pick you up."

She pounded the bed with her fist and Harm put his hand on her shoulder. "Ah, Sir?" she said, about to launch into a strenuous protest. "That's not ..."

He knew what was coming so he interrupted her, "I'm waiting out front," he said, and hung up.

"Shit," she said, slamming the phone down on the bedside table.

"What's going on?"

"He's out front waiting."

He tossed off the covers and as he put on his shorts he said, only half-jokingly, "I think he's got a thing for you."

Kat let out a short laugh. "Yeah, and his thing is to drive me crazy. He doesn't want me to be with you."

"He can't break us up," he said, angrily.

"True, but that won't stop him from trying," she said, "Give me a kiss and I'll talk to you soon."

After she dressed, she said, I love you so much, Harm."

"I'll love you till the day I die," he said. They kissed one last time before she left Harm in the room.

She saw her CO's car parked by the hotel entrance. This time Devlyn was driving a Camaro and she took note of the white racing stripes and the big wide wheels.

The trunk lid popped open and she tossed in her suitcase noticing the Maryland license plate. Before she opened the passenger door she stooped down and knocked the window. He rolled it down for her. "Morning Sir. You must really like muscle cars." Delivering a little jibe, she said, "It's sort of like a girl in every port thing with you, isn't it?"

"Just get in," he snapped. "What kept you?"

He was pissed that she still carried a torch for Toucksberry. It had to stop. "I was just saying goodbye, Sir," she said, as she eased herself in next to him and put on her seatbelt as he pulled out into the street.

The engine roared and farted as he changed gears. He had her new assignment sealed a manila envelope. She took out the contents and read the opening paragraph.

"What's at Fort Rucker?"

"Be patient, we'll get to that."

As they made the short trip to her new billet, he once again insisted that she end the relationship with Harm. She told him that if he didn't like it, she would be happy to resign.

"That's not going to happen. I have too much invested in you to let you go now. What do you know about helicopters?"

"Helicopters? Nothing."

"Ever wanted to fly?"

134

"Uh, no."

"Wrong answer. From this point forward if anyone asks you how you feel about flying a helicopter you will say it has always been my number one dream."

"Has it really?"

"It says so on your recruitment form," he said.

"I must have been sleeping when I wrote that."

"Are you telling me you lied to the Army?"

"Sir, what the hell are you ...?"

"Careful Fernando."

"At least can you tell me why?"

"Okay, Wolfson is handing you a promotion. Does that work for you?" And it wasn't the promotion she was expecting. She was being sent to the Warrant Office Course (WOC) at Fort Rucker, Alabama.

After the WOC she was to move into the helicopter pilot training and by the end of that program she'd be promoted again to Chief Warrant Officer Second Level (CWO2 is the NCO equivalent of a 2nd Lieutenant). "Then there's the SERE course. You'll need to take that to go operational in enemy territory."

"But you've already put the cart before that particular horse. Is that what this is all about, you're sending me into combat again?"

"No, but I want you to be eligible to liaison with Special Forces."

She knew about the SERE program and it was not for the faint of heart. Learning to fly a helicopter didn't sound like fun either so she asked, "What happens if I don't get through these courses?"

"You'd better fucking pass it or I'll send you back to driving trucks till you retire."

"Understood."

"Prepare yourself for a whole lot of special training, Fernando. I want you to be ready for anything I throw at you."

"What if I don't want ...?"

"Now get this, you have no fucking choice. I want you on the sharp end of the stick when the shit hits the fan."

"What shit are we talking about?"

"You'll know about it soon enough." He was working on a bit of intel that hadn't been confirmed yet but it had bad news written all over it. "For now, just keep you mind focused on the assignment. Get packed, your flight to Rucker leaves at thirteen hundred. Don't be late."

WARRANT OFFICER'S COURSE

Fort Rucker, Alabama

To her surprise, Kat felt comfortable with the people at Fort Rucker and Devlyn was right, she did very well in the five-week Warrant Officer Candidate School. She graduated as a Warrant Officer and moved smoothly on to the next challenge.

At Rucker the trainees were assigned a 'Stick Buddy.' Kat's Stick Buddy was WO Gail Forester, and their instructor was CWO 3 Dutch Patterson. They'd all be together until the end of the course. Dutch and Gail were both really good people and made the whole training program a pleasure.

Harm came over from San Diego for a quick visit and they spent the evening at an inn.

Though Devlyn would have objected to Harm's visiting during training, he didn't know about it and couldn't have stopped it if he did.

During their protracted separations, Harm's retirement project quickly grew in reputation and had become tremendously successful. Without telling Kat, Harm had had a Partnership Agreement drawn up making her full partner, but because she was still in the Army, he thought it wise to make her partnership silent.

He placed the document on the table in front of her. Confused, she said, "Um Harm, what's this?"

"It's a Partnership Agreement."

"Yeah, but …"

"I had it drawn up a couple of months ago but as you know only too well, this is the first time I've had a chance to present it to you."

"Duty before pleasure." She began to read it over and was taken aback and rather distressed, "But ..." She put the document down and pushed it back to him, "I don't understand. What are you doing, Harm?"

"What does it look like?" he said, with a half-smile. He didn't understand what her problem was.

"Yeah, I get that, Harm. But no, this is your baby; you don't need me horning in on it."

He pushed the document back to her. "This is what I want, Kat. From now on you will legally be known as Madam X."

She put her hands in her lap and said, "This is ridiculous, really I mean you can't give me a share in ENA."

"It's not just a share, Kat," He took a pen from his pocket and laid it on the paper, "it's half of ENA. I've split right down the middle."

"Wow," she was stunned. "I don't know what to say."

"You don't have to say anything. You just have to sign it. Put your X here by the sticker." She did. "Thank you. And then," he flipped to the last page, "sign your name here on the dotted line and put your X there."

"What's this?"

"This page is an addendum to the agreement which states that Madam X is you and that this supersedes that other one. The document will go into the safe and remain secret until you join ENA fulltime."

"Okay, but I hope you won't regret this."

"Not a chance." She signed it and handed back the pen. "You're still going to need that. I have one here, without the last page." He placed a document file on the table. "put your X on it.

"What's this now?"

"It's a statement of ENA's profits and losses since I started the academe. It's a declaration that says you understand what this partnership requires of you."

She opened it and began to scan the columns. Her eyes grew wider the closer she got to the bottom line. "Holy crap, Harm! That's a lot of money. How is that possible?"

"I didn't tell you about it before because I didn't know how it would fly. It takes a lot of management participation, but I won't be calling on you to take it on until you're ready for it. I've got Doug Laymen looking after that for me and he's doing a great job. It's a really big money maker."

"I can see that, but what …?"

"Kat, all I can say now is that ENA is more than just the Academy for Strategic Studies, but I can't get into that now."

"Really? You're so mysterious all of a sudden."

He seemed so anxious to get this done and she wondered why. "It just needs your X here at the sticker."

She found something that confused her on the last page and hesitated. "What's this down here? The Madam X numbered account? What's that for?"

"You are Madam X, right?"

"If you say so."

"Then that's your account."

"Holy crap, Harm you can't be serious!"

"Please," he said, and waited expectantly.

"Wait a second, I can't accept that. That's … that's … god, that's ridiculous. No, it's too much. I can't accept that."

"Well, there's nothing either of us can do about it now. It's in the agreement you just signed, so that's your account."

"No, seriously, I mean, god it's wonderful for you to think of me like that and I am totally honored, but Harm, it's too much."

"I couldn't have done any of this without you. Please, just sign it." She did finally then, producing a slip of paper from the folder he handed it to her.

"What's this"?

"That's your access code, you can use Chase here, The Royal Bank in Canada, and Lloyds of London in Europe. There are banks in Africa, South Asia and Asia that have reciprocal agreements. You just have to find them."

"OK, but ..."

"Remember that number. When you go to the Chase bank for the first time, they'll scan your thumb print. You can access your account anywhere in the world whenever you want and do whatever you want with it."

"Harm ..."

"It's yours and you deserve every penny."

"Thank you. I don't know what else to say."

"Good, because I want you to keep it our little secret, okay? And whatever you do, don't tell Devlyn."

"That won't be a problem."

As usual they ended the visit in bed. They were comfortable lovers now and their lovemaking was slower and more sensual.

Kat drove Harm back to the airport and as he flew back to San Diego with the agreement Kat found her stick buddy heading off to the airfield. "How was your weekend?"

"It was quite an experience."

"Really, then I want details."

"Sorry, Top Secret, need to know."

"You'd tell me if there was a ring involved, wouldn't you?"

"You can count on that. Are you ready for this?"

"I am so ready." Gail Forester said. "How about you?"

Kat smiled then put her arm around her friend's shoulders and said, "Absolutely."

The second phase was challenging, but now she was totally hooked on flying.

The first part was learning how to fly the training helicopter. The second phase was choosing a ship in which to specialize. It wasn't just knowing how to fly, she also had to know every inch of the bird and how it worked.

After her experience in Honduras she chose the UH60 A Blackhawk. Learning every nut and bolt was 70% tedium and 30% interesting. The computer system was challenging but she got a handle on it and it was smooth flying from there on.

It was something she'd never considered before, but being in control up there felt like it was what she was born to do.

After helicopters she qualified on fixed wing, dual engine and multi engine jets, and graduated as a CWO 2nd Level combat helicopter pilot.

She went through SERE (Survival, Evasion, Resistance and Escape), a course combat pilots, among others, have to go through in case they have to ditch in enemy territory and are captured.

It was tougher than she'd anticipated and she was glad to get through it alive.

SIX-SIX-MI

66th Military Intelligence, Rome Office, Italy

While she was at Rucker, intel suggested there was a growing threat to US security within Europe. What it was wasn't clear, but Devlyn had been right to worry.

Something was going on, it was going to erupt soon, and Devlyn wanted her there with the 66th Brigade otherwise known as the Six-Six-MI to prepare for it. Kat went to the field office in Rome using the alias, Special Agent Barbara Carr.

Her passport said she was from Billings, South Dakota, but she kept her age and birthdate.

Special Agent Carr was the new Assistant Liaison and Operational Coordinator working with local law enforcement, security, and intelligence agencies.

Her real assignment was to direct surveillance ops and collect intel from field agents to send back to Maryland for analysis.

Her fluent Italian helped her blend in seamlessly but being undercover meant she had to refrain from making contact with anyone who knew her as Kat Fernando.

I'll bet this is just another attempt to separate Harm and me. But she was wrong this time. "How long am I going to be stationed here?"

"It's indefinite," he said.

"What does indefinite mean though Sir? Six months, a year?"

"Indefinite means for as long as it takes. I'd think about getting rid of your apartment. I don't think you'll be going back there any time soon."

I'm really beginning to despise this man.

She wrote on the back of the postcard with a picture of the Coliseum, "Hi from Rome. The weather is great here and the people in the office are a lot of fun, I don't know how long management will keep me here. I hope it's not too long. All my love, Madam X."

She couldn't say any more and perhaps even that was too much.

11

THE PHOENIX PROJECT

Toronto, Canada

Dr. Deacon Loats PhD, started small with Dectron Aerospace, designing and building experimental aircraft in Toronto.

He was twenty-eight with doctorates in aeronautical engineering and mechanical engineering. He liked titles, so he always asked people to referred to him as Doctor Loats. It was his secret ambition to someday build a fully electric powered aircraft. After designing several concept-planes he put them aside and waited until he didn't need an extension cord to give the idea wings.

The issue was never really about the aircraft design, his ideas were constantly changing anyway. It was about the replacement for the extension cord, the independent and dependable power supply.

Over the next thirteen years Deacon's little start-up became a large and successful company with hundreds of employees.

Leaving the aircraft company in the reliable hands of Dectron Aerospace president Clive Thorn, Deacon quietly moved away from aircraft design altogether to create a new low-profile affiliate company called Dectron R&D. His research was devoted to the creation of a solar powered fuel cell and the initial research showed enormous potential. The one problem was that the project development was extremely expensive, and he needed a backer.

Jasper Cleveland, a childhood friend, had started a one-man software development company in Palo Alto, California. He developed a unique piece of software that became extremely valuable and sold his company for a huge amount of money.

Jasper told Deacon that he was getting bored so Deacon proposed that they go into partnership on his new Phoenix Project and that they keep it as a secret for the time being.

Two years down the road and after rigorous testing, the new power cell proved to be one-hundred percent successful. Jasper was elated and wanted to get it into production right away. Deacon agreed but insisted that the project remain top secret until it was fully market-ready.

He started looking for companies to build the tooling and production equipment he'd designed for the manufacturing plant.

Jasper's job then, was to find the raw materials and the location for the first Phoenix Project plant. Deacon's dream of an electric VTOL aircraft could become a very successful reality and potentially replace the conventional aircraft. But not only that; the implications of the fuel cell he created would be far greater than that.

While Kat was stationed in Rome, Deacon was in Toronto wrestling with that issue. The economic and social effects of potentially inexhaustible free energy his invention could have on the world were incalculable. To say the least, he thought, it would potentially unbalance the global economy. Eventually, when everyone would be able to have their own affordable source of energy directly from the sun the petroleum industry would fall into a dismal second place.

The person who controlled this energy would have power and wealth beyond imagining. The possibility for this power to be used maliciously was also beyond imagining. That frightened Deacon more than he could say.

His fear was well founded because there was an organization in Russia building its power base and looking for a doorway to infinite power. How long would it take before it found that portal?

12

BACK STATESIDE

Fort Mead, Maryland

Kat had a bit of intel from an agent in Milan. At first it didn't seem to be of any real interest in Maryland, but Kat asked for more details. She was told that the company's executive team changed almost overnight, with little explanation. He said it seemed to follow right after a tragic accident that took the life of the company's president.

She had another report of a second company in Genoa that underwent the same sort of abrupt change. The agents found a common thread, Dectron Aerospace R&D in Canada. The companies in Milan and Genoa were building high tech precision machinery for Dectron.

"Any idea what this machinery was for?" she asked the agents.

"No."

"Did you find out anything else about those companies?"

"Only that they were both taken over at about the same time by a numbered company registered outside of Italy. We haven't been able to track its origins down yet."

Kat sent in her report and a day after she filed it, she was ordered home. Devlyn met her at the airport.

"That shit I mentioned has hit the fan." He gave her the details as they drove back to Fort Mead.

Devlyn changed gears as he merged into traffic. "It matches what I've been hearing from an agent in St. Petersburg. A crime syndicate specializing in corporate takeovers. Now the concern is that the syndicate could jeopardize the security of NATO member-states."

Devlyn appeared agitated but focused.

"Then shouldn't I be over there?" she asked eagerly. He was surprised because it just sounded like she was asking to go back to Europe.

"I'll come to that," he said, as he looked over his shoulder before changing lanes. "There's an agent working deep-cover on the inside of a Russian syndicate. I worked alongside her partner, Agent Raymond Holst, two years ago on a European drug cartel takedown. They just found Holst's body in a pond in The Hague. Now Harken thinks they're coming after her."

"What agency is she with?"

"Europol."

"Never heard of it."

"Didn't you encounter them in Italy?"

"Interpol yes, not Europol."

"They're a new player in The Hague, established to investigate drug dealing and organized crime. They don't have the authority to arrest yet, but they think they're in the Bigs now, so we're supposed to play nice."

"Okay, so who's the agent?" she asked.

"Petra Harken. According to her the syndicate is doing a purge and she's afraid that she's next and wants to come in."

"Then shouldn't Europol get her out of there?"

"Apparently they have no jurisdiction in Russia, so they say they can't."

To think an agency would leave one of their people hanging out to dry really pissed Kat off. "That didn't seem to stop them from sending them in."

"That's just it, they didn't. Holst and Harken did it on their own. Harken worked her way inside and Holst was her handler."

"Christ. So, I suppose one of our people in Russia will have to do that for them?"

"No Kat. I'm sending you."

"Excuse me?"

"You speak Russian and you're young enough to pass as a student."

"Why a student?"

"Petra feels more comfortable with a college aged woman."

"What does comfort have to do with it? We've got people there, don't we?"

"One of them just goes in and gets her out."

"And that someone is you," replied Devlyn.

She balled up her fists and stared out the window. They drove the rest of the way in silence. When they arrived in his office Kat posed a question that she'd been gnawing on most of the way.

"You know I'm twenty-nine, right?" Devlyn just looked at her. "So, how am I going to pass myself off as a college kid?"

"You're a post grad student working on your doctorate in languages. It's all been arranged." He sat down and opened his desk drawer. Taking out a manila envelope he slid it across to her. Kat picked it up and looked inside.

He'd prepared a dossier that covered details of her counterfeit life from kindergarten on. It covered parents and grandparents, address, favorite haunts in Toronto, some facts about the university, and Canadian history and geography. There was also a pair of reading glasses with plain plastic lenses. "You're Canadian, eh."

"They don't really say that, do they?"

"I don't know, you're the language expert. The intel Harken has could help us take the organization down before it gets serious."

"Who am I going in with?"

"You're on your own."

She counted to eight as that woody feeling crept in again. "Will I at least have someone to contact over there?"

"Don't get your tits in a wringer. You're a soldier, Fernando, a veteran, you've earned the Medal of Honor, for Christ's sake. Look, all you have to do is make contact, set up an extraction plan, and get out her of Russia in one piece."

"And if I can't?"

"Then get yourself the fuck out of there and don't die."

He picked up a manila envelope an dumped the contents on the desk. She picked up the Canadian passport and thumbed to the photo and information page. "Samantha Dole, female, born January 12, 1971, in Toronto." She looked at him. "We're sticking with my real birthdate again."

"Easy to remember."

"Perfect. What about the photo?"

"Take it over to the art department in Procurement." Devlyn took out another envelope and slid it across to her. She dumped the contents on his desk. Passports, visas, and money. "Do I take a weapon?"

"Those items will be issued to you at Procurement. You're going to go to New York first. Set up a safe house, use the name Janice Ferraro in case I need to find you. Get a safety deposit box and stash some cash and ID in it just in case. And stick to cash only."

"Copy that." She thumbed through the money. US dollars, Canadian, Euros, and Rubles.

"The rubles are in case you've got to bribe your way out of trouble. Take some Euros and Canadian with you, but just enough to make you look like a student."

I should find a place in Europe to establish another safe house and leave some Euros in a bank there too.

"Arrange your escape route ahead of time to get her out of St Petersburg. There's a CIA safe house for you there, the key and the address are in this envelope." He passed it over to her.

She looked inside and removed the card and key. "Okay."

"Take Harken there. Wait for things to cool off, then get her out. Your itinerary is New York today nineteen hundred. Find an apartment, don't be too picky. Friday, 14:40 Air Canada to Toronto connect with KLM to Amsterdam. You'll have a three-hour layover, then at twenty-thirty-five Amsterdam time take the Aeroflot flight to St. Petersburg. Have you got that?"

"Yes, Sir."

"Okay get to Procurement and pick up your wardrobe. They'll help you to alter your look for the ID photos. I've ordered a special suitcase for you. They'll show you how to use it. I suggest you keep the Barbara Carr ID. Put it somewhere safe, it might come in handy someday. I'll keep it active and the paychecks will continue to be deposited in the same account. Use it as a reserve."

"Yes Sir," Kat said. "When they ask me why Samantha Dole is in St Petersburg, I tell them what?"

"You're there to brush up on your Russian," Devlyn told her. "Make like a tourist, see the sights, do touristy things until you make contact."

"That's it?"

"That's it. Katrina," he said, with a grave, almost apologetic expression. "Okay, a word of warning. As soon as you get on that plane in Toronto, you're on your own, there's no backup for you on this.

"If you're caught, we can't bail you out. My advice is don't get caught. If there's a possibility that they're on to you, leave Harken and get yourself out. I guarantee you, Katrina, they'll torture you and then shoot you in the head. Save yourself a lot of pain. Don't let them take you alive."

Kat had no immediate response for that.

The asshole just told me that this is basically a one-way trip. Is Harken that valuable that I have to risk my life to get her out?

"Yes Sir, I understand."

Bullshit, I don't fucking understand.

148

The people in the art department took her passport pictures to finish the documents. While they were doing that Kat went to be fitted out with a new set of clothes to put in the suitcase. It had a false bottom to hold the weapons, money, and documents. They told her that it would pass through the most stringent examination anywhere. It goddamn-well better, or I'm dead. She showered and dressed as Samantha Dole, Canadian post grad languages student from U of T, Toronto, then headed for Ronald Regan.

She didn't have time to call Harm, but while she was waiting for her plane, she took a moment to write him a postcard with a picture of D. C. on the front. It was one of the hardest things she'd ever done.

"Hi Lover,

Back from Italy early, but the company has asked me to take a meeting at a branch plant in Russia before I get some time off. I'm rushing to catch the plane now. Sorry I didn't get a chance to see you this time. I'll call you as soon as I get back. All my love, Madam X."

She dropped it in a mailbox at the airport.

ASSIGNMENT ST. PETERSBURG

New York, NY

Kat took American airlines to New York and then took a taxi to Manhattan. She stopped for an early dinner at a deli on Madison.

The dining room was up on the second floor, so she dragged her suitcase up and ordered eggs over easy, crisp bacon and coffee. The bank she chose was just up the street.

While she ate, she went through the death notices in The New York Times. Seinfeld once said that that was how New Yorkers found their apartments. There was a small, one bedroom in the Village. She called and made an appointment for 1:00 pm the next day and then found a small hotel for the night.

When the bank opened, Kat got a safety deposit box using the name Janice Ferraro as instructed and left the money and some of the passports, keeping the French and Italian documents as backups. She had three guns with her in the suitcase, tucked away in an x-ray-defeating sub floor along with a K-bar folding knife. Her small armory had passed through the security checks without trouble.

She left a SIG P226, with a suppressor and four, twenty-round clips, in the box. Keeping the compact SIG P220 in the case to take to St. Petersburg she intended to leave the second P226 and accessories in a bank box in Toronto.

After a quick lunch, she viewed the apartment and decided that it was perfect and leased it on the spot. She paid the deposit and the first six months' rent in cash. With that done she headed to Toronto for the connecting flight to St. Petersburg.

PLANNED EXTRACTION

St. Petersburg, Russia

Customs and Immigration in Russia was not a problem. She took a taxi to the Matisov Domik Hotel on a small island bounded by the Bolshaya Neva River on one side and the River Pryazhka on the other. The cab drove in through a bright blue iron gate and stopped in a small parking lot.

The hotel wasn't much, but she figured that she wouldn't be staying long so it didn't matter.

150

An odd-looking woman in her fifties came out of a back room to greet her. She stood behind a small counter embellished with a simulated piano keyboard surface. "How can I help you pretty young girl?"

Bemused, Kat smiled back. "You have a reservation for Samantha Dole?"

"I will look, just a second." While the woman was occupied, Kat's eyes were drawn to the wall behind. It was covered with signed photographs of all the 'famous' musicians who had stayed there. Apparently, their fame was not international.

"Yes, yes, yes, here you are. Samantha Dole. Why have you come to Russia my dear?"

"I'm studying Russian at university and I wanted to see St. Petersburg, so here I am."

"How delightful. You speak our language so well that I thought you must be Russian but you have such an odd name for a Russian. We have the very best room for you. You will be very happy. Passport please."

Minutes later she found the room and dropped her suitcase by the closet and locked the door behind her. She took her laptop over to the desk in the corner by the window and plugged it in. While it booted up, she looked out at the view. Across the narrow road lay a strip of weedy grass with a few spindly trees and a dirt track that passed for a sidewalk.

Just beyond that was the river, actually it was more like a canal with concrete sides. Some old men stood at the edge on the far side with their fishing poles, their lines dipped into the black, seemingly lifeless, river.

Behind them was a row of tired old buildings. The one right across from her should have been torn down years ago, she thought. Her first impression of St. Petersburg was that this place was not the romantic summer playground of the Czars she'd imagined.

At eight she made the scheduled call to her 'parents' to report that she had made it to Russia safely. "Hello Mom, I'm here."

"How was the flight, dear?"

"Long and tiring, but I survived." That was code for everything is okay. "Oh, the room is great, by the way. Tell Daddy thanks a bunch."

"I am so glad Sam. Your father is on the line too," said the female agent. Kat had no idea who she was, but that didn't matter. This was all theater to allow her to speak to Devlyn.

"Hi Dad. This room you booked for me, what can I say, it's interesting."

"Nothing but the best for my baby." Devlyn said, smiling. It was a serious downgrade from the place she had in Rome.

It was the sort of place a student would stay in, and he thought it served her right.

"Yeah thanks," she said, sounding less than thrilled, "you're the best. I'm on a tiny island in the middle of the city."

"I'm glad you like it Honey. You have fun now and be careful."

"I will. Okay, bye Mom, bye Daddy." Asshole.

Kat's instructions for the meeting were to go to the Mirage Cinema on Bolshoy St. at 2:00 on Sunday carrying a St. Petersburg guidebook. It had to be held upside down in her left hand. She was to buy a ticket and sit through the matinee at the back of the theater.

After the movie, she was to walk around the corner to the Molly Sullivan restaurant on Shamshevea. She would take a table, order a beer, and give the server the code phrase, 'I am expecting friends.' The counter-phrase was, 'Aren't we all?' If the server said anything other than that there would be no meeting.

MAKING CONTACT

Bolshoy Street, St Petersburg

The following morning Kat went to the front desk and asked about a cab. The concierge suggested, "Cab is too expensive. Big strong girl like you should walk."

"Right, well then could you recommend some places I should see?"

"The Peter and Paul Fortress, you must see."

Not that anybody was watching her, the first full day was spent establishing her cover as a tourist. She joined a tour at the Peter and Paul Fortress, took lots of pictures, and recorded the details in her trip diary.

Day two arrived and her gut was tied up in knots as she anticipated the contact with Harken. Kat was a bundle of nerves as she left the hotel early. She had her gun tucked in her belt at the small of her back and hidden under her bulky white sweater. She didn't expect to use it, but who knew? Maybe a little recon first to make sure there was nothing to impede her exit strategy.

The day before she'd seen a few Russians and a lot of tourists from Moscow and was not overly impressed. This time she took a cab to Bolshoy Street and the downtown showed her a different St. Petersburg. Most of the people seemed to be about her age, many were quite beautiful, well dressed, and appeared affluent.

Bolshoy was a busy one-way street with high-end shops across from the theater. The smaller side streets were also one-way. She quickly began to understand the pattern of the city. The street where the restaurant was had cars parked on both sides. On the restaurant side they were parked diagonally, on the other side parallel.

Across from the restaurant was a hotel, the Vvedensky. All the buildings, save for that one, were old and neglected. The windows on the hotel's main floor bore the name, Beverly Hills, Beyond Beauty & Spa. Had anyone in there ever been to Beverly Hills, or even America for that matter? The Americana struck her as odd.

The spa was on the main landing behind a glass wall. The spa employees, all blond, slim, young, and gorgeous were gathered by the desk and seated cross-legged on a plush red sofa against the side wall. She casually walked to the lobby and seeing no quick exit, turned around and went back out to the street.

After wandering for a couple of hours Kat needed to sit and have something to eat. Avoiding Molly's, she went looking for another place nearby. A cute little place called The Viking in a basement just up the street, appealed to her.

The menu was written on a chalkboard on the wall out front and decorated with a drawing of Bart Simpson in a Viking helmet.

Just before the movie started, she crossed the street following her instructions. The theater looked like every other small cinema she'd ever been in. It was nearly empty and it didn't take long to figure out why. As far as she could tell it was an art film shot in black and white. A confusing love story set on a farm in the steppes during Stalin's reign of terror. A young soldier and a beleaguered farmer's daughter. The relationship was doomed from the outset and she didn't need to see that.

She left early and as she rounded the corner she wondered if it was humanly possible to make a more stupid, confusing, and depressing film.

As soon as she sat down in Molly Sullivan's restaurant a waiter came over and asked her what she wanted. "A beer," she said.

"Are you going to order anything else?"

"Not just yet, I am expecting friends," Kat said, making slight eye contact.

"Aren't we all?" he said, and she felt her gut begin to twist again. She looked up at him as calmly as possible. This was not Petra Harken. "You are early," he said.

Her hand casually moved to her back and her fingertips touched the grip of her gun. She responded coolly saying, "The film was terrible, so I walked out. And, who the fuck are you?"

"A messenger." Here it comes, she thought. She wrapped her hand around the grip and began to lift the gun from her belt. "The woman is waiting for you outside. The black car. She said you would give me a thousand rubles."

"Oh, how generous of her." He nodded quickly and stuck out his hand. She took out the money and handed it to him.

"What kind of beer do you want?"

"Forget the beer," Kat said, slipping out of the booth

155

"Suit yourself," he said, and turned away. Kat headed for the exit fully expecting that a bullet was waiting for her outside.

THE ASSET

Outside Molly Sullivan's

The black car wasn't at all what she expected. It was low, loud and looked very expensive. She crossed the street tentatively, keeping her distance while she checked the woman out.

Petra was watching her with a cigarette between her lips. She flashed the headlights impatiently and gestured for Kat to hurry up. As Kat approached, the passenger door swung open.

Waving away the smoke, Kat made it clear that she wasn't happy. "Harken?"

"Oui, oui. Okay get in quickly, ma chérie." Harken's voice was low and soft, colored by years of smoking and Scotch.

Her dark brown eyes stared out at her from beneath awning-like blue lids weighed down by heavy fake lashes and black eye shadow. Her lip gloss had stained the end of her cigarette, but not her perfect teeth. Kat assumed they had been acquired recently.

She was petit, unmistakably Mediterranean and forty-something. Her shoulder length hair was pulled back behind her ears to show expensive long jeweled earrings. Leaving no doubt that she had nothing on underneath, her black leather jumpsuit was unzipped almost to her navel. It was stretched tight over her lean body like a second skin. She had a dragon tattoo over her tiny right breast.

As soon as Kat placed her bum in the seat, the woman tossed her cigarette out the window and reached for her.

"What are you ..." Before Kat knew what was going on Harken slipped her hand under Kat's sweater, grabbed her breast and began kissing her hungrily. Pulling back Kat quickly removed her hand. "Stop that!"

"Shut up stupid girl they're watching," Harken said, and resumed her assault.

Blocking her, Kat said, "Who's watching us? And I told you to cut it out!"

"Oh, for God's sake, act like you're enjoying it!"

"Now why the fuck would I do that?" she asked calmly. Kat was much stronger than Harken, so the woman finally backed off. "This is not playtime, Harken. We have some business to discuss," Kat said, wiping the second-hand lipstick from her mouth with the back of her hand.

"Bitch! I was told you would cooperate."

"Funny, I was told the same thing. Listen, if you want to survive then give me the information and I will see to it that you get out of Russia alive.

"We are being watched," the woman said. Kat's eyes darted to the mirror and then up the street. "No don't look, you idiot! They are a block up the street. Two men in a black Audi. They have field glasses. If you play the part they may go away."

"Forget them Petra. I wasn't sent here to be a snuggle-bunny. Do you have the intel or not?"

"Not here," Petra said furtively.

"Shit. Okay, let's go to my safe house and you can tell me there."

"No, I know where to go."

Petra dropped the shifter down into first, popped the clutch and stomped on the accelerator. The twelve-cylinder engine roared, the tires squealed and left a trail of burnt rubber on the road. The g-force pressed Kat against her seat, pressing her gun into her spine.

Harken went through the gears as if she was on a racetrack. She was doing 160 kph by the beginning of the next block. "Slow down!" Kat shouted. Harken paid no attention. Shouting like a drill sergeant, Kat repeated her demand and added "I didn't come all this way to die in a car crash!"

Beginning a zigzag course north through the sprawling city Harken turned at the next corner and slowed down. Blending with the traffic flow she asked with a sneer, "Is this better?"

"It's a start, now pull over. We'll leave the car here and take a cab to the safe house."

"I'm not going to your American safe house. The Russians know all of them."

Kat had no idea if that was true or not but she had a contingency plan worked out. "Alright a cab will take us to the airport. I have rented a plane to get us across to Finland."

"No planes, we will drive to Helsinki in my car."

"Be reasonable, we can't make it in this flashy thing."

"That's what makes it perfect. Who would think we were running away in a Ferrari? We are going on vacation."

"Some vacation." Once she had what she needed she could always stop the car and get out. "Alright, we'll do it your way, but I want the intel you promised."

"Not now, when we get to Helsinki." Petra didn't seem to be interested in compromise and continued heading north.

Kat removed the gun from her belt and pressed it against Harken's ribs. "That's not the way this is going to happen. Start giving me the intel now or the trip stops here."

Petra looked at the gun, recognized Kat's expression, and had no doubt that Kat would shoot her. "Fine, in the syndicate that I have infiltrated there has been a coup. Someone is taking over the entire organization and the people I've been working with have begun to disappear.

The word is that anyone who was loyal to the organization is being eliminated."

"I don't see how that effects US Military security."

"I'm not finished. The people behind this are building an army. They are taking over corporations and government positions all over Europe. They want to be the real power behind the governments. After Europe they will move on to America."

"How do you know this?"

"I have my sources."

"Alright, I'll accept that but I want the names of your sources and the people behind this new syndicate. Start with who is at the top."

"I don't know his name, but I know that he is a friend of Putin."

"I need more than that?"

"There is a rumor that Delph Petros is involved in some way but there is no proof of that." She continued to drive her meandering course through the city so that now Kat had no idea where they were.

"I can't take rumors back to the States. We need proof. Have you any other names in this organization?"

"The ones with the money are the people who were behind the Rote Armee Fraktion."

"Okay, now hang on they were from the '70s and they don't exist anymore. How could they be part of this?"

"There was a Stasi officer who supported their activities back then. He was getting the money and his orders from the Russians. His name was Karl Holbïn."

"Where would we find this Holbïn guy?"

"He may be dead already, I don't know."

"Then why bring him up?"

"There is another man who has suddenly been appearing with big political ideas and he is not happy with the United States."

"And …?"

"There is something familiar about the way he does business. It is just as Holbïn worked. And it is said that he works with a Stasi officer."

Kat prodded her with the gun. "You haven't finished yet give me another name."

"Stephan Gelenko."

"Who is he?"

"He is the president of a company in Berlin, S. G. Data Services. It struck me as unusual at the time because when they mention a name like that then he would already be dead. But not Gelenko. I think he may be working for Petrus. That's all I have."

"I don't believe you. I want the names of your sources now or we don't have a deal."

"When I am safely out of the country."

"That wasn't the deal. You give me the information then I get you out."

"That's all I will give you. I don't believe you will keep up your end of the bargain. I don't trust you anymore. I want you to get out."

"Don't be a fool, I said I'd ..."

"No, It's too late for that now." Her eyes flashed. She yanked on the emergency brake and as Kat held on Petra drifted through a sloppy 180.

"If you give me some time ...," Kat said.

"There is no time! You have run out of time."

"I can get you out of here. Let me help you."

Petra made a last second turn into the parking lot of the Ozerki Station and stopped. "Get out!" she screamed pushing Kat.

"Please Petra."

"Your time is up." Petra reached across Kat to pull the handle and pushed the door open. "Get out!"

"We have ..."

"Samantha!" she screamed, *"GET OUT NOW!"*

Kat barely managed to set her feet down on the asphalt before Petra dropped it down into first and sped off. The car sped away slamming the door behind her. Kat just stood there shaking.

THE YOUNG WOMAN

Petrogradsky District, St. Petersburg

Petra drove south like a maniac threading through traffic while constantly looking behind her. Heading south she entered Udelnyy Park. When she was sure that there was no one behind her she slowed down. Reaching Marka Gallaya she drove through the inner-city forest at a more reasonable speed. She noticed a helicopter above her and for a terrifying second, she thought it was following her.

No, she had just spooked herself needlessly, obviously there was no one tailing her. She was certain of that now.

Her plans for leaving town began to take shape. She would go to her bank first to get some travelling money.

And then ... where? People would be watching the airport, so that was out. Maybe she should have kept on going to Helsinki. She could still do that, fly out from there and go home to France. Home had a nice ring to it.

Traversing the narrows of the Bolshaya Nevka River on the Ushakovskyi Bridge she passed over the tiny island through Park Tikhiy Otykh. Then the Kamennoostrovskiy Bridge with a name almost as wide as the Reka Malaya Nevka Rived it spanned. Much relieved she entered the Petrogradsky District an island community of commerce and banking.

Just up ahead a young woman stepped out into a crosswalk. From a distance she seemed quite pretty, tall and slim with short blond hair. As Petra drew nearer there was something about her that she found irresistible.

She stopped. The blond was paying no attention to the traffic her focus was on something in her handbag.

Petra was admiring her as she walked in front of the Ferrari. What would it be like to take her to bed? My-god, she is in incredible shape, what a lover she would be.

The woman paused and looked at Petra. She smiled, Petra's heart quickened, and she smiled back. Yes, she's very beautiful. I wonder if I have time to do more than flirt through the glass. There's a hotel near ...

The blonde's hand came out of the bag gripping a gun equipped with a silencer and pointed it at her.

Petra froze, her thought left unfinished. She'd been so stupid. They had people everywhere.

The kill shot cut a neat hole between her small breasts, through her sternum to stop her heart. The second drilled a hole through the center of her forehead pushing a part of her brain out the back of her skull.

Her head lolled back, her ruby lips parted, and the blood dribbled over her carefully sculpted eyebrows and into her dead brown eyes.

Her hands fell to her lap and her foot slipped off the clutch. The powerful car jerked forward and stalled only inches from the killer.

The blond didn't flinch. She calmly put the gun back in her bag and walked on, making her way to a parked car at the corner.

ON HER TAIL

Ozerki Station, St. Petersburg

As Kat walked to the metro station a car stopped behind her. She heard the door open and close. A man's footsteps quickened to close in behind her. Kat didn't dare look back.

It would be stupid to go for my gun now. A professional would be ready for that and I'd be dead. Maybe I'm already dead. Perhaps he's just a commuter. Maybe there's nothing to worry about. It occurred to her that the word maybe wasn't really all that comforting. She merged with the crowd in the station wondering if he was still behind her. She bought her ticket and surveyed around her. She couldn't tell who it was, there were so many men with hard-soled shoes.

Heading down to the platform Kat was sure the man was following when she heard his distinctive footsteps on the tiled floor.

There was a route map on the wall, so she took a moment to locate Ozerki Station and traced the route down to the station nearest to her hotel.

That was Nevsky. She'd have to take a bus the rest of the way. Casually she turned and faced the track and looked to see if he was there, but everyone was just standing waiting for the train. She took out her phone, went through the protocol and heard Devlyn's voice.

"Katrina, what's happened?"

"She kicked me out of the car."

"Did she pass along the intel?"

"Just things we already knew about, world domination through corporate takeovers and three names she'd heard. She didn't know if they were involved."

"What were the names?"

"An oligarch, Delph Petrus, he could be Russian or German, an ex-Stasi freak named Karl Holbïn, and a businessman named Stephan Gelenko, his company is S. G. Data."

"I'll check them out."

"That's it."

"Shit. And she's gone?"

"Oh yeah."

"Okay, wrap it up and come home."

"I'm on my way."

Crammed in like a sardine in the overcrowded train, it was impossible to see past the man next to her.

Maybe the man got into a different car? Perhaps it was all just a coincidence.

Don't be stupid dummy, be prepared. I still have a long way to go. Okay Kat just stay alert and just try not to be too obvious about it. God it's fucking crowded in here.

Several minutes later she was practically dragged from the train in the crush of people getting off at Nevsky prospect. She worked her way across the platform to a column and watched carefully to see if she'd been followed.

There'd been a switch during the stop at Pionerskaya, the man who followed her down had now been replaced.

The new man stepped out of the train and was staring at her.

As she turned her head he quickly looked away and that furtive movement was all she needed. Now it was her turn to watch him as he casually moved off down the hall. He stopped to read a paper.

Oh, very subtle, she thought.

When the crowd thinned, he walked to the stairs and headed up to the street level. Kat followed. He must have known she would because he went over to a kiosk on the middle level to looked at the magazines. She kept on going up.

He knew he'd been blown, but he wasn't alone. After she was out of sight a third man took over and followed her up to the surface.

She located her bus stop and waited. Soon the third man spotted her and got in the line behind a large woman. Kat was keenly aware of everyone around her now. The way the man studiously ignored her was so un-Russian that she knew he had to be involved. When the bus arrived, he sat across from her and one back. She would have to kill him when he followed her off the bus and began considering her options during the half-hour trip to her stop.

The bus stop was a long block away from the river, which in turn was just a block away from her hotel. What could happen between here and there?

The man got off first and when he reached the sidewalk, he opened his cell phone. She overheard him mention the cross streets and arrange for someone to pick him up. Perhaps she was wrong about him. Paranoia was part of the job. Vigilance was what would keep her safe.

He stayed put as she headed to the river crossing about two hundred yards down the road. She thought about Petra. She tried to convince herself that there was nothing she could have done.

But it wasn't working. Kat regretted leaving without her. She'd failed. She looked around, but there was no one else on the wide barren street. There was no comfort in being alone beside the Moyka River.

Just ahead the road came to a fork. The main road doglegged to the left while Kat's route would take her straight across the bridge that spanned the smaller Pryazhka. She hurriedly crossed the road to reach the threshold of the bridge. From there it was less than a quarter of a mile to the hotel. She'd be safe soon.

TROLLS AND OTHER MONSTERS

Moyka Bridge, St. Petersburg

Kat's sense of security vanished as soon as she stepped onto the bridge. Her shoes echoed ominously, triggering an irrational childlike fear that something bad was underfoot, perhaps a troll.

Why was it always a troll?

There had to be one under the bridge and she was totally alone. She was exhausted.

She had to remind herself that it was just a short walk across the bridge, perhaps half the width of a football field and there were no goddamn trolls. Needing to hear a reassuring voice she took out her phone and went through the protocol again. She'd never have guessed that Devlyn's voice would be comforting.

"Katrina, where are you?"

"I'm nearly at my hotel now, I'm on the bridge."

"Has something happened?"

"No. I'm sorry, I know it's stupid." From her vantage point the river looked like a hostile thing, cold and black, slicked with oil.

Surely it was filled with monsters.

She shivered and quickened her pace. Soon she would be safe in the hotel. "I just needed some reassurance."

"Keep your head and you'll be alright," he said. Perhaps he'd pushed her too hard, placed too much pressure on her after all.

"I'm going to head to the airport as soon as I get my ..." She looked into the gaping mouth of the Pryazhka River;

its black water swirled beneath her. It was the strangest feeling, as if there was a malevolent spirit under the bridge counting her footsteps.

"Katrina, what is it?"

"I don't know. Something isn't right."

"What do you see, what's going on?"

"That's just it, there's nothing here. I just ..."

A powerful car roared up behind her. A black Mercedes swept by her and screeched to a halt drifting sideways to block the far end of the bridge. The doors flew open and two men jumped out. "Oh, fuck no!"

"Katrina! Jesus Christ, Katrina, what's happening?"

Forgetting about the phone she turned and ran. They chased her. She needed her hand, so she dropped the phone and reached for her gun. Devlyn's distant voice called to her from the deck.

Kat remembered there was already a round in the chamber. She also knew that if she didn't aim the bullet wouldn't count. All she could hope for was to keep them back while she ran. Without turning, she swung her arm back and fired a shot. It hit the car door with a loud thunk.

As she was wheeling around to take aim, a second car pulled up right behind her. Her arms were extended holding the gun ready to fire, but she twisted to look. There was a man leaning out of the window with his gun levelled at her.

It was a split-second decision. The two men didn't have guns and the man in the car wasn't going to miss at that range. She redirected her gun toward him and fired.

Blood erupted from his cheek just below his eye, his gun hit the road, he slipped back into the car and she ran. She was heading away from the hotel now.

Taking that shot had cost her precious seconds. The men were catching up to her.

Before she reached the end of the bridge, huge iron-like hands slammed down onto her shoulders stopping her in her tracks with a bone crushing grip. She lifted her foot to kick back and take out his knee, but something hit her at the base of her skull and the world suddenly went grey.

She sagged into the iron man's arms, dazed but `conscious, her gun clattered to the pavement.

The second man put the leather-bound lead club in his pocket.

She had the sensation that one of the men was holding her up under her arms, the other one was picking up her feet. Then she felt herself swinging, then flying. She felt weightless. As she rolled in the air, she saw the black river rushing up to meet her. She hit the water face first. It felt like she had slammed onto a sheet of ice. Then, like a sucking mouth, it opened up and swallowed her whole.

They just tossed me away like a bag of garbage.

Face down it took a moment for her to bob to the surface with her arms and legs stretched out. Spinning slowly with the current she floated as still as death, staring down into the black void.

A LITTLE DEATH

The Pryazhka River

The blow had stunned her, but Kat was still conscious. She lay perfectly still, unable to move. She sensed a splash beside her as her gun hit the water, then another plunk as the phone followed.

They left her purse where it fell, perhaps to suggest a suicide. Her assailants looked to see if she moved. She didn't, not a muscle.

The driver of the second car had retrieved the fallen weapon then backed off the bridge and sped away. The other two returned to their car, spun around in a cloud of smoke from squealing tires and followed him.

For more than two minutes Kat drifted face down in the swirling current.

To the north, just beyond the bridge she'd just left, was the Moyka River. It and the Pryazhka were linked like an intersection of a small city street to a main road.

In turn the Moyka drained out to the superhighway, the Neva River. If the current was dragging her out there ..., well at this point, she thought, what would it matter? Soon the monsters would rise from the depths and take her. Maybe it wouldn't be too painful.

After all dead is dead, isn't it?

It was another half-minute before she could sort out what she had to do to stay alive. Cupping her hands, she pushed down on the water, lifted her head and gasped for air.

She wondered why it was so dark and then she realized that she was under the bridge. The crippling cold had seeped down into her bones and it took a great deal of effort to struggle to the edge.

The concrete walls of the Pryazhka River rose four feet to a narrow strip of grass on the bank above the water line.

Dredged for barges, there was no shallow bottom at the edge, no beach to clamber up, just a slime-slicked wall that stretched as far as she could see.

She was having trouble keeping her head above water and the taste of the polluted soup the river served up made her want to vomit. She realized that no matter what she did, she was going to drown.

But that didn't mean she was going to give up. She clawed at the wall trying to gain a purchase, but all she did was shred her nails down to the quick.

Clinging to the rough wall was impossible. Slowly she kicked her feet to keep her head above water as the current carried her further under the bridge.

Her legs and arms were cramping, and her sodden sweater was dragging her down. Her throat tightened into a panicked groan.

This is it, she thought. Death. I can't do this anymore.

Her life began to slip away.

Something grabbed her by the hair and pulled her back up. She gasped for air. The pain of being yanked up by the hair while at the same time being sucked down by the river was indescribable. She had no idea where this magical hand had come from. With a pathetic scream, she reached up for it and seized a handful of his sleeve.

The hair pulling stopped and current dragged her away from the wall and she began to sink again.

"Oh go- ...!" She choked as water filled her mouth. Coughing and gasping, all she could think of was that she had a chance and now it was gone. The numbness was taking over and her mind was shutting down, but she still clung to that sleeve.

Another hand took hold of her sweater at the shoulder. The hand extending from that sleeve grabbed her other shoulder. Then the hand moved under her right arm. The other reached under her left. She heard a man's voice shouting something unintelligible.

She thought she should be able to understand it, but her brain had switched off Russian. Spanish, her primary language, had taken over. Nothing he said was making any sense, but he kept prattling on. Then other excited voices joined in as she was pulled from the river.

But the river didn't want to give her up, and she thought in the tug of war she might split in two. It sucked and slurped at her, pulling off her shoes and socks, and tugging her jeans down to her ankles. None of that mattered because she was going up. She could feel the cool air and then the warmth of the sun on her exposed skin. That warm sensation flooded over her stomach and bare legs and, at last, the water released her. Another pair of hands reached for her legs and lifted her beyond the concrete onto the grass.

She hadn't noticed them, but three old men had been fishing nearby. They saw her on the bridge, witnessed the cars cutting her off. "We heard the shots and saw them throw you in. We came as soon as the men were gone."

They moved her up to the sidewalk and one of the men was attempting to perform an entirely unique version of CPR. Alternating between blowing hot vodka breath into her mouth and delivering painful compressions to her chest. He kept it up until she found her Russian voice once more.

She began coughing, sputtering, and shivering, she tried to hold his wrists to stop him before he could apply another painful compression. Then, managing to speak just above a whisper she said, "Thank you. I'm okay, I can breathe on my own now."

"Good, we are so relieved. You are safe now, pretty lady."

She sat up coughing as she pulled the sweater down over her exposed breasts and slid her knees up to her chest. "You were like angels, thank you for saving my life. I would have died if you weren't here."

A small crowd was beginning to gather around them from the school across the street. Cars stopped on the other side of the river.

Someone must have called for help because presently an ambulance pulled up to the curb. The medics wrapped a blanket around her.

Her relief was soon replaced by anxiety when she remembered that she had just killed someone, and the police would be coming.

The police arrived with lights and noise, but only one car, just two officers. Not much of a response for a shooting, she thought. She had been moved to the tailgate of the ambulance and was sitting with a reflective blanket wrapped around her. One officer came to her while his partner went over to the bridge.

"You try to commit suicide, why?"

"What?" *How could they be here and not known about the shooting? Surely someone must have told them what happened.* "No, I didn't, I was thrown off the bridge. There were three ..."

She was going to continue with the story then thought better of it.

If they don't know what happened, why go into details?

"I saw no sign of a mugging," the officer said, and Kat shrugged and looked bewildered.

His partner joined them with her purse. "Is this yours?"

"Yes."

"There's still money inside."

He handed it to the first officer who stared into the bag as if it would reveal some deep secret. "They took nothing." Looking back to Kat suspiciously he said, "If this was a mugging then why is it that they took nothing?"

"I have no idea Officer," she said, her voice was trembling because of the cold but she milked it for all it was worth. "It was horrible, I was so frightened."

She didn't have to fake that; they scared the shit out of her. "They tried to kill me!" She turned on the waterworks and trembled so convincingly that the ambulance attendant put his arm around her trying to comfort her.

The cop wasn't particularly moved by the tears, but he wasn't totally unsympathetic. "Do you have any other injuries?"

"No, I don't think so." She tried to ramp it down just a little and show a brave face.

"Is there anything else you can tell me?"

She rubbed her eyes with the palms of her hands, cleared her throat and said, "All I know is that two men attacked me, hit me on the back of the head," she winced as she put her hand on the lump at the base of her skull, "and threw me in the river."

"Why would they do that if they had not intended to rob you?"

It's interesting that the old men haven't told them what really happened.

Kat looked over at them watching her performance from the other side of the fence. She smiled at them and they all waved back. "I honestly have no idea."

The policeman looked at her passport. "You are from Canada."

"Yes."

"How is it that you speak Russian so well?"

She read his nameplate, Officer Uri Rostov.

They said using a man's name brings him closer to you, use it get him on your side. Okay let's see if it works.

"I am a student of languages, Officer Rostov. I speak twelve fluently." She let the tears dry up.

"Impressive. You are a student where?"

"The University of Toronto."

"It's a good school, yes?"

"It is."

"And why are you in St. Petersburg?"

Officer, to tell the truth, I'm and American agent, here to help a spy come in from the cold. Why don't you just shoot me now and get it over with? Or I could just go with ...

"I'm just here as a tourist, I wanted to see the city and improve my Russian."

"How long have you been here?"

"Three days," she said.

The partner took her purse back, then removed her wallet. Kat read his nameplate, Officer Anatol Demitov. He was not a sympathetic listener. After extracting her driver's license and student card he studied them then asked Rostov for her passport. Rostov handed it to him and Demitov compared them. "You are Samantha Dole?"

"Yes."

"Where are you from, Samantha Dole?"

"I told your partner. I'm from Toronto, that's in Ontario, Canada."

He was watching her closely then he asked, "What were you doing this afternoon?"

She looked at Rostov for help and got none.

Shit, he's making connections and this is just going to get nasty. What are my options here? It's a tie between fuck-all and none. Unless I start playing the dumb bimbo bit. Hey, I can do dumb bimbo.

"I'm sorry Officer Demitov, I don't understand the question."

"Your activities today. Where did you go, what did you do?"

"Oh, well I had lunch at that Viking place, and then I went to the movies. Ah, can I ..., can I have my passport back now, please?"

"I'll keep it for now. Where did you see this movie?" He produced a notebook and pencil from his shirt pocket and began writing.

"It was at the Mirage Cinema," she said, and watched as he wrote it down carefully.

"Which one?" he asked.

Her brow wrinkled, "I didn't know there was more than one."

"There are two. What did you see?"

"I have no idea now, but it was awful and depressing, so I walked out. Does it matter?"

Rostov smiled and said, "No, I suppose not."

Hey, it's working on him!

"What did you do after that?" he asked, taking over the questioning.

"I met with a friend for a beer and we went for a drive."

He wrote that down and moved on. "After that, what did you do?"

"Nothing, I left her and was just heading back to my hotel when the men attacked me."

"Which hotel?"

She pointed across the river. "That one over there, the Matisov Domik. My dad booked me in there."

He looked then shook his head sadly. "You were so close. What is the name of this friend?"

"Why?"

"Please miss, humor me."

Oh god. Well if he asked the question then he probably already knows the answer, so I can't lie about it.

"It was Petra something."

"You don't know her last name?" Demitov asked and Kat just shrugged. "What is her address?" he asked.

"How would I know that?"

Demitov whispered something in Rostov's ear. He nodded and Demitov resumed the inquisition. "You went for a drive with a woman and you didn't know her name. You are either very foolish or you are trying to protect this woman. I assure you; she does not need your protection. Do you know her name, or not?"

"Alright yes it's Petra Harken."

"Are you long time acquaintances?"

"No, we just met this afternoon."

177

He nodded at Rostov as if he had scored some sort of victory. Rostov studied her and that worried her.

Does he believed me or is he preparing to try to trip me up? "What did you do with this person you just met?" he asked.

"I don't know. I guess we ... just talked. Why?"

"Talked, that's all?"

"Yes ...," she said, guardedly. "Look, I don't know what you want me to tell you. We talked and then she dropped me off at the metro station."

"She dropped you off at what station?"

"Why are you asking me about her?"

"Which station?" he asked again.

"Ozerki." *I don't like the way this is going at all. I've got to change the subject.* "Why are you asking me about her? Two men just tried to kill me. If those men down there hadn't pulled me out when they did, I'd be dead. I'm afraid they'll come back for me."

"I doubt that they would do that, Miss Dole. Were you alone with her?"

She took a breath and steadied herself. "Yes, there were only two seats in her car."

"A black Ferrari California?" the Demitov asked.

I'm not going to get away with this am I?

"It could have been, I don't know anything about cars. Has something happened to her?"

Ignoring her question, he started working his way down the chain of events, "From the metro, you then came here by bus, yes?" Kat nodded. "Did you see someone following you from the bus?"

178

"There was a man. He got on the bus behind me at the metro and got off at my stop, but he didn't follow me."

No, he called his buddies and they all came after me.

"What were you thinking just then? I saw it in your eyes. What was it?"

Shit, can you read my mind?

"I was just having a flashback of them coming after me."

"Of course, I'm sorry. Was the man on the bus one of the men who attacked you?"

"I don't know." She flashed on the man's face.

Yes, he was the man from the bus and I killed the bastard.

"It all happened so fast, they grabbed me, hit me with something hard, then tossed me in the river. I didn't see their faces."

"But you saw the man on the bus. If we showed you pictures ..."

"I'm sorry. I could try, but I don't think I could identify him. What's happened to Petra?"

"You say you only talked to her, nothing else?"

"What else would you think we'd be doing?"

"You are a very beautiful woman, Miss Dole. I wonder if you are a student as you say. Perhaps you are a working girl, yes? Were you working for Petra Harken?"

"Wait what? Working for her? Oh ... no! I told you, I just ... you think I am a prostitute. I am not a prostitute, Officer Rostov."

"So, you didn't know she was a Madame?"

Kat had to pause to catch her breath. "You are really beginning to frighten me now."

No lie there.

"I only want the truth, Miss Dole."

"I'm telling you the truth. Something has happened to her, hasn't it? Please, you've got to tell me. Is she alright?"

Was it the police chasing us, the police that followed me, hit me and dumped me in the river? No, don't be stupid, these guys don't know anything. So how can I spin this?

"Okay, listen I had no idea that she was a lesbian until I got in the car with her."

"She picked you up?"

"I wouldn't say she picked me up. We had a beer and ..." She stopped and tried to have a second go.

"Look, I'm not a lesbian if that's what you're thinking. Okay, yes, she picked me up. She said we were going to a party. When I told her that I wasn't into girls she got angry. She drove me all the way up to the north end of the city and told me to get out. I did, she drove off, end of story. Can you please just tell me what happened to her?"

"She was found murdered in her car a short time ago."

"Oh-my-god! And, you think I did it?"

"No, we have a description of the killer and she was certainly nothing like you." *The syndicate was cleaning house and she was a loose end. None of it should have been a surprise.* Still Kat felt upset. She thought about their brief time together.

It could have ended differently if Petra hadn't panicked.

"What do you know about this?"

"Someone really doesn't like gay people?" she offered. At that point the medic intervened, insisting that she be taken to the hospital. The police agreed but they followed to ask more questions.

She was taken to a cubicle in the emergency department.

The police wanted to stay with her, but the nurse pushed them out and began to close the curtain when Rostov pushed back. "Hold on nurse. Miss Dole, give us your hotel key and we will get you some dry clothes from your room."

Okay now that's really weird. Why would he offer to do that? Cops don't step and fetch like gofers. Either he has the hots for me, or he wants to search my room. That's the more likely scenario. They're going to do it no matter what I say so ...

She handed him the key from her purse and said, "That is very kind. Thank you. Oh ..., I wonder if you could do me a favor."

How far can I push this?

"Perhaps," Rostov said.

"Maybe it would be easier if you would just toss all my things into the suitcase and bring it to me. Oh, and could you tell them at the hotel that I'm checking out? They can put the charges on my credit card."

"May I ask you what you plan to do?"

"This had been a terrible experience, Officer Rostov, I don't feel safe here anymore and I want to go home now, back to Canada."

And that's the truth, so help me God.

"Of course, I understand. We will bring all of your things to you and when you are released from the hospital, we would be happy escort you to the airport."

"I can't believe how kind you are, thank you," she said.

Now they'll find the false bottom with the fake passports, the secure cell phone, the silencer and the ammunition and that will be it. I'm never going to get out of Russia alive. But I'm not going to let them kill me while I smell like the river. "Nurse may I take a shower?"

"Yes of course, but the doctor must see you first."

A doctor had given her a clean bill of health and Kat had her shower. When she returned to the cubicle with wet hair and wearing the flimsy hospital gown, she felt clean, but vulnerable.

She thought about the three old men. She'd seen them out there when she arrived that first day, or men just like them. They were just part of the scenery, unimportant, completely forgettable ... and yet without them she'd be dead.

Did I thank them enough for that? Would it ever be enough? Thank god they were there.

Her mind wandered.

Did they eat the fish they caught in that polluted water? If so, then how can they still be alive? Maybe the vodka kills off the bad stuff.

She shut her eyes and thought of the fish that lived in that water.

Once again visions of monstrous, deformed sharks, great evil things appearing out of the blackness to rip her to shreds. Great slimy lamprey eels latching on to her body to suck her dry. *Oh, holy shit!* Kat screamed, and opened her eyes.

The nurse ran to her side. "What's wrong?"

"Nothing, sorry. I ... I just had an awful flashback." Whatever terrible things that might have happened didn't. She was spared by the grace of three drunken old men.

The curtain suddenly parted and Officer Rostov appeared, "How are you feeling now, Miss Dole?"

Startled, she looked up and for a moment thought the end was coming. "I'm feeling ..., um, I'm feeling much better, thanks."

She was relieved to see her suitcase. "Thank you for bringing my things Officer Rostov."

He lifted the case onto the end of her bed and smiled. "When you have dressed, we will take you to the airport."

"You are very kind, Officer Rostov, thank you."

A LUCKY BREAK

St. Petersburg Airport, Russia

There was a flight to Amsterdam with a connecting flight to Toronto on KLM, scheduled to leave at 6:30 pm. She wanted to check in before she booked it. It was a good thing that she did. Devlyn was relieved to hear from her. "Jesus Katrina, what the fuck happened?" She relayed the gist of the story and told him she was in rough shape. He said, "Shake it off, I've got one more detail that needs your full attention."

"What's that?" No Sirs this time. He seemed to have no sympathy for what she'd been through and she was too tired and too stressed to play nice with Devlyn.

"Right. Okay, stop off in The Hague on your way home. The head of Europol wants to know what happened to his agent. His name is Dael Van Haanrade. Give him a report and then fly back to D. C. Got it?"

"Sir, I just ..."

"You just what? I said suck it up and grow a pair, you're a soldier Fernando."

"Yes, I got it, but my ID's in a box in Toronto, so I'm still Samantha Dole. How do I deal with that?"

"Don't worry about it. I'll make sure they know who you are. You can go to Toronto and retrieve your property some other time, I want you in Maryland ASAP. Now get to The Hague. I'll have them send someone to the airport to pick you up."

"How will they know me?"

"I'll send them a photo," he said. "Oh, and Katrina?"

"Yes Sir?"

"I'm glad you didn't die." he said, and disconnected.

"Oh, well thanks a bunch asshole, you're a peach," she said quietly.

She was looking over her shoulder the whole time as she booked her flight and went through the documents check and security. She even felt vulnerable sitting on the plane at the departure gate. She was expecting a syndicate killer to appear at any moment and blow her away.

She couldn't relax until the plane was in the air over Estonia, heading for Amsterdam.

13

MEETING IN THE HAGUE

Amsterdam-Rotterdam Airport

A Europol agent was waiting for her at the baggage claim. A very tall, thin man with a soft voice. "Welcome to the Netherlands Agent Fernando," he said in English.

His voice was quiet, and respectful but the heavy accent made him difficult to understand. Maybe it was just because she was tired. "Who are you?"

"Sorry, yes. I should have introduced myself. I am Agent De Jonckheer, from Europol."

"Thank you for coming to pick me up."

"Not at all." He waited beside her at the carousel until her suitcase came around and as she reached for it, he said, "Allow me."

"Thank you." She stood back without protest then walked beside him like a zombie as they worked their way through the crowd to the customs area.

He'd already made contact with them at the gate so the customs agent offered a quick smile and salute and allowed them to pass without question.

"It is not too far to my car. Did you have a pleasant journey?" It was still difficult to understand him and more so in the crowd of people waiting for their loved ones outside the arrival's gate.

"Agent De Jonckheer, I'm sorry but I have a terrible headache and I'm having trouble understanding you. It's strange I know but do you speak German?"

"Of course, yes. Is this better?" he asked, immediately switching languages.

"Yes. Have you come a long way?"

"60 km, it's just under an hour."

She nodded as they stepped out into the warm evening. *I wonder what Harm's doing right now.* She looked at her watch.

9:35 pm, so it must be about 12:35 in California. He's probably up to his ears with work. God, I miss him. I wonder if the asshole has a new assignment for me, or is he going to let me go see Harm for a while. A couple of weeks would be nice. It feels like forever since I've seen him. I need to go home. Home.

"Agent Fernando?" She hadn't really noticed that he was standing in front of her.

She'd been walking on auto pilot when she started thinking about home and Harm. "Excuse me, Ms. Fernando."

"Sorry, I was drifting, Yes?"

"We are here, this is my car." He put the suitcase down and opened the door for her. She waited for him inside while he put the case in the back seat. A moment later he was sitting beside her with the engine was running.

He's very kind, I like this man.

"Are you ready to go?"

"Yes. If you don't mind, let's dispense with the last name, friends call me Kat."

"Not at all, thank you Kat. My name is Henrick. Will you do up your seat belt now," he said softly.

"Oh, sure. Sorry, drifting again." she laughed weakly.

"Henrick, would it be possible to take me to a hotel now? I can meet the Director in the morning if that's possible. I really need to get some sleep."

"I was instructed by your colonel to take care of that for you." Henrick.

My Colonel? So the rat bastard's a colonel now.

"There is a reservation for you at a hotel near our office. Your appointment with the director is scheduled for 9:00 tomorrow morning. Just relax now while we drive to The Hague. He pulled away from the parking lot and began the trip from Amsterdam-Rotterdam Airport to The Hague.

She thought about Henrick for a moment, wondering what sort of man this quiet agent was.

In his mid-thirties, a pleasant looking man. A middle management office worker type, probably suffering from chronic boredom. If he was a field agent, he'd stick out like the Space Needle.

"Henrick, could you be able to do me one more favor?"

"Anything you like."

"Would you be able to book a flight to D. C. for me? I want to head out tomorrow afternoon."

"It has already been taken care of. You're on the 1:42 pm flight to Washington D. C., I booked a First-Class seat for you."

She responded with a smile. "Henrick, I think I love you."

He smiled.

Her hotel was near the Europol Headquarters, and it seemed like the trip took no time at all. She checked in and hit the bed as soon as she found the room.

HEADING TO EUROPOL HQ

The hotel food court

Kat was up and showered by 6:40 am wondering what to wear. The wardrobe people in Procurement had only packed one dress for the trip, a flower print spring frock they did not expect her to wear. It was warm so she decided to wear it anyway.

Sitting in the food court with her suitcase beside her, Kat nursed a cup of coffee and nibbled on a tosti while she waited for Agent De Jonckheer.

She'd folded a copy of Der Spiegel on the table so that she could read it hands free and scanned the story about the murder in St. Petersburg.

A woman, identified as the infamous Madam Petra Harken, was shot dead in her car while stopped at a crosswalk yesterday afternoon. They included a gory picture of the murder scene.

"She didn't deserve that epitaph," Kat said, in English.

She said it quietly, but a man with a heavy accent spoke to her in English, "Who didn't?"

She recognized his voice immediately and looked up at her new friend with a sad smile.

"A woman I met in St. Petersburg."

"Ah, yes I read about that and assumed that she had something to do with your mission. I am sorry that it turned out that way."

"Thank you Henrick."

"Did you manage to sleep?"

"I suppose so. I'm feeling slightly more rested, thanks."

"Good. That is a very pretty dress."

"What, this old thing?" she joked, suddenly feeling very self-conscious. "Is it appropriate? It was this or jeans and a sweatshirt."

"You look very nice, but either would have worked."

When they arrived at the Europol building, Henrick drove down the ramp into the underground parking past an armed security man who waved them through. They took the elevator to the main floor then Henrick escorted her through to a waiting room. "The Director will be with you shortly. May I get you something, coffee or tea, Kat?"

"No, I'm fine thanks."

"Very well then, I will see you after your meeting and take you back to the hotel."

"Thanks."

She still had a headache after sleep and pills and she wished it would go away. Presently a slim, cultured looking man came in, bowed politely and introduced himself.

"Good morning Special Agent Fernando, I am Director Van Haanrade."

Kat stood up. "Good morning, Sir."

"Walk with me, please." He turned and walked away, forcing her to catch up. "As I am sure you are aware, this is a very delicate matter," he said, leading her down a long corridor. "Understand that it must be handled with discretion."

"If you say so, Sir."

"I must insist upon it, Special Agent Fernando." He rushed her along to his office and she noticed that while all the others were simply numbered his had his name and title on the glass.

"This was a Catholic boy's school before the war. Not a very glamorous situation, I'm afraid, but we make do." He opened the door of a small classroom. The Dutch flag hung from a pole in the corner behind an Ikea desk and chair. There were four chairs, two of them were well used, leather armchairs, the other two wooden were refugees from the original school furniture.

"Please, take a seat."

Choosing something comfortable seemed reasonable, so she moved to the leather chair and was about to sit ... "No," he snapped, "not there! Those are reserved for people above your station."

"Excuse me?" She stared at him in disbelief.

"Be good enough to sit there," he said, pointing to a wooden chair. Was his rudeness because she was an American or a woman? *Perhaps he's one of those people who only behaved well toward women when there were witnesses.*

Kat sat and smoothed her skirt, then folded her hands on her lap again and waited for him to begin. He rested his elbows on the arms of his comfortable chair, steepled his hands and stared at her with a supercilious smile. When he noticed that she didn't smile back, he cleared his throat. "What we discuss here must be held in the strictest of confidence."

"Of course, you mentioned that before," she said, giving him some attitude. He was pushing all her buttons.

"Yes. Ah, you know what we do here, don't you?"

The condescending bastard was really pissing her off now and she'd just about had enough, so she decided to be blunt. "Not really. Until I was handed this assignment, I had never heard of Europol."

"Ah hah. There it is, do you see?" he said, pointing at her with an accusing finger.

"Do I see what?"

"You Americans never change."

"Oh?"

"You Americans are painfully ill-informed about the world outside the continental US."

How could I argue with that? It described a lot of Americans. He took a pipe from his breast pocket and proceeded to fill it. Without bothering to ask, he struck a match on the sole of his shoe and held it to the tobacco. The sickly-sweet aroma instantly filled the room.

Speaking into a series of well-practiced smoke rings he'd blown in her direction, he continued, "Since you don't pay much attention to what we are doing here in Europe, I'll give you a précis, shall I?"

"I'm sure that could be entertaining, but," she said with a cough, "before you do, would you mind opening a window?"

Without a hint of apology, he said, "Oh, does the smoke bother you?"

"It does," she said crossly.

"Then I suppose, if you must." He didn't move so she went to the window and opened it as wide as it would go before returning to her seat. "Where was I? ... Oh yes, the European Police Office, or Europol as you now know it ..., is very new. Following a Ministerial Agreement ..."

"Director, forgive me, but I really don't need the history lecture from you. I came here to give you the intel I received from your agent. I get that you don't operate in Russia and that she, excuse me, they shouldn't have been there. But the fact of the matter is that they were, and they uncovered a new criminal organization that is threatening the security of both Europe and the United States."

Kat decided to gloss over Petra's behavior. "What they did for us was very brave and they both sacrificed their lives to get the information to us."

"Officer Holst acted without the sanction of our unit when he sent Agent Chouinard to St. Petersburg." He stood up angrily and moved to the open window and struck a dramatic pose as he stared into the small courtyard.

Kat balked. "Excuse me, who is Agent Chouinard?"

"That harlot you met in St. Petersburg. Please try to keep up, will you?"

"Oh, Sir ..., I'll do my very best. But you see, I knew your agent as Petra Harken."

He tapped out the tobacco on the window ledge returned the hot pipe to his pocket keeping his back to Kat he said, "Agent Fernando I ..."

"Let me tell you about Agent Chouinard first. After working undercover in an extremely dangerous situation, she provided me with valuable intel, intel she died getting to us. So, I think the very least you could do is show her some fucking respect."

"I don't appreciate your attitude."

"You abandoned her and let her die. So, let's just chalk that up to my being American and move on."

"Really, I must ..."

"You were the one who wanted a briefing so here it is. We're talking about a Europol agent who gave her life doing her job. And her partner also died while uncovering this plot, so what is it going to take to get you to pull your head out of your ...?"

"I don't have to tolerate this kind of treatment!"

"Well, neither do I, so it's time to go," Kat said, and stormed out. She looked at her watch as she stood in the hall waiting for Henrick. It was only 9:11.

Jesus that lasted eleven minutes? It seemed like a goddam lifetime.

The hall was empty so she decided to leave unescorted.

Henrick was waiting for her at the front. She walked right past him and headed for the elevator. As they got in the tiny car he said, "I gather it didn't go well."

"He is un-fucking-believable!" she fumed.

She led the way this time and held her tongue until she was past the security and out into the garage. "Bad? The man is a pompous buffoon. Is he like that with everyone or is it just with women? I'm sorry Henrick, but I ..."

"Not at all, your conversation was overheard by several people and they applaud you. I should have warned you about him. I am sorry."

"I don't think it would have made it any easier, but thanks for the thought."

"Now that you have been assaulted ..."

"Oh, good word."

"Thank you, Katrina. Now that you have been assaulted by the old man, I consider you as one of us. It's something akin to a baptism of fire around here."

"Compared to being shot at he was a fart in the wind, but it still pissed me off."

"Point taken."

"I know it's early, but I'd like to get to the airport, if that's okay with you."

"Certainly." Henrick drove on for a bit then looked at her and said, "I am only sorry you couldn't stay longer. I would have liked to get to know you better."

"It's always a pleasure to make new friends. I'm sure we'll meet again sometime." Kat said, smiled and left it at that.

Once she was alone at the airport, she took out her phone and called Harm.

"Oh Christ Kat, I've been so worried about you. Are you okay?"

"Better now that I'm talking to you. I've missed you so much Harm."

"I've missed you too. Are you coming home now?"

"I have to go to Washington first. After that I don't know what I'm doing. I'll ask for some leave, but you know Devlyn. He may send me out on another assignment."

"Where are you now?"

"Amsterdam airport. I can't really talk now, I just wanted to hear your voice before I get on the plane. I love you Harm. I'll talk to you again when I get to D. C."

ONE MAN WELCOMING COMMITTEE

Returning to Maryland

Kat was surprised that Devlyn was at the airport to meet her. Like the first time she met him, he was right there as she came off the plane.

He was looking very urban casual this time in a short sleeve shirt, Khaki trousers and loafers. And he was actually smiling. "How was your flight?" he asked.

"Acceptable, thank you, Sir."

"Good." He hustled her through baggage claim and customs flashing his badge at every opportunity. Outside in the hot humid fume filled air she finally felt safe, she was home, well home in America at least.

All she could do was hope that Devlyn would let her go to California. They crossed the traffic to the parking garage and got into his Camaro and they drove to her apartment.

"I know this mission was rough on you, Katrina. I want you to stay home, put your feet up and rest for a while. Your report can wait until tomorrow."

That sounded hopeful but there was no commitment to a leave. She was curious about his apparent good mood. "Has Wolfson heard from Van Haanrade yet?"

He laughed. "Oh yeah. I gather you were very entertaining. But forget about it, water under the bridge," he said. "Sorry, couldn't resist it."

Was he just twisting the knife in there?

"I hear you got a promotion, congratulations Colonel."

"I think that from now on when we're out of uniform you can call me Paul."

Whoa, that was unexpected.

"How are you holding up?"

"Honestly?"

"It's just you and me here, so talk," he said.

"I can't get the taste of that river out of my mouth and I feel like shit."

"Do you need to see a doctor?"

"I don't know, maybe I just need some more sleep. But if I sleep, I dream, if I dream, I see bad guys with clubs and monsters in the water. It's all I can do not to scream."

"Okay, listen to me. Talk like that could be a career killer. Write your report, stick to the facts, hand it in and then go take some R&R." He paused before he said something that must have been really difficult. "I heard somewhere that they have gliders in Warner Springs and I understand Harm has a helicopter now."

"I can go to California now?"

"Why not, you've earned it. Go flying, get some airtime and try to put that monster crap out of your mind."

"I don't know if I can keep doing this anymore, Paul."

"No, no, no," he said, as if they were going to crash. "I'm counting on you, Katrina. I've got too much invested in you to lose you now, so you've gotta suck it up."

"And grow a pair? Yeah I got that."

"Get some rest, get laid and then get your head back in the game. Look, I'm trying to be nice here. I know I've been hard on you in the past and I've come to realize that that isn't doing either of us any good. So, if it's possible I'd like to try to get past that."

"If that's what you want then I'm prepared do that, Paul."

"Good, I want you to be on my team, heart and soul."

"You can count on me, of course," she answered. *I'm not sure that I trust you, but for now I'll give you the benefit of the doubt.* "What are we doing with the information we got from Petra?"

"We're still building up the intel and planning the strategy to deal with it. But it looks like you're going to have to get involved over there again. I'm going to need you at your best." He could read what was going on in her mind just by the look on her face. Before she could say something regrettable, he continued, "I tell you what. Why don't you write that report now? I'll come over to pick it up in a couple of hours, then you can head off to Warner Springs today. By tomorrow you'll be sitting in the sun with lover boy, sipping Margaritas. How does that sound?" He stopped the car in front of her building.

"Okay," she said, wondering how they got all the way there without her noticing.

"You'll have the report in a couple of hours."

I am so tired I can't even think straight. What did I just agree to?

THE NEST

Warner Springs, CA

Harm was looking tired and drawn when he met her at the heliport, but he was so happy to see her that she thought it best just to stick with the welcome home and save the interrogation for later.

They spent the first day in bed together, then at the kitchen table talking long into the night. Day two Harm took Kat horseback riding on the mountain trails and later went soaring in a rented glider over the Hot Springs Mountain.

After a super afternoon in the air riding the mountain wave, Harm was looking like he'd had enough. She ordered some takeout food from the Academy restaurant and while they were having dinner in his apartment she leaned across the table and took his hand.

She knew he was sick. He'd never been as ill as this before.

She could see the pain in his face and his skin was sallow. Deeply worried Kat had to find how sick he was, "You look like hell and I know there's something going on with you. What is it?"

"Don't get all upset Honey, it's really nothing, nothing to worry about at all."

"I don't believe you, Harm. There's something you're not telling me."

He withdrew his hand and sat back, which only made her more frightened. "Harm level with me. She got up and then sat on the floor next to his chair. She hugged him around his middle and he figured that he had to say something.

He put his arm around her shoulders and stroked her back. "Maybe I'm a little over worked. Have you noticed how busy we are here? ENA was the best idea ever. We've got clients on a two-year waiting list."

"That's wonderful, I'm so happy for you."

"You are a rich woman."

"I don't need to be rich, Harm. I just need you and I certainly don't want you to work yourself to death either."

"Don't worry about me, I'm fine. It's you that I'm worried about. Make sure you don't take any more unnecessary chances out there."

Everything I do is dangerous these days, she thought, but she said, "I promise."

"Good. Tomorrow, why don't you take over some classes. I think they could use you over at defensive driving."

"Sure, I can do that."

"I knew I could count on you. Always."

"Yes, always. What are you going to do?"

"I've got mountains of paperwork, but I'm bushed, I think I'll turn in early."

"Come on there's something wrong here. What is it?"

"Nothing. Altitude gets to me sometimes. That's all."

Kat wasn't really buying it, but he was obviously done talking.

She joined the teaching staff in the morning for the threat avoidance driving class which was part of their condensed Survival, Evasion, Resistance and Escape. As intensive as it was, she'd do anything for him.

Mid-afternoon on day six a call came in from Devlyn. "Something has come up, Katrina. I need you on it, so I'm cutting your leave short."

"What?! You have got to be kidding me, I still have a week left!"

"You'll make it up later. Our syndicate has shown up in France. I want you back here right away."

"Am I the only fucking agent in CI now?"

"Don't give me attitude, Fernando. This one has you written all over it."

"But … I just told Harm …" She shut her eyes and swallowed.

"Your leave is cancelled, end of discussion."

"Yes, Sir. May I ask if I'm doing this solo again?"

"No, I'm putting you with Special Agent Flynn." He paused, "Look, I know you're upset and I don't blame you. But here's a word of advice."

"Sir?"

"In this business, we have to make sacrifices. You've gotta bring your 'A Game' to this, anything less than 100% is unacceptable. You can't give 100% if you're thinking about your boyfriend."

"Jesus. Harm is ..."

"Katrina, your duty is to the county and its security.

"Yes, Sir."

"Nothing else matters. Do you understand me?"

"Yes."

"I hope you do. My office at zero-seven-thirty tomorrow," he said, and hung up.

14

SPECIAL AGENT GEORGE FLYNN

Fort Mead, Maryland

As soon as Kat entered his office Devlyn said, "We caught a lead in France that has the syndicate written all over it," "We hit on something in your report on that company in Milan.

"There was an offer, then intimidation, followed by murder and acquisition. Somehow you have to find out how they do it. I want to know who makes this happen, who is at the top. You're going in, your mission is to team up with the General Directorate for External Security."

"DGSI (Direction Générale de la Sécurité Intérieure) wants to work with us?"

"No, but we asked them nicely and they say they'll cooperate in a joint investigation. They've got something that fits the Milan methodology. A company called Vacon Industrial was recently acquired by a corporate-raider new on the scene.

"Before the takeover Vacon's CEO, Gerard deFuss, was murdered. His body was found in the public toilet of a rest stop on the highway just outside Nancy. Two days later Vacon announced that they were under new management. The whole executive staff was replaced. The new CEO is a man named François Arnaud and his VP is Elene Mainhard. I think they're all dirty."

"They don't waste any time, do they?"

"And neither should we."

"What's the name of the predator company?"

"Muenchenstadder, it's supposedly German, but it's a shell buried so deep that the principals are untraceable. What's concerning us now is that Muenchenstadder has taken over seven companies over the last three months. All with contracts with US and Canadian companies. There is one name that is on every client list, it's the one you found in Italy."

"Dectron R&D."

"Yes. It's raised some red flags here in D. C."

"Do we know anything about them?"

"Other than it's a Canadian company, building a factory somewhere in Nevada, nothing at all. They're hiding something behind some very sophisticated security, hence the red flags."

"Okay."

"We put in a call to Interpol and Europol to invite us to join their task force, but after you lipped off at their director we were shut out. G-2 had to make some promises to get the French on side."

"Sorry about that."

"Don't worry about it. It was your heads-up that gave us the connection between Italy and Russia, so you're the lead agent on this investigation."

"Thank you, Sir."

"The French are holding out on us, we know that. But this is an asteroid and it's heading straight for us, so don't let them bully you."

"It'll be just the two of us then?"

"St. Petersburg really got under your skin, didn't it?"

"I'm fine, Sir."

"Good answer. You're heading out in two hours. You'll meet up with Flynn at Kennedy and then go on from there. FYI, if you do need reinforcements, contact Special Agent Harry Welsh at the Six-Six-M-I."

"And they are not handling this because ..."

"Because I am sending you two to do it."

THIS MUST BE PARIS

France

Their 'official' French welcome began with a cold reception as Kat and Flynn presented their credentials at customs. Two scruffy looking men took them by the arms and escorted them to a security office. People around them thought they'd been caught smuggling.

"Oh, how lovely to be in Paris again. Parisians are such warm and friendly people aren't they Flynn," Kat said.

"Without a doubt, Kat."

"You are the Americans agents, no?" asked the first man.

"Oui," replied Kat, expecting to continue in French.

"Passports." He studied them as if he was sure they were forgeries.

"Now you know who we are. Who are you?"

His tone was sharp and unfriendly. "We are French Internal Security," he said.

"All of it?" she quipped. "I'd like to see some proof if you don't mind."

They flashed their IDs "I am Frontier," he thumbed at the other man, "my partner, Villanova. You are armed, I take it?"

"Yes," she said.

"You Americans always carry guns."

"Federal Agents always do, it's the law. I noticed that you also have guns. I don't see the problem."

"We are in charge here."

"Oh, absolutely. Think of us as just part of the team. Isn't that right, Flynn?"

"Team players all the way," Flynn said dryly.

Soon they were splashing down the streets of La Défense District and turned onto the Rue Voltaire, heading for what they were told was a business hotel near DGSI headquarters. Kat couldn't believe that this rundown flea palace was where they were expected to stay. Villanova turned in his seat and said, "We have booked rooms for you."

"Here?" Flynn asked, astonished.

"You need only to pick the keys up at the desk. I would suggest that you get some rest."

"Is this the best you could do?"

"What do I look like to you, a fucking travel agent?" Frontier said. "A car will come for you at 8:00 am, the briefing will begin at 9:00."

As soon as Kat and Flynn were standing on the sidewalk the Alfa peeled away with its siren blaring.

Kat shook her head. "Boy, I love Paris already, don't you?"

"It's always a little more than one expects, and a lot less than one hopes for," said Flynn, "People are so courteous and friendly here."

"We're getting another hotel," Kat said, and Flynn called the DGSI office to advise them of the change and they'd make their own way to the meeting.

DISAPPOINTING BEGINNING

8 :00 am

Flynn rented a car and drove them to the DGSI headquarters in Levallois-Perret, in the north-western suburbs of Paris. Their escort took them to the eighth floor. They were expecting they'd be meeting the task force.

It was a surprise to find the same two agents from the night before and their boss Inspector Noël Bussing were the only people in the room

Bussing was standing impatiently at the front of the long room with a cigarette hanging from his mouth.

His mane of dark black hair was slicked back as if he'd been caught in a strong wind. The expression on his thin face managed to broadcast how unhappy he was at the thought of dealing with Americans.

"Finally," he said, setting the tone for the meeting, "here they are at last."

Flynn looked at his watch. "You did say 9:00, correct? We're ten minutes early."

"You know Frontier and Villanova," Bussing said, then using the cigarette as a natural extension of his hand he described the murder without embellishment. His conclusion was that the Americans were overreacting, trying too hard to appear relevant and wasting his time.

Kat declined to enter into a pointless argument with the pompous blowhard. "When can we interview the witnesses?" she asked.

"That will not be necessary. If you wish to hear them, all the interviews were recorded and have been transcribed and translated into English."

"I'm sure you must have noticed, M. Bussing, that we both speak French fluently," Kat said. "We would prefer to hear the original recordings."

"Perhaps M. Flynn, your partner's French isn't as good as she thinks. You will, I am sure, be able to explain it to her at your convenience."

"There is nothing wrong with my language skills, M. Bussing," Kat said, "and I insist that you make all the original evidence available to us."

He listened to her but looked at Flynn when he replied, "M. Flynn, perhaps you could tell this woman that that will not be possible."

"M. Bussing," Kat said, controlling the urge to pulverize him, "we are Special Agents with the US Army's Counterintelligence and as the senior agent, I suggest that you address your comments to me with respect."

"But of course, Special Agent." He smiled with a sneer.

"In the spirit of cooperation between our two countries, I'm sure that DGSI will do everything it can to assist us in our investigation," Kat said, with icy precision.

"What could you possibly expect to learn that we have not already put in our reports?"

"We won't know that until we have begun our inquiry, will we? We would like to go to the service station where M. deFuss was found."

"No witnesses have come forward. All we have is the physical evidence found in the washroom and on the body."

"We will want to see that and have access to the body of M. deFuss as well."

"That is impossible, Special Agent. The body has been cremated."

"Excuse me?! This is an open investigation, how could you ...?"

"What I am telling you Special Agent, is that the investigation is no longer ongoing."

"This is bullshit," she said. "Reopen it."

"Impossible," he said heatedly, as he placed another cigarette in his mouth and lit it. He let the smoke slowly curl out of his mouth then said, "The investigation was a waste of our time. It is done!"

"That is unacceptable."

"Frankly, I don't give a fuck what you think, woman. You Americans should not be here, this is strictly a European matter."

Kat had to hold Flynn back. She took a deep breath then let it out slowly. "Inspector, our instructions are very clear. We are here to do all we can to ensure that this security threat does not spill over into North America."

"Why would we care?"

"Unbelievable. We will interview the witnesses involved in this incident and all materials collected during your investigation. I ... will be the one to determine how this affects American concerns and you will cooperate."

"I refuse, this is too much."

"Then I'll go over your head."

"I am in charge here!"

"You said that already but it doesn't make it so."

When Kat brought it to his attention, the Director Gustav Canton, felt compelled to explain to Inspector Bussing the arrangement he and MGen Wolfson had made. "The agents are here to do a job and you are to assist them with their investigation. Am I clear?"

Later Flynn said, "I am sensing that Bussing's people don't like us very much."

"Me too, but let's pretend that we're all friends, okay?"

THE COLD SHOULDER

Vacon Industries, La Défense District

One thing that inspector Bussing said was true. The hard evidence they collected was a waste of time. As the Vacon head office was practically next door in Courbevoie, La Défense District, Kat decided to pay them a visit. Vacon occupied the 40th and 41st floors of the Tour UAP.

Seated in a chair behind the lobby desk was a guard reading a magazine about wine, cheese, and naked women. It was obvious from his body language that he was determined to ignore them. So, they walked right by without checking in.

Suddenly he popped up. "Halt! You have to check in first."

Kat turned on him and glared. He shrank behind his magazine and said, "Madame if you please, what can I do for you?"

"Vacon Industries, where is it?" she demanded, sounding like the Ice Queen.

"Fortieth floor," he stammered.

"That will be all." She turned to Flynn and said softly, "My, everyone here is so friendly and helpful. Isn't it just wonderful?" Flynn snorted as they headed for the elevator.

The carriage doors opened at the fortieth floor onto a wide hall that looked more like an art gallery than an industrial head office.

"Remind me, Kat, what do they do here?" Flynn asked.

"They build robotic systems."

"A lot of money in that, I guess," he said.

"No doubt." The building was a three-pointed star. Each wing had a glass wall that slid back into the wall when approached.

The wall of the north wing had the company logo and 'Vacon' rendered in large gold lettering.

"I suppose we'll find the reception through there," she said.

An attractive woman wearing an expensive silk suit came to greet them. While she wasn't frowning or smiling, her eyes were not friendly.

"Madam/Monsieur, welcome to Vacon," she said in English, while gracefully spreading her arms as a welcoming gesture. Kat mused that if she was a spider that would indicate that she was about to attack. "Have you an appointment?"

Since the greeting was in English, Kat went with it. Perhaps these people would say things that they didn't want her to understand. "No, but we have come to speak with Mme. Mainhard."

Any hint of a smile flatlined. "And you are ..."

She flashed her badge. "Special Agents Fernando and Flynn, US Army Counterintelligence."

The woman's tone turned frigid, letting them know that she wasn't about to spend her limited charm needlessly. "One moment." She went behind the desk and made a phone call. "Two American agents are here to see Madame Mainhard." She listened for a moment, "They are from the American Army... Oui." She paused to listen, "No, they didn't say." A pause. "Of course," she paused again, "Oui, monsieur."

Looking up at them she said, "Madame/Monsieur, I am sorry, but Madame Mainhard is unavailable this morning. But Monsieur Chauvette, will come down to have a word with you. You may wait over there."

More than fifteen minutes later the glass panel swished open and a tall, square jawed man in his late forties stepped in.

He stared at them then retreated into the gallery hall. "Well, isn't he a sweetheart," she said.

"Do you think he wants us to follow him?" asked Flynn coolly.

Kat nodded. "I think that's what he had in mind."

Chauvette was waiting by the elevators. "You are here to speak to Madam Elene Mainhard?"

"Yes."

"Why?" he asked. His English was quite good. Kat wondered if the hostility was because they were Americans, federal officers, or was this just his winning personality shining through. Perhaps it was all of the above. She immediately began assessing his threat level. He was a little over six feet tall, 215 lbs., probably ex-military, thickly muscled, lean, and aggressive. Everything about him said, don't mess with me.

"Our business is with her," Kat said.

If he's going to be a problem then perhaps, I should just step out of the way and let Flynn deal with him. How would I put it?

Maybe being direct would be the best policy. Flynn, I would say, kill him for me. Yeah, that might work.

"Again, I must ask you, why?" he was becoming agitated.

"Persistent, aren't you?" she said, giving herself some time to think of a reason. "Because, she has a unique perspective pertaining to our investigation."

"What investigation?"

"I am not at liberty to discuss that with you."

"What could she possible have to say that would be of any interest to the US Army?"

"Again, that is none of your business. So, if you would kindly point us in her direction."

"Madame Mainhard is no longer available."

"What do you mean by no longer?"

"I mean, she is not available for interviews."

"It's still unclear to me. Does that mean that she is here, but not receiving visitors, or are you saying that she was here, but she has gone out?" He didn't reply.

"Perhaps she no longer works here. Is that what you're saying?"

As if responding to some invisible signal, four men appeared behind them. Kat had a peek over her shoulder. Obviously, they were chosen for their brawn and cleverly disguised as security guards in blues and greys, white shirts, and ties. The earbuds were a nice touch too.

"Too cheeky, was I?" she asked.

"These men will escort you out of the building."

"Hold on a second, Pepe le Pew, I asked you a question. Where is she? This is official police business and we demand to be taken to her now."

"You have no authority here, official or otherwise."

"Perhaps she went home." He didn't respond but his eyes told her what she wanted to know. "Sudden, was it? I'm only asking because, until just a second ago, you were suggesting that she was here."

He flicked his fingers at them dismissively, as if shooing away ill-disciplined children.

The gorillas moved on cue, grabbing them by the arms and to steered them to the elevator. "Not so fast!" Kat wrenched her arms free and Flynn kept them at bay for a second. "While we're here, we may as well save time and interview your CEO, François Arnaud. That is if he hasn't suddenly gone home as well."

The elevator doors opened, "Take them away." Once again, the guards took hold of them and dragged them into the carriage.

The moment the doors opened on the ground floor the thugs literally carried them out the door and shoved them away from the building. They staggered to the edge of the road.

Flynn was ready to bust a few heads, but Kat stopped him. "Hang on. Let's give them this one. We have other fish to fry." Flynn growled in frustration. "Did you just growl at me?"

"Maybe," he said cautiously.

"Now George, you know that I'm the growler around here."

He grinned. "You should have let me pop him one."

"Would it have made you feel any better?" she asked.

"Probably," he said. "What do we do now, Tiger?"

"Tiger eh? Okay, we go to Madame Mainhard's place and see just how sick she really is. Her address is in the file in the car."

As they walked down the ramp Flynn said, "I'm beginning to wonder if all Frenchmen are hostile."

"Don't forget the French women." Kat smiled over the top of the car. "Did it ever occur to you that maybe we're just hitting them on a bad day, er days?"

He growled again. "Maybe it's you." Flynn said, settling in his seat.

"I'll have you know that I am an exceptionally sweet person."

"Oh yeah, you're all sugar and spice ... Tiger."

"Shut up. And what did I tell you about growling?"

Flynn took the wheel, "I'm just saying ..."

"Nu huh, you've hurt my feelings, so I'm not listening to you anymore." He laughed as they headed out of the underground labyrinth. Merging into traffic they missed the black Audi exiting behind them. It slipped into the flow three cars back.

LADIES FIRST

Le Marais District, Paris, France

Elene Mainhard lived in the Le Marais district, a chic residential area on the north bank of the Seine.

Flynn was dealing with Paris traffic while Kat was watching the side mirror and happened to recognize the faces in the Audi two cars behind them. "We have a tail."

"Can you see who it is?"

"Oh yeah. Two of the gorillas from the elevator."

"What do you want me to do?"

"They must know where we're going so there's not much point in trying to lose them. Maybe they are just keeping an eye on us."

"So, we just continue as if we don't see them?"

"Sounds good."

"Okay."

Mainhard's apartment was on the second floor of an attractive old building. It sat on the corner of Rue du Roi de Sicile, a one-way street heading east, and a narrow side street on the right.

The side street had been transformed into an open-air salon in front of the L'Alivi Bistro. Several people sat at small tables under umbrellas, chatting over cappuccino and croissants.

By some miracle, a car pulled out of a parking space a block up the road giving Flynn a place to put the Peugeot. They were walking back to her building when their tail drove by. "There's the Audi," Flynn said. "But the passenger is gone. That's not good."

"Aw fuck that's not good at all," said Kat, and they both began to run.

Before they reached the corner, there was a crash of glass followed by a loud thud as a body slammed through a table on its way to the pavement.

The screaming customers immediately retreated under the awning as if they expected more bodies to rain down on them. They stood open mouthed, staring at the woman sprawled on the ground in an expanding pool of blood.

"I'm guessing that whatever it was that kept her home suddenly became fatal," Flynn said.

"You think?" The woman had landed face down, but they both assumed that it was Mme. Mainhard. In the ensuing confusion, a big man in a blue blazer came out of her apartment building and headed west.

Kat took off after him. He broke into a run pushing through the crowd like an icebreaker. Kat was gaining on him. He made it to the corner just as his buddy drove up and he jumped in. By the time Kat got there the car was gone.

'Jesus, did they rehearse that?' she asked herself.

"And?" Flynn asked when she returned.

She shrugged, "Nothing left to do here." She pointed to their car. A moment later they heard the see-saw siren of a police vehicle approaching.

"Should we stick around?"

"No. I think we have to get back to the Tour UAP and talk to François Arnaud before someone sends him out a window."

RETURNING TO VACON

Vacon Industries, La Défense District

Kat called Bussing and told him what just happened to the woman and requested backup. "And detain Chauvette and everyone on his security team. Consider them armed and dangerous."

Bussing said he would take care of it, but when they arrived, the police backup she'd asked for was nowhere in sight.

"Where is everybody?" asked Flynn.

"The place should have been crawling with cops. Call the Six-Six and tell them we may need help."

Flynn made the call. "There sending some people from the Paris office."

Avoiding reception, they went right to the 41st floor and were greeted by their favorite agents Tweedledee and Tweedledum standing in the hall. "Oh shit, we should have called the Field Office sooner."

"They'll be here soon," Flynn said, eyeing the DGSI agents warily.

"I hope so." She took in their antagonistic expressions and asked, "Are you the only DGSI people here?"

"No," said Frontier, while Agent Villanova continued to stare malevolently. "Ins. Bussing is in there," he said, thumbing toward the wall.

Flynn was regarding Villanova's hostile expression and asked, "What the fuck is your problem?"

Kat wanted to de-escalate. "Where is he exactly?"

"Through there, interviewing Garnell Chauvette. It would seem that he knows something of Madame Mainhard's suicide."

"Oh, Chauvette told you it was suicide, did he?"

"Yes."

"Idiots," she said, heading for the door. "He's the one who had her killed."

"Wait, you can't go in there," Frontier said.

"Are you going to stop me?" A movement through the glass caught her eye and she turned just in time to see the man who threw Mainhard through her window. She drew her gun and shouted, "Stop!"

"Drop the gun," demanded Frontier, drawing his weapon. The guard hesitated in the open doorway.

Kat was alarmed by this twist, "What the fuck are you doing? This is the killer!" The security guard began to back away. "Uh, Uh, Uh, stop right there! Raise your hands!"

"Drop your gun," Frontier repeated.

"You are making a big mistake, Frontier!" Kat kept her gun pointed at the killer and Villanova went for his weapon.

Flynn didn't hesitate, he stopped the smaller man's hand as he was pulling the pistol from his leather jacket and the gun went off taking a chunk out of his hip.

Distracted, Frontier turned to look, and the security guard drew his gun and fired. Kat was already moving as the bullet zipped past her ear. She fired twice hitting him in the center of his chest. Again, Frontier turned his gun on her.

Fed up, she spun and kicked him, sending him flying back into a bronze bust by Picasso. His gun flipped out of his hand as he dropped to the floor and the sculpture tipped over and landed on him. Frontier let out a blood curdling scream.

Pushing the bronze away he looked to his partner for help, but there was no help there. Flynn had shoved Villanova face first into the fabric wall and snapped the cuffs on him. His blood was beginning to pool on the nice wood floor.

"Hands where I can see them and get up," she demanded. Frontier tried to stand. "Are you part of this?"

"Part of what?" he said, getting to his feet. He was about to say something else, but Kat interrupted him. "You know what, forget it. Just stand there and shut the fuck up."

Frontier had other plans. He threw out a high kick aimed at her head. He didn't consider that the bronze had done some damage. Kat ducked his foot and kicked out his knee causing a loud crack as it moved out to the side. He went down, and she was on him instantly.

She flipped him over, shoving his face into the floor and dropped her knee on his back cuffed him.

Agent Bussing appeared standing over the body in the doorway. "I heard the shots! My-god, what the fuck is this?!" He went for his gun.

Flynn shouted, "Stop!" His gun was up and ready. Bussing froze.

Kat went to Bussing and pushed his gun aside then with her gun under his chin. "Let's just not do this anymore, okay?" she said, taking his gun.

"What are you people doing?"

"We have some concerns about who these two idiots are working for. Now tell me Bussing, whose side are you on?"

"What are you talking about?" he asked. "We are not the criminals here."

"After what these goons did, I'm not really convinced," she said. "Where is Chauvette?"

"I left him down the hall in the boardroom."

"Christ, I told you on the phone that he was dirty. Flynn cover this asshole!" Kat ran toward the office area.

"Wait! What are you going to do?" Bussing said, following her.

Flynn shouted at him to stop but he was out of sight before Flynn could reach him.

At least he doesn't have a gun, Flynn thought.

Running down the corridor she looked back and saw him coming up behind. When she arrived at the main offices she whispered over her shoulder, "Stay back or so help me I will shoot you!"

"No, I am on your side."

"Still not convinced. Chauvette better not get away."

"What did you do to my men?" he demanded.

"Oops, we broke them, sorry. I'd use this opportunity to get some smarter guys next time," she said, slightly out of breath. "Are there more people back there?"

"Yes, maybe ten or fifteen."

"Jesus!" She pressed her back against the wall. "They could all be part of this!" She took a quick glance into the big room and saw several terrorized people crouched against the far wall. "Where is ..."

A gunshot cut her off. It came from the far door on the right. "You left Chauvette with a gun?!"

"No, I ..." Bussing began.

She ran forward and took cover in a workstation. The shooter fired from the boardroom hitting the barrier above her head. Kat caught a glimpse of him before he ducked back and recognized him from his photo. "François Arnaud. Throw the gun out and come out with your hands raised."

Bussing had taken cover behind another partition. Arnaud lunged out again and fired. Two shots came through the cubicle divider over her shoulder. "Shit! Arnaud give it up!"

Bussing spoke in a stage whisper, "I can't help you without a gun!"

"I don't trust you! Arnaud, listen to me. There is no way out." Kat signaled for the office workers to head for the exit. They quickly obeyed, keeping their heads down, but there were still more people in the room. She could hear them whimpering under the desks.

"Arnaud, there's no need for anyone else to get hurt here. Throw your gun down and come out."

"No!"

"We can talk, make some sort of deal," she said, but he fired again. His round punched through the thin wall just behind her head. Kat quickly moved up one cubicle and was now no more than ten feet from his open door. Behind her she heard another door open. She looked back.

The room had two doors.

"Oh shit," she whispered. He could appear from either door at any second. "Listen to me! All we want to do is talk."

"There is nothing to talk about!" Arnaud shouted, then reached out to fire again.

Another bullet sailed over her head.

Kat could have fired into the wall by the door and it would be over, but dead men don't answer questions.

"Tell me, what will it take to get you to surrender?"

Bussing remained hidden behind the buffer. Several seconds ticked by before she heard movement from behind and turned.

Arnaud jumped out.

He'd caught her wide open and all her options were gone.

She fired a single shot to his head. She went to the door and paused just long enough to reposition her gun and then stepped into the room. Chauvette was in the end chair with his face planted on the table. There was a small hole through the right temple. Bussing appeared at the door stepping over Arnaud's body. She looked up leading with her gun, unsure of what he would do next. "I'd be much happier, Bussing, if you would put your hands up."

"You know I am not armed," he said, lifting his hands above his head.

She watched him carefully and he seemed more frightened than anything else. "Clear!" she shouted, holstering her gun.

Flynn came running down the corridor. "Kat, are you good?"

"Yeah, you?"

"Yeah." Kat relaxed.

"Why would he kill Chauvette?" asked Flynn.

Kat shrugged, "Christ, who knows? They're all batshit crazy people in here."

"Thanks to you, we'll get no answers from either of them now," Bussing said, as if he had nothing to do with the way it turned out. "Now, I want my men released at once."

"Inspector Bussing, I'm still not sure whose side you're on. Would you care to explain why your men drew on us?"

"They were simply told to detain you."

"Why would you want us detained? And why did you leave a suspect unattended? He's dead because of you. Do you get that Chauvette and Arnaud are dead directly because of your actions? Do you realize how bad this looks?"

"You are not in charge here Special Agent Fernando, I am."

"You are completely delusional, Bussing, but if it makes you happy then whatever floats your boat. Flynn, you can let them go."

"Do you think that's a good idea?" he asked.

"No, but we're out of here now, so they can do what they like." She pushed by Bussing and stepped out into the corridor. "For all we know Bussing, all of these people are part of the syndicate." Kat jerked her head back at the dead man at the table. "Chauvette's security men are part of it. There are three wings in this building. They have two floors of offices full of people who could be bent. You do the math."

It wasn't long before agents from the Paris Office joined them. When they saw the mess, the AIC said, "It might have been better if Devlyn had brought us in on this at the beginning."

"I told him that back in Maryland." Kat ushered Flynn to the elevator. "It's all yours now."

As soon as the office staff was rounded up and the questioning began, Kat and Flynn were escorted back to the airport by the police.

15

THE DEBRIEFING

Fort Mead, Maryland

There was nothing to follow up on, the French were handling the investigation and they weren't sharing. Devlyn grilled them both during the debriefing.

He was looking for anything that might implicate any of the men Harken mentioned in St. Petersburg, but there was nothing.

Special Agents of the 66th Brigade were asked to look into the activities of Delph Petrus and Stephan Gelenko again. And again, that investigation found nothing.

The companies that had gone through similar hostile takeovers were examined. Several of them were raided and people arrested, but no one talked. A few of those arrested were later released due to lack of evidence and others were murdered in prison.

As far as Six-Six-MI knew the 'infection' hadn't spread across the Atlantic yet.

Kat was given back the week she lost because of the assignment and flew to San Diego. Harm had the academy's pilot Roger Beech fly down to Montgomery Airfield to pick her up. Roger let her fly the Blackhawk home. It was a wonderful feeling to be flying again, and great to be coming back to the Nest. That was until she asked Roger about Harm.

"I think he's doing okay. The chemo isn't wearing him down as much now."

"Chemo? What chemo? Oh holy ... why didn't anyone tell me what was going on?"

"Oh boy, I thought you knew."

"Well, you were wrong." She radioed Harm as she passed over Lake Henshaw in the valley at the foot of Hot Springs Mountain. "We're a couple of minutes out and I thought I'd give you some time to put the coffee on."

"It'll be ready for you."

As she came over the rise, she saw him standing at the entrance of the Hacienda with a ball cap on and his hand up waving. He looked happy. She set the chopper down on the pad and he walked out to meet her. He looked like he hadn't slept since she left. When they hugged, he held her for a moment longer than usual.

He saw her concern and knew she was afraid. "Was it a rough mission?"

"I don't think the French like me anymore, but I'm okay. How are you?"

"Yeah, I'm good. God, I have missed you Kat."

"I've missed you too. I'm back for another week and I'm spending it all with you." He put his arm about her waist and hustled her up to the Hacienda. "Harm, you can talk to me, you know that, right?"

"Now don't fuss, I'm fine, never better."

"I'm a big girl now, Harm, so stop lying to me. Roger told me about the chemo."

"He did? Crap! I'm gonna have to get a pilot who can keep his goddamn mouth shut."

He took a deep breath, then said quietly, "Not here." He tossed an angry look back at Roger before they went inside. Roger just shook his head.

"First tell me how the mission went. Tell me everything."

"Forget it. I'll tell you later." They walked down to his apartment with their arms around each other. "I want to hear what's happening to you."

"Okay. Have a seat and I'll get us some brew."

Leaning on his folded arms he watched her fill the cups. "Harm," she said, placing her hand on his arm, "you have to tell me everything."

"You were under so much pressure already and I didn't want to worry you. But since the secret's out I suppose it's for the best. Honestly, I don't think I can manage much longer without you."

"Harm." It was all she could say because her eyes were filling up.

"Now there's nothing to be scared about, Kat, it's all just another part of life. It's just coming a little sooner than I'd care for."

"When did it start?"

"Well, I had a bit of a stomach problem, thought it was maybe a touch of flu or food poisoning, but it wasn't getting any better.

"So, about eight months ago, I had my doctor run some tests down at the hospital. The doctor told me ..." He stopped to take a deep breath. She squeezed his arm impatiently. "Ah jeeze Kat, this really sucks. I think telling you is the hardest part."

"I am so sorry Harm. I... ah... what did he tell you?"

"I've got pancreatic cancer."

It felt just like it did when she was being pulled under the surface in that river. She was drowning in the darkest place she had ever been. She shut her eyes. She wanted to be strong for him, but she couldn't stop the tears from spilling out.

"I don't know what that is. Is pancreatic cancer as bad as it sounds?" Kat asked, trying to dry her eyes enough so she could see him. "I mean they can cure it, can't they? The chemo is working, and they can fix you, right? Tell me they can fix you, Harm."

"No, there's no fix for this."

"Aw Jesus." She paused, unable to speak for a while. "This isn't happening. This can't be real. What if ..., what if he got it wrong? We can go to see another doctor, a specialist up in LA, or New York. Somebody's got to be able the do something."

"Kat ..., shush now. I've been to other doctors. I've been to the USC Medical Center in LA and they all say the same thing. There's no cure for this. I tried the chemo a couple of times, but it made me feel sicker and I was beginning to lose my hair." He took off the ball cap.

"Oh ...," She covered her mouth with her hands. "Your beautiful hair."

"I didn't see that it was worth it. Kat listen to me. Listen to me now, the only thing we can do is make the most of the time we have left."

Sliding off the chair, she got down on the floor beside him, and wrapped her arms around his waist. "I can't lose you. I just can't, Harm. I'm not strong enough."

"Honey, you're a lot stronger than you think." He held her head to his chest. "Shush now, crying isn't going to change anything."

"I'm sorry. I wish there was something I could do."

"Actually, there is something I'd like you to do." She looked up at him knowing that she would give him anything. "I want you to marry me, Kat. Will you do that for me?"

"Oh, Harm," she said, and pressed her face against him and put her hand on his heart, just so she could feel it beating, to reassure herself that he was alive.

"I love you so much. Yes of course, I'll marry you." They remained in each other's arms for what felt like days.

FOR THE SAKE OF LOVE

The Hacienda Courtyard

Kat and Harm WERE married in a civil ceremony by a Justice of the Peace from Warner Springs, then she immediately put in for compassionate leave.

She got some serious resistance from Devlyn, which was not unexpected. The silent war that raged between them only intensified. He had stolen precious time from her, time she could have been with Harm and that she would never forgive.

She'd been standing at attention in front of his desk listening to him lecture on esprit de corps when she finally lost it. "If you don't approve this leave then I'm putting in for an immediate discharge."

"No, hang on there. I'm not going to let you throw all my hard work away."

"Your hard work!? I think you're forgetting who has been get shot at, attacked and dumped in the river." He gave no indication that he cared.

"I fought those drug cartel thugs in Honduras, that fire in Kuwait. I learned how to fly a helicopter for you, and for what? You just keep fucking me over. Well I've had it, Sir. My man is dying and you're not going to keep me away from him any longer!"

He stood up ready to give her both barrels then he stopped himself and considered the optics if this got to the press. He sat back down. "Okay, I'm going to forget about that outburst, but hear this, if I get any more insubordination from you then there will be serious repercussions. Am I clear?" She just stood at attention. "Am I clear?!"

"Yes Sir."

"Alright then. I'm going to look into granting you an LWOP, it'll give you a year to look after him."

"Is that a promise, Sir?"

"Yeah, it's a promise. Will it be enough?"

"No, but I'll take it. Can I have that in writing, Sir?"

He grabbed a pen and a sheet of paper and quickly wrote a promissory note and signed it.

"There, happy?"

"May I be excused now, Sir?"

"Yeah you're dismissed, now get out of here."

Kat temporarily took over the administration of the academy with Harm's guidance, but her mind wasn't on the job. She called Doug Leman, and asked him to take over management of the academy as well as the contract defense force. After Doug was settled in, Kat took Harm down to San Diego for his weekly treatments for pain. And from that time on she never once left his side.

THE TWIN TOWERS

Harm's apartment

They were up very early as usual on a cool September morning. Sitting at the breakfast table with coffee and toast they were watching the NBC News Today.

The station cut away from a commercial with the news reader saying, 'Yeah ..., this just in, we are looking at obviously a very disturbing live shot there. That is the World Trade Center and we have unconfirmed reports this morning that a plane has crashed into one of the towers ...'

They sat there for the rest of the day watching in horror as the world as they knew it came crashing down.

All leaves were cancelled, and Kat was ordered back to Maryland to join a new task force to find the people responsible for the worst acts of terror in American history.

It was mass confusion, made worse by false rumors and territorial behavior by competing agencies who refused to share information.

The country lived in constant fear of more attacks.

Every day she talked with Harm by phone and every day his condition worsened. Finally, she was given permission to resume her leave and hurried back to the nest and devoted herself to his care.

BETRAYED

Eagle's Nest, Warner Springs, CA

Ramsey Hershoff had been in touch with Harm weekly since the diagnosis and flown over to visit a few times.

When he phoned to say that he was coming to ENA to see them in the morning, it was a welcome diversion for both of them. They had an animated conversation then Harm said he needed to lie down. After he hung up Ramsey said, "Kat the reason I called was to talk to you about something I need your help with."

"Sure Ramsey. Just let me get Harm to bed and I'll call you back. How's that?"

"That's fine."

She rang him back five minutes later. "What did you want to talk about?"

"The reason for my visit this time is business, Kat. A security problem has just been brought to my attention."

"Does this have anything to do with Iraq?"

"No, I've talked with Wolfson about it and he agreed that this would be the best way to handle it."

Her voice turned cold. "What's the security problem about, Ramsey?"

"Hasn't Col. Devlyn contacted you?"

"No, about what?"

"This is very awkward for me, Kat. I hope you understand. I have a friend, a Russian friend who is coming to San Diego to speak at the Art of Security Conference."

"When is that?"

"Wednesday. Our government is not and cannot be perceived to be involved. He and I have a history, which I can't go into, but I have promised him protection while he's here."

"Bottom line is, you'd like us to put him up here before he makes his appearance. We can do that."

"Great, but there's more to it than that. He'll be in San Diego for the week and I need you to provide the security for him."

"It's rather short notice, but I'll ask Doug to arrange a team for you. I think we can handle that without a problem."

"No, I don't think you understand. I need you to do it."

"Me. I'm sorry Ramsey, but I'm not leaving Harm for an hour let alone a week. Now I have some very good people on ..."

"That's not going to cut it, Kat. The Pentagon has an arrangement with ENA that covers this situation, and ..."

"I know all about the arrangement, Ramsey. But nowhere does it say that I have to be personally involved."

"Kat, MGen. Wolfson has ordered you and George Flynn to handle this for us."

"Ramsey, no I can't ..."

"You have no choice. You and Flynn will be acting as employees of ENA."

"Ramsey ..."

"I'm sorry Kat, but this is how it has to be. I need someone on this detail that I can trust completely and that's you. Now don't worry about Harm, I'm bringing two nurses with me to take over while you are away."

"Ramsey please ..."

"Kat, we'll be there in the morning. I'm sorry to do this to you, but you have to comply or lose the Academy. We'll be at the airfield at 07:00 hrs."

DEATH ON A STAGE

Convention Center, San Diego

Kat and Flynn blended with the crowd at the Convention Center. She was pretending to be alone, just an independent businesswoman interested in everything new. Always staying within easy reach of Mogilevski, while giving the impression that she had no connection with him. Flynn was taking the bigger risk because Mogilevski and Hershoff, who insisted on being there, couldn't move without him.

The conference was devoted to security, related hardware and technologies. They were surrounded by tools, systems, and people that could be turned against them at any time.

They were both painfully aware that contrary to California law most of the people crowding around them were probably carrying concealed weapons.

Every move toward something inside a jacket or behind the back got a reaction from them.

It was amazing how many times people in that place reached for their wallets or business cards, or a pen, or a tissue. It was exhausting.

Kat wandered about from booth to booth, tagging behind the client, vigilant and sensitive to danger while appearing indifferent. It was all about reading the intent in the faces in the crowd. Looking for the Devil in the crowd with the bored ones, the engaged ones, and the people demonstrating whatever it was they were selling.

Guarding Mogilevski meant trying to find the assassin lurking behind every pair of eyes in the hall. So far neither of them had spotted a hint of murderous intent. It was crowded and noisy with all kinds of distractions.

A perfect place to jab in a needle, to stab with a pick or a knife, fire a silenced bullet from a few paces away, or spray a toxic chemical.

Unlike combat, which was ninety-five percent boredom and five percent terror, this was just non-stop, 'Holy crap, what the fuck is that guy doing?'

It was nothing but one false alarm after another right up until the final evening when Mogilevski was scheduled to give his speech. He had his remarks in his hand and they were making their way to the stage when Kat saw something. She read it in the man's eyes and his furtive movements. She studied him carefully. He was a newcomer to the press corps. Something about him just didn't fit. Kat had contrived to have a small interaction with all of them during the week and by 10:00 only the die-hards were left, waiting to cover Mogilevski's speech.

All the other photographers and reporters had been there from the beginning, asking questions, doing interviews, but not this guy. Kat looked, but she couldn't see his press pass clearly, so she moved to a better vantage point. Fortunately, her strategy for protecting the Russian meant that the assassin hadn't put them together.

He wasn't snapping pictures like the other journalists, and his camera didn't look right.

The telephoto lens bothered her. He was the only photographer who had one. Equipment designed for shooting sports events and wildlife, not closeups and candid shots.

The lens had to be a weapon.

When he moved up onto the stage behind the curtain, she knew it was going happen during the speech. Either it was a suicide mission, or he wasn't alone.

She had to move on him now before he had an opportunity to fire. She kept her eyes on him as she moved between the assassin and the Russian to speak to Flynn. "We've got a problem," she said, over her back. "Possible shooter, stage right."

The man lifted the camera to his eye and aimed it directly at Mogilevski. Kat turned toward him smiling brightly thinking he was going to shoot right through her to get his target.

This is it. I'm going to die this time for sure.

"Where?" asked Flynn, closing in on her as he began to scan the crowd.

"The stage, edge of the curtain."

He wasn't the only one up there. "Describe him."

"Jesus Flynn! Male, short brown hair and beard, plaid shirt, jeans, and he's got a fucking cannon stuck on his Canon."

"Got him," he said, but he was careful not to make eye contact. "What do you want to do?"

"I don't think he's alone. Move our guy behind the booth. I'm going over to get a better angle on him. If anyone pops up, you play whack-a-mole."

"Copy that. Be careful," he said, and immediately directed Mogilevski and Hershoff to the other side of the display.

While the assassin wondered where his target had gone, Kat moved toward the stage focusing her gaze on a group of men talking just behind him. One of them was the show's MC.

She was trying to be as conspicuous as possible as she closed on him. It wasn't difficult to attract male attention. All she had to do was open her jacket and undo enough shirt buttons to threaten a wardrobe-malfunction.

Her hand was holding the jacket flap so that it didn't expose the SIG in her shoulder holster.

They were watching alright, as a matter of fact they were just talking about her; each man fantasizing about having her between the sheets for an hour. She turned on a big smile and called out to him.

"Well, if it isn't Drag-Net Jack. You old rascal!" She waved and called out, so her voice would carry, "Oh-my-god, Webb, where'd you go last night?"

She thought the reference was cute because after all, this was Friday in San Diego. The man looked stunned.

Confused, the MC whose name was Bob Vance pointed questioningly at himself. Yup, he thought, grinning like a fool, she's looking at me.

The assassin couldn't help having a look, then he turned back hoping to find where Mogilevski had gone. Kat was close enough now to see the gun in the lens. She ignored Bob and went for the gunman. He was too busy trying to reacquire the target to notice her coming up from behind.

It wasn't until she snatched him by the collar and stomped on the back of his knee that he knew he was finished. She drove the knee onto the stage floor and heard the nasty but satisfying crunch.

He cried out in pain, but somehow managed to hold on to his weapon. He tried to turn it on her, but she drove a half fist punch down on his forearm hard enough to snap the radius just below his elbow.

As the camera-gun crashed to the floor her SIG was in her hand and she pressed it against his temple. "Security," she shouted, "don't move!"

"GUN!" yelled the MC.

With shrieks and gasps the crowd instantly pushed back away from the stage and ducked to the floor.

"I'm Security!" she shouted again, in case some hero in the crowd decided to pull out an illegally concealed weapon and shoot her. A woman in the crowd wouldn't stop screaming, a man dialed 911, and someone in a nearby booth called for building security.

"Is there anyone else?" Kat demanded, roughly twisting his collar. He began to choke.

At the same time, she scanned the audience for someone who might be targeting her. He shook his head but didn't answer. She tried the same question in Russian, Is there anyone else?

"No," he said.

"Hands where I can see them." He raised his hands as ordered. Continuing in Russian so there'd be no confusion she said. "Face on the floor." He lay face down on the floor. She replaced the gun to the back of his head and knelt on his legs to immobilize him.

235

Kat had come prepared with nylon quick tie wrist cuffs. "Hands behind your back," she ordered. He complied with one hand, then she pulled the broken arm back, slipped the double loops over his wrists and pulled them tight.

He winced as she jerked his arms up his back.

She used a second set to secure his legs. When he was trussed like an oven ready turkey, she scanned the crowd.

Was there someone else? There had to be. Where were they?

Quickly she examined the camera, using a pen so as not to disturb the suspect's prints.

It was a very professional bit of work, cleverly fitted inside was a Russian Army 9 mm semi-automatic Strizh, with a suppressor.

A Russian hit man as advertised and captured alive as ordered. Was it a State sanctioned hit? If so, how high up did it go?

There was an aggressive movement from the far side of the crowd and once again people scattered screaming, "GUN."

Kat dove to the side as a man fired a burst from a sub machine gun, and the bullets ripped into the stage and the wall behind her.

Kat's prisoner was his first target. Kat used his mistake to fire twice and she never missed. Her rounds hit the gunman's left eye and forehead.

Almost simultaneously a third gunman appeared aiming at her this time, and it was Flynn's turn to fire from behind the display.

A quick double tap and his man dropped to the ground. Without hesitating, Flynn began shepherding Mogilevski and Hershoff toward the exit.

Could there be another shooter? Kat desperately scanned the room.

If there were others, they left when building security arrived with guns drawn. Kat put her gun away, stood up and raised her hands. "It's over now," she told them, and carefully reached into her jacket pocket to produce her ENA ID card. "I'm private security."

One of the guards reached for the camera. "Don't touch that!" she snapped, "It's evidence." The security guard flinched back.

As planned, Flynn took the clients straight to a waiting limo. While they drove to Montgomery Airfield he couldn't help thinking that once again, she'd impressed the hell out of him.

Knowing that Flynn would stick to the plan she was confident that the client was safe, she could relax.

Survival was bitter-sweet.

She had killed another man, her body count was climbing and as necessary as the killings were, it sickened her.

No matter what the reason, it was still murder. She was a murderer. She looked down at the bloody body of the man in the plaid shirt and jeans, thinking how close she came to be down there too.

Did she deserve that? Her depression was barely manageable because of Harm, and now this. Guilt was eating her alive.

The room began to fill up with police, her cue to hurry off the stage.

She was buttoning her shirt up to the throat when a cop said, "Okay, secure the crime scene and let's start gathering statements. Move the witnesses over there and I'll take them one at a time."

She checked in with Flynn who was waiting with the clients in the Gibbs lobby. She gave her statement and contact numbers, then called Roger from the cab to say she was on the way to the Blackhawk. The rotor was winding up and he was just finishing the check list as she arrived. "Do you want to fly the bird?" he asked.

"Thanks, but I think I'll sit this one out." Minutes later they were in the air and heading for the Nest with Hershoff sitting in the left seat. She was back with the Russian sitting next to her. Flynn sat behind them looking out the window.

"Don't be sad, Katrina, you are a hero today. You saved my life. Ramsey said this was suicide, but you ..."

"If you knew that, why did you come here?"

"I was prepared to give up my life for this. Please believe that I am sorry to have risked yours as well. But I had to go through with it to bring them out into the open. To get people to see them for what they are."

"Them? Who are you talking about?"

"My speech was about the threat to world security from a crime syndicate that is becoming a terrorist organization."

"I wish we could have heard it. Tell me about it."

"It started in Russia by taking over an existing syndicate and is sanctioned at the highest level. I believe that it could turn out to be a far larger threat to America than Al Qaeda."

Her eyes widened. "I have had some experience with this syndicate. Did you know that I work for Army Counterintelligence?"

"Yes."

"Then you know that we have been trying for months to find out who is behind this. Please, tell me, do you know who it is? It is imperative that we take him out."

"Yes, I agree completely, and we will talk about it. But first, you and your partner saved my life and I will be eternally grateful.

"Anything you want Katrina; all you have to do is ask." He embraced her and kissed her on both cheeks several times.

"Thank you, Mr. Mogilevski," she said, gently putting some space between them, "That is very kind of you."

"Nonsense, you are smart and brave and of course very beautiful, a deadly combination. You are now as a daughter to me. What you have done today, this I will never forget."

"Mr. Mogilevski ..."

"Vlad, please."

"Alright ... Vlad, now that it's over could you tell me who you think was behind it."

"Excuse me for one moment." He turned and offered his hand to Flynn and said in English. "Mr. Flynn, I am in your debt, Sir. Thank you for saving my life."

Flynn's chin pushed up into an expression of modest satisfaction and offered a slight bow.

Mogilevski turned back to Kat and speaking in Russian said, "You were about to ask me something, Katrina?"

"Vlad ..., please."

"You are persistent, Katrina. It is another quality that I admire. His name is Delph Petrus, he is the one you want."

"Jesus Christ." The helicopter followed the slope of the mountain to the top and hovered over the Hacienda.

"You have heard of this man?"

"Yes.

RETURN SAFELY

ENA's landing pad

Harm was standing out on the front patio Charley waiting for the Blackhawk to return from San Diego. The idea that his oldest friend would take advantage of Kat was very upsetting and he was beyond angry. "I can't believe that he would do this to us."

"Listen to me Harm, you have got to keep it together. It's going to happen whether you like it or not."

"I know about the goddamn agreement, Charley! But why did he have to choose her?"

"Because she's the best and you made her part owner of ENA. She's got no choice, and neither do you."

"I'll never forgive him, Charley. Never."

The chopper could be heard coming up the mountain, "Okay, there they are now. Remember, she's a soldier and so were you once, so man up."

"Remind me why I like you, Charley."

"You do?" he asked, making it sound like a dream come true. "Aw shucks Harm, how come you never told me that before?"

"Shut up. You're such a dick."

240

"And you're an asshole," Charley said.

"Yeah?"

"Yeah."

They stood together with Charley holding on to his arm to keep him from being blown away. "But there's an old saying, Harm, if you save a life, it's yours forever. So, I'm stuck with ya."

Harm chuckled. "Yeah."

A BITTERSWEET HOMECOMING

The Hacienda porch

As the helicopter came down, she saw Harm standing with Charley on the steps. She waved to him and smiled. She could barely see his smile and it struck her like lightening.

Oh Harm, I am so sorry. Look at you. We've lost another week together. Why is life so unfair?

Mogilevski touched her arm. "You were saying ..."

"Sorry. A source in St. Petersburg mentioned his name and told me he was East German. Our people in Germany checked him out and they reported that he couldn't possibly be involved. How does he manage that?"

"I'm not surprised they found nothing, and your first source was correct, he is German. He pays President Putin to maintain his position, and the Kremlin protects him. European authorities won't touch him. We had hoped that one of the assassins would be taken alive to give evidence. But sadly, that was not to be. It probably would have been a waste of time anyway. No one speaks against Petrus."

"Perhaps there is another way to get to him," she said.

As the chopper touched down, he said, "Perhaps. Time will tell."

LOVE CAN'T SAVE A LIFE

Warner Springs, CA

Harm's relief at seeing her back safe was almost as taxing as the anxiety he felt when she left. Kat was happy to pass on her information and leave it to someone else to worry about.

Her only concern now was Harm. His pain was terrible, but he was trying to make light of it. "Harm I can't bear to see you suffer like this."

"You could euthanize me," he offered.

Kat snapped. "Jesus Harm, how can you joke about it like that? There has to be something we can do."

"I'm sorry." He held her and just let her cry. "But, Kat, there's nothing left, we've tried everything. You have to accept that you can't save me from this."

"I just can't. I can't lose you, Harm. I don't know what I'll do without you."

"I know you, Kat, you've survived things a lot worse than this."

"No, nothing is worse than this. I love you so much."

"I know, and I'm sorry to do this to you."

She gripped him as if she'd never let him go "And you still love me?"

"Uh huh, you are the strongest person I have ever met and, yes, I still love you. Do this one thing for me, Kat.

Promise me that when I am gone, you'll move on. I need to know that you will try to find some happiness."

"Happiness? There is no happiness without you."

"There will be if you open yourself up to the possibility. Hopefully you'll meet someone who will love you as much as I do. Love them back, Kat. It's what I want."

Harm had come to terms with his death. On December 20th he collapsed, and Kat rushed him to the hospital.

On New Year's Eve 2002, Kat was lying beside him, holding him at the end.

THE NEST

Hot Springs Mountain

Kat and Charley were sitting at the kitchen table in Harm's apartment. Kat was just staring into her coffee cup. The brew had gone cold and he could see what was happening to her. He'd been there. If he was being honest with himself, he was still there and if he wanted to help her now, he'd have to face those emotions he'd buried down deep so many years ago.

"Kat, I know how rough it's been for you, it's hard on all of us. I've tried the therapy bit, the shrinks from Veterans Admin but I couldn't deal with it then."

That seemed to wake her up and she looked at him. "What are talking about?"

"The experts say you can't keep it all locked up inside you, you have to let it out and face it, talk about it." He began to spin his cup around slowly as he tried to figure out what he wanted to tell her.

243

"Charley what are you trying to tell me?"

"From my experience, when you've been surrounded by death, by the loss of those close to you and responsible for the death of others you shut down. You don't do it consciously it just happens. I can see that that's what you've done.

"Now that Harm's gone those things you've been holding back are ripping you apart. All that bad stuff is coming out. You're going to need some help to deal with it, Harm told me you would. He was a brilliant man Kat and he knew you very well. He loved you more than life itself and well, I'm kind-a fond of you myself. So, as a friend I'm here for you. Whatever you need."

"Thank you. I love you Charley, you're a good friend. I don't think I'll ever be able to get over losing Harm, but I'll be alright, I promise."

"Well the offer stands. Whenever you need me, I'll be here for you."

They had a quiet funeral for Harm with just a few friends. Ramsey and Bernice had come over from Maryland, Vlad came up from Arizona, and a few of the guys from his unit also paid their respects. His ashes were spread on top of Hot Springs Mountain.

Charley was nervous and noticed his heart racing, like he was giving a speech in grade school.

Standing on that mountaintop with Kat by his side Charley had to deal with it now. The pain of memories long buried was overwhelming. "Harm was my comrade," Charley began, "there was so much I wanted to tell him, things that I couldn't say at the time, things that I shouldn't have left unsaid. It hard for an old soldier like me to talk about my feelings, so I wrote him this poem."

244

Charley took a crinkly piece of paper from his pocket and began to read his poem for Harm.

"I was alone, adrift in a troubled land,
Then you came to fight alongside me,
You brought me friendship and strength.
Peace and kindness in a time of war,
I almost lost you there ..."

He was overcome and couldn't finish Doug went to him and placed his hand on Charley's shoulder. "I've got your back Charley." The old sergeant simply looked at him with tears in his eyes and handed over the poem. Kat took his hand while Doug continued from where Charley left off.

"I almost lost you there on that hill,
I almost lost myself then too,
But you came back to me, to us,
And you gave us all of this,
A new life, a new purpose,
You made us all whole again,
My friend, my friend,
My brother,
Goodbye."

It was hard to tell who was supporting whom as Charley and Kat clung to each other on their way back to the Hacienda.

Kat remained at ENA for a month after the funeral, seldom leaving Harm's apartment. The tipping point came when Harm's lawyer came to read the will. It dealt with the dispersal of the few things he'd bequeathed to his friends and a letter to Kat. According to Harm's wishes it was not to be opened until the 12th of January, Kat's thirty-first birthday.

At Charley's request Kat returned to Eagle's Nest so that he could be with her when she opened it. Harm had written it right after 9/11 when she was away with the task force.

It explained that he wanted her to have everything when he was gone. ENA was hers to do with as she wished. He had transferred the bulk of his money to the numbered account he'd set up for her. Its balance was nearly a hundred million dollars. She nearly fainted.

"Harm invested everything," Charley said, "never spent a dime on himself. It was always for you, Kat. He told me that everything he did since he met you was for you."

"Oh god. I had no idea. Where did all this money come from?"

"There is more to ENA than most people know, Kat, a lot more. Government contracts with this place and the private security force Doug was running."

"I can't run something like that, Charley."

"Don't worry, Harm knew how you'd feel about it. Doug has agreed to stay and run things for you. It's all under control.

Part 3

16

BLACK HAT HACKER

Zaventem, Belgium

Lo Gi worked from his blacked-out top floor apartment in a five-story building in Zaventem, a Flemish village not far from Luchthaven, Brussel's National Airport.

He was both a computer genius and a deeply flawed human being all packed into a five-foot-three, hundred-and-ten-pound frame. Hiding his pimply face under a mass of dirty long black hair, bony little Lo Gi had been breaking through firewalls and installing back doors without detection since he was twelve. Always in and out before the victims noticed they'd been hacked.

Now he worked at arm's length for the syndicate targeting companies for acquisition. It was his wide-ranging experience accessing American companies and institutions and stealing their information, that drew the syndicate to him.

He powered up his computer at dawn and bit into a cold slice of pizza from his nightstand while he waited for it to boot up. The monitor came to life illuminating his gloomy mancave with a soft yellow light. It was all the light he needed. "Good morning my beauty," he said, as he entered an 18-digit code to open his system. Then he started his first search of the day with Dectron R&D.

Dectron Aerospace in Toronto was a well-known company that designed and built small aircraft. He could find nothing to describe what Dectron R&D was doing nor what their facility in Jean, Nevada was for. So, why were they spending millions all over the world having components built for manufacturing systems?

This was something that warranted further research.

Lo Gi's breakthrough came with his second slice of pepperoni pizza. The link was between Dectron R&D and The Cleveland Foundation.

He hacked into the foundation and created a remote access protocol to follow everything it did.

He discovered that Cleveland had been negotiating with the California State Planning Board to take over a Rare Earth Mine in the mountains in southern California. The mine had gone bankrupt trying to compete with China's vast resources, so why would someone buy that?

Then he linked the REM to Nevada and something called the Phoenix Project, a name on the client list of Vacon Robotics. He read further and discovered the Phoenix Project was located in Jean, Nevada. Coincidence? No. It led him to the agreement between the States of California and Nevada and Dectron R&D of Toronto a division of Dectron Aerospace owned by Dr. Deacon Loats. So why was Dectron hiding the existence of R&D?

He broke into the California Government system and found the file dealing with the industrial development program. It described the Phoenix Project as 'experimental battery development.' The grants from California and Nevada were substantial. As usual, he sent a report to his employer, but it was light on the details.

The report went to Herbig Co., an investigative, intelligence service in Spandau, Germany, run by Karl Herbig. An analyst took the information and then began looking into it.

Normally that would be the end of it, the syndicate would pay him and he'd go on to something else. But this time Lo Gi wanted to extort a little something for himself before the syndicate took over Dectron.

EXTORTION

Dectron International

It was after 1:00 am when Deacon got off the phone with Jasper and turned off his computer.

It had been another marathon day in the office and as he stood up the phone rang. Thinking that it was Jasper again, he touched the speaker phone. "Forget something?"

"Dr. Deacon Loats," said the strange voice.

"Who is this? Do you know what time it is?"

"If you want to keep your Phoenix Project secret, you'll just shut up and listen. I know all about it, Dr. Loats."

"I don't have any idea what you are talking about."

"You have too much to lose to take that chance."

Deacon had known this day might come. He'd hoped to complete the project and announce it on his terms, but apparently time had run out. "You couldn't know anything about that."

"I know about the battery, the factory in Jean, Nevada, and the rare-earth mine in California. Need I say more?"

"What do you want?"

"I thought you'd see it my way. A hundred thousand American, or I sell it to the highest bidder."

"You're bluffing."

"Try me. What do you think I could get for it?"

"I'm calling the police."

"That would be a big mistake. Be smart, turn on your computer. You will see The Niche icon on your desktop. Open it, make a bank transfer and your secret is safe. Otherwise someone else will have it by sunup."

Deacon turned on his computer and saw the icon. "Alright, how do I do this?"

The NSA was given Vacon's client list and was monitoring international communications searching for any mention of companies on that list. When the Phoenix Project appeared in the conversation, they notified their affiliate agencies that someone was interested in Dectron R&D.

TO THE HIGHEST BIDDER

Zaventem, Belgium

Diving into the dark web, Lo Gi entered his eighteen-digit password and opened his virtual storefront; the place where he listed everything he had to offer.

Stolen personal information, credit card numbers, bank accounts, and Social Security information were his stock and trade. Occasionally he had something special, like the Phoenix Project. His clients found him by using a key word from a notice board called Quick Sale Zaventem to get to the domain. Then they'd enter the temporary password found in a personal ad in The Niche. He had hundreds of regular users who bought IDs and credit cards, but there were always a few whales looking for something specific.

He added a teaser about the Phoenix Project, sat back waiting for the whale to surface. Greg Bokken kept an eye on the site and when he saw the posting, he called in the Director

Former Stasi officer Karl Herbig was used to dealing with duplicity, he practiced it himself from time to time. He understood it and knew how to deal with it, but the syndicate had a protocol and he followed it. He put a call through to the syndicate's chief operating officer.

"We have a problem with Lo Gi, Sir. It appears he has gone into business for himself, offering our information to the highest bidder."

"Thank you. The problem will be remedied immediately. Have you found any details in the information he is selling that we don't have?"

"No, Sir. It is simply a tease, but the implication is that he has been holding out on us."

"Good, anything else?"

"No, Sir." Herbig was always impressed by the man's self-control. These business problems ended with a death, yet the psychopath never exhibited the delight he took from the pain and suffering of others. Perhaps it was Gelenko's own Stasi background showing through.

Stephan Gelenko was supposed to be a Wunderkind, a genetically perfect little Nazi.

That was why the Russians put his perfect pregnant Nazi mother in a concentration camp in 1945 and waited for his birth before they executed her.

Delph Petrus was told about the boy in 1953 and was drawn to him. Stephan was a handsome and intelligent child, but deeply troubled. His sadistic nature emerged when he was very young. That intrigued Petrus and the institution didn't hesitate to give him the boy.

As if he was training an attack dog, Petrus cultivated those traits. On several occasions, he took Stephan to an abandoned warehouse close to the Berlin Wall.

He would give Stephan someone the Stasi had captured, a few basic implements to play with, then allow his sadistic instincts to flow. Nobody heard the screams from the ruins.

With time the technique became more refined and each new victim was kept alive longer. He always tasted the blood of his victims and noted the subtle differences in a journal as if he was discussing wine.

After 'home schooling' Stephan in the social arts of polite society, Petrus sent Gelenko to England to attend Eton College.

His only demand was that the boy restrained his homicidal tendencies until he graduated. He was there to learn English and how to be a gentleman.

While there, when several people in the area disappeared, the authorities suspected they were dealing with a serial killer. The disappearances were never solved.

When Gelenko graduated from Oxford after reading European history, Petrus saw to it that he had a good position in the Stasi. He was free to pursue his pleasures with government sanction. Gelenko enjoyed his pleasures with both sexes and the disappearances continued until the wall came down in 1989.

The goal Petrus had in mind for the young man had changed with time. Stephan's brilliance made Petrus consider him as his successor when he retired and, following unification, he set Gelenko up in business in Berlin.

A CONTRACT

Spandau, Germany

Tobias Keirken was resting on top of his bed when his phone chirped by his pillow. He reached for it without looking and flipped it open. "Keirken."

"I have a contract for you in Zaventem." Gelenko supplied the address then said, "The plane is waiting for you at Schönefeld Airport. Remove all the data storage devices you can find and destroy everything else. Call me when the job is done."

Keirken rolled off the bed and slipped into his leather jacket, grabbed his backpack and bike helmet, and headed for the door. It took twenty minutes to get to the airport and as soon as he was strapped in, the plane took off for Brussels.

It was a simple matter for him to steal a car from the long-term parking lot and drive into Zaventem. Lo Gi's apartment was at the south end of the town, just ten minutes from the airport.

He parked in the lane beside the building then, with a pair of latex gloves on, he used a bit of electronic high tech to open the lock on the front door.

Taking the stairs, Keirken casually climbed to the fifth floor. At Lo Gi's door he withdrew a small camera system from his backpack and fed the flexi camera under the door.

His tiny monitor showed that the main room was empty. Using a pair of slim tools to unlock the door he pushed it open with a fingertip then entered.

He was in no hurry, as he screwed the suppressor onto the barrel, he heard Lo Gi in the bedroom talking to himself. Keirken smiled, it was easy money.

Very gently he placed his hand on the doorknob, turned it, then pushed it open with his finger. Instantly the bedroom filled with light and Lo Gi spun around in his chair temporarily blinded. Keirken waited until Lo Gi could see.

"What do you want?"

Keirken turned on the lights and put his finger to his lips. Pointing the gun at the young man he said, "Not a sound." The Swede spoke English without a trace of an accent. The room reeked like a locker room after football practice, with overtones of old pizza and stale beer. The only window was shut and blacked out with a large sheet of black foam core board. "This place is disgusting; did you know that?"

"Look man you've got the wrong guy ..."

"Shush," Keirken said. "You have cheated on the syndicate. Never a good idea," Keirken said. His gun coughed twice creating two holes in the hacker's forehead.

Lo Gi slumped to the floor. Bits of brain and skull stuck to the wall above him. Keirken policed his brass and placed them in his pocket. Then he took out his knife and dug the slugs out of the bloodstained wall.

After taking the memory devices and destroying the computers, he left the building and headed back to the airport. In the air he called Gelenko. "The job is done. I have the material you requested."

"Very good Mr. Keirken. I will have another job for your team soon. Please see that they are available. I will give you the details later."

"I'll be waiting."

THE REPRIEVE

Dectron, Toronto

Deacon had stewed for days after paying the blackmailer. He'd been wrong not to first report it to the police. They told him as much. They might have been able to catch the guy, they said. Now he'd never get his money back.

Three things they didn't consider. The blackmailer didn't give him time to think, he didn't care about the money, and it was the security of his project that mattered. There was one positive thing to look forward to, the blackmailer would come back, they always did, and they'd get him then.

Jasper was mortified that he'd been hacked. His fortune came from a program he wrote that was supposed to prevent hackers from getting in.

"Well, you don't own the program anymore, and nothing lasts forever," Deacon said.

"You're right. Look, I'll reimburse you, but we both know that there is no way the guy could know any details of the Phoenix Project. He just pieced together something he heard and drew conclusions. Anybody could have done that. I don't think your genie is out of the bottle yet."

"You're right, but still ... it freaks me out."

"Don't blame ya. But don't worry, I'll fix it."

The NSA passed on the information to their affiliates.

Kat was working alongside the FBI in Washington on leads to a possible terrorist cell in Baltimore when Devlyn brought her back into the loop.

"We're looking at that Canadian connection with the Vacon takeover now. Do you remember the company Dectron Aerospace?"

"Sure, the robotic assembly line for the Phoenix R&D Project. I thought the syndicate had given up on Vacon."

"On Vacon yes, but not on the move into North America. The CEO of Dectron paid off an extortionist to keep his project secret. It may be the syndicate's first move and we have a chance to get in there before they get a foothold. Dectron has just hired RAM Security."

"That's Tom Holly's company in San Diego. He and Harm were buddies."

"Exactly. I want you to contact Holly and lay the groundwork for us."

"Okay, I'll give him call. Have we had any success tying this to Petrus yet?"

"No, I think your Russian was wrong about him."

"I wouldn't rule him out, Vlad was certain about him and he was right about the assassins. I'll call Tom now and set up a meeting."

HELP FROM A FRIEND

RAM Security, San Diego

Tom Holly was pleasantly surprised to hear from her. "It is so good to hear from you, Kat. How are you coping?"

"I'm keeping busy, but I still can't quite believe he is gone, Tom."

"He was a wonderful friend. I'm sorry I didn't get a chance to speak with you on the mountain, but you left so quickly."

"I thought Charley needed to sit down and I wasn't feeling very stable either."

"His poem was a fitting tribute to Harm."

"Tom the reason I called was that M-CI has been informed of a possible national security threat and you have some new clients who are directly in their crosshairs."

"That is disturbing. Who are they?"

"A Mr. Jasper Cleveland and ..."

"Dr. Deacon Loats, yes. Loats says he is being blackmailed by a corporate spy. That doesn't sound like something you would be interested in."

"We believe that it goes way beyond blackmail. Dectron's R&D Project is being targeted by a criminal syndicate planning a hostile takeover. We believe this may be state sponsored terrorism.

"For the past few years, we have been trying to break up this syndicate before they get here. If we can cut the head off this group, we can stop it. So far we haven't been able to prove that our suspect is involved."

"How can I help you?"

She smiled. "We believe that your clients will need around the clock security."

"I have a couple of my best people working with them now."

"I'm sure you do. Do you remember that incident that I was involved in at the convention center last year?"

"Who could forget that? You were a media sensation for a while. It's lucky that they blocked any images of your face."

He paused as he connected the dots.

"Wait ..., are you saying that these are the same people that were responsible for that?"

"Yes, we believe that they are."

"My god!"

"And we're concerned that they'll come after your people. We don't know when they'll make their move. CI wants to take over your clients' personal security while you put alarm systems in their homes."

"I can't argue with that. How do you suggest we proceed?"

"As Dectron Aerospace is the primary target, and experience tells us that its CEO is the one at risk, I'll be making him my responsibility. I'd like to get to know him in a controlled safe environment first, so I want you to invite them to stay at ENA while you're doing your thing."

"If I understand you correctly, you want to ease them into the idea that their lives are in danger."

"I think that covers it, yes."

"This will be a full military operation."

"No. I don't want to overwhelm them, and I don't want to scare off the syndicate. If we're going to stop them, we have to catch them in the act. I'm asking you to tell your clients that this is your plan and that you will be using security personnel from ENA."

"I'll set things up."

"Thank you. The situation is level RED, Tom. There's no time to waste here. I'll have the accommodations ready for them. So, call me when you have it set up."

"I'll call Jasper right now."

17

FAILURE IS UNACCEPTABLE

Petrus' Office, Berlin, Germany

By summer the syndicate should have established a foothold in North America, but it had stalled in Paris and Petrus was furious. He called Gelenko in to discuss it.

The younger man entered the top floor office, a futuristic fusion of steel, stone, glass and fabric in black, grey and chrome. Petrus sat behind a huge desk of two-inch-thick glass on a black granite and steel base. The surface was clear of clutter.

"I want to talk to you about this Phoenix Project problem, Stephan, this delay is unacceptable."

Gelenko remained calm in the face of the storm. "Our concern has been that the American's are watching everything surrounding Vacon. They will have determined our next target. Any action we take against Dectron could end very badly."

"The Americans?! The Americans know nothing! Their agents were expelled before they could do any serious damage."

"I think you are missing the inherent ..."

260

He banged his fist on the table. "I miss nothing! What you fail to see is the long-term effect it will have when we assume control of this company. It is the perfect vehicle for us to enter the US. They are already setting up manufacturing facilities."

"But we don't really have any idea what Dectron plans to build."

"We know enough to proceed, Stephan. It is an important steppingstone."

The view from the eastern window looked out over a heavily industrialized park and next to it the Nordhafen Canal where long and narrow river boats plied their trade in slow motion. There was something very calming about it. Gelenko took a breath and said, "Sir," perhaps you are putting too much stock into the remote possibility that Dectron will do what you think it will."

"No. You have been procrastinating so long you have lost the vision. I want America and I want it now!"

"Sir, there is an industrial complex in Hungary that ..."

"Stop! Stop wasting my time. Have your people move on Dectron now. In fact, it is time for you to get down onto the battlefield. Prove to me that I haven't put my trust in the wrong man."

"Sir I ..."

"Understand me, Stephan. I will not accept failure."

"Of course, Sir, I understand."

INVITATION ACCEPTED

Kat's apartment, Eagle's Nest Academy

Kat was in her apartment when Tom called back. "How did you make out with the clients?"

"It has all been arranged, Loats is flying down to San Diego in the morning. He and Mr. Cleveland will meet you at Gibbs."

"Perfect. Did they seem concerned about staying at ENA?"

"Both men are wondering why we are increasing their security."

"What did you tell them?"

"I just told them that there were similar cases where threats escalated and it was better to be safe than sorry."

"Good, I'll head over to the coast tonight. At noon tomorrow we'll have the helicopter on the pad at Montgomery Airfield to pick them up."

She briefed Devlyn on what had transpired and asked to have Flynn and two other agents fly out with her. She'd bring them up to speed on the plane. They flew out of Davison Air Force Base on a small military jet to San Diego.

Once she was in the air, she briefed her team, then called Doug Leman to say it was on and they were coming.

THE CLIENTS

Montgomery Airfield, San Diego

She spent the remainder of the night in a San Diego hotel then took a cab to Montgomery at 11:00 am. When she pushed through the door at the Gibbs building the staff greeted her like an old friend.

"Has the Bird Man arrived yet?"

"Yeah, he's in the assistant manager's office."

"Oh. Okay well, bang on the door will ya and tell him I'm here and I'd like to get that whirly-bird in the air sometime today."

"Sure thing, Kat."

She turned and spotted Tom Holly peeking over the half wall around the waiting room. "Hi there, Tom," she said brightly. "I wasn't expecting to see you here."

"Kat, lovely to see you, as always."

She went around to give him a hug and he responded with a sympathetic fatherly squeeze that almost made her cry. She cleared her throat with a little cough and asked, "Are you coming up to the Nest too?"

"No, I just wanted to put a face to our new Canadian client and introduce them both to you. It's been a while and you look great as usual."

"Thank you," she said. She liked him, there was something about him that always reminded her of Harm.

"Maybe I can convince you to come down to the city for dinner with Sharon and me sometime."

"I'd like that." Kat heard the door open and looked over the room divider as the two men entered.

263

Tom looked at his watch. "That should be them now. As usual Kat, your timing is perfect." Jasper Cleveland appeared around the corner first. "Good morning Mr. Cleveland, nice to see you." They shook hands then Deacon stepped up. "And you must be Dr. Loats. I'm Tom Holly, RAM Security." They shook hands. "How was your flight?"

"It was fine, thanks."

"Well ..., gentlemen, I'd like you to meet Katrina Fernando." Kat smiled and said, "Hi." Jasper grinned at her like she was a Christmas gift. Deacon's reaction was more subtle.

"She is the owner of Eagle's Nest Academy and will be in charge of your personal security. Her team will be with you 24/7 until this unhappy situation is resolved. Since you are the primary target Dr. Loats, Ms. Fernando and her partner will be with you."

"Great," said Deacon. "I looked ENA up online on the way over here. It looks like quite a place, Ms. Fernando."

"Harm wanted to make sure his clients were comfortable while they're taking it easy after class." Deacon gave her one of those you're kidding me looks. "The first week is quite strenuous; it takes some people a day or so to get used to the pace. And we tend to be less formal about titles at ENA. Everyone calls me Kat."

"Well then I'm Deacon and the guy with the grin is Jasper. I was told that you fly the helicopter."

"Yes, I share the duty with Roger Beech."

"Great. Is it possible to sit up front?"

"Sure, I don't see why not."

"Will we be meeting Harm?"

Hearing his name punched a hole in her carefully crafted armor and, unfortunately, she let it show. "Ah, no. Sadly, my husband died recently."

"Oh, I am so sorry."

Tom immediately felt it was time for an exit. "Yes, he was a great man. Well Kat, you know where to reach me," he said.

"Thanks Tom." He sketched a quick wave and was gone. She used the interval to collect herself then turning back to Deacon said, "Okay, our ride is out this way."

It was a bit of a walk to the helipad at the north end of the lot so Kat kept the conversation going, "Jasper, you'll meet your bodyguards at the chopper. They'll have lots of things to keep you busy while you're with us."

"Me too?" Deacon shouted over the noise from the twin jets winding up.

"For sure, Deacon. My partner Flynn is waiting out there and you can say hi before takeoff."

"What's his first name?"

She smiled. "It's George but he hates his first name, so, it's just Flynn. The guy in the OIC chair is Roger Beech and he seems to be all set to take off, so let's get your suitcases aboard and climb in."

"What does OIC stand for?" asked Jasper.

"Officer in Command." She waved to Roger and signaled that she needed a word.

He opened the right-side door and took off his earphones.

"Roger, I'd like to fly us home and have Dr. Loats sit up front with me."

"Not a problem, Kat."

"Thanks."

When everyone was strapped in Kat said, "Okay boys, how about a little tour?"

Soon they were at a thousand feet and flying out over the harbor, across the North Island.

"Jasper lives down there," Deacon said, pointing to Coronado.

"Lucky him," Kat said. Seconds later they were out over the Pacific, then back over the land at La Jolla and up to the mountains.

She watched Deacon admire the view and began to size him up.

He's a couple of years younger than Harm, a nice-looking man with a pleasant, honest smile. And tall too, perhaps as tall as ...Whoa, what am I doing? Okay the comparisons are done now.

She needed conversation to distract herself. "You're an aircraft designer?"

"Yeah, among other things, small planes mostly."

"How do you like helicopters?"

"This one's terrific," he said. "I've never seen one dressed up like an executive jet before. They did a really nice job. You're a hell of a pilot, by the way."

She smiled, he was a lovely man and she was attracted to him. The way he looked at her just made her feel good.

ENTERTAINING THE CLIENTS

Eagle's Nest Academy

The agents Devlyn chose to protect Jasper had never been to ENA before, so Kat handed them off to Charley to familiarize them with campus protocol. Flynn used the time as a bit of a vacation while Kat spent her time coming up with things for Deacon to do.

"We teach survival skills for diplomats and executives, most of them are guys like you. It's serious training because where they're going survival can be touch and go. Have you ever fired a gun or done any martial arts training?"

"None of the above. I live a very quiet life."

"Well it's time to learn some new skills."

The first week was spent finding his strengths, the second developing each one of them. Deacon didn't like guns but enjoyed martial arts.

Okay, first impression still holds up, he's nice guy and I like him and all that, but is this going to be a problem down the road?

18

NAIROBI LAWYER

Nairobi, Kenya

The syndicate had established a pattern for their corporate takeovers. It started with a Nairobi lawyer with no traceable connection to the organization. The lawyer was a master at starting the process of intimidation. He began with a lowball offer, followed by the threat of a hostile takeover.

His victim would try to fend him off, but he would come back with a second offer, higher but still unreasonable. When that was turned down, he'd follow with the threat of violence. Then the syndicate heavies would step in the victim would die, the company would collapse, and they would step in and take over.

Gelenko got in touch with Niko Umbutto. "I have a new project for you. I want you to contact Dectron Aerospace in Toronto, ask to speak to Dr. Loats."

"And what should I offer?"

"Something insulting, as usual. I'll leave that up to you. Rattle his cage, get him angry, threaten him, all our standard incentives."

"I know the drill, Herr Gelenko. When I am done, they'll be begging to sell."

MAKE HIM AN OFFER

Dectron Aerospace, Toronto

Clive Thorn was working his way through the new budget when his secretary buzzed him, "There is a Mr. Umbutto on the line from Nairobi."

"Is he a client?"

"No. He says he is a lawyer."

"A lawyer from Nairobi? We don't have any princely relatives, there do we? Is he asking for money?"

"I don't think so. He asked to speak to Dr. Loats."

"Alright, put him through." She transferred the call. "Hello, Mr. Umbutto, this is Clive Thorn, VP of Dectron. What can I do for you?"

"Mr. Thorn, I wanted to speak with Dr. Loats. Is he unavailable?"

"Yes, he's away from the office for a few days. What is this about?"

"I have a business offer I would like to discuss with him. Please tell me where I might find him."

"I'm sorry ... Mr. ... Umbutto is it? Dr. Loats has asked not to be disturbed. If it isn't urgent, then I suggest you leave your number and I will have him contact you when he returns."

"As I told your receptionist, this is a matter that must be discussed immediately."

"I see, then you'll have to discuss it with me."

"Very well, I am acting for a large multinational company, which, for the moment, chooses to remain

269

anonymous. They are very interested in your company and have asked me to begin the negotiations."

"I'm sorry, what negotiations are you talking about?"

"We intend to buy Dectron Aerospace."

That broke Thorn up. "Pardon me for laughing, Mr. Umbutto, but you have been misinformed. Dectron is not for sale. Thank you. Good b..."

"You are the man in charge at the moment, are you not?"

"I am, but as I said, Dectron is not for sale."

"My client is prepared to offer twenty-five million dollars."

"Goodbye, Mr. Umbutto."

"Mr. Thorn!" he said urgently, and then continued with ominous calm, "dismissing me out of hand would be a very serious mistake."

"I'm sure you think so, Mr. Umbutto. But your offer couldn't possibly be taken seriously," said Thorn. "Goodbye." He hung up and looked over at his secretary, who had been standing by the door dying to ask what that was all about.

She asked, "Should I try to get in touch with Dr. Loats?"

"No, it was just some African loon who wanted to buy the company. I mean, what planet are these people on anyway?"

"Do you want me to inform Dr. Loats?"

"No," Thorn said. "Let the guy have his vacation."

"SCHOOL" IS OUT

Eagle's Nest Academy, CA

On the second last day of their stay at ENA, the whole school had been out on the mountain since lunch playing capture the flag.

It was a great game with a very serious set of lessons for them. It gave them a sense of what it would be like to be hunted, to look for sanctuary with the enemy all around. When taken seriously it could be a life changing experience.

After the blue flag was brought in everybody wandered into the Hacienda for a coffee break. It was just past 4:00, Kat assessed Deacon's condition and asked, "Do you have any energy left?"

"What did you have in mind?" Deacon replied, taking a sip of coffee.

"An hour of MA in the dojo."

"Really, you want me to fight you ... now?" She noticed how sweaty he was.

"We'll have the place to ourselves, and you look like you could go a few rounds. So, what do you say?"

"I say, let's do it. And by the way ..., you're going down," he smirked.

"Sure. I like a man who can dream big."

They went in and changed into shorts, t-shirts, and helmets then met out on the mats. "Okay, bring it on lady."

"Settle down now, Dr. D, we should warm up first."

"I'm warm enough. Come on let's go."

"So, hit me." He threw a punch which she deflected and followed with a move that was so fast he hit the mat before he knew what was happening.

"Whoa! What did you just do?" He looked up at her, then rolled over on his stomach and pushed himself up.

"Did you see how that worked?"

"No ..., and ..., JESUS CHRIST!"

"Okay get up and I'll show you." She offered her hand and he took it. "Now you can try it on me. I'll throw the punch." She struck out slowly, "And deflect..., that's right. Good." And he tried to put her on the mat, but he missed the most important part, to use the attacker's momentum against them.

"Sorry."

"It's okay, you can let go now. This time try to make it flow so you're using my momentum to carry me over your hip, but let's do it faster and put me down on the mat." Kat threw a punch, he parried, twisted and pulled, then she hit the mat. "Good. Again." They worked at those moves for an hour. "I think I'm getting the hang of this," he said."

"Oh, you're getting better ..." she threw the punch, he did what he was supposed to do, but she turned it back on him and he was on the mat again. "But there's always a counter move."

"Did you ever have to use it on anyone for real?"

"Yes, once or twice," she said, with no details.

"Were you frightened?"

"Yeah of course, in combat everyone is afraid. If they're not, then there's something wrong. Okay, that's it for today."

"Oh, show me one more take-down first. Please."

"Fine, just one."

"Whoops!" It was a similar move ending with him on his back this time. "And then you punch your opponent in the throat." Her punch came very close.

"Yikes." She was kneeling beside him and, without thinking, he sat up and kissed her. From her surprised expression, he thought he'd made a big mistake and backed off. "Um, sorry I ... uh."

"I didn't complain, did I?"

"No, you didn't, did you?"

"Come on, tough guy, up we get."

"You know something?"

"What?" she said, towering over him.

"I've wanted to do that since I got here."

"Really?"

"Yeah. I could do it again."

"I think you've had your smooch ration. Come on, it's time for a shower. And I suggest a cold one." Before he had a chance to object, she held out her hand to him.

"Oh ..., okay. And then what?"

"We'll get ready for dinner. If that's alright with you?"

"Sure. In the restaurant or the Mess Hall?"

"Your choice," she said.

"I brought a suit so why don't we dress for dinner in the restaurant?"

"You've got it. We'll meet at seven in the lobby."

They walked over to the Hacienda and as they parted company, he asked her, "What time do we leave tomorrow?"

"The chopper leaves for the airport at twelve-thirty and our flight departs at sixteen-thirty hours, that's 4:30 to you. There are no classes for you tomorrow, so you'll have all morning to pack."

19

FINDING LOATS

Back to Berlin

Like it or not, Stephan Gelenko was committed to something that he considered irresponsible folly. He called Keirken, "I have a job for you.

There is a man I need you to locate for me. His name is Dr. Deacon Loats. I've heard from one of my operatives that he isn't in Toronto. I suspect that he may be in San Diego, California, with a business associate, Jasper Cleveland. If not, perhaps his associate knows where he is."

"What is the associate's address?"

"He lives on Coronado Island, that's all I can tell you. This is important, I need Dr. Loats alive, he is key to an existing project."

"What about this Cleveland?"

"After he tells us where Loats is, he is expendable. Concentrate on finding Loats. He lives in Toronto, so I'm heading there in case he shows up."

"I'll need two men, so the price is doubled"

"Fine, get whatever you need and leave today.

Keirken and co. arrived in San Diego expecting to be in and out in a day. They found Cleveland's house with a male housekeeper, but there was no sign of either target.

After two days, he called the house claiming to be from a foundation Jasper was supporting, "So sorry, Mr. Cleveland is not here."

"When will he be back?"

"I not know this, Sir," said Mr. Win, Jasper's Cambodian houseman. "He away maybe two weeks, maybe more. Sorry."

"It's important that I meet with him, where is he?"

"Did not say. Please call back some other time," Win said, and hung up the phone.

Keirken phoned Gelenko asking for new instructions.

"Find them."

"But we have no indication where they are."

"Damn. Alright, Cleveland is bound to turn up eventually. Stay put and watch his house."

"What about Loats?"

"He too will eventually turn up. I will wait for him here."

LANDING IN TORONTO

Toronto International Airport

To avoid disclosing that they were M-CI Special Agents, Kat took Deacon aside while Flynn arranged to clear their guns with the airline in private. The guns were packed away in the checked luggage and Flynn had the paperwork to show the Canadian authorities at the other end. They boarded the Air Canada flight in Business Class and arrived at 12:15 am, Toronto time.

This was the first time that Kat had ventured beyond the airport strip into Toronto and even though she'd seen it from the air she was surprised by how big and busy it was up close.

It was impressive at night too, all lit up. The downside was that Toronto had been in the grip of a heat wave for several days. A thunderstorm was heading their way and people were hoping that it would finally bring an end to the heat.

The cab was heading to Deacon's newly renovated Georgian house on a quiet tree lined street in Rosedale, 45 minutes from the airport.

As they drove up to the house thunder was rumbling quietly in the distance and the sky was crackling with heat lightning. It was weather one could smell, taste, and see as the wind picked up.

"It's going to be quite the storm," the driver said. "They have been talking about it on the radio since yesterday."

"I guess we got in just in time," Kat said, and Flynn agreed silently. He had a headache and he blamed it on the weather.

As they pulled into driveway the floodlights came on. A moment later the front door opened and Deacon's housekeeper appeared on the stoop.

Kat looked at her suspiciously and Deacon said, 'Don't worry, she doesn't bite. Mrs. D has been with me for years. Hi Mrs. D."

"I've been waiting by the window for you, Dr. Loats. Welcome home."

"Kat left the car and ventured up the short path while the driver removed their luggage from the trunk.

While Deacon paid the driver, Flynn stood beside him wishing that he had his gun.

"Well, my goodness, you must be Ms. Fernando. Come right in," she said, beckoning with both hands. "Dr. Loats told me all about you and Mr. Flynn over the phone. My word, if you don't look just as he described you. And you as well Mr. Flynn." He relaxed a bit and smiled at her. "I made you a snack in case they didn't feed you on the plane. And your rooms are all ready for you."

Kat went right up to change into something cooler. When she came down, she found Deacon in his study, Flynn was on guard at the door and feeling a little more secure now that he was armed.

"I'll call the office in the morning to let them know that I'm back," Deacon said.

"Do you need to go back to the office right away?" Kat asked.

"I suppose not. Why?"

"If you could handle your business over the phone for a few more days, we can maintain the illusion that you're still in California. I think that from a security standpoint, it would be best if no one knows that you're back yet."

"Oh, okay. But what if Jasper calls the office asking for me?"

"Call him now, tell him what we're doing and ask him to only use your cell number."

"Then maybe we can eat something?" suggested Flynn from the door.

"Why don't you help yourself now while I make the call?" Deacon said.

"Wait a second. Do you have a cottage or a ski chalet, some place out of the city?"

"Yes, I have a farm, why?"

"It's a big city, I'm worried that it would be too easy for someone to sneak up on us here. We'd never know if the car going by is just a neighbor or someone doing a recon. Maybe the farm would give us an advantage."

"I think you're right Kat," Flynn said.

"If that's the best way to handle it the farm would be perfect. It's hard to find if you don't know the area and it's large enough to accommodate all of us without getting in each other's way."

"Sounds perfect. I suggest you make your call to Jasper and get some sleep. We can head up there first thing in the morning."

The building wind provided no relief from muggy weather and the thick, humid air inside added to their discomfort. While Deacon made the call from his office, they watched the trees bend and branches whip about in the light of the streetlamp as they finished eating their sandwiches. "This would have been a good night for air conditioning," Deacon said, "but I'm afraid it's not working."

"Oh, I had a man in to fix it, Dr. Loats. It is on, but it's not helping much is it? This heat wave is too much for the poor thing."

Deacon yawned saying, "Damn. Okay, I'm bushed, so I'm going bed. Goodnight everyone." Flynn and Mrs. D followed. Kat went to her room but it was impossible to settle. For hours she lay naked on top of the bed, drenched in perspiration and as usual her thoughts tormented her.

The flashbacks of combat and killing and her life with Harm, the good times in the house in Durham, the brief, stolen moments of happiness during the training courses and when she was deployed.

Finally, she got up and opened the window to see if that would help.

It didn't. She pulled a wooden press-back chair away from the little desk, placed it in front of the open window, and sat down to watch the light show.

The rain arrived with a vengeance, but Kat was oblivious until she felt the rain sting her body and noticed that the floor was getting wet. She got up, shut the window, returned to the chair, and sat spellbound by the storm.

It ended with the dawn so she opened the window. It was cool now and she sat down again thankful for the quiet. Kat had just nodded off when the silence was broken by a knock at the door. Oh god, she thought. "Yes?"

"Kat, I uh ...," Deacon said, through the door. "Are you still in bed?"

"No, I've been watching the storm." She looked at the time on the bedside clock. "Is there a problem Deacon?"

"No ..., I was just wondering how you were." he faltered. "Who could sleep with all that noise?"

"I know, but I'm fine thank you." In the silence that followed she thought he may be having a problem. "Are you alright? Is there anything I can do for you?"

"Look, it's hard to talk through the door. Can I join you in there, or can you come out?" He turned the handle and opened the door. At first all he could see was her silhouette. Then as his eyes became accustomed to the dawn light, he realized she was naked. She was so beautiful.

"Deacon," she said quietly.

"Yes? Oh, Christ, I'm so sorry. I thought you'd be ...,
um, okay, sorry." He quickly withdrew then said through the
door. "I'll wait for you downstairs. We'll have some
breakfast."

"Deacon," she said, thinking how easy it would have
been to invite him in.

"Yes?"

*All I have to do is ask him to come in. How it would
feel to make love to another man. God, I need to feel loved
again. I've been so desperately lonely since Harm died. She
felt like crying. No, I'm not ready, not yet.*

"I'll be down in a few minutes."

A COUNTRY HOUSE

Mulmur, Ontario

Deacon was behind the wheel of his big Mercedes with
Kat beside him. Mrs. D was in the back, thrilled to get out of
the city.

Deacon thought it would be a good idea to have two
cars up there so Flynn was in male-heaven alone following in
Deacon's Porsche.

The drive up to the highlands was beautiful. An hour
and forty-five minutes from the city Deacon left the paved
highways for Mulmur's country dirt roads. The trip got more
interesting as he drove them up the 4th Line which turned
sharply after the intersection then snaked uphill.

In places, it seemed like nothing more than a tractor path. They came to a deep narrow valley with a shallow stream at the bottom.

The township didn't bother putting in a culvert, so the cars splashed through the tiny gravel riverbed then charged up the hill on the other side.

A couple of minutes later he said, "This is it."

"Where? I don't see anything," Kat said.

"That's the beauty of it." His lane was long and gently curved through the old growth forest. "No one is going to find us in here," he said. They came out into a clearing where the drive circled a small island in front of the house.

The building was like something out of a futuristic Japanese sci-fi movie. Timber frame and stucco structure, simple and yet elegant. There were three pavilions with hip gabled roofs clad with blue tile and linked together by glass hallways.

The largest section was open to the world with sliding glass walls and surrounded by a wide veranda.

Standing in the doorway Kat could see through the open concept house to the interior bamboo garden at its heart and the field behind.

She explored the place and then returned to main room.

"It is absolutely incredible, Deacon."

"When I had this built, I thought that I'd be married and start a family."

"What happened?"

"I got too busy," he said.

"I'm sorry that didn't work out for you. But Deacon, this is the most beautiful house I have ever seen. And then

281

there's so much out there, the forest and fields to play in. If Harm and I had had a family I would have loved to have my kids grow up in a place like this."

"That's only the second time that you've mentioned him."

"He told me to move on, so I'm trying. But it's difficult."

"I can imagine." Three loud beeps sounded an alarm coming from the kitchen. "What's that?" Kat asked, drawing her gun.

Flynn had his out and rushed to the porch. "Someone's coming down the drive."

"That'll be my neighbor, Earl Brown. He watches the place like a hawk. He and his wife Ronda, look after the place for me."

The truck stopped near the front steps and Earl stuck his head out the window, grinning broadly, "Deacon, it's been a long time since you bin up. I was out to the barn when the bell sounded, so the wife come out to say it must be you."

"How've you been keeping. Earl?"

"Good, yeah no complaints. I thought you'd forgotten about the place."

"Never."

"You stayin' for a while, then?"

"Yes, I don't know for how long. These are my friends Kat Fernando and Flynn."

"Afternoon to yous."

"The wife will b' wonderin' what's what by now, so I best get back, so I should."

"Well, say hi to her for me and thanks for stopping by Earl."

Kat looked over at Deacon and saw that he had been watching her with a hint of a smile on his face. Everything about him was extraordinary, his work, his dreams, this house. Deacon should have been a real catch for some woman, yet somehow that never happened.

"We should go inside and get settled," Kat said.

"You know, I was thinking of going for a walk. Care to join me?"

"Sure. Are you up for a walk Flynn?"

Aware that Kat had been attracted to Deacon from the beginning. "No, I'm good right now. You two go ahead."

HACKER UNPLUGGED

From San Diego

Kat had been anticipating trouble from the get-go and she was feeling like a caged beast not knowing how or when it was coming. Like war, it was 90% boredom 10% terror. They talked about it and Flynn was feeling pretty much the same way. It was like they were under siege, and there was some tension developing in the house.

She was on her cell phone with Tom Holly, he often called just to check in to see how they were doing. But this time he had news.

"It was quite a job, but our IT people traced the hacker through his IP address. The investigator I hired from Paris found his home near the Brussel's airport. When he arrived, the police were already there, and the blackmailer was dead."

"The question is, was his murder connected to the blackmail or something unrelated?"

"I agree," Holley said, "but there's no way of answering that now. He'd been dead for several days, my man said it looked professional, two shots to the head. My sense is that the threat is over, so I'd say that you are free to go at any time."

"No, I don't think so. Blackmail wasn't part of the other takeovers. There's a chance that his appearance was purely coincidental. Or for whatever reason, the guy decided to freelance and the syndicate terminated his account."

"Okay, I see your point," said Tom.

"The main show hasn't started yet. We'll stay where we are for now. Thanks for the heads up, Tom." Kat hung up.

Flynn had been listening in. "It's not over is it?"

"No. It will start out like Vacon with an offer. When we hear about that then this shit will get serious."

"What now?"

"We have some quiet time, so I suggest we should take advantage of it."

20

A FISHING EXPEDITION

Toronto

Passing himself off as a potential client, Gelenko called Dectron and asked to speak to Deacon hoping to find out exactly where he was.

The receptionist told him, "I'm sorry Sir, Dr. Loats is out of the country for a while. Would you care to leave a message?"

"No. When do you expect him back?"

"He didn't say, Sir."

"Perhaps you could tell me where he is. It is urgent that I meet with him."

"I am sorry, Sir. The best I can do is forward your message. If it is urgent, I could put you through to our vice president Clive Thorn, perhaps he could assist you."

Gelenko hung up frustrated. It was likely that Loats was with his partner in California and he hoped Keirken would find them soon. He reread the report Herbig had written on Loats and then concentrated on the list of assets.

Nothing jumped out at him until he saw the name Township of Mulmur.

Loats had owned a house north of the city. Herbig hadn't found out whether he still owned it. He circled Mulmur, then put the report away.

PICNIC LUNCH

Snake River Ranch, Mulmur

Deacon was in no hurry to have Kat leave, but when she said, "Listen, I have a feeling that trouble's coming."

"On a scale of 1 to 10 how concerned are you?" he asked,

"It's about a 3, I'd say. We expect they will contact Dectron first to make an offer. When that happens, we'll know we have a serious problem."

"So, you're not leaving me yet."

"Not until we're sure you are safe."

"Great."

"Flynn is going stir crazy and having you cooped up in your office all day is not good, Deacon. You have to get out and get physical. The trails are nice, but we should go further afield, do some serious hiking."

"I'm not a big fan of hikes."

"Really, okay then we could ..." she began.

"Do you ride?"

I do. Harm and I used to ride all over the mountain, she remembered fondly. "I love riding."

"There's a place not far from here."

"Sounds good. Flynn, what about you?"

"I'll pass on the horses, but I'll go with you."

They arrived at the Snake River Ranch just before 11:00 and got two horses saddled up and ready to go. Flynn stayed in the car. After packing their picnic in a saddlebag Kat hopped up into the stirrup and swung her leg over the horse's back.

Deacon tried to copy her, but it didn't go as well. His horse chose that moment to back up, leaving Deacon hanging with one foot in the stirrup while clinging to the saddle horn. Kat reached over and caught the reins and held him steady giving him a second chance.

"I think you just saved my life," he said, as he settled into the saddle.

"That's what I'm here for."

"Yeah," he said sheepishly. "I guess you are."

"Ready to head off now?"

"Absolutely."

Kat laughed and spurred on her horse. Deacon quickly matched her pace. His old rhythm gradually came back, and he had the confidence to settle into the saddle as they raced over the hills and across the fields.

The sun was high when they reached the lake Deacon mentioned. It was little more than a seven-acre oval shaped pond with an island in the center, tethered to the mainland by a rustic bridge.

The bridge had been rebuilt recently, its cedar log deck rested on a cedar log trestle, paved with pounded earth and a thick blanket of grass. Deacon led the way to the other side and stopped under the three huge pines that lorded over the island, their reflections reached deep into the lake. It was crystal clear in the shallows, but a couple of yards from shore the water was deep and dark as night.

It looked peaceful but, since St. Petersburg, Kat had acquired a fear of deep, black water. "Are there any monsters in there?"

"Maybe some frogs but that's it. No trout or turtles."

She refused to allow her phobias to spoil this. She took a deep breath and let it out slowly. "Fantastic. How about a dip?"

"I didn't bring a suit. Did you?"

"No." She laughed impishly, got off her horse and said, "Does it matter?"

Deacon watched open mouthed as she tossed her boots aside, peeled off her clothes, and with a shriek of delight, ran into the cold water.

Splashing like a kid she ran out till she was up to her waist, then dove below the surface.

She surfaced like a water nymph, floating on her back with her firm breasts peeking out of the water. She loved that he couldn't take his eyes off her and she willed him to come to her. He hesitated.

He needs to be encouraged.

She touched the bottom and stood so the water just covered her nipples. He wasn't moving yet, so obviously he needed a stronger enticement. She stood taller, lifting her breasts above the surface and raised her arms up to smooth her long, black hair away from her face.

She arched her back rocking slowly from side to side so that the sun glistened off the beading water on her caramel skin. He groaned audibly in the presence of perfection.

She pulled her hair into a ponytail and then draped the end over her shoulder. His eyes were filled with nothing but her, her body, her lips, and her amber eyes.

"Are you sure you won't come in? The water is wonderful!"

Deacon's shyness crumbled. He looked around to make sure they were completely alone and when he turned back Kat was gone. She had ducked underwater and was swimming toward the bridge. He could see the color of her body, an indistinct shape beneath the dark water.

He shed his clothes, hurried into the lake, and kept going until the water was up to his chest. It was cold. He wrapped his arms around himself to hold in the warmth and waited to surprise her when she surfaced.

But she didn't surface.

Kat watched him from the far side of the island then swam to him underwater and waited to look at his lean body beneath the surface. As he turned his head searching for her, she burst up in front of him.

He gasped from shock and embarrassment then laughed with delight.

"Hi there," she purred. She was so close that her warm breath touched his face. "Are you cold?" He nodded. "Here," she pried his arms open and pressed her body against his. "Let me warm you." And she was warm, incredibly so, and soft too. She pressed her breasts against his chest and felt his temperature begin to rise. "Feeling better?"

Spellbound, all he could manage was, "Uh huh." His acceptance and desire mirrored hers. His body responded and pressed against her thigh.

"Oh! That's nice. Is it for me?" She slipped below the surface again and taking hold of his legs, she took him into her mouth.

Slowly stroking him with her lips, touching him with her tongue, she sent waves of heat shooting up through his body. She felt him trembling with pleasure and it thrilled her.

She came up for air, pressing her body against his, and held his erect penis between her legs, then leaned back, to sweep the water from her face. How could he resist? She took his hands and pressed them against her breasts. He squeezed them gently and kissed them and she shut her eyes, delighting in his tenderness.

She moved in close, kissed him, "I want you."

Her arms went about his neck, she pressed her mouth against his, searching for his tongue with hers. She sensed that he was drawing his power from her. He had become stronger now, more in tune with what he was doing.

She needed this, to be wild and free, even if it was just this once and only for a moment. Deacon's effect on her had been unexpected. Suddenly all she wanted was to have him inside her, she wanted him to make her feel whole again, to feel loved again.

Lifting herself up onto his hips she guided him with her hand and in that moment, he felt so good that nothing else mattered.

The feeling of being surrounded by the cold water with him inside her was incredible.

She kissed him as she moved against him; he was hers now, all of him. They found a rhythm together and lost the world around them. He filled her up and she was happy.

As powerful as it was, the climax came too soon.

It had been too cold and her pleasure too intense to be paced out or controlled. They were floating now, still clinging together after his knees had buckled from the exertion.

The cold water swirled about them with a sobering sting, and they finally dragged themselves to the shore.

For a short time, they lay together naked on the grass in the hot sun, hands touching, small happy smiles on their faces.

He looked at her, enjoying the curves of her body but then he saw a jagged scar across her ribs just below her right breast. "Jesus, how did you get that?"

"A branch did that as I fell through a tree."

"What do you mean by fell through a tree?"

"Let's make that a story for another time, okay?" They shut their eyes as the sun dried their skin.

The horses began to nuzzle them, their hot, grassy breath on their faces forced them to stir, "Holy Jesus, what time is it?" Deacon said.

"Time to eat Mrs. D's picnic, dress and head home, I guess. Unless ... you want to do it again."

This time it was slower and, in a different way, more satisfying. Deacon turned out to be a very good and generous lover. How lucky was that?

The mood on their return trip was quite different from the ride out. She felt contented and peaceful for the first time in ages. Now she knew what it was about him that made him so disturbingly attractive. The guy didn't have a mean bone in his body.

"Kat, I think I'm falling in love with you."

And there it is. As much as I like him, I'm not ready for love. "Don't be silly, you don't know anything about me."

"I have a pretty good idea, and that's all I really need to know."

She reached over and caressed his cheek with the back of her hand. "You are a very sweet man, Dr. Deacon Loats."

UMBUTTO'S PREDICAMENT

The Hilton, Toronto

Time was slipping by and they hadn't made any progress. Loats and Cleveland were nowhere to be found and Gelenko knew the state Petrus would be in. He had to do something radical now, his survival depended on it.

If this operation failed, he would be the one swinging from the lamp post regardless of who was to blame. He called Umbutto. "Have you contacted the man again ..., what was his name?"

"Clive Thorn. Yes, Herr Gelenko."

"And ..."

"He said he would not negotiate with me and was going to report me to the authorities here in Kenya if I called again."

"Did you threaten him?"

"Most dreadfully, yes I did."

"And what happened?"

"He reported me to the authorities. I am under house arrest pending an investigation. There is nothing more I can do."

"Idiot!" He hung up and called Keirken.

"What is Cleveland's status?"

"He arrived this morning with two bodyguards," said Keirken.

"Well thank the gods for that. What about Loats?"

"No. No sign of him yet."

"Did you question Cleveland about him?"

"I called him saying I was with the FBI. The man told me I had to meet with him face to face before he would talk about anything."

"Well, did you meet with him?"

"I had no FBI ID, so no."

"Shit! Stop fucking about Keirken, get in there and take him. Find a place where he can be questioned then storm his house, kill his guards, and take him. Do you hear me? Do it right now. Call me the moment you have secured him, and I will fly down to meet you." He hung up without waiting for a response.

WHEN SOMEONE KNOCKS

North Island, San Diego

Posing as a parcel deliveryman, Keirken's man Westerhoff rang Jasper's doorbell.

He had a Ruger with a suppressor hidden in the package.

As soon as Jasper's bodyguard answered the door he was shot. Henning, the second gunman, ran by Westerhoff to take out the other Special Agent and Mr. Win with his silenced submachine gun. Keirken was the last one through the door.

He seized Jasper and knocked him unconscious, gagged him with duct tape, put a hood over his head and carried him to the waiting van.

In less than thirty seconds they were away, heading for the San Diego-Coronado Bridge. Their destination was the town of Oceanside. As instructed, Keirken had rented an isolated house on the outskirts. There they waited for Gelenko to join them.

MORE BAD NEWS

Deacon's house, Toronto

Kat was in the hall beside the indoor garden when her cell rang for the first time in days. She assumed they were calling to say that it was over "Tom, hello. How are you?"

"Kat, I have terrible news. Jasper has been taken. His housekeeper and your agents are dead."

293

"Oh ..." She wasn't prepared for that and the news literally took her breath away.

For a moment she couldn't speak as she slowly sat down at the bottom of the staircase.

"Kat, are you still there?"

"Yes, sorry ... Who took him, does anybody know?"

"The neighbors say they heard nothing. Someone on the golf course across the street saw his door open and the bodies on the floor. We have very clear images from the security cameras, but these people aren't in our database. We got there as quickly as we could, but there was nothing we could do. I am so sorry."

"This is unbelievable."

"Kat, is it safe where are you?"

"Yes, for now. No one knows that we're here. I'd like to keep it that way."

"Deacon should be told right away."

"I'll tell him."

"Does Jasper know where Deacon is?"

"Jesus, that's why they took him, isn't it?"

"I'm afraid so. Tell Deacon that the FBI are doing everything they can to find him."

"I will. Tom, what went wrong?"

"Jasper was easy to find. They were dressed as a delivery service. Oh, hang on ... damnit, I've gotta go. I'll call later."

"Tom ..., Tom, hello?"

"Someone took Jasper?" asked Flynn.

Kat nodded. "Spencer and McBrian are dead." She noticed Deacon had come out of his bedroom and was standing at the top of the stairs.

"I could tell by your voice that something was wrong. Tell me."

"Deacon I'm sorry, that was Tom. Jasper has been kidnapped."

"Oh God." He sank to the floor. "And the guards?"

"Dead."

"Oh Christ. How?"

"I don't know what to tell you. The FBI is looking for him. This is just ..." Her phone rang again, and she tapped on. "Hello?"

"Katrina," Devlyn said, "have you heard about Spencer and McBrian?"

"Yes, just a moment ago. Have you come up with any new information?"

"No, I was just on the horn with the FBI. They've got nothing. There's something else now. What do you know about an offer to purchase Dectron?"

Good God, when did it happen?"

"A couple of weeks ago, why."

"What!"

"Deacon, is there something I should have be aware of?"

Deacon got up and came down the stairs. Kat moved over to let him get by.

"The African has already made an offer?"

"Yes."

"What's happening?" asked Deacon. Kat put her hand up to hold off the interruption. He sat on the step next to here and waited.

"Thorn thought it was a hoax and didn't report it to the RCMP until yesterday after he got a second call. They put a request through to the Kenyan police. They had him under house arrest until last night."

"Had him?"

"Someone killed him. I want to know why Thorn didn't tell Loats about this."

"Devlyn, can you hold on a second." She took the phone from her ear and covered the mouthpiece. "Deacon did Thorn call you about someone making an offer to buy Dectron?"

"No! Why, what's happened?"

"The syndicate's opening move against you happened two weeks ago. Thorn didn't report it until yesterday."

"I can't believe it."

Kat considered the information they had so far and none of it was good news. "Does Jasper know you're here?"

"No, I told him to use my cell number."

"Yes, I know, but does he know about this place?"

"Oh-god." He practically fell off the top step. Yes, he's been here but that was years ago. I don't think he could tell them where it is."

She put the phone to her ear. "Hello Paul?"

"Yeah."

"He had no idea about the calls."

"Fuck!" He took a breath. "So, does Cleveland know where you are?"

"I just asked Deacon and he doesn't think it's a problem."

"You know he's as good as dead."

"Yes," she said, looking at Deacon, knowing how he must be feeling. "What are your orders?"

"Work out an escape plan, find an alternate location for Loats, and don't die. We'll talk soon."

IN SECLUSION

Oceanside, CA

Gelenko drove to the abandoned house Keirken had found up on the northwest edge of Oceanside. Westerhoff met him at the door with a gun in his hand. Gelenko pushed by him saying, "Where is he?"

"In the back," Westerhoff said, tilting his head in the direction.

Gelenko strode to the back of the house and found Keirken in a dingy little room standing beside Jasper with a gun to his head. Jasper was tied to an old metal kitchen chair. "Put that away and remove the gag," he ordered.

As soon as Jasper was able, he stammered "W-who are you people?"

"Does it really matter?" Gelenko said, as he signaled Keirken to leave him with the prisoner. The hired killer went out and took his men to the car.

"Why have you done this? What do you want from me? Money, is that it?"

"I'll get to that soon."

"What are you going to do to me?" Jasper demanded.

"I just want to ask you some questions. That's all. Now tell me, where is Deacon Loats?"

"Deacon? I have no idea."

"I don't believe you." He took out his knife and stabbed him in the leg. Jasper screamed. "You will tell me eventually, so why prolong the pain?"

"I don't know. I haven't heard from him for weeks."

"I don't believe you." Gelenko cut his arm and pressed his thumb into the wound. Jasper screamed again. "Now tell me where your partner is. Where will I find him?"

"Go fuck yourself."

While Gelenko enjoyed his pleasures, Jasper continued to scream. He kept screaming for twenty minutes as Gelenko kept cutting him building up the level of pain.

"I can keep you alive for a very long time while I do this. You don't want that, do you?" Jasper knew how this would end and shook his head. "Tell where his is and this will end." Jasper told him about everything.

"And where does he keep the plans for Phoenix Project?"

"His laptop, it's always it with him."

"And, where is he? The property in Mulmur. Is that where he is?"

"Maybe."

"I want to know exactly where it is."

"It's near Mansfield. That's all I know."

"Near Mansfield. That's it?"

"I've told you everything."

"I believe you."

Jasper opened his mouth but Gelenko rammed the blade into his ear ending his screams forever. He simply slumped back in the chair, his face a frozen mask of horror and surprise. His body was covered in blood from the dozens of cuts and stab wounds. Gelenko left the knife in his ear and the stream from it joined the expanding pool of blood on the floor behind him.

21

WAITING

Mansfield, Ontario

Before sunrise two days later, Keirken's men were parked next to the Mansfield General Store. It was a rundown building at the intersection of Airport Road and County Rd. 17. They were standing by their cars waiting for directions.

Henning's phone finally rang. He was tired, overheated, and cranky, so before he answered he checked the time, 9:20, and sighed. "Henning."

Gelenko rattled off his instruction. Herbig had finally come through with the location of the house. The 4th Line East, north of County Rd. 21, he'd said. It wasn't enough but that's all he had.

Gelenko ended the call by saying, "... and I want you two to block the road in front of the house. If Loats tries to leave you can kill his guards. But be sure to take Loats alive."

He'd said that repeatedly and Henning was sick of it. "Yes, Sir." He signaled to his partner to mount up. Heading west, they took off down the dirt road in a great cloud of dust with Henning leading the way.

Both men struggled to maintain control through the corners on the loose gravel. It was like driving on ice with bald tires and the road had more kinks than a snake. Westerhoff was having the most trouble, because he was driving blind in Henning's dust.

Careening along a relatively straight and flat stretch Henning swept over the crest of a hill, missing the hidden intersection of the 4th Line North. The road plunged into a valley much steeper than either man expected.

Henning read the sign for 4th Line South and realized that he had gone too far. He slammed on his brakes catching Westerhoff by surprise. Westerhoff swerved, narrowly avoiding a crash and continued up the hill on the other side.

Henning backed down to the intersection to turn around then throwing up a rooster tail of dirt, raced back to the blind intersection near the top. He drifted into the corner, silently wondering if the graveyard behind him was for the people who didn't make it around that corner. Angry and frightened Westerhoff reached the top, spun into a 180° turn and followed in Henning's dust once again.

The 4th Line North was even more dangerous than the road they had just left. It hadn't been graded for weeks, and between negotiating the nasty ruts and deep potholes that jarred them to the bone it seemed to be interminable.

When they crossed County Rd. 21, the road immediately jogged to the right and snaked up into the hills. "How far up do we have to go?" Henning shouted at the road. "Holy Jesus! What now?" he raged, as it turned into little more than a tractor path forcing them to slow down.

It narrowed to the width of a car and dipped down sharply into a gully with a tiny stream running over it. On the other side it twisted through a series of tight curves in a dense forest. Henning slowed down even more looking for the lane Gelenko told him would be there.

As far as he could tell there was no sign of a house anywhere. He stopped high up in a clearing on a hill.

He got out and could see a large lake in the distance. Westerhoff stopped behind him and waited as Henning walked back to talk. Opening his window Westerhoff shouted, "What's the matter?"

"Do you have any idea where we are?"

"I have no fucking idea." He reached for the map that had slipped to the floor. "That must be Georgian Bay up there. Do you think we should keep going north?"

"It can't be this far north."

"We've missed it then. Let's go back."

Henning agreed, returning to his car they turned around and went back into the forest at a crawl.

Westerhoff stopped before he reached the valley with the stream and Henning got out to have another conversation. "We've missed it again, haven't we?"

Westerhoff shrugged and said, "I have no fucking idea where we are."

"Okay, we go north again."

Both men were looking for a conventional driveway like normal people had. Something that went straight from the road to the house. Mulmur was anything but normal.

Many of the lanes purposefully meandered through the bush down into hidden valleys, or across wide fields. They could be as short as a hundred yards or as long as a mile. They poked down one of the obscure trails and saw an old farmhouse.

Henning was sure that wasn't the place they were looking for, so they backed out.

301

The one next to it was much longer with a long curve. It was impossible to see what lay beyond, but something told Henning that this was it. They backed out onto the road again and parked on the shoulder. Henning called Gelenko.

ALARM

Deacon's House

Back at the house a call came in, which alarmed Deacon. "That was Earl. He said his driveway alarm went off and now ours has too."

"What? Why didn't we hear it?" Kat said.

"I have no idea but he saw two cars drive down his lane. Now they're parked out front."

"Here?"

"He said there was nobody in them. What do you think that means?"

"It means we're out of time. Get your computer Deacon, we have to go now."

"Really?"

"Yes! Right now. Hurry." She ran to the door. "Flynn ..., they're here!" she yelled."

She turned again wondering where Flynn was. "Goddamnit, where is he? Flynn!" she shouted again, but louder this time. "Oh, for Christ's sake Flynn!"

Flynn came bursting through the back door with his gun in hand. "What's happening?"

"We've got company and they're coming down the lane right now."

"You've got to take him out of here."

"Yes. Get Mrs. D."

"She's gone off on a walk. You take him now. I'll find her and follow."

"Fuck that, I'm not leaving you here alone."

"You have to take Deacon away. I can take care of myself, Tiger."

"Jezzus, Flynn. I don't like this."

"What choice do we have, Kat? I'll call 911. If the hostiles come in, then I'll deal with them." Kat hesitated; she had already lost two men. She couldn't bear the thought of losing Flynn too. "Kat! You have to go!"

"Okay. Be safe, George." Using his first name like that seemed so personal, like a goodbye and she regretted it. Deacon was by the door with his computer.

"Okay, let's move it."

As they ran to the car he asked, "Where are we going?"

"The OPP station. Flynn's calling them now to tell them we're on our way."

"Kat, they'll take forever to get up here."

"Flynn will hold them off till they get here."

The instant the Mercedes roared to life she pulled the shifter in to drive and speed off. Flynn was already running down the path, shouting into the cell phone at the 911 operator. Then he called Devlyn.

A WAR ZONE

4th Line, Mulmur

Deacon was still putting on his seat belt when Kat sped off down the lane, hoping she didn't meet the opposition on their way in.

That hope was dashed as she swung around the wide turn in the driveway. Henning and Westerhoff were in the middle of the road.

"Shit! Deacon, get down!" She floored it heading straight for them. Westerhoff dove left, Henning went right and rolled out of it on his feet and opened fire.

As the warning left Kat's lips bullets slammed into the car. One went through the front door window just behind her head, another slammed through the door itself, into the dashboard.

Deacon was on the floor with his hands over his head. She ducked down too as more bullets from Westerhoff came smashing through the rear window.

The car drifted out onto the 4th Line heading south, kicking up a cloud of dust. Kat skillfully guided the big car through the turn as they flashed by the two parked cars and raced across the plateau chewing up the road. Soon they were heading down into the gulley. "Do you think they're alright?" Deacon asked from the floor

"I don't know. I think you're safer in the seat now," she said. He climbed back into his chair and put on his seat belt. The car splashed through the stream, forcing her to turn on the wipers.

304

"Flynn must have heard those shots," as they sped up the other side. "Call him. Use my phone." Deacon had difficulty hitting the right numbers. "His phone is on speed dial press #2."

"Oh, right." He pressed the call button and listened. "It's busy."

"Shit! Okay, are you alright?" He nodded. "Good."

"How the hell did they find us?" he asked, looking back though the shattered window.

"I don't know, maybe Jasper told them."

"No. He wouldn't do that."

"I'm sorry, Deacon, but sooner or later everybody talks."

He said nothing after that, he just sat there being tossed around like a rag doll. She didn't blame him; she just wished for a better ending. "I'm going to cut across to the 2nd Line." The Mercedes soared off the tops of the hills and landed hard each time sending up sparks and clouds of dust.

She couldn't see behind her, so she had no idea where the killers were or even if they were back there.

Their pursuers were driving like mad men in a demolition derby, making up for lost time. She caught sight of them as they broke over a hill just seconds behind them. "Shit! I thought we'd have more of a lead by now."

"Try Flynn again."

Kat came to another sharp curve and drifted into it then stomped down on the gas into the straightaway. Her tires threw up a hail of stones and a huge cloud of dust as she flew down the road.

Putting the car sideways again preparing for the last 'S' curve, she drifted over the apex to the right, lining up for the left turn and out onto the straightaway. She lined up for the quick sharp right onto County Road 21, braked put it sideways to finish the sequence then floored it heading west.

Henning and Westerhoff were expecting her to go south on the 4th and slowed.

When Henning realized his mistake, the separation between Kat and the pursuing vehicles was significant.

He had to push hard to catch up, but she had the more powerful car.

At Ruskview Kat turned onto the 2nd Line and hurtled south down the steep hill toward Terra Nova. She knew the road well. Her pursuers didn't. That downward stretch of hills was treacherous at speed.

The Mercedes was catching air as they crested each hill and that gave her an idea. The 2nd Line snaked up the south side of the Pine River Valley.

That would force them to slow down and give her time to reach 15 Sideroad and turn without being seen. She knew the road and drove the line as if it were a racetrack. Down through the last difficult 'S' turns she turned right onto 15th Sideroad leaving another thick dust cloud behind.

Henning and Westerhoff were stretched to the limit.

Both men were terrified and blew right through the intersection before they realized that there was no longer a dust cloud, she wasn't in front of them anymore.

Deacon tried the phone again. "It's ringing."

"Finally."

"Flynn," he said, and Deacon could tell that he was running.

"I've got him."

"Okay, tell him there are two cars chasing us. There may be more back there."

"I think he heard that."

"I did," said Flynn. "I haven't found Mrs. D yet. What does she want me to do?"

"He hasn't found her yet; wants to know what he should do now."

"Tell him to get out in that little car as soon as he can and head north to Creemore. Ask if the cops are on the way."

"Yes, the cops are sending someone up now. They said it will take twenty to thirty minutes to get here." Deacon relayed the message.

"Shit." If he didn't find her and move soon, they'd be in serious trouble. "Okay, tell him …," she was desperately worried about Flynn. "Oh fuck! Tell him …, to stay safe."

"I heard that. Tell her I will. You too, and good luck Deacon."

Deacon passed on the message as Kat kept on going, across the top of the ridge. The pursuit cars hadn't made the turn yet and she knew there was a hard-left coming up. She drifted into it and her mood became very dark as a plan formulate in her mind.

Those men are going to pay for this.

The engine roared as she straightened out of the turn, kicking up dust on the 1st Line East.

It was impossible to see if the cars were still on their tail, but it was a safe bet that they'd catch up soon.

Like the 4th, this road hadn't been graded in a long time and it was a rutted nightmare of twists and hills. Up ahead there was a steep hill impossible to see until you crested it.

Henning was closing the gap, but he'd lost sight of the Mercedes. It must have looked as if they were playing leapfrog as their cars flew into the air over every bump.

When Kat reached that special spot, she slammed on the brakes and slid to the side of the road.

"Jesus, what are you doing?"

She jumped out, shouting, "Stay there!" She pulled out her gun and ran back halfway up the hill.

"Kat ..., what are you going to do?"

"My job Deacon," she said, her voice was cold and frightening. "Just stay put."

She anchored her feet, reached out with the gun in her right hand and her left supporting her elbow. She aimed at the most likely spot where the car would be. She could hear the sound of Henning's screaming engine closing in. It would appear any second now.

Then there it was cresting the hill in the air like a giant blue Hot Wheels.

The Ford tilted forward and as the front wheels touched the ground Kat fired twice. Henning took one in the chest and one in the neck. As soon as his car careened into the ditch, the second car popped up.

Westerhoff saw the car turning end over end. He slammed on the brakes but was too late. He was in the air pitching forward; his Chrysler was shedding dust from its bronze hood as if his ghost was already on its way out. He saw her standing at the side of the road and knew what was coming.

Again, Kat waited until the front wheels touched down.

Two shots.

Her bullets pierced his side window, one struck him in the temple just behind his eye.

His car continued straight by the Mercedes, sailed across the ditch and ploughed through a split rail fence onto a pasture. It came to rest in the mud at the edge of a cattle pond.

Deacon was overwhelmed by the violence.

SERGEANT CORNFIELD

OPP Detachment, Shelburne

Twenty minutes after leaving the house, Kat escorted Deacon into the small Ontario Provincial Police station. They were greeted by the anxious Supervisor, Sgt. Howard Cornfield, who came out from behind a large window of bullet proof glass. "Special Agent Fernando?"

"Yes." She showed her badge.

"Why did you call her special agent?"

"Deacon ..."

"No, she works for RAM Security, she's my bodyguard."

"Deacon, please ..."

"You're a special agent of what?"

"Deacon ..., okay, I'm sorry I lied to you. I work for US Military Counterintelligence." Deacon stood open mouthed but didn't say anything. Kat turned to Sgt. Cornfield, "You talked to my partner?"

"Flynn? Yeah. He told me you were heading down. He said he heard shots fired, but there was no sign of anyone else."

"That's a relief."

"She killed them both," Deacon said, as if in a dream. "Shot them dead."

"Deacon please, sit down and try to put it out of your mind. Sgt. Cornfield, I'm going back for him now."

"Do you think that's wise?" Cornfield asked.

"As far as I know he hasn't found the housekeeper yet. They may still be there, so I have to go back."

"Alright. Call me if the situation changes, I've already dispatched an officer to his location."

"Just one?"

"He's all I have at the moment. I've called for backup, but who knows how long it will take."

She headed for the door without looking back.

Cornfield turned to Deacon, "Alright, what happened up there?"

23

MEN WHO FAIL

Mulmur Township

It had taken Gelenko and Keirken longer to get to Mansfield than expected, and as they turned onto the Mulmur sideroad Keirken's men weren't answering their phones.

Gelenko found the 4th Line East without trouble and headed north, expecting Henning and Westerhoff to be in position at the driveway. The plan was to go in together, but the road was deserted.

"Where are they? They should be here," Gelenko said.

"They may have taken the house already. I'll call them again," Keirken said, taking out his phone.

He speed-dialed Henning's number while Gelenko complained, "I gave explicate instructions ..."

"There is no answer," said Keirken.

"Where the hell is this place?"

Gelenko drove right by the driveway just as the others had done and had to turn around.

He stopped about a hundred yards from the driveway. His eye was drawn to the rear-view mirror and he saw a police car stop on the narrow verge. Keirken looked over his shoulder. "So, that's where they are. Loats must have called for help."

"Scheiße," Gelenko swore, "If those idiots have failed ..."

"We don't know that."

"We kill the policeman and go in. I am going to drive up to the car, so you can deal with him." He turned the car around and drove back to the squad car.

The officer was on the radio to Sgt. Cornfield when he saw the car approaching from the north. "Ah ..., hold on Sergeant, I've got some visitors." Anticipating trouble, he drew his gun and held it in his lap, ready. Gelenko stopped beside the patrol car and rolled down his window. The officer waited until the glass was all the way down before he said, "Can I help ..."

Keirken leaned across Gelenko, lifted his gun and fired into the young man's face.

Cornfield heard the officer's last words and shouted into the phone, "Chris what's happening? Chris ..., come in."

"Turn that thing off," Gelenko said. Keirken got out and pushed the man out of the way and switched off the radio.

"There will be more of them soon," said Keirken.

"I agree. We have to get in there and take care of business before they arrive." He looked at the patrol car and an idea came to mind.

"Get rid of the body, put on the man's hat and drive his unit to the house with the lights flashing. If there are any guards left, they'll come out. Kill them, but ..."

"I know, leave Loats for you." He dragged the dead officer's body into the ditch then returned to the car.

"I don't want Loats harmed."

"Yes, I heard you," he said irritably.

"He has the computer with the Phoenix Project. It is imperative that I get that."

"I understand, now may I go?!"

"I'll follow you in a minute or two."

Gelenko pulled away from the driveway. Keirken donned the policeman's hat and headed to the house with the roof lights flashing.

Flynn had just returned with Mrs. D and they were heading for the sports car when he heard the shot. He took out his gun and waited by the car. He felt a sense of relief when he saw the emergency lights coming down the drive. "I think we'll be alright now. You just stay here while I go out and meet the cop.

The black and white pulled up just short, forcing Flynn to move closer. The glare of the sun on the windshield made it impossible to see inside, so Flynn approached cautiously saying, "I'm Special Agent Flynn, US Army

Counterintelligence. Officer? I can't see you. Show me your hands," he said, with his gun up and ready.

Keirken rolled the window down and said, "Is everything alright here, Sir?"

Flynn saw the street clothes and fired but Keirken was just a millisecond faster. While Flynn's bulled sailed by nicking Keirken's ear, his bullet found it's mark in the center of Flynn's forehead.

Gelenko waited the full two minutes before he drove in. He strode by Flynn's body without looking down and found Keirken inside holding Mrs. D at gunpoint. His neck was covered with blood from the wound, but Gelenko ignored that too. "Is there anyone else in the house?"

"She says it was just the two of them."

"And you believed her?" Keirken shrugged. Gelenko turned to the woman. "Where is Dr. Loats?" She didn't answer him right away, so he grabbed her by the throat "Where are they, woman!"

"She …, she has taken him away."

"She? His bodyguard is a woman?" He thought for a moment, picturing the pleasure he could have with her.

"How very interesting. And who might she be?" Again, she refused to answer. "Very well, a simpler question. Where is the good doctor's computer?"

"I don't know. He must have taken it with him."

"Well then you are of no use to me." He opened his folding blade. "Keirken, hold her for me."

She struggled frantically, but Keirken's grip was too strong to shake off. "No please, no please don't!" Gelenko placed the edge of the knife against her neck.

She could hardly breathe. "Please don't. I don't want to die."

"But you will." Her eyes bulged with horror and she opened her mouth to scream as Gelenko's cut deep into her throat. Her head rolled back toward Keirken as if it were hinged.

He jumped back away from the stream of blood shooting up into the air and she dropped to the floor. Now drenched in her blood Gelenko said, "Bring the man's body inside and put him next to the woman while I look for the computer."

"But she said it wasn't here."

"And you still believed her?"

"She wasn't lying before," he protested.

Keirken dumped Flynn's body next to Mrs. D's and said, "No luck?"

"I want you to take this place apart!" Gelenko shouted.

"What for?"

"We don't leave here without it."

"It won't magically appear because you want it to."

"Find it!" he screamed.

As long as he was paying Keirken would follow orders. They were so preoccupied that neither of them noticed the arrival of the officer from Shelburne.

Officer Jake Pemberton had found the body of Const. Foley in the ditch. He'd called it in, also requesting backup.

His chief responded, "Backup is on the way, Jake. Stay put until it gets there."

"I'm going in."

"No! Hold your position. Do not go in alone! ... Jake! ... Jake!"

314

He had been too upset to listen and too angry to just stay with the car. He lit out on foot down the lane. Carrying his shotgun loaded with slugs, he ran across the drive and the small island hill at the center to take cover behind a spruce tree. He took a knee to catch his breath, then after a brief pause to look at the house, he dashed over behind Foley's car.

He crouched down leaning against the door. He saw the blood stain in the gravel. Someone else had died here. He took a deep breath, popped up to see if he could spot any movement inside then crouched down again.

Keirken was walking by the open front door just at that moment and saw the movement out of the corner of his eye. He went out onto the front porch pointing his gun at the squad car.

Pemberton heard the footsteps and popped up once more, swinging the shotgun over the hood. Keirken's bullet struck him right between the collar bones. The shotgun went off and the slug hit the roof of the house. The assassin jumped back through the door and waited for more fire. When it didn't come, he went out and collected the young man's body and put it with the others.

Too much time had passed without a report from his people so Keirken made one last call to Henning's phone and let it ring. He found Gelenko in the back bedroom slashing the mattress "I called Henning, I think they must be dead."

Gelenko couldn't believe that he'd failed so completely. Failure was unacceptable. "And why must they be dead?"

"I know my people; they wouldn't run away."

"So, it would seem that it is just the two of us now."

Keirken leaned against the door jamb and said, "We should go while we still can." Gelenko didn't hear him. As he stood there with the remnants of the mattress stuffing in his hands all he could think about was Petrus. "What's the matter with you? This is a failed mission. We have to go now."

"Men who fail die."

He slapped the wood trim with the flat of his hand hoping to snap Gelenko out of it. "Don't talk nonsense. Let's get out of here while we still can."

He came at Keirken with the knife held in his fist. "We have to get Loats."

The professional killer easily parried it away. "Stop this nonsense. Loats is gone, Gelenko. I'm getting out of here." He turned and walked up the hall to the front door.

"No."

Keirken spun around ready to fend off another attack. "What?"

"The woman, she will come back for her partner and the old woman."

"Even if she does, she won't bring Loats or the computer, so what's the point?"

Gelenko put the knife away. Keirken relaxed and resumed his march to the door. "Wait!" The hired gun heard the change in Gelenko's voice and turned around again, but slowly this time. "I suggest you take that weapon out of the car and go into the woods to wait for her."

"Didn't you hear me? There is no point to this. It's gone, we can't get it now."

Unable to control his anger Gelenko pressed the gun against Keirken's forehead. "I will not ask you again."

It was suicidal and Gelenko knew it. Keirken could see it in his eyes and backed down. "Fine, I'll do it your way. But I expect to be paid double for this."

"Of course. Kill anyone who comes down that lane."

Keirken realized that Gelenko had lost it and walked out of the house weighing his options.

He removed his sniper rifle from the trunk of the car and walked toward the bush. He had some time to think it over. After looking around and getting the lay of the land he found the best vantage point for his sniper's nest. He could see the approach to the house and the surrounding area clearly. He also had a good view of the house.

If he gets any crazier, I'll just kill him and to hell with the money.

After building his blind he settled in to wait.

BACK IN THE FIGHT

Deacon's House

Kat returned to Mulmur hoping that there would be some backup on the way. Seeing the Shelburne Police car parked by the lane was a surprise. The backup had already arrived. Why only one car? She had no idea how many had responded but at least she wasn't alone.

She went closer to investigate and found the body of the officer in the ditch.

He was OPP, the squad car was from Shelburne and it was too quiet down there. Whatever hope she'd had for reinforcements was gone now.

Was Flynn okay? Had he found Mrs. D? Had they been captured? She went back to the Mercedes and drove it into Earl Brown's driveway then walked back to Deacon's lane through the bush.

She'd trained for jungle warfare with Special Forces in Georgia and could move through the bush like a ghost. Slowly picking each spot to place her foot so carefully that she made no sound.

Once Kat got close enough to a deer to touch it, then walked by leaving it undisturbed. She could close in on a target and take him down before he knew she was there.

Knife in hand she instinctively returned to that practiced rhythm. She was the predator now, Flynn's tiger. She moved, keeping low and using every bit of cover there was to hide her progress. She pushed Deacon's shock from her mind. It no longer mattered what he thought of her; this was all that mattered now.

It took ages to approach the clearing, but now the house was visible, and she was watching for the slightest movement. Her right foot was just reaching out, as if to test the ice before she put her weight on it and she froze. It was a flash of color in the scrub near a fallen tree. His cover was very good; he was nearly invisible. Kat waited for him to move again.

Yes, there!

Killing the men back on the road was one thing, doing what she was trained to do. But somehow, after seeing the dead policeman she felt different, something had changed inside her.

He had no idea he'd been seen. Like that deer she caught grazing, he was distracted, careless.

She moved forward stealthily, totally focused on her prey.

THE PREY

Deacon's country home, Mulmur

Keirken felt invisible in his sniper's nest, confident in his superior skills. His silencer would hide the flash and he never missed. They wouldn't know what hit them. Let them come, he thought, *I'll kill them all before they know where I am.*

He hadn't counted on it taking this long though. He was getting stiff and his mind began to wander. He couldn't stop thinking about how the job had been bungled by Gelenko. He'd never lost a man before and now he had lost two.

It was a sign. He should cut and run. But the money Gelenko was paying was going to make things infinitely more comfortable for a long while. Perhaps he would finally get that house in Kotor, right down by the shore on the bay. Montenegro was a perfect place. He looked to his left and checked his watch. *Where the hell were ...?*

RETRIBUTION

In the Mulmur woods

That thought was never finished. All he felt was her hot breath on the back of his neck as her hand clamped over his mouth and nose. He had no time to understand what was happening.

Kat pulled his head back onto the blade slicing into his neck at the base of the skull and his life was over.

She lifted the rifle from his slack hand, then carefully eased him back before she withdrew the knife and pushed him out of the way. She cleaned the knife on his shirt, folded it and put it in her pocket. Then lifting his rifle, she scanned the building through the scope. Once again, she was looking for movement.

It was barely perceptible through the glare on the large glass wall, a dark shape, a man shifting his weight. He'd moved just enough to be seen, then stopped and remained completely still.

It wasn't Flynn. This dead man beside her wouldn't be here unless Flynn had been captured.

She wouldn't accept any other explanation. He and Mrs. D were prisoners and she would rescue them. That man inside had to be taken down.

He moved again. It was enough to give Kat a clear choice of targets. She used the gun rest Keirken had made. She shut her eyes to steady her breathing, to calm herself. Thankfully he was still there when she opened them.

She chose the spot to hit, not a kill shot, merely one to put him down. If there were others inside, they would start firing and she would kill them. But this one she would keep alive to answer her questions. She took a slow breath and as she let it out, she stopped ... and gently squeezed the trigger.

There was a soft cough as the bullet left the rifle and a curl of smoke rose from its mouth. In a millisecond the glass imploded as the slug pierced it.

The bullet carried a punch that ripped through the man's shoulder.

It smashed his collar bone, shattered his scapula, and tore a chunk of muscle and skin away as it exited.

Gelenko pirouetted like a dancer as he fell face first onto the floor. He writhed and screamed just like his victims had as he tortured them.

Kat waited for return fire, but there was none. Had there just been the two of them? Was it just him now? She watched through the scope as he squirmed on the floor. Seconds passed, but nobody went to help him. He was in full view now without the glass to hide his features.

Yes, he was alone, and he had things she needed to hear.

She dropped the rifle, took out her side arm and broke from the cover running across the drive to the front door. Without hesitation, she bounded up onto the porch, kicked through the door and came to a stop in the hall.

She knew exactly where her man was. Gelenko was still thrashing about, but he wasn't going to go anywhere. She turned to look in the kitchen and the breath caught in her throat.

When she could breathe again it came out as a scream. "NO!"

Flynn, Mrs. D, and the policeman, all dead.

She felt something inside her head snap as if a part of her had been torn away and left her panting. White hot with rage she spun on the fallen man. He was watching her, panting with pain and she could see a hint of pleasure in his eyes.

"Are you actually gloating?" she growled. Any semblance of humanity she'd had was gone now, that part was left behind with Flynn.

In that instant Gelenko saw it happen. His expression of pleasure was replaced by terror.

He had wanted to die, but what was coming for him now was incomprehensible.

He struggled to his feet. Unsteady, he tried to back away as she entered the living room. Leaning to the left, his blood drenched arm hung uselessly at his side. In his trembling right hand was his gun, his face was ashen, his skin sweaty. He didn't look like he had the strength to do anything, but he tried to control his trembling chin and look fierce as he lifted the gun to point it at her.

Without a pause she shot out his knee before his gun was levelled. He shrieked in agony as his leg folded back unnaturally and he went down face first again. The gun bounced from his hand as he hit the floor.

Spitting out the blood from his broken nose, he tried to reach for it. She kept coming, slowly, menacingly, there was no hurry now.

She picked up the gun and placed it on a table. "You won't be needing that anymore."

She took a knee beside him; her eyes were shining brightly as she took hold of his good shoulder. With seemingly super strength, she flipped him over onto his back and in a low husky growl she asked, "Who are you?"

The words caught in his throat. The only thing he could manage was a guttural noise. It took more self-control than she thought possible, but she gritted her teeth and asked again, "Tell me ..., who are you?"

"Stephan Gelenko."

"The syndicate's point man I suppose." He didn't respond but she didn't need an answer. "Who was the man outside?"

"Keirken."

"Very good. Now I want to hear you give me the name of the man you work for."

"Go fuck yourself," he said in German.

"Now that's just rude," she said, "We're in Canada now and they have two official languages, English and French. I'd let you choose but then I don't like you, so let's do this in English, shall we? When you are rude to me, I will hurt you."

She pressed her hand on his wounded shoulder then, without hesitation, she pressed her gun against his other knee and fired. She waited for his screams to die down, then began again. "Who ..., do you work for?"

Gelenko tried to keep his mouth shut but he couldn't breathe through his broken nose. She moved the gun to the middle of his thigh. "The femur is next. I'll bet it's really going to hurt."

It was the strangest feeling, as if somewhere Kat was outside of herself watching and horrified by this sudden desire to inflict pain. Gelenko's eyes widened as she pressed the tip of the hot barrel against his leg. She waited, but only for a few seconds. With that same malicious growl, she said, "I can keep shattering your bones until you give me the answer I want." She pressed the gun down harder. "Say his name!"

He shrieked and shouted, "Nein, warten Sie! Wait, wait! Alright, alright ..., I'll tell you." She lifted the gun. "Please don't shoot again, I'll tell you."

"Yes?" She released the pressure. "Go on, give me his name!"

"Petrus," he said in panic, "It's Delph Petrus."

"Yes, very good, now, who is Holbïn?"

"I … I don't know a Holbïn."

She moved the gun to the side away from the bone and pulled the trigger. "Karl Holbïn, he has a new name what is it? Tell me …, now!"

"Alright, Herbig, Karl Herbig."

"Herbig? He was a member of the Stasi?"

"Yes, but how …, how would you know that?"

"Where will I find him?"

"Spandau. He's in Spandau."

"And Petrus, is he in Berlin?"

"Yes. But you will never get to him."

"Oh, but Stephan, I got to you, didn't I?"

"You are already dead. You can kill me, but his people will find you."

"His people? They seem to be dropping like flies."

The gun went off again and the bullet just grazed his inner thigh. His screams were deafening before he passed out. She waited for a moment then began slapping his face until he opened his eyes. "Stephan, I am growing very impatient with you. How do I get to him?"

"Please, stop it."

She moved the gun to his other leg. "I said …, how do I get to him?"

"I'm going to kill you, I'll do it. I'll kill you if it's the last thing I do." Then his voice trailed off into a high-pitched cry.

"No Stephan, I don't think you'll live long enough to kill anyone ever again. And we're speaking English, remember? English."

"Oh God."

She leaned over him. "He never helped me, so I can promise you that he won't help you either, Stephan. You're already in hell. Now tell me, how do I get to Petrus?" She pressed down again.

"Yes-s-s-, yes alright," he said, only slightly more clearly that before. His speech was slurring, and she was finding it difficult to understand him. "Berlin," he said

"I know he's in Berlin, where in Berlin?"

"We always ... meet away from his office. I ... have never been ... there."

"I don't believe you."

"F-f-find Karl ... find Karl Herbig ... he will take you to Petrus."

"Herbig?" He nodded.

"Where will I find Herbig?"

"Herbig ... Investigations ... Spandau ... Arcaden ... near ... train station."

It wasn't a full address, but she would find him. "Now tell me, why would he take me to Petrus?" He shut his eyes, so once again, she slapped his face until he opened them. "Why would Herbig take me to Petrus?!"

"Finish me," he said, the words came out as a whisper.

"No! Tell me," she demanded, but he couldn't talk anymore and for an instant, she felt a twinge of something. She put the gun against his forehead, about to pull the trigger.

But his eyes opened again and he smiled at her with bloodstained teeth. "Yes, kill me now."

She drew back and moved the gun to his genitals. "No, but I will give you something else to scream about. Answer me, why would he take me there?"

"You are a whore ... like all the rest. Petrus toys with his whores ..., then ... he cuts them up, slaughters them alive like pigs. He will do that to you."

"That is disgusting. You are disgusting. Normally I wouldn't let an animal suffer, but for you I'll make an exception," she said, and walked away.

Kat put her gun on the table next to Gelenko's then returned to the kitchen and sat down on the floor beside Flynn. After closing his eyes, she took his hand and lay her head on his chest. There were no tears now. They'd all been boiled away.

She waited silently for the others to come. Sgt. Cornfield had promised they would.

THE POLICE

Kat is in the Kitchen

Shortly after Gelenko stopped making noises, she heard a car approaching in the driveway.

"Special Agent Fernando?" a voice blasted from a bullhorn.

Without moving Kat whispered, "I'm in here."

Two officers came in cautiously with guns drawn expecting to find everyone dead. The lead man saw her move. "Special Agent Fernando? What happened here?"

"They are all dead," she said, still leaning over with her head on Flynn's chest.

The corporal spoke to Kat from the veranda. "Yes, I can see that. Are you armed?"

"No."

"Okay Sam," the man said, "you can put away the gun now.

She looked up. "There are only two of you?"

The middle-aged corporal said, "Yes Ma'am." The young man was drawn into the living room by the horror of the bloody corpse. "Alright, I'm calling for backup and an ambulance."

"They're way past help now," she said.

"The ambulance is for you, Ma'am." She was drenched in Gelenko's blood.

Like the matted fur of a dog that had been rolling in burs, Kat's hair hung down over her face, tangled in clumps of congealed blood. Blood stained her face, her arms, it had soaked into her clothes and all the men could smell was the scent of death.

"God, will you look at her. That's disgusting," said the younger man.

"That's unhelpful, Sam. Keep your comments to yourself." He came back inside. "Now can you tell me what happened?"

"I don't know." she said, without looking up at him.

"Well somebody has to and you're the only one left."

DEVLYN'S SOLUTION

At the Crime Scene

Flynn had called Devlyn to give him a Sit Rep. and Devlyn immediately headed for Toronto. On his way he tried to contact both Kat and Flynn without success.

The young OPP corporal picked up Flynn's phone. Devlyn asked him what the situation was up there. The corporal could only tell him what they found.

"Alright listen to me, officer. This is a matter of US national security. Is the ambulance there yet?"

"Yes Sir, it just arrived."

"Good. Now this is vital. Do you understand me?"

"Yes Sir, I know what vital means."

"Alright, put Special Agent Fernando in it and keep her isolated until I get there. No one, repeat no one, other than the EMT people is to have any contact with her whatsoever. Is that clear corporal?"

"Yes, sir."

"What's your name?"

"Casson Sir."

"Alright, Cpl. Casson, this is very important, so I'm counting on you. Absolutely no exceptions, do you understand?"

"No, I don't, Sir. Why would I do that?"

"Cpl. Casson, as far as anyone there is concerned, Special Agent Fernando died in the gun battle. Have I made myself clear?"

"No. I'm a police officer and you have no authority in Canada, Sir. It's not our ..."

"Do you honestly think you are in a position to make that kind of judgement, Officer?"

"Sir, I ..."

"Now you listen to me. I am a Federal Law Enforcement Agent and this incident affects the national security of both Canada and the Unites States. Will you do it, yes or no?"

The man paused to think about it.

"Casson, yes or no?"

Devlyn said nothing more, he let the silence stretched on until the officer finally said, "Yes, Sir."

Nearly a half hour later more OPP officers began arriving. They came from all over South/Central Ontario. Sgt. Cornfield arrived with Deacon in tow and Deacon immediately asked, "Where is Kat?"

"Is your cat missing Sir?"

"No, I mean Special Agent Katrina Fernando."

"She is in the ambulance, Sir."

"I need to speak with her."

"I'm sorry, Sir, Special Agent Fernando has passed away."

"What?"

"She's dead, Sir. I've been instructed that no one is to be allowed to see her."

"She's dead?"

"I'm sorry, she died of wounds sustained during the gun battle. That is all I can say."

"It is eh? Well that's not good enough! Get out of my way!"

Deacon tried to break away from them and run to the ambulance, but the officers held him fast. "Let me go, goddamn you let me go!"

"I'm sorry sir but you shouldn't see her like that," Casson said. Deacon seemed to lose every ounce of strength he had and collapsed to his knees. Cornfield help him back on his feet and guided him inside. They had done a thorough search of the house and Cornfield had been told about Deacon's upstairs office. "Can you make it upstairs, Sir? I think you would be more comfortable there."

"Yes, yes I can do that. Thank you."

After he was interviewed, Deacon stayed in his office as the OPP detectives conducted the investigation downstairs.

THE CAVALRY ARRIVED

On Deacon's Lawn

The US Army Blackhawk helicopter came in out of the black night like a glowing star and it's propwash had everyone scrambling to hang on to their hats.

Finally, the Senior Special Agent with US Military Counterintelligence had arrived and with him was a CSIS agent named Daniel Sinclair.

Devlyn left his travelling companion with Sgt. Cornfield and sought out the OPP officer guarding the ambulance. "Senior Special Agent Paul Devlyn, M-CI, are you Cpl. Casson?" he said, flashing his badge.

The officer was obviously not thrilled to see him. "Yes, Sir."

"Has anyone tried to see her?"

330

"Yes, Dr. Loats, but I told him it was impossible."

"Good. What is her condition?"

"The ambulance attendant said he gave her a sedative and she's sleeping now. She should be out for quite a while."

"Excellent. What about the attendants, have they talked to anyone?"

Both EMTs had been sitting in the truck with Kat and heard Devlyn talking outside. "We're here, and we haven't talked to anyone."

"Good. Alright, from now on Special Agent Fernando is to be listed as deceased, death by gun shot. Now this is what I want you to do." He explained what he wanted in great detail, reminding everyone that jobs were on the line here. "This is covered under the Official Secrets Act so you forget everything you've seen and heard here today. You get me?!" He got nods from three very overwhelmed public servants.

Devlyn walked back to the house and rejoined the CSIS agent. "Who's in charge here?"

"I am," the man in the sports jacket and slacks said. "OPP Detective Foster."

"Okay, Detective Foster bring me up to speed."

"As I was telling Agent Sinclair here, Special Agent Fernando tortured and murdered one of the suspects. She will be charged on all counts."

"I thought you knew. My agent died in the ambulance. As I'm taking the bodies of my people home with me, you won't have anyone left here to charge."

"You can't do that, Special Agent Devlyn."

"Well that's the way it's going to be and if you have a problem with that, take it up with Agent Sinclair. I'm leaving now."

Foster grabbed Devlyn's arm as he turned away. Devlyn jabbed his finger into Foster's chest and presented the world according to Paul Devlyn. "Let me explain something to you detective, and Agent Sinclair will confirm this, I'm sure. What happened here is covered under the International Official Secrets Act. Everything you have seen today is classified Top Secret for the National Security of both Canada and the US.

We have lost four good agents, agents who have sacrificed their lives to prevent these terrorists from setting up operations here in Canada and in the US. So, don't fuck with this. I hope we understand each other gentlemen."

"I don't, but I suppose I can't stop you."

"Yes. You see, you do understand me after all. Outstanding."

Kat's body was placed in a body bag then in the helicopter. The crew chief and crewman bagged and carried Flynn's body to the helicopter on a litter and placed him beside Kat. Devlyn climbed aboard they took off, leaving Sinclair behind.

As he stood by the window watching the helicopter fly away into the night, Deacon's world fell apart. It looked like it would never be whole again. She was gone, and all he had now was regret. Regret for the things he'd said and things he didn't say. He sat at his desk and began to sob.

23

WITHOUT HUMANITY

Petrus' Office, Berlin

Petrus raked back his short blond hair with his fingers and lowered his rimless glasses and looked up as his personal secretary entered. He adjusted the French cuffs of his shirt and smoothed his tie before he buttoned his suit coat, an idiosyncrasy he no longer noticed. "Yes, what is it?"

"Excuse me, sir, Herr Herbig is here to see you, he says it is urgent."

He closed the file he was reading and folded his laptop to receive his most trusted advisor.

"Alright, send him through." Herbig entered and she shut the door after him. Petrus stared at him and then stood. Herbig noted, as he usually did at meetings like this, that his employer's suit still looked immaculate at the end of a hot humid day. "Something has happened, Karl. Well, what is it?"

"Sir, I am sorry to report ..." Petrus' face had been quite calm almost expressionless to this point, but Herbig's hesitation irritated him.

"Yes, what is it?"

"Regrettably Sir, Stephan Gelenko is dead."

The trim sixty-seven-year-old man waivered and pressed his knuckles against the desktop to steady himself before he sat down again. "He failed."

"Yes sir. He and his men are all dead."

His dark, cruel blue eyes softened and his narrow lips parted momentarily, then his expression hardened and, in a heartbeat, turned from grief to rage. "How could he let this happen?"

"I have an official report which says that there was a police raid following a home invasion of a residence belonging to Dr. Loats. Dr. Loats is the head of ..."

"Yes, yes, I know who he is," he snapped. "What about Gelenko, how did he die?"

"Apparently, he was tortured to death, sir."

"How appropriate. What of the Phoenix Project? Is Loats dead?"

"Dr. Loats was the only one to survive the incident. His project is secure for now."

"A total failure then. Is there any good news to come out of this?"

"I have been informed that his bodyguards, Flynn and Fernando, were the same Army Counterintelligence agents that acted in the Vacon investigation. Our agent tells me that much of the intelligence the Americans had concerning us came from them."

"And how much do they know about us now?"

"There is no indication that any of our people had the opportunity to talk before they died. There will no doubt be an investigation but ..."

"Umbutto will be a problem."

"I have already dealt with both him and his staff, sir. I sent a specialist to Nairobi to do the job. Umbutto's building was destroyed by a fire during the night. There is nothing left to connect him with you."

"Excellent."

"As well, I took the liberty of eliminating Gelenko's employees and all his records."

"Well done."

"Sir, have you any instructions as to what we should do about Loats?"

Faced with the validity of Gelenko's warning that it was unwise to go after Dectron Petrus decided to pretend it was his position all along.

"I warned Stephan that it was foolhardy to go after Loats, but he wouldn't listen. I insist that we maintain a less conspicuous profile in America for now."

Herbig knew that it was Gelenko who said that not Petrus, but it would be ill-advised to antagonize a viper. "I agree, Sir, that is the most prudent course of action."

"We will regroup and continue here in Europe. Thank you, Karl."

"If that is all, Herr Petrus, I will take my leave now."

"One more thing. Find someone to replace Gelenko. I will leave it to you to select a few suitable candidates for me to interview."

"Of course, Sir."

"That will be all."

Herbig clicked his heels and bowed before he made his exit.

24

A HERO'S BURIAL

Arlington National Cemetery

Devlyn gave his report to MGen Wolfson, recommending that the situation in Canada had to be handled quickly. Avoiding an international squabble over the incident he suggested it would all be over if Fernando was dead.

"I don't like the sound of that Colonel. The US Army does not kill its own people."

"I'm not suggesting that we kill her, Sir. But if we list Fernando as KIA and quietly drop her from the roster there would be no one to prosecute."

"Oh, now that's something I can go along with," the general said, and issued an official statement.

Special Agents Katrina Fernando and George Flynn died while battling terrorists in a foreign country. A grateful Nation thanks them for their sacrifice.

Two flag draped coffins were prepared for burial.

The Canadian official report echoed Devlyn's, leaving out any and all references to the Dectron Phoenix Project. The Dectron affair was sealed and forgotten.

MGen Wolfson spoke to the small gathering during Kat's burial ceremony in Arlington. "She was a soldier's soldier, courageous in the face of the enemy. A soldier who more than once risked her own life to save the lives of her comrades. She was committed to the defense of the United States of America and its people. She served with distinction and honor and made the ultimate sacrifice. She will be missed by all who knew and served with her. I salute her."

The Honor Guard fired the salute, the bugler played The Last Post and the flag was folded into a tight triangle for the presentation.

Deacon stood beside Charley as he was presented with the flag. Doug Leman and a few others were also there representing the family she never had.

Deacon was devastated by the loss of Kat and his lifelong friend Jasper. He had the Mulmur house torn down and rededicated himself to the Phoenix Project in solitude

Part 4

25

DISAVOWED

Tucson, Arizona

The general had written her off. He didn't care if she was dead or alive, he just wanted her gone. Kat didn't care about that either. She was devastated that Flynn had died and that she had lost Deacon forever.

Devlyn was treating it as a Witness Relocation, thinking that Tucson, Arizona was a good place to conceal a Mexican woman.

The Red Roof Inn just off Route 10 would do while he figured out how to set her up. It wasn't much, so he was certain that nobody would stumble on her there. Kat was in no condition to complain.

She was haunted and ashamed by what she had done to Gelenko. She swore she'd never do that again.

A week after the funeral Devlyn flew to Tucson to tell her about her future. It was dusk and he had thought he'd take her out for a burger or something. Nothing fancy, just some little joint where she wouldn't be noticed, a place where the charge on his expense account wouldn't be of interest to anyone.

He knocked and stood waiting impatiently for her to open door. She let him in without saying a word.

Hit by the stale air his first concern was for his comfort not hers. "Jesus, doesn't the air conditioning work in this place?" She just looked at him. "Okay, sit down, I want to talk to you."

339

She sat at the small round table by the window, he spun the other chair around and straddled it.

Leaning on the backrest he said, "Now listen, here's what I want you to do, fade out of the picture, don't make waves, disappear." He laid out his plan, she'd get a small house in town, he'd help her with the mortgage.

She'd choose a job, a waitress in a restaurant or salesperson in a shop somewhere. But the point was, she'd start living her low key, off the radar life as a civilian.

"No, that's not going to happen."

Devlyn sat back and asked, "Well then what the fuck are you going to do?"

"I'm going to find Petrus and kill him."

"Now look ..., do you get that you blew it up in Canada? No one at the agency wants to have any part of you now. Face up to it, Katrina, you're done."

She stood up and moved to the window, peeled back the curtain and looked out at the bland and unappealing view. Then turning around, she looked at him with dead eyes. "Does that include you, Paul? Do you want to be rid of me too?"

"Fuck Katrina ..., what's gotten into you? I mean, you really screwed the pooch when you killed that guy."

"Gelenko deserved everything I did to him."

"Katrina, come on, that was ..."

"He told me something before he died. I know how to get Petrus now and that's exactly what I'm going to do."

"Katrina, you can't do a fucking thing about it. You're off the team."

"I was never really on the team though, was I Paul? All that time I was your private test case."

"Don't flatter yourself."

"Really? You think I couldn't figure it out. Why was it that I only reported to you? Why was it that you gave me all my assignments? People talked, Paul."

"So why didn't you say something?"

"You fucking bastard. After all you've done to screw me over, all the times you threatened me when I told you I wanted out?"

Her voice became louder with each point. "You kept me from Harm, you fucking bastard! How dare you say that to me now?"

"Katrina ..."

Her voice went flat again, but it revealed the underlying threat she was sending. "Hey, no, I get it. I'm invisible now, no biggie, Paul, I grew up invisible. But that means you don't pull my strings anymore."

"Katrina ..."

"What?" she said quietly, but to him it was like a shout.

That single word signaled the end of the relationship as he knew it. The tables had turned.

The people around her saw her as a leader, they trusted her. A few people who opposed her eventually had the good sense to be afraid and yield.

Devlyn was not in that group, he missed all the signs. She wasn't what he'd thought she was at all. He wasn't the man he thought he was either and she just made him aware of that.

Devlyn was sitting in the cage with a predator, he'd pulled the tiger's tail. Now he realized that at any moment she could spin around and bite him and suddenly he was afraid.

"Okay Katrina I get it, you're pissed. I don't blame you." He was trying to find a way to retake control, but he was grasping at straws. "Look, alright if you want payback there may be a way, I can get you back into CI. On the downlow of course. I'll go back to Washington, talk it over with Wolfson and see what I can come up with. While I'm gone, I want you to stay put. Do you understand?"

She didn't reply. He waited expecting her to say something, but then he realized that wasn't going happen, so he got up and left her by the window.

NOT WHAT HE HAD IN MIND

La Paloma Resort, In the Arizona desert

After taking care of business in Washington Devlyn flew back to Tucson, During the flight he received a text message saying, "Janice has moved out of town." He was so pissed he thought he'd burst a blood vessel.

Just as he was about to start shouting obscenities he remembered where he was. Instead he sent a text back. 'Janice, where the hell are you now?'

Her reply was simple. 'La Paloma Resort.'

'Is it at least in Tucson?'

'Yup. Take a cab.' Her response was nothing like his reception at the Red Roof Motel which made him wonder what had changed. He landed in Tucson under the burning noonday sun and quickly hailed a cab. "La Paloma Resort," he said, and sat in the back fuming. It carried him away from Tucson, into the Catalina Foothills. As he neared the place, he began to get angrier, if that was possible. How was she paying for a place like this?

He walked into the cool pale-yellow cathedral-like lobby, rehearsing the tirade he was going to lay on her. It was hard to do in a place like that.

"May I help you, Sir?" asked the young woman at the desk.

"Janice Ferraro," he said, letting a hint of his anger spill out.

"Ms. Ferraro? Ah, of course, Sir ..., I'll call up and see if she is in. "Hello, Ms. Ferraro, this is Jamie at the front desk, how are you today?" She paused to listen. "Wonderful. Ah, Ms. Ferrero there's a gentleman here to see you." She paused. "I'll ask." She placed the receiver against her shoulder and asked, "May I have your name please, Sir?"

"Paul," he snapped. "Tell her it's Paul."

"He says his name is Paul. Would you like to meet him in the lobby?" she hinted diplomatically. "Oh ... uh huh okay, thank you." She hung up the phone and this time she tried to smile but it was unconvincing.

"Ms. Ferraro said you can go right up. She is staying in La Resort Suite. Take the elevator to the second floor."

As soon as Kat opened the door his jaw dropped to the floor. "Jezzus will you look at this place. It's bigger than my goddamn house!"

"I'm fine thanks, Paul. How nice of you to ask." He just stared at her. Where did she get those expensive clothes? "Well, are you coming in?"

"Have you got a drink in this mausoleum?" He brushed by her and went straight to one of the comfortable chairs and dropped himself into it. "New outfit too I see?"

"I found some really beautiful things downstairs," Kat said evenly. "Do you like this?" she asked, offering him a view from all sides. She looked absolutely beautiful but he didn't comment. "It's like that is it?"

"My drink?"

"Scotch, bourbon, or vodka?"

The last time he'd seen her he thought she was suicidal, but now she seemed like a different person. He wondered what had triggered this drastic change. "Bourbon, three fingers with lots of ice."

"Would you like a cherry with that?"

"No ..., I don't want a fucking cherry. Will ya just get the fucking bourbon and si'-down." He looked at the fireplace and the pictures on the wall. "You know they send people to the electric chair for credit card fraud in this state."

"I thought you might have remembered that Harm left me a little money. And nobody uses the chair anymore, Paul," she said. He grunted as she splashed the booze over ice "Why are you so angry?" she asked, handing him the glass.

"For one thing, I told you to stay put."

"I heard you." Ignoring his mood, she curled up on the couch. "I didn't want to stay put, so, shoot me. Oh wait, you can't because I'm already dead."

"It doesn't mean I can't shoot you."

"Well you could try I suppose." That gave him a chill. She looked out the sliding doors onto the patio.

"You keep looking out the window," he said, watching her over the top of his glass. "What do you see out there?"

"I see my future."

Kat was a good name for her, he thought, she's spotted an antelope and she wants to pounce. He almost laughed at his own joke. Everything about her was feline. "What's gotten into you Kat?"

"Paul, everything I've ever cared about has been taken away, everyone I ever loved is either dead or thinks I am. I'm starting over now. This is the new me."

"Don't kid yourself, this isn't you Kat, this is rich-bitch territory and you're as phony as a three-dollar bill."

"I am whatever I say I am," she replied calmly. "I have a new purpose now."

"Oh, shit," he thought aloud, then asked cautiously. "And that is ...?"

"I've already told you that. I'm going to put an end to Delph Petrus. Nothing else matters."

"I spoke to Wolfson and CI isn't going to let you kill him, so you can forget about that right now."

"I know where he is now."

"Who?"

"Karl Holbïn."

"Wait a second, Gelenko told you about him too? We looked everywhere for that guy."

"No, Vladimir told me about Petrus and Holbïn after the convention in San Diego. Gelenko told me that Holbïn's new name is Herbig. I'll find him, and he'll take me to Petrus."

"Fuck. Mogilevski has known where he was all this time?"

"Why does that surprise you? The point is, if Petrus wants a 'Ho', then I'm going to give him one?"

"Does Mogilevski have anything to do with this? Have you been talking to him?"

"No, not yet, but I'm going to. I'm going to ask him to help me."

"No! I forbid it."

"You can't forbid shit. Gelenko told me all I need to know."

"I'm not going to let you do this."

"You've got no say in it, Paul. I don't work for you anymore."

"You have no idea what you'd be heading into."

"No? My uncle was a monster, maybe not as bad as Petrus, but he taught me all about that dirty world. He used me like a scullery maid from the day I moved in with him. I was four!" She put her hands on her breasts. "I got these when I was thirteen, so he rented me out as a fuck doll to his pal, Sebastiano. He screwed me and passed me around to his disgusting friends until I was seventeen and ..."

She saw the shock on Devlyn's face, so she stopped talking. It all came back to her though, the pain, the fear and loathing she felt as a child, the need to make them pay, to make them suffer. It was like hot lava in her gut. Holy shit, I can't believe I just said that out loud.

"Katrina ..., my God, I had no idea."

"No? I thought you knew all about me. Anyway, my point is, Ernesto and Sebastiano were choirboys compared to Petrus. Anyone who uses women like disposable garbage should be put down."

He'd never thought about how frightening she could be, but now he was beginning to understand the light in her eyes that belied that look of calm. It was the look of a predator before the kill and she couldn't fake that. He drained his glass. "I told you that the Government isn't going to sanction an assassination."

"You forget. I don't work for the government anymore. And a dead woman can do things CI can't."

"Fuckin' hell," he said, and tried to get more bourbon from the empty glass. "I hope you've got a refill."

"Help yourself," she said, pointing to the tray on the wet bar.

He got up and went to the bar. "Look Kat ..., what I'm trying to say is, this idea of yours ..., it's crazy, I can't let you do it."

He remembered what she had with Harm and for the first time realized what he had taken from her. Feeling ashamed he asked, "What do you want to do?"

"All I have to do is present myself to Herbig and he'll do the rest."

"And you think he won't kill you?"

"Oh, I think he'll try." Kat began to lay out her plan, and Devlyn said, "That's just nuts. And believe me, Mogilevski will say you're nuts too."

"Perhaps, but I don't give a shit anymore. Will you help me?"

"Let me think about it, just don't do anything without telling me."

"I'll make no promises." She stared at the desert beyond her terrace. "Paul."

"What?"

"I am going to need help with this, help from a friend."

"Yeah, but how many of those do you have left?"

"Well, if I can count on you ... that'll make ... one."

BREAKFAST ON THE BALCONY

Kat's Suite

Devlyn was too drunk to leave so he spent the night in Kat's guest room and woke with a hangover. He went looking for her and found her on the terrace. He joined her while she ate her eggs over easy, bacon, toast, and fruit salad. All he could stomach was Tylenol, orange juice, and coffee.

She tried to get a conversation going but his hangover left him with little to say.

She filled the void with the pointless details of a trail ride she took while he lay passed out in bed.

"Okay, stop it alright? I'm sorry I got drunk. It won't happen again, but for Christ's sake please ..., just stop talking."

"Not a problem."

She left him with a pad of paper as she heading for the door. "Hey, what am I supposed to do with this?"

"You're the strategist, figure out how I'm going to get the buggers to notice me."

"Christ, all you have to do is show up."

"I expect something a little more provocative than that. Get busy. While you're doing that, I'm going down to play tennis with the pro."

"Since when do you play tennis."

She smiled sweetly and left.

Devlyn began to doodle aimlessly on the pad as he thought about her. He thought he knew her better than anyone.

348

He'd been under the impression that he'd created her. Now he realized that all he did was set a wild thing free.

That sparked an idea.

He started to think about an abused woman. As he began to write it down, he set the stage based on some of the small truths about her, her first language, her father's accidental death, her uncle's abuse, and her homelessness.

Those things that should have destroyed her just made her stronger.

With some tweaking to hide her deadly skills he developed a character who would fit the profile of the perfect victim.

His new character would have to have mobility which would take money. Apparently, Kat already had that covered.

With the right staging this character could gain the instant and meaningless celebrity, something that a Petrus type could find irresistible.

The meaningless flash in the pan celebrity was the important detail. All he needed to do was invent something that would create a ridiculous 'fifteen minutes of fame.'

Devlyn started writing down a series of sexually provocative events, starting off with something trivial which he could spin into something with a big finish.

He was reading it over when Kat returned. "So, feeling better, I hope."

"As a matter of fact, I am," he said. "I've got the basic plan now. I'm just working out the details."

"What have you come up with?" she said, shaking her shirt to cool off.

He tried not to watch but failed. "Okay, listen to this." Referring to his notes he began, "Here it is. Since you have all of that money ..."

"You know how much it is now, do you?"

"I have no idea, but I'm guessing it's gotta be a million or so." She smiled, he hasn't a clue. Anyway, it's going to be a titillating story the European media wouldn't be able to resist. The Who, would be you, the sexy woman and a middle-aged millionaire."

"I'm guessing that would be you."

"Of course."

'The What, everybody loves a human tragedy, right?"

And what would that be?"

"My untimely death."

"Oh, I'm beginning to like this," Kat said, gulping down some ice-cold water.

"Shut up. And you, the wrongly accused. The Where, is some exotic location, I don't know where right now, but it'll come to me. The How, is tragic misadventure following some heavy-duty sex."

"Dream on."

"It's imperative," he said, with conviction and hope.

"Fine, then it'll be implied just like your death. I am assuming that your death will be implied," she said, and smiled sweetly.

He exhaled in frustration. "Very funny, okay so it's implied sex, and booze. Okay so far?" She nodded. "The When, of course, is right after we get married."

"Are you writing this for the National Enquirer?"

"I'm being serious here, and, yeah, that's the goal, trashy news for trashy newspapers. You'll be the kind of woman that grabs the attention of people for about a week and then they'll forget all about you as soon as the next sensation comes along."

"Oh, gee, thanks a lot. What am I now, a hooker?"

"Not exactly," he said, hedging slightly.

"What does 'not exactly' mean, precisely?" Kat asked, using air quotes.

"You said it yourself, he wants a whore so you're a part time working girl."

"As long as it's just part of the background. I'm not having sex with you or anyone else, Paul."

"I didn't say you had to go out and sell it. You just have to give everyone the impression that you do. You're practically every guy's wet dream."

She was about to protest but he put up his hands. "Let's be frank here, you're extremely beautiful, incredibly sexy and you can look downright dangerous. The papers will eat you up!"

"Well as flattering as all those adjectives are, Paul, I think I'll try to find some other ..."

"Let me stop you right there. I've given this a lot of thought."

"Obviously, but ..."

"Let me finish. Your cover story is Anita Vargas, a former street kid from Valencia, that's in Spain."

"I know where Valencia is."

"Your parents died when you were fourteen. You survived by begging and picking pockets."

"So. I'm a gypsy now?"

"You can pick a pocket, can't you?"

"Oh, shut up."

"Spain is full of that, right? Then, when you developed your ..." he paused.

"My what?" she challenged.

"Jesus, I'm just giving back what you told me the other day. Look at yourself, will you? Are you trying to tell me you're not trying to look like that? I can see your nipples through that top for Christsake. Come on now. You had something to sell; so occasionally you turned tricks."

"There it is! That's why you sent me to get the dyke out of Russia. You think I'm a hooker."

"That's not true. Listen, do you want to get this guy?"

"Of course, I do, but ..."

"I'm going to give it to you straight, this mission you're dying to go on, it's a one-way street. You're going to die, so what do you care if people think you put out for cash?"

"Oh." She sat down feeling very uncomfortable. What he was proposing was ridiculous, embarrassing and depressing all at once, but he wasn't wrong.

"You're hot and intelligent and you need money. Along comes some rich sucker; a modern-day King Pygmalion, and he transforms you into a Galatea."

"Who the hell are they?"

"Do you know My Fair Lady?"

"My Fair Lady? Yeah, sort of, An English asshole latches onto some poor street kid and makes her say that rain in Spain crap. But what has that got to do with Pig-what's-its?"

"You haven't read any Greek mythology, have you?"

"No."

"Come on, the Iliad and the Odyssey maybe?"

"Oh, the Iliad and the Odyssey? Oh sure, when I was a kid my uncle used to read it to me before he tucked me into bed ..., in the original Greek."

"I'll take that as a no. Okay, well ..., long story short, the king of Cyprus, Pygmalion, had a dim view of the women of his kingdom. He thought they were all whores and he wouldn't marry any of them. He carved an ivory statue of a virtuous woman and fell in love with it. The statue was the most beautiful woman in the world."

"He must have been a very talented sculptor. But you're not making me even remotely virtuous, are you?"

"No, and it's just a story, Kat. Well, anyway he fell in love with it because it was perfection. He was so obsessed with it that eventually he wished it was real."

"Oh, goodie, a female Pinocchio."

"Shut up will ya? Aphrodite was listening. You know about her?"

"Uh huh, the goddess of love."

"Right and beauty, sexuality, and hunting. Sound familiar?"

"We couldn't forget about sexuality, could we?"

"Not in this story. Anyway, she heard his wish and changed the statue into a real woman named Galatea."

"Does it have a happy ending? I mean does her nose grow when she gets horny?"

"This was true love, they get married, have kids, the whole nine yards."

"But that's not how our story is going to end, is it?"

"No, you have a history of using wealthy men, like me."

"Yeah, just like you."

Ignoring her barb, he continued, "You learn their languages, you make them love you and you take their money."

"Wonderful! So, I'm an extortionist, hooker, con artist. That's my back story?"

"Yeah, you do what you've gotta do to survive."

"Oh fabulous, you're a peach. The whole thing is just peachy. Who are you in all of this?"

"I'm a Spaniard, Paulino Ricardo Esteves Franco. I've been away, living in ..., Venezuela let's say."

"So okay, how do you fall into my trap?"

"I come home to Spain, to Valencia, and I meet you. I've got to have you, so I propose."

"How romantic, and I accept of course."

"Yeah, you jump at the chance to marry someone like me."

"Because you're so gorgeous."

"And rich. I'll strut like a peacock playing it up so that the media gets interested and takes it from there."

"So far it's a fairy tale. Where does the tragedy come in?" He realized that she had her own tragedies that would bring on the tears he was looking for. But he had no idea who she really was and until now, he hadn't cared enough to find out. He had discounted the effect Harm had on her because it inconvenienced him. She had proven beyond a doubt that she had no trouble with killing people. She was a soldier, soldiers bitch and whine but in the end, they would get the job done. That's all she was to him and he had dismissed the idea that a woman like her could experience love.

But he couldn't explain the cause of that horrible grief that wouldn't let go. That was because he had been interfering with her life for years yet and never took the time to appreciate what he had put her through.

She grieved for the one person whose existence had given her a reason to live, to survive. He thought he was beginning to understand that now, but he never considered the possibility that she might have had feelings for Deacon Loats.

There's nothing Devlyn could possibly dream up that could compare to the loss of Harm. He said this was a suicide mission. Well I don't care anymore; death would be a merciful release.

"Right after the wedding, I go fishing ... or no, scuba diving ..."

"Yeah, diving for sure, then you go down and never come up."

"Exactly. Okay, so after I disappear the police think you killed me."

"Oh, now that's perfect. I'm an extortionist, hooker, con artist and now a murderer. It just gets better and better. They're going to throw my ass in jail and toss away the key! That's wonderful. Just curious, do I kill you?"

"No, no. It'll be an accident. There'll be no doubt that it was all my fault. I'll make a show of going out alone while you are with friends, so you're totally in the clear."

"Where am I going to get the friends?"

"Don't worry about it, you'll have lots of people hanging around you."

"What kind of people?"

"Don't get caught up in the minutia now, we'll find people, okay?"

"Fine, but have you noticed that when it comes to sex, you've got all kinds of details."

"Okay, everybody loves rich people. We invite some strangers to our wedding."

"Where will that be?"

"I was getting to that. We'll need a boat."

"A boat? What kind of a boat?"

"A cabin cruiser."

"You're talking about a yacht. You want me to rent a yacht."

"Yeah, I'll go out in the yacht and disappear while you're ashore with your new friends."

"Aw, couldn't I give you a push?"

She thought about his plan, and it sounded like it would work.

He was right, if I'm going to die then it doesn't it matter what people think of me.

26

SHOW TIME

Heading to Spain

Eventually Kat warmed up to Devlyn's plan. By the end of lunch, they sat down together inside to work out the details. Valencia's beach area was perfect for the meet and it was just a ferry ride to Ibiza.

Kat rented a yacht for the wedding to make their little soap opera work. Ibiza was very popular so finding the supporting cast wouldn't be difficult. While Kat did her research, Devlyn returned to Maryland and quietly created the paper trail. Agents who were loyal to Devlyn electronically planted the documents in government files. Another agent in Barcelona was able to plant the back story in the papers' archives.

She found a fully furnished apartment to rent on the beach and a Justice of the Peace in St Antoni de Portmany, Ibiza to marry them. Then, acting as Paulino Franco's secretary, she phoned and engaged His Worship Ferdinand de Gordano to perform the civil ceremony.

She also called the yacht brokerage and rented the biggest boat they had for the wedding. She was given a seventy-five-footer called Amigo de Mar, which came with a captain and cook. It was all set up.

Kat stayed in her suite for two more days and when Devlyn to return from Maryland with her passport she flew to Valencia. The apartment was better than she'd expected, and it was right on the Malva-Rosa beach, a perfect address for a fun-loving gold digger. She'd already paid three months in advance through a bank transfer.

It took two weeks of strolling on the beach and sitting in the bars to establish her credentials and draw enough attention to herself that people began to think of her as a local.

In her big hat, small bikini, and flimsy cover-up she became an instant favorite with the boys of all ages.

She didn't do anything particularly provocative; she was just enormously friendly with everyone. Men hit on her constantly, bought her drinks, made propositions. But they were all sardines and she made it clear that she was after a whale. Almost everyone recognized her, knew her name and shared stories about fabulous Anita Vargas.

THE WHALE

Valencia, Spain

When Devlyn arrived from Caracas he took a suite at Las Arenas Balneario Resort just down the beach from Kat's apartment. He made sure that everyone knew he was originally from Malaga. Those who enjoyed the show quickly identified Paulino as an eligible whale and made sure Anita knew he was there.

With some help from a bartender, she set her trap at a table near the bar and her mark walked right into it. Devlyn's bushy moustache surprised her, she thought it looked ridiculous, but she didn't say anything.

Much to the delight of a small, but appreciative audience, she somehow managed to involve her entire body when she smiled at him. Landing him took no time at all. Everyone thought he was the luckiest man to walk into the place. They watched and took pictures as if it was a sporting event, as she reeled him in.

After only four days of walks on the beach and evenings in the clubs he took her out by the pool and very publicly proposed. There were gasps and cheers when she accepted. Lots of pictures were snapped with hotel guests and staff to document practically everything they did.

Anita made a bit of a show when she went to Paulino's suite and people talked just like Devlyn thought they would. "As Shakespeare said, the play is the thing and all the world is a stage."

But much to Paulino's continued disappointment, the play went into intermission the moment the door shut.

The day before leaving for Ibiza, an article appeared on page two of the Castellón Diario.

The headline read, Valencia Beach Beauty Weds Malaga Millionaire.

The story ran with five, large, very colorful, and revealing photos of Anita and a small blurry shot of Paulino.

THEIR WEDDING

Ibiza, Spain

The day they left for Ibiza, Kat was stunned by the crowd of curious well-wishers who came to see them off. Among them were a few reporters and paparazzi who showed up to record the event and follow them onto the ferry.

With waves and kisses blown for the cameras they boarded the Valencia - St Antoni de Portmany ferry.

A cab took them from the ferry to the marina at Aes Nãutic with a couple of paparazzi on motor scooters following. Word spread through the harbor and several people from other boats gathered to see them as they arrived. Fellow yachtsmen followed them into the marina office and they had a spontaneous celebration with sparkling wine. The paparazzi ate it up. More hugs and pictures.

"I told you we'd find some friends for you," Paulino said.

"I had no idea it would be like this," Anita said.

As the play continued, the script called for a separation.

Anita said, "Darling, I'm tired, I want to go to the yacht now."

Paulino just shrugged, "Fine, you go and I'll finish up here. You, boy, see that she gets to the Amigo de Mar."

The eager employee walked down the dock with her, but when Anita spotted the yacht's captain, she had an idea that would certainly boost the drama. She ditched the dock boy and prepared a surprise for her dear Paulino.

The captain, a tall pleasant looking Englishman in a white uniform, deck shoes and cap, was standing on the poop deck beside the gangway. She waved to him from the dock and he greeted her with a polite salute.

"Welcome aboard the Amigo de Mar, Señorina Vargas. Where is the lucky man?" he asked, mimicking an upper-class English accent.

Apart from saying Señorina, he made no attempt to speak to her in Spanish, which pissed her off.

"Oh, don't worry about him," she said with a strong Spanish accent. "He's taking care of business." As she stroked his epaulette with her finger she asked, "What is your name, my handsome Capitan?"

"Eden Phillips, Señorina," he said, letting his professional detachment slip just a little.

"Oh my, how very English you are." Then, tracing a lazy S on his chest she asked, "Do you handle this beautiful big boat all by your lonesome?"

"Ah," he cleared his throat. "There is a cook in the galley who helps with the lines when we get underway."

"Oh my ... that sounds so impressive. Will you give me the full tour?" she asked, reaching for his hand.

"Er ..., certainly," he said, surprised and slightly aroused. He was imagining that this was going to be one of those dream cruises.

"Would you care to meet the cook?" he asked.

"Tempting, but not now, I think. Perhaps you can show me to my stateroom, I'd like to slip on my bikini."

"It would be my great pleasure, Señorina."

"How sweet you are." Pointing to her suitcases she said, "I would be very grateful if you would carry my bags for me," she cooed with a come-hither smile, and saw Paulino on the dock walking toward them. As he picked up the suitcases she purred, "Such a strong man you are, Capitan."

Her timing couldn't have been better because, right on cue, Paulino appeared on the gangway. "Never mind that, Captain. I think I can handle those for my fiancé."

"My goodness, there you are Paulino. What kept you? I was just saying hello to this nice ..."

"Yes, well I'm sure the Captain has more important things to take care of just now, Anita," he said. His jealousy was very convincing, so the captain beat a hasty retreat to the wheelhouse, while Kat hurried below laughing.

As soon as they were in the security of the master cabin, Devlyn snapped, "What the fuck were you doing up there, Katrina?"

"My name ..., is Anita. And if your plan is going to work, we can't have any crew on board to get in the way, now can we? Go tell them in the office that the captain came on to me and you want both of them off the boat."

"Wow, I had no idea you could be so devious."

"Whatever it takes, remember? Now get out, I want to change."

"Hey, who's in charge here?"

"If you must ask, Paulino dearest, then it isn't you, is it? Now go up there and deal with him."

As he stormed off to fire the crew she changed into a small, but tasteful, white bikini, then went out onto the bow deck with a beach towel and stretched out provocatively in the sun.

Both the captain and cook left the yacht spitting mad. The agent apologized and said he would try to find another crew, but it would take time.

Paulino said, "You can forget about it, I don't need a crew."

"But it is company policy. The boat cannot leave the dock without a crew."

"Who said anything about leaving the dock?" Devlyn said.

The story circulated through the yacht harbor like a virus. Anita was going to cause her future-husband serious trouble.

It was perfect.

That night Anita and Paulino had dinner on shore where they were spotted by several tourists and locals. The untimely exit of the captain and cook filled the papers and made Anita and Paulino the hot topic in the yacht club bar.

They met Roselyn and Johnathon at the bar, a young English honeymoon couple who arrived earlier on a sailboat. It was moored at a slip nearby. Anita liked them immediately and asked them to be a part of the wedding party.

The four of them talked past two, then staggered back to their yachts drunk. Anita and Paulino put on a good show, but they were sober and slept in separate cabins.

A SPLASHY CEREMONY

Aboard the yacht, Ibiza

As arranged, the justice of the Peace arrived at 11:00 am.

Roselyn and Johnathon arrived with bright smiles and flowers and were rewarded with champagne and caviar when they boarded.

Standing with the Justice of the Peace by the wheel of the flying bridge, Paulino was wearing white shorts and an open shirt that showed off several gold chains he'd recently acquired. The JP turned on a recording of the Pachelbel's Canon in D minor to begin the ceremony cuing Anita's dramatic appearance on the stairs. She wore a simple white satin dress, a double strand of pearls and high heel sandals. They all said she looked like a Vogue model.

Paparazzi had filled the dock and were constantly snapping pictures of the beautiful gold digger and the hapless millionaire. Their stories would be filled with salacious details and revealing photos.

The whole affair just screamed big payoffs for them. The honeymoon couple took lots of pictures too. After the ceremony, they talked and laughed and mugged for the cameras while drinking champagne with the JP.

The caterers produced a lovely lunch of langoustine/calamari salad with cheese and figs for dessert and they all sat down to enjoy it. Roselyn monopolized Anita with talk about shopping in town.

(Kat had never had the opportunity to talk with another woman like that before.) When they finished, they convinced

Johnathon to go into town with them, but Paulino wouldn't leave the yacht.

"Paulino sweetheart, you must come with us," Anita pleaded, clasping her hands together.

"No, you young-people go on ahead. I heard about the perfect spot for scuba diving, I think I'll check it out."

"Alright, but you be careful. You know you are not supposed to dive alone."

When they were gone, he powered up the engines, hoisted the anchor, and asked a couple of neighboring yachtsmen to help him cast off. They made perfect witnesses that he was all alone. Paulino piloted the yacht out of the slip and went out through the breakwater.

By the time the man in the office noticed what was happening it was too late to stop him. He sailed out into the open sea and that was the last anyone ever saw of him.

Shopping took most of the afternoon and when they returned to the marina the slip was still empty. Anita began to panic and tried to reach him on his cell phone. When he didn't answer, Johnathon tried to reach him on the ship to shore. When that failed, Anita insisted that the authorities conduct a search.

Johnathon stood by her as she was interviewed by the police. "Why did he take the yacht out by himself?" the policeman asked.

Anita looked perplexed and frightened. "I don't know. He never mentioned that he wanted to do that. To be honest Señor we have only known each other for a few weeks. I was just beginning to get to know him."

"When we find him, he will be charged with theft, you understand that Señora?"

"I suppose so, I guess. I don't even know if he has ever driven a boat like that before. I'm afraid he will get lost. Señor please, I just want him back safely."

The Coast Guard was already looking for him. The yacht charter people were going to charge him with piracy.

Devlyn wasted no time getting away. Ignoring the anchor, he shaved off the moustache as he studied the chart of Ibiza, searching for a place to go ashore. He added weights to the diving gear and sent it over the side. He emptied a scotch bottle, put it beside a glass tumbler, then left his clothes in a pile on the back deck. He let the boat drift towards a small bay north of Santa Agnès de Corona. He lowered the yacht's outboard and ran it up to the rocks, jumped ashore and pushed it off to drift in the current.

Having discarded everything related to Paulino Franco, he walked back to town and waited for the ferry to Valencia. He had his return ticket to Washington and left Spain without being noticed.

The Coast Guard located the Amigo de Mar but before they arrived a local fisherman boarded the yacht and claimed right of salvage. The Coast Guard chased him off, "It looks like he went in the water drunk. The current or a shark must have taken him away," said the ship's captain.

A tragic story like that one was impossible to ignore. It was front page in the Diario de Ibiza with a photo of Paulino and Anita right after the wedding.

Inside there were more pictures. The yacht broker supplied a photo of the boat, but they were mostly candid shots of Anita in a bikini.

It gained momentum when mainland papers picked up the story later that day. Just as Devlyn had predicted, a rumor started suggesting that Anita had murdered him for his money. The Black Widow story became a sensation and drew in readers all over Spain.

Anita was hounded by reporters and critics and fled to a hotel to hide.

She had to stay on Ibiza until it was established that Paulino Franco's disappearance was death by misadventure.

The new headline shouted *ANITA ES INOCENTE,* (Anita Is Innocent) as if it really mattered to people. She was amazed that people were so passionate about it. Retractions began appearing everywhere, and, after a brief funeral service which ended with her throwing a wreath into the sea, she was free to leave the island.

By the time Anita boarded the ferry to Valencia, the story had truly gone viral. The press was waiting for her when the ferry docked.

She walked off the ship in a bright yellow dress and a shy smile.

When they saw the yellow dress, they created a new title for her. Now she was Anita Franco, La Feliz viuda de Ibiza, (The Happy Widow of Ibiza).

JETTING OFF TO MADRID

Madrid, Spain

Paparazzi were hounding her, making it impossible to stay in Valencia. She had planned to deal with the apartment and let things simmer for a couple of days, but she had to move up her schedule.

She decided to decompress in Madrid for a while. A chartered jet whisked her to the capital and she arranged to have it on standby for the next five days. It would cost a fortune, a detail no paper would miss mentioning in the ongoing saga of Anita Franco, the Happy Widow of Ibiza.

She thought that would give her enough time to establish a pattern of behavior before she met with Vlad in Russia. Things would begin to move very quickly after that. Hopefully, Vlad would arrange for some backup for her in Berlin, but she was uncertain about that. Regardless of what happened there, she would head to Berlin and set her trap.

During the flight to Madrid she booked a suite at a trendy boutique hotel called, Only You. It was easy to do it all over the phone, because now almost everyone in Spain had heard her name. As ridiculous as she imagined it would be, people by the thousands seemed to care about what she did.

She called her friend in Moscow. "Vlad, I am in play now."

"I know. I have been reading all about you. You are quite a sensation. Any problems?"

"No, it seems to be going as planned. I'm on my way to Madrid now."

"I have heard you rented a jet."

"Oh god, really? This is totally ridiculous."

"It is the way of the world Katrina. When can I expect to see you?"

"You must call me Anita, Vlad."

Of course, I apologize for my mistake."

"I'll make a spectacle of myself there for two or three days and then I'll fly to Moscow."

"I'll be waiting."

Everything she did seemed to spark interest with the media. Paparazzi followed her from her hotel as she went shopping and clubbing. She spent a small fortune in expensive shops, visited an exclusive spa, and had her hair done in a very trendy and unbelievably expensive salon. Wealth made everything so easy.

Shopping made Kat feel like everything was alright and she became aware that it was like a narcotic that she could easily become addicted to. That was, if she lived long enough.

While all this freewheeling was going on, Anita began to feel like a prisoner, constantly surrounded by an insatiable crowd. The relentless clicking of cameras, the pawing and lewd remarks began to sting. She was experiencing a warped reality she'd never known existed before.

As she embraced the alter ego of Anita Vargas Franco she thought about the celebrities who were going through this every day.

Even though most of them brought it on themselves as she had, she sympathized. Someone was always watching. She was walking a high wire without a net and if she slipped up ... just once ... she was dead.

A ONE NIGHT STAND

Club Vila, Madrid

Being on the prowl with people watching made life more exciting. Everything she did brought her closer to her goal.

368

The plan demanded that she go out and be seen, constantly on show and looking into the lens. It was exhausting, and she needed a new distraction.

On her third night, she went to one of the hottest clubs in the city. Her limousine stopped at the curb in front of the club. Behind a thick velvet rope stood a huge black man holding back the unwashed masses.

He spotted her immediately and rushed forward to open her door and escorted her beyond the barrier. People stared, those people who would never be going inside.

They knew who she was too and whistled, cheered, jeered and shouted her name.

Anita pretended not to notice them as she glided by.

The music seemed loud outside but inside it was deafening, and the room shook with a frenetic energy that made her dizzy. It was full of Madrileños (the young elite of Madrid) who drank and laughed, danced and groped each other.

It was as if they were having sex right there on the crowded dance floor. Perhaps they were.

She paused for a moment simply trying to acclimatize. Then she noticed an elevated area where the people seemed to able to talk to one another without shouting.

She headed in that direction, bumping into the velvet rope. A man with bulging muscles and a spray on T-shirt with 'Security', written across his chest smiled and opened the way for her. As soon as she stepped up, she was rewarded with a significantly lower decibel level.

A pretty young blond in a tight dress approached and offered her a glass of champagne from her tray. Anita accepted with a smile.

Before her first sip a tall handsome man approached her and clinked his glass against hers. He stared into her eyes as he lifted the glass to his lips.

"Salut," she said.

"Hola," he replied. "Interesting."

"Oh, what is interesting?"

"That you would use a French greeting."

"It is just a greeting like any other."

"Perhaps, but the French have not been popular in Spain since Napoleon's last visit. But I don't need to tell you that do I? No, I would like to think that it had a much deeper meaning."

"Really?! And what meaning might that be, Signor Alvarez?"

"Ah, then you know me."

"What woman in Spain does not?" she said. She had seen him in an action movie on television while she was waiting for Devlyn to arrive. Alverez was very handsome, extremely sexy, and a surprisingly good actor.

"And what man in Spain today would not recognize the lovely Señora Anita Vargas Franco? I've been watching you from the moment you came in."

"I am more than a little embarrassed by such notoriety, Señor."

"Fame is not always something we choose. I am sorry that yours has come at such a cost."

"Thank you," she said, with genuine surprise. "That was a very sensitive thing to say after some of the comments in the tabloids. They are calling me the Happy Widow of Ibiza. It makes me sound so wicked."

"Being a little wicked is not always such a bad thing, is it?" he replied, with a raised eyebrow and a crooked smile.

"I suppose," she said, allowing the corners of her mouth to curl up slightly.

"Will you join me at my table?" And without waiting for a reply he took her by the hand and led her to an oasis within an oasis.

"I have been reading about your tragedy and I am truly sorry. It is a terrible thing to lose your love like that."

"Thank you. Something confuses me, Señor Alvarez. Do you know why they call me that, the Happy Widow?"

"You do not know? That is another thing that surprises me. It is because of your yellow dress. Spanish widows always wear black."

"Of course, but I don't like being dictated to by tradition."

"Brava." He took her glass from her and set it down on the table. "I would be honored if you would dance with me."

"Would you?" she asked, raising an eyebrow. She looked out on the dance floor and what they were doing out there was not really dancing.

"Oh yes," he said, turning on his most charming expression, "I certainly would. And call me Antonio."

"Alright, Antonio." They made their way to the dance floor and as the thumping bass cut out nearly all communication, she leaned toward his ear and said, "If I had any friends, they would call me Anita."

"You must permit me to be a friend," he shouted back. He was a very interesting, attentive and inventive dancer. Just as she began to enjoy his touch, she noticed people staring.

"I feel very vulnerable out here."

It was after three when the actor suggested he take her home. That made Kat think of an ancient phrase, the one that gladiators would recite as they stood in the circus facing Caesar. Her version would be, 'Those who are about to die should first make love with a handsome movie star.' "Care to join me in my room?"

A nightmare woke her, but by the time she was sitting up she couldn't remember it at all. A small mercy. She looked at the clock as the red digits changed to 2:35 pm. "Shit," she said, reaching for the phone she pressed 0.

"Hola, buenos días Señora Franco."

"Buenos, would you get my bill ready for me please? I'll be right down to check out. Oh, and could you call a cab for me please." She made another call to get the plane ready.

27

FLIGHT TO RUSSIA

Muromtzevo Mansion

Her business jet was sitting with the engines running just waiting for her to board, and within a few minutes they were wheels up and heading for Moscow. As soon as they were in the air, she called Vlad to say she was on her way. He said there would be a driver at the airport to meet her.

The rest of the flight was as somber as a funeral procession because all she could think about was the upcoming execution. It was Petrus' head on the block, but would she lose hers in the process?

She'd gained two hours when she landed at Domodedovo International Airport. Vlad's driver stood by the exit, holding a sign in Cyrillic script, Anita Franco, written crudely with a black marker.

She went to him and handed him her bags. No words were said as he led her out to the car and she was thankful not to have to deal with small talk.

They headed north on a superhighway to the outskirts of Moscow. She stared without seeing as they passed vast stretches of drab apartment buildings that circled the city.

The car sped along the Gorkovskoye Highway reaching out through farmland, small towns, and forests heading to Sudogda

He turned off the highway bearing south toward Muromtzevo a tiny village which had grown up into a small town surrounding the castle, Vladimir's country home.

The flight to Moscow and the long silent drive in the back of the limousine left her with too much time to think. That night with Antonio had carried her away from reality. Surrounded by his warmth it was so easy to forget who, or, more precisely, what she had become. But it was impossible to forget that she had become an assassin.

By the time the car reached the stand of trees that encircled Vlad's castle Anita was deeply depressed. It was as if all the color had been drained leaving nothing but shades of grey. And what lay at the end of driveway only made things more surreal. Vlad's home was a French style fairy-tale castle; but she was light-years away from a happy ending.

His castle had a tenuous grasp on its past grandeur clinging to the center of the considerably reduced estate.

Somehow, it had survived the desolation of the Bolshevik Uprising relatively intact.

The driver must have called ahead because Vlad was outside waiting for her, flanked by armed guards. As the car came to rest, he opened her door to welcome her.

"My dear Anita," he said, with a wink, "I must tell you that I was deeply saddened to hear of Ms. Fernando's death." His smile was infectious, so she smiled allowing her mood to lighten a little. "But here you are, looking remarkable well. How are you feeling?"

"All I can say for sure is that I'm alive, Vlad."

"My dear, you are so much more than that."

"Thank you," she said, "and you, how have you been?"

"I am in perfect health, thank you. You know, I had thought that I would never see your lovely face again. And yet here you are, more beautiful than ever."

"I promised I would come," she said, ignoring his flattery.

"And for that I am grateful. Now that we are far away from the prying eyes of the press, may I be permitted to call you Katrina?"

"I'd like that."

"You must be tired, no?"

"Not at all, I'd like to get started right away if that's alright with you."

"Certainly, anything you want." The driver placed her luggage beside her and she began to reach for it. "Don't worry about that. You are now a woman of great wealth, you must learn to enjoy it," he said, taking her by the arm.

"Lev will see to that. Come in." She took his arm and he led her in through the grand entrance, and pointing to the left said, "We can talk through there."

It was a large sitting room filled with antique Russian treasures. "This is quite the house, Vladimir."

"It is, isn't it? It's famous also. It's called the Muromtzevo Mansion." He looked about him admiring the work that had been done. "I have spent several years and many rubles renovating it. There is an interesting story behind it. Perhaps you would like to hear it."

"Yes, I'd love to. But another time perhaps."

"Of course, this is not the time for stories." He'd spent all morning rehearsing the tale and was disappointed, but he understood and moved on. "Now, tell me, what you are planning?"

She sat down in the antique chair next to his and began. "Officially, there is no doubt now that Petrus is behind this business, but the authorities are afraid to go after him."

"It is just as I said. He has built up such a large base of supporters now who believe every lie he utters. President Putin would never allow him to be touched."

"I intend to do more than just touch him I'm going to kill him at his estate."

"That is ridiculous, you would never get past the gate alive."

"I agree that there is an excellent chance that I won't survive, but my plan will get me close enough to kill him."

"I don't like this, Katrina, I will tell you that right now. But you asked for backup, what do you have in mind?"

"I assume that he is well protected."

"A sizable security force, yes."

375

"Vlad, forgive me for being so forward, but Gen. Hershoff told me that you also have a small army."

"My old friend is too boastful. It is but a modest compliment."

"Russian Special Forces I was told." Vlad cocked an eyebrow to go with his lopsided smile. She took that as a yes and continued. "You told me once that you had not gone after him because Putin would retaliate."

"Nothing has changed."

"If a lone assassin were to take him out, President Putin would have no one to go after, would he?"

"He would go after the assassin and her family, my dear."

"But what if her family was already dead?"

"Do you think you cannot die twice?" he asked, with the tone fathers save for their daughters.

"I'm a cat, Vlad, I may have a few more lives left," she lied.

"But if I help you it would be like assisting you in suicide, Katrina. I have no desire to allow him to butcher you."

"What if a platoon of Russian Special Forces were to enter the estate before me? They would think that Putin had abandoned him. Perhaps they would simply surrender without a fight, leaving the field open for me. Then I would have a better chance of getting to him and possibly getting away as well."

"Ah hah, yes, it an ingenious idea, but they will probably put up a fight. I will admit that my force would best his, but not without losses."

"True." She lowered her eyes and concentrated on the rings on her finger, the rings Harm had given her, the same rings that Devlyn had used at the fake wedding.

"I can see that you grieve your husband still. It was a great loss to be sure Katrina, but you have a chance for long life, another man to love, children ..."

"Please Vlad, don't make this more difficult that it is already." This was a terrible thing to ask but she had to make Petrus pay. "The loss of even one of your men is something I would like to avoid. I have no wish for them to sacrifice their lives for me. But if Petrus is allowed to continue, how many more innocent people will die? He must be eliminated, even if I have to die in the process."

"Spoken like a hero. I have no doubt of your bravery, my young friend, but isn't there another way to deal with this problem?"

"Have you found one?" she asked. He shrugged and shook his head. "No Vlad, there isn't."

"Yes, I see." He fell silent while he thought about his response and Kat waited patiently. At last he said, "He tried to have me killed. You stopped that from happening so I made you a promise. I will do whatever I can to help you."

"Thank you, Vlad."

"I'm not convinced that there is anything to be thankful for, Katrina, but you are right, Petrus thinks he is a lion. In truth, he is a perverted parasite and if he can be eliminated then the world will be a better place. Let me think." He got up from his chair and walked to the window.

Kat watched him stare into the distance for a long time.

She wondered what he saw out there that gave him inspiration, because something obviously had. He returned to the chair with a plan. "I will help you, but you must appear to be working on your own."

"Thank you."

"You are welcome. Petrus has been a thorn in my side for a long time. You have brought an opportunity to my door to make this right. I said you should appear to be on your own. I will see to it that you have all the protection you need. You just won't be able to see them. At least, that is my hope. I will use your idea for the raid. If it causes Putin some difficulty, then that is a bonus."

"Thank you again."

She began to tell him what she had in mind.

"A word of caution about your first target, appearances can be deceiving. Herbig is not so old and frail as he looks. Take you for example. On the surface you are simply a beautiful woman."

"I don't need flattery."

"Nonetheless, it's true, a very beautiful woman and men often don't see beyond that. You are an intelligent woman so I am sure that you are keenly aware of this. You use your beauty like the tiger uses her stripes. Those stripes hide the predator by distracting the prey."

"My partner Flynn used to call me a tiger."

"I remember Flynn and I am sorry that he is gone."

"Me too. Is that how you see me, as a tiger?"

"Oh, yes my dear, you are an apex predator with very sharp claws. The moment I saw you in action I knew. You are an extraordinarily dangerous woman, Katrina. I would hate to cross you and suspect that I am one of the lucky few who have seen that side of you and lived." As if to add weight to his comment, Vlad filled his glass and tossed it back. "Returning to Herbig for a moment. How do you think you will approach him?"

"I agree that if I present myself to him it could end there, but Devlyn's plan was to make Petrus ask for me. That would force Herbig to follow through with the delivery."

"It is an interesting idea to have the tiger play the part of the tethered goat."

"That's funny, you've compared me to a tiger and a goat. Devlyn said I was Pygmalion's ivory woman and a Trojan horse."

"The ivory statue analogy is interesting, and the Trojan Horse is apt. Is the man a Greek?"

"No, he's just in love with mythology. But, which of the four am I?"

"You will be all of them temporarily, but you will always be the tiger. The other things are the grasses the tiger uses to distract the victim before the kill."

"I like the feeling of being a tiger," she said, with a coy smile.

Vlad laughed. "I'm sure you do and your plan to force Herbig to play along is sound."

"Where should I set my trap?"

"Spandau, it is not unusual for tourists to wander about in his area. There is a restaurant on the street level called the Fritz. His dossier says he lunches there every day. Let's have dinner and talk of happier things. You can study the file tonight."

"Agreed, but first tell me, what do you think will attract his attention?"

"I assure you, with your ample bosom you will have no problem attracting his attention."

"Why is it always about breasts?"

"Because my dear, it just is. More vodka?"

"Please."

SUITING UP

Berlin

Saying goodbye to Vlad was harder than she'd expected. It felt like preparing to jump into a firefight, knowing death was just a bullet away.

At Berlin's Schönefeld Airport she breezed through customs without leaving a ripple. What was different from her arrival in Moscow, was that she greeted by a throng of noisy reporters who had been tipped off that the Happy Widow of Ibiza was arriving by private jet. Vlad primed the pump by arranging for her driver to meet her with a large Anita Franco sign.

She struggled through the crush of men, camera flashes, and rude questions to the driver who spoke English saying, "Welcome to Berlin, Señora Franco. Your escape is just outside."

"Thank you, and where are you taking me?"

He tucked the sign under his arm took her luggage and escorted her to the door where they lost the crowd. "Mr. Mogilevski has arranged a suite for you at the Ackselhaus Hotel. There will be a car for you as well, Señora."

As soon as she was sitting comfortably in the back of the limousine, he passed a wrapped package through the privacy window. "I was instructed to give you this."

"Thank you."

As he pulled away Anita tore off the paper and found a wooden box weighing about two pounds.

Without opening it she knew what it was. "How did he manage all of this so quickly?"

"We received our instructions shortly after you arrived at his castle, Señora."

She smiled at the mention of the castle. "That was very kind of him. What car will I be looking for?"

"It is a black Mercedes S-Class sedan, Señora. If you call the concierge, he will bring it up for you. You will find maps and directions in the glove box."

"Perfect." He raised the barrier and Kat watched Berlin pass by her window in silence, holding the box on her lap like a precious treasure. They drove up the peaceful tree lined Belforter Str. and, finding a scooter and delivery van parked in the drop off zone, stopped in the street.

He walked around to her door. "I am sorry, Señora. If you wouldn't mind getting out here, I will bring your luggage in."

"Thank you. This is a charming place. I must tell Mr. Mogilevski how perfect everything is."

"Before you go, Señora Franco, I was instructed to inform you that while you are here, we will never be far away. Should you see me again, please ignore me."

"Of course. And please tell your companions that I am very grateful."

She walked into the shaded entrance of the upscale boutique hotel in Prenzl'berg, a very trendy neighborhood of Berlin.

As she entered the lobby she was greeted again in English by the trim and very formal middle-aged man behind the desk.

She replied in German. "I'm sorry, I don't speak English well. But I am quite comfortable with German."

"My compliments Fräulein. You must have learned it here in Berlin. Your accent is very good. I am also pleased to say that the suite you requested is ready for you as is the car you requested."

He handed her a registration card and a pen. "When you wish to use it, just call the desk and we will bring it to the front."

"Thank you." She signed and put the pen down.

"Here is your key and we hope you enjoy your stay with us, Señora Franco." When he made the reservation, Vlad had insisted that she be made very comfortable.

"I'm sure I will." She was escorted to her suite by the bell captain. "This is lovely, thank you," she said, as she tipped the man.

When a soldier is in the field there is little time for rest, so while she had a chance, she decided to take an hour. The moment the door was shut she stripped off her clothes and climbed into bed.

Part 5

28

SPANDAU RECON

Berlin

She was up an hour later as if she'd set an alarm. She showered to wash off the effects of travel, then dressed in jeans and a light blouse.

The box was on the desk and it was time to see what was inside. It contained a SIG Sauer P938 Nightmare. Aptly named, the pocket-size 9 mm semi-automatic shared the space with four extended 7-round magazines.

Anita took it out and studied it. It weighed just 16 ounces and fit in her hand nicely. She slid in a clip and chambered a round, then ejected it, pulled out the clip and checked the safety. It was easy to operate with her thumb.

What a lovely present, thank you, Vlad.

She returned the ejected shell to the magazine and slid it back into place. Satisfied, she dropped it in her purse and snapped it shut.

The next step was to do some reconnaissance in Spandau. She called down to have her car brought to the door. The Mercedes looked brand new and was quite comfortable. In the glove box, she found a map of Berlin/Spandau and the instructions to get to Herbig's building.

The Spandau Arcaden was in a busy commercial part of town, lacking the charm of Berlin's Prenzl'berg neighborhood. She parked near his office and opened his dossier to read it through again.

Information gleaned from wiretaps and surveillance gave a detailed picture of the man and his routine. He would arrive at the office 7:30. Out for lunch at 12:15 and return at 1:00 pm, then leave for the day at 5:30.

Occasionally, he would be away from the office attending to business all over the continent, but this week he had no travel plans.

His only regular contact with Petrus was a standing Friday morning briefing by phone. If something came up, he would call Petrus regardless of the hour.

For those occasions when a suitable subject became available for Petrus there was a special protocol. Herbig would phone a private number to ask if he could bring over a 'house guest'. Herbig would deliver her to the country estate, a secluded compound near Werneuchen. There they would sit down for a leisurely cup of tea while they waited for the host to arrive. The tea would be drugged. The woman would awaken to find herself chained in a dungeon, ready for an evening of horror.

The information in the report was extremely unsettling and she needed to clear her head and calm down. It didn't seem to matter what she did though; she couldn't put it out of her mind.

Kat wanted to see him up close, to bring the troll out from under the bridge, and expose him for the pathetic, weakling he was. She needed to hear him cry out in fear before she killed him. Anita demanded it.

She studied the patio of the Fritz and the little pedestrian mall beside it.

After a moment's reflection, she settled on the presentation of Anita, the tethered goat, then headed back to her hotel.

She was calmer after the coffee break and decided to go shopping. She found an exclusive little designer shop that had the perfect things to wear to make the goat irresistible.

She also found an international bookstore and bought a foreign language best seller to help with the staging and then returned to the hotel. Just as she stepped through the hotel door it began to rain. It seemed to match her mood exactly.

THE BRINGER OF DEATH

Spandau, Germany

The next morning was also overcast, another day with the threat of rain. Even so, it was very warm which suited her purpose. She donned her new clothes as if she was dressing for battle, though it was far from body armor.

She stepped into a pair of sleek cream-colored cotton pants that accentuated her long legs. She slipped on an exquisite Egyptian cotton blouse the color of vanilla ice cream. It was so light that it practically floated across her body as she moved.

With golden bangles on her wrists and hoops in her ears, she tied her silky black hair back with a creamy white bow. With just a hint of eye shadow and deep red lip-gloss she completed her battle dress and stood back to assess the effect in the full-length mirror.

That works, I think.

She practiced her most engaging smile, though smiling was the last thing she wanted to do. Once again, she took the SIG from her purse and checked the action. She released the magazine and ejected the bullet from the chamber. When she was satisfied, she reloaded the bullet, reinserted the magazine and chambered the round.

With the safety on, she put it back in the shoulder bag. One last look in the mirror, turning this way and that.

Thinking she looked like a high-priced call girl Kat couldn't believe that she was going out like that. But if she was going to get anywhere near Petrus, the bait had to be ripe.

She called down to have her car brought round, picked up her new book and took the stairs to the lobby. The paparazzi had camped outside on the street, banking on a return engagement and she didn't disappoint, causing a minor sensation as soon as she stepped into their viewfinders.

She crossed the wide pedestrian walk like a movie star at a premier, providing them with a view that was sure to sell papers and videos.

She ignored them as she slid gracefully behind the wheel. The car was surrounded by frantic men with their clicking cameras, but her mind was focused on the mission to the exclusion of everything else. She placed the book and purse on the seat next to her. After accepting the ten Euros she offered, the valet closed the door for her and she drove away.

She had no way of knowing that Petrus was aware that she was in town and had already left instructions for Herbig to bring her to him.

The book she'd selected was an important prop, a Spanish translation of a novel by a renowned German author. To succeed, she felt she had to give Herbig as many visual clues as possible to encourage him to recognize her and spirit her away to her doom.

Returning to the area she had scoped out earlier, she left the car in a multi-level parking garage, but before venturing out, she checked the SIG one last time.

Oh please! Stop fussing, as she looked in the mirror to reapply her lip-gloss. You are ready for this.

She tossed the tube into her bag and was about to leave the car when saw the stress in her eyes and realized that lip-gloss wasn't going to hide that. She shut her eyes and took a few long breaths to calm down.

You are Anita, you're ready for this, so get on with it! Sunglasses weren't necessary, but she put them on anyway.

It was a short walk along the narrow pedestrian mall that separated the office building from the Berlin-Spandau train station.

She took a patio table with an umbrella in front of the restaurant. There was a light breeze that tossed her hair over her shoulder and tugged at the buttons making her blouse flutter provocatively. Once again, she had to force herself to relax and breathe.

A young waiter arrived at her table. "A cappuccino and pastry, whatever you have"

"Of course, Fräulein."

Her hands were rock steady as she opened Robert Musil's novel. She turned to the first page and began reading The Man Without Qualities.

Time passed slowly. Her second cappuccino had gone cold while the pastry she'd been ignoring was attracting the attention of a pair of hungry sparrows. She was relaxed enough to smile as she got into the book.

A honking horn brought her eyes up momentarily. She lay the book down against her chest and glanced at her watch. The female sparrow flew away, but the hungry male would not be put off. "Typical," she said.

It was a quarter past twelve. Picking up her book again she caught a movement out of the corner of her eye. A quick glance to the side confirmed it. Show time, she thought, going back to the book.

He noticed her at once and was surprised that his quest had been so effortless. Casually, he took the table next to hers. Had he done this so often that there was no mystery left, she wondered? She almost laughed thinking, look who's talking about the loss of mystery!

She read the same sentence for the third time before he spoke. Trying out his limited Spanish he said, "You have an admirer."

"Excuse me?" she said, looking at him over her book.

He pointed to the sparrow, "It will ..., how do you say it ..., take your pastry if you are not careful."

She briefly turned her attention to the little bird before returning to her book. As if that was his invitation, the sparrow hopped onto the table and broke off a crumb. Anita had to smile now.

"He is very bold," she answered in German, and with a casual glance looked over at Herbig. "How is it that you knew to address me in Spanish?"

"It was the book you are reading. A Spanish translation."

"You are very observant."

"I try to be." His smile was sly and suggestive. "I wanted to say that it is hard to blame the little fellow when so tantalizing a morsel sits within his grasp."

She shot an accusatory glance his way and asked, "Are you referring to the pastry, or to me?"

"Ah ..., I have been caught. I won't apologize for it though. I am happy to say that though I am old, I am not yet dead."

His voice was reedy and higher than she expected.

I'd always imagined that trolls were bigger with a growly baritone voice.

"Obviously," she said, positioning the book to obstruct his view.

"Admiring beautiful women has always been my weakness."

He was just as his pictures had shown. His pinched face narrowed from his high cheekbones to his jutting chin. What remained of his hair was long and slicked back behind his rather large ears, held in place with grease. His pale grey eyes were cruel and devoured her through thick, horn-rimmed glasses.

She had no delusions about what he was thinking. He wanted to watch as Petrus raped, tortured, and killed her. The thing that she found particularly disturbing was that she was going to let him try.

"May I ask you something?"

"I suppose," she said, guardedly.

"Your German is very good."

"Thank you." Laying the book against her chest again she smiled as if she enjoyed the compliment.

"So why you are reading that book in the Spanish translation?"

"I am more comfortable in my own language. I find that Spanish is more romantic."

"A matter of opinion." He paused. "I must confess, Señora Franco, that I am surprised to find you here, so close to my office."

"Ah," she removed the sunglasses. "I thought that by coming away from Prenzl'berg I would avoid being recognized."

"Oh, this meeting would have happened no matter where you were. I was prepared to spend the rest of the day searching for you."

"I don't understand," she said, genuinely alarmed.

"I am an investigator. A very wealthy client commissioned me to locate you and invite you to visit him at his estate."

"Oh, how odd. Well thank him for the invitation but I'm not interested."

"I hope you will reconsider; he has become intrigued by your story and would very much like to meet you."

"As flattering as that sounds, I'm afraid it is out of the question. Now if I could just get back to my book."

"Señora Franco, you are famous for your attraction to wealthy single men. My client is exceptionally wealthy, and he thought you might be interested in a mutually beneficial introduction."

"Uh hah," she said, "people have written such awful things about me. You should know that you can't believe everything you read."

"I don't mean to offend, but seeing you dressed as you are, suggests to me that there is more truth in the written word than you are prepared to admit."

"But I am offended, Herr ..."

"Herbig, Karl Herbig at your service. Do you know the story of the scorpion and the frog?"

"Do you really intend to tell me a story?" she asked.

"I do, if only to prove my point."

"Fine. No, I have not, and I hope it is short."

"The scorpion needed to get across a wide river. He saw a frog in the shallows, so he asked it to carry him across. The frog said, 'I will not because if I did you would sting me, and I would die.'

The scorpion pointed out how absurd that would be. 'If I were to do that,' he said, 'we would both drown. I promise that I will not sting you and we will reach the other side in safety.'

The frog said, 'Very well, get on and I will take you across.'

The scorpion hoped on his back and they set off. As they approached mid-way the scorpion stung the frog and as they sank into the depths the frog asked, 'Why did you sting me? Now we are both going to die.' The scorpion replied, 'It is in my nature.'"

"What a sad little story. So, you think I am the scorpion."

"It is simply an observation."

"I see. So, it is inevitable that I meet your client because it is in my nature."

"Exactly."

"But your story suggests that my nature will carry me to my death. Under the circumstances I don't think I can accept an invitation from a stranger."

"I assure you that my client is only interested in the pursuit of pleasure."

"Why do I feel like I have suddenly become the frog?" He shrugged his shoulders with his palms turned upwards. "What is this estate like?"

"Werneuchen is magnificent. Just seeing it is worth the drive. It was the hunting lodge once owned by an infamous Chancellor of Germany. It will be a thrill like none other, of that I am certain."

"This Chancellor, what was his name?"

"Adolph Hitler, he entertained special guests there during the war. My client, Delph Petrus, restored it to its original beauty."

"It sounds impressive but let me think about it."

"He is a very generous man," he said, taking out his cell phone and pressing speed dial. "You would find it a most rewarding experience, I promise you." He raised the phone to his ear. "Do you have a car, Señora Franco?"

"Yes."

"Wonderful, if we take yours then you will be able to leave whenever you wish."

She had strung it out as far as she dared, it was time to give in and accept. "Alright, I ..."

He held up a finger and spoke into the phone, "Hello, Herr Petrus, it is Herbig. I have found her."

"So soon?"

"As it happened, she was just around the corner."

"Then bring her to my estate. I have some business to attend to and will be along as soon as I am free. In the meantime, see that she is entertained."

"I will, sir," he said, and put the phone away. "He has some business to complete in Berlin first. We are to go ahead, and he will join us in time for tea."

"Then I'll have time to go back to my hotel to change."

"But you are perfectly exquisite as you are," he said, "The lodge is very casual."

AT THE POINT OF A GUN

Werneuchen

Throughout the trip he prattled on about the estate and the further they went the more effusive, and creepy he became. Nearing Werneuchen she interrupted him to asked, "Is it much further?"

"We're almost there." She noticed the change in his tone and she had a horrible feeling that his plan had changed. "It's just on the other side of the village."

Nervously he readjusted himself in his seat so that he was facing her. She could tell that he had given over to his obsession as he stripped her naked with his eyes. They were nearing the Lidl supermarket at the far eastern edge of the village. "Pull into the mall."

"What is it?"

"Keep away from the other cars and stop."

"Why, is there something wrong?"

"Don't ask questions, just do as I say." He drew a Phoenix HP25A .25 semi-automatic pistol from a shoulder holster. She gasped with surprise and looked suitably frightened. "Why do have a gun?"

"It occurred to me that Petrus enjoys the cream while I merely look on and I am tired of it."

"What are you talking about?"

"Give me your cell phone."

"You're not taking me to see your friend, are you?"

"I have changed my mind. You will pleasure me instead."

"I beg your pardon?" Her gun was useless now, he would certainly shoot her if she tried to use it. She removed the phone and gave it to him. "What do you want from me?"

"A little cooperation, that's all."

"But ..."

"A-a-a, you will thank me for this. I am prepared to save you from the certain and terrible death that waits for you behind those walls."

"Are you going to kill me?"

"No, I am giving you the opportunity to save yourself. But you must do something for me."

"What?"

"Simply give me the pleasure you have given to so many men. Do it for me without complaint and I promise I will set you free. If you refuse, then he can have you."

"You have done this before, haven't you?"

"You have only yourself to blame. You are after all the scorpion."

"No, actually I am something else entirely."

"What?"

She was so much stronger and quicker than him. She stripped the gun from his hand, took him by the back of his head and slammed his face into the dashboard. There was a resounding crack and he sagged. She put the car in gear and headed for the road.

He lifted his head with blood spurting from his nose and yelled, "Bitch!" His blood speckled her beautiful blouse with dots of red. "I am going to kill you."

"I doubt that," she said calmly. "And, you've ruined my blouse."

His eyes widened as his anger turned to fear. "What? Who are you?"

"I am your worst nightmare, Karl Holbïn."

Her hand shot out like the blade of an axe and slammed into his throat.

As he choked, she held the steering wheel steady with her thigh and reached for his jaw and the crown of his head. With a sharp and violent twist, she snapped his neck. He sagged again but this time he would not get up.

She pushed him back, unfastened his seatbelt, reached across for the door handle and flung him out onto the road. As she sped away, she took out her SIG, checked the safety, then placed it on her lap.

Okay, one down and one to go. The front gate is out now, so how the hell am I going to get into the lodge? The road was empty and driving alone helped her think.

Vlad had said they'd go in ahead of me and clear the way. How the hell will I know if they've done it?

She saw the wall ahead of her.

Holy fuck, that's gotta be ten feet tall! What the hell am I going to do now?

And an opportunity presented itself.

Hold on, what's that?

THE GARDEN WALL

Werneuchen Farm

Anita noticed a tractor path running alongside the western barrier into the forest. She pulled off the road and followed it for a couple of kilometers or more. Ahead she saw a setback in the wall with a gate large enough to accommodate farm machinery.

She stopped the car and got out to have a closer look.

I doubt that it's guarded, they would have heard me drive up if it was. So that's one plus. Downside, that thing is solid oak, I'd probably kill the car if I tried to drive through it. Okay, so I've got to get over it. How am I going to do that? Oh! She looked at the car and back at the gate. Yeah, that might work.

She moved the car up against it and tossed her shoes over to the other side. After buttoning her shirt up to the neck, she placed her gun at the small of her back in the waist band. The gun had a seven-round clip, without pockets there was no way to carry extra magazines and it was a sure thing that she'd need more than one clip. "Aw screw it!" she said, and put the purse strap over her head.

She hopped onto the roof of the car and, using it as a sort of springboard, jumped up and grabbed the top of the gate. Going with the momentum she pulled herself up and threw a leg over the top. Once comfortably perched on the top she scanned the area for danger. Spread out before her was a managed forest as neat as any city park and not a guard in sight.

She was about to drop down when she heard the faint sound of a helicopter.

Vlad's men? Christ, I hope so. The question is, are they coming or going?

She looked at her shoes and then the soft ground.

So those would be totally useless on that. I'll just have to go bare foot.

She jumped, tucked, and rolled out onto the thick damp grass and came up running, heading for the trees.

Dropping to a knee she waited to see if she'd been spotted. She let a couple minutes go by before she set off again. Pacing herself, she ran toward the compound's center, keeping parallel to the tractor path.

The next obstacle was a large open pasture with a herd of rare Hungarian Grey cattle grazing in her way. Their huge black tipped horns were intimidating, and she hoped to hell that's all they were.

Walking slowly, she crossed to the far side then picked up the pace through another stand of trees.

This forest was deeper than the first. Before she cleared it, she made certain that she wasn't spotted before moving on. Her heart was pounding but her breathing was controlled.

PURSUING HIS OBSESSION

Heading to Werneuchen

Petrus never tired of his obsession with beautiful women and this one was going to be deliciously exciting. The

398

prospect of what was to come made him burn with anticipation.

He wrapped up his business for the day and headed down to his car. The four men who went everywhere with him weren't interested in his perversions. They would be elsewhere while he amused himself and thankful for it. The big Mercedes sped along the highway to Werneuchen in silence, but as they neared the village his phone chimed. "Yes?"

"Sir," his butler said, "we have been attacked."

"Attacked? By whom?!"

"It was terrible. The cook and I are lucky to be alive."

"Max! Who attacked you?"

"I could only see a little of what went on. They came out of nowhere, sir. It was so fast!"

Petrus tried to think of who would be foolish enough to attack him. He practically owned the police and his silent partner, Ahern Jäger, would have no possible reason to cross him. "Max tell me, damn you, who were they?"

"They were Russians."

"Russians!?"

"Yes, sir. They were wearing uniforms of the Spetsgruppa 'A'. They just appeared without warning. It was over so quickly. They killed them all, then loaded them into their helicopter and flew away."

"All of them?"

"Yes, sir, every man. The ones that surrendered were executed right out in front of the house. There is now just Hilda and me here, sir. I don't know what to do."

"Have they left?"

"Yes, I believe so."

"I am glad that you were spared, Max. I am very close now. I should be there in a few minutes. I want you and Hilda to remain where you are and wait for me. I may call for you, Max. If I do, see that you bring your knives. Do you understand me?"

"Yes, of course, sir."

He folded the phone and his head of security said, "Sir, did you say the Russians had taken the compound?"

"Yes, the Special Forces he said. All of the men are gone. They took their bodies and left. What do you make of that, Kastner? If they were after me, why leave before I got there?"

"It is a hoax, sir. President Putin would never send troops into Germany like that. It would be a declaration of war."

"Then who were they?"

"Someone who wants you to think it is the President?"

"Of course," he said, considering the implications. "That makes more sense. Then who would want to put ..., oh!" and then it came to him. "Very clever. That woman Herbig is bringing, Anita Franco, she must be a part of this. A distraction."

"But sir, everyone knows her, she's nothing but a common whore. Herbig must have checked her out before bringing her."

"You are right of course; it is a coincidence." Petrus called his butler back. "Max, has Herr Herbig arrived with a guest?"

"No, sir."

He ended the call then called Herbig's number. He let it ring until it went to voice mail. "This could be Mogilevski's

400

retaliation for California! Didn't he command a unit of Spetsgruppa "A"? And it was a woman who killed our people there."

"Yes."

Petrus shut his eyes and concentrated on the images he'd seen trying to picture Anita.

They had obscured the surveillance video but there were civilian photos. Then it hit him like a physical slap. "How could I have been so blind?"

"Excuse me, sir?"

"Franco, she must be the woman from California. That bitch works for Mogilevski. I thought he wasn't worth the trouble, obviously I was wrong. I should have expected some form of retaliation, but this? This is war."

"Sir, we should return to Berlin."

"No! He would have sent someone to the office as well. Not a force perhaps, but maybe a sniper, or a bomb. If he set up such an elaborate plot to get his assassin inside Werneuchen, then he would have planned for that as well.

"Herbig will have the woman under control. She will be expecting that her people have cleared the way for her, so she won't try to do anything until she is at the house."

"But sir, she may have already taken him out. I think it would be wise to return to Berlin."

"I can't imagine a woman turning the tables on Herbig. We will go in and prepare our welcome."

"As head of your security, Sir, I must insist ..."

"Your mercenaries failed. Will you fail me too?"

"But ..." Kastner saw the warning signs and changed his mind. "No, Sir."

"Good." The men exchanged looks, which Petrus chose to ignore. They drove through the village and came across a police investigation blocking the roadway. Petrus said, "Just drive around it."

"But Sir, the police are flagging us down," his driver told him, and stopped near the barricade.

The officer came over and knocked on the driver's window and before he rolled it down Petrus opened his window. "What is the problem here?"

"I'm sorry, but you can't go through, you'll have to go around."

"We are just going to the lodge, surely you can let us pass."

"Oh, it is you Herr Petrus. There has been a murder, sir. We found a man in the road. Someone just dumped his body here."

"How did he die?"

"It appears that he may have fallen out of a car."

"Have you identified him yet?"

"Sir, I am not permitted to ..."

"You are obligated to do whatever I tell you to do. Quickly, who it is!"

"His name was Karl Herbig, sir."

"Herbig?"

"Did you know him?"

Petrus ignored his question. "When did this happen?"

"We received the call twenty minutes ago."

"Has there been any trouble further up the road?"

"No sir, we have had no reports of anything. Have you something you would like to report?"

"Hurry, move the barricade and let us pass."

"But ..."

"Do it and be quick about it!"

The barricade was moved aside "You were right, the woman has done this."

"It would also appear that she is an experienced assassin. It would be safer to turn back to Berlin."

"I said no!" he repeated, irritably. "She is quite good, but she will fail. You will see to that, yes?"

"Sir, if she has killed Herbig, we must assume that she will be waiting for you at the house."

"Even if that were possible, are you telling me that you afraid of one woman?"

"But ..."

"If Kastner tells me to turn around once more," he said to the guard in the jump seat, "shoot him." The guard drew his weapon and pointed it at his superior.

"Now, Max would have called if someone had entered the house." His chief of security did not look happy. "I will not be beaten by a fucking woman. The car is bullet proof. We are going in. If we draw fire, you will know where she is and will deal with her."

In the chilled silence that followed, Petrus began to formulate a plan.

"Alright, this is what we will do. When we get to the house, send two men to the farm. They are to tell Hans that if he sees her, he is to do nothing, understand? He is to let her pass."

"Yes, sir."

"Then have them hurry back and join us inside."

At the entrance to the estate, the driver pressed the button to open the gate then drove up to the house. While

Petrus waited in the car with the security chief, the men from the front seat drove off in the utility vehicle to deliver the message. When they returned ten minutes later, they joined the others at the door.

"Had he seen the woman?"

"No, sir."

"Alright, we are going inside. Kastner, lead the way." Cautiously they entered the house and checked it carefully. Max and the cook were in the kitchen and said no one had entered the house.

Surrounded by his men Petrus continued to his office where he laid out his plan for the ambush. "Remember, when I call you out you are to restrain her; that is all. I want her alive."

"You," he pointed to one of the men, "see to it that the cameras are all working, and the system is recording everything. I want to have something to show Mogilevski when we take him. I want him to see what I have done to his whore assassin before I kill him."

"Yes, sir."

"This is just the beginning. I will rebuild my force stronger than ever. No one will ever cross me again."

A FARMER'S REGRET

Werneuchen Farm

It had taken time to cross the fields and go through the woods. The tractor path eventually brought her to the original farm buildings.

Built like an ancient fortress, the brown brick farmhouse was linked to the barn and several sheds with a high wall enclosing a large courtyard.

The air was filled with the sweet smell of freshly mowed grass and cow manure.

Anita saw a portal in the wall with a low wooden gate. She moved carefully up to it and peeked over the top. Except for the chirping of songbirds, the crickets, and the clucking of chickens, all was still and serene.

The barnyard was paved with cobblestones, wet from a recent rain. Where was the farmer?

She heard a new sound. Someone was hammering on metal. She moved to get a better view. The sound was coming from the largest of the sheds. The doors stood open and, in the gloom, she saw movement. She could make out the shape of a man working on a tractor.

Suddenly a bright light from a welding torch made her shield her eyes.

The man was thoroughly engrossed in what he was doing, and she decided she would just let him be.

As she was about to move on, a vehicle stormed up the gravel road and through a carriage pass into the courtyard. Two men in dark suits and carrying machine guns emerged. The farmer came out wiping his hands with a dirty red rag. They exchanged a few words, then they argued. The argument ended abruptly, the men got back into the truck and drove off.

The farmer stood there glaring at them until they were out of sight. He tossed the rag on the ground and hurried back into the shed. When he appeared a moment later, he had a double-barreled shotgun cracked open in the crook of his arm. He fed two shells into the barrels then with the expression of a man determined to prove something, snapped it shut and headed to the gate.

She backed away looking over her shoulder, judging the distance to the end of the wall. There was no time to run. She was only a few meters away as his hand took hold of the latch, flipped it up and pulled the gate open.

He spotted her the instant he stepped out and was raising his gun to shoot, but she had already taken aim.

The little 9 mm SIG sounded sharp in that pastoral setting. It echoed off the walls in the yard sending chickens scurrying away, pigeons took to the air, and the man collapsed. There was a bloody hole where his eye used to be.

Someone must have heard the shot.

She ran.

Beyond the corner of the wall she saw the track the truck had taken. It had to lead to the house, so she followed it.

The track was lined on both sides with giant white oaks, their canopies were so wide and full that they merged one into the other like a gigantic hedge. She sprinted until she came to a fork where the dirt path ended and the paved driveway began.

The muddy tire tracks headed off to the left and she could just see the roof line of a mammoth house. She covered most of the distance running hard, then did the last fifty meters crouched down across the rain-soaked lawn, taking cover behind the hedges surrounding the house.

Drawing close, she stopped to watch and listen. Vlad's Special Forces must have done their job to allow her to get this far. She would be grateful to them until the day she died. Which, by all accounts, was probably going to be today unless she was unbelievably lucky.

The lodge was huge and strangely familiar. Then she remembered seeing it in a documentary of the Second World War containing footage from home movies. In that particular film clip, Hitler stood at that huge doorway mugging for the camera with Eva Braun and a King shepherd at his side.

The main structure was brick on a field stone foundation. Above, pale ochre stucco filled the spaces between dark oak timber frames like the cream in a Black Forest cake.

Tall dormers jutted out from the red tiled roof with heavy timber balconies and flower boxes filled with carnations. The balconies were the perfect cover for snipers.

But there were none.

She circled the mansion and found the truck the men had used and parked next to it was a black limousine.

It's still warm, so Petrus must have just arrived and he's inside. Alright, what now? He's got at least two men with him? Where the hell are they?

She scanned the length of the house looking for some sign of cc cameras but saw none.

Maybe Petrus isn't concerned about trespassers. Yeah right. They must be hidden up there in the woodwork, so they've gotta know that I'm here now. They'll be waiting for me. But where?

She leaned against the stone wall to think but there wasn't really anything to think about. She had to keep moving. She pushed away from the wall and headed for the door

Crouching low she moved quickly to the front door and stepped up to the landing.

The door had been left ajar.

Oh, now wasn't that kind of them.

407

She slowly pushed on it leading with her small gun.

I wonder if I'll feel the bullet when it hits me? Probably not. I've heard them say that you don't hear the shot that kills you.

She entered the house barefoot and silent.

Now how the fuck would they know that?

TO DIE FOR

The Petrus Mansion

The great paneled hall with the vaulted ceiling spanned the width of the house. Twelve feet above her head was a gallery that surrounded the hall. She waited, but no one popped up.

She walked to the center of the huge open space. On the left was a large room. It was too big to see it all from her position, so tentatively she crept closer to peek inside.

It looked empty.

She moved through the arched portal and stepped into the ballroom. The walls were paneled with caramel colored fruitwood. Every panel was adorned with either an elaborately carved hunting scene in bas-relief, or a beveled gold marbled mirror.

Now that is one big fireplace, she thought, looking at the massive fieldstone construction directly across from the door.

Moving into the room she saw what lay beyond a second smaller arch to her left. It was a short hall leading to another smaller room.

She had to get closer to see inside.

408

Her heart was drumming so loudly, she was sure they'd be able to hear it.

Leading with her shoulder she crept forward, her lips pressed tightly together, her gun held up in both hands and tight to her body. With each step, she could see more of the room.

There was a man sitting behind a huge desk.

At his back was a wide bank of windows. With the backlight, all she could make out was his silhouette.

Is that Petrus or one of his guards?

Confirmation came quickly.

"Ah hah, here you are at last, Anita. I was beginning to think you weren't coming." He appeared to be relaxed, unconcerned by the threat she posed.

"Look at you ..., my assassin." He stood up. "I must say, Anita, you are even more beautiful in person." He was trying to distract her while reaching for something on the desktop.

"Stop moving," she warned him.

"Do you honestly think you will be able to kill me now? Put away the gun, you've already lost."

"From where I stand, I don't see it that way. Keep your hands where I can see them."

"As you wish," he said smoothly, and raised them to shoulder height. She moved closer to the mark he'd made on the floor. "That is far enough I should think."

She stopped.

Now why would he say that?

She looked down and saw a chalk mark on the floor then quickly looked around her for a threat she had missed. She was just outside the arched hall; a step to the right would give her cover if they popped out. She took that step and put her back to the wall.

"I couldn't help noticing that you left poor Karl on the road. He was very useful to me you know. I shall miss him."

"Trust me, you're not going to live long enough to miss anything."

"If that were true, I would already be dead. No, I am afraid, my dear, unless you put your weapon down you will die long before I do."

"Move away from your desk."

"Why don't you just give up now?"

"Move!"

"My men are all around you, waiting for my command. It's hopeless." He began to lower his hands.

"So, give your command."

"I would rather deal with you myself," Petrus said venomously.

"Oh, Gelenko gave me a pretty good idea of what you have in mind."

"Ah hah, you killed Gelenko as well. How kind of you, you saved me the trouble of doing it myself."

"And the three thugs he brought with him; so, if it's all the same to you, I'd rather pass on that and take my chances with your guards."

"Very well then," he said, then shouted, "Now!"

The panels surrounding her swung open and four men jumped out. Their guns were out but they expected her to just give up and they hesitated.

Anita didn't, swinging around she fired four times.

Her response was so fast and unexpected none of them had the time to react. Each bullet she sent out was a kill shot and the men fell back into their hideaways.

Petrus was utterly stunned. He had never seen anyone move so fast. She reached into her purse and took out a fresh clip, pressed the release button and let the first one drop to the floor.

The reload was also quick and smooth, so quick he wasn't aware of her actions at all. She had one in the chamber and seven more ready to follow it.

"No, that is impossible." He had assumed that he was infallible, that something like this could never happen to him. But this woman had obliterated that notion in the space of an afternoon.

"I'd say we are alone now, unless you have someone else stashed away in the wall somewhere?"

Petrus reached for something on his desk and she fired. Her bullet took three fingers from his outstretched hand.

He screamed in pain and snatched his hand away.

"Why Herr Petrus," she said, sounding surprised. "I believe you are bleeding. Come away from the desk." Covering the stubs of his missing digits with his other hand he cautiously obeyed.

"Keep coming, that's right, out here onto the dance floor." She moved back as he approached her, the nerves in the back of her neck were tingling. "Keep coming, I want you out here, in the middle." Her instincts told her someone else was in the house.

She looked behind and to her left but saw no one. "Where are they?"

"Where are who?"

"The others you have hidden away."

"There is no one else."

"I don't believe you. I can sense them." She moved back and to her left until she was up against the wall. From there she could see the whole room and part of the hallway. "Call them out."

He was bewildered. "Why don't you just kill me and be done with it?"

"I said, call them out."

"It is what you came for, isn't it, to kill me? Do it! Do it!"

"I began by putting a huge hole in Gelenko's shoulder before I shot out his knees. Consider yourself lucky that I started with your fingers." She aimed lower. "Come closer," she beckoned him with her gun. "Keep coming to me while you can still walk." He was now standing facing her in the middle of the room.

Reverting to English she said, "For the last time call them out."

"Your English sounds American," he said, "You are good with languages. Very useful no doubt. I had assumed that Mogilevski's assassin would be Russian."

Aiming at his crotch she warned, "I won't ask you again."

"But you are American aren't you. That Special Agent in France that ruined the Vacon takeover. An officer of the law, aren't you? So, you aren't going to kill me after all, are you?"

"No?"

"American police don't kill their prisoners, yes? I must confess that it was very clever of you to blame the Russians."

"Will it be the right ball, or the left?" she said.

He covered his crotch. "If you want to get out of here alive, perhaps we can come to some ..."

She interrupted him. "Okay, I'll choose. The right one I think and, by the way, your hand won't stop the bullet." Her finger moved to the trigger.

"No, no wait! Alright! I'll call them. I have to go back to my desk."

"I'll bet that if you call loud enough, they will hear you," she said.

"Alright. Hilda! ... Max! Come to my office now."

She didn't have long to wait. She heard a door open on the far side of the great hall, then the heavy sound of a man's flat shoes followed by the staccato of a woman's heels as they crossed the ornate canyon. They stopped at the entrance.

She looked over and in German she said, "Come in. All the way in where I can see you with your hands over your heads."

They obeyed and stopped facing their employer. The cook was a broad little woman in her forties with a puffy face and hard eyes. Her blond hair was wrapped in a tight braid around her head like a helmet. She leaned forward to meet Anita's eyes.

Max was a different story. He was tall and thickly built and glared furiously at her, clenching and unclenching his overlarge fists. He had the hands of a bare-knuckle boxer and the broken nose to complete the picture. His stiff collar looked like it was ready to pop, the only thing holding it back was the white bow tie.

"Hilda, move out so that I can see you," Kat said, but the woman didn't budge.

413

"What will you do now," Petrus asked.

"Hilda if you do as I tell you, there is a chance that you may live through this. Move, I said!" levelling the gun at them. "I won't ask again."

As she waited for the woman to obey, the butler performed a very clever bit of conjuring. A small, double edged throwing knife slipped from his sleeve into his hand and, with a smooth and powerful underarm swing, he launched the blade at her.

She fired as soon as she saw the movement, but she couldn't stop the knife. It struck her chest below the collar bone. The force of his throw buried the razor-sharp blade deep.

Her shot tore through the butler's neck snapping his spine and kept on going. The deformed projectile struck Hilda high on her braided helmet, opening a large hole going in and a larger one as it exited.

The braid instantly released as if it was spring loaded and the woman collapsed. But Max remained on his feet for a moment. Blood erupted from both sides of his neck.

He dropped to his knees, his head flopped onto his chest tipping him forward and he hit the floor with a resounding thud. Blood pooled around them and began to spread out across the floor.

Petrus was stunned. Failure was unacceptable and yet everyone he relied on had failed him.

Anita had fallen back against the wall; her hand instinctively went to the knife. The blade pivoted painfully, slicing god-knows-what inside. A big mistake. She cried out and let go. Her heart pumped like it would burst and her breathing became rapid and shallow.

414

Petrus regained control and began to smile as if what had just happened was the entertainment he'd been waiting for.

Anita's knees began to buckle so she slid down the wall slowly, easing herself to the floor.

"Two with one shot, with that knife in your chest," he said. "I must say, that was truly amazing."

"Shut up!" She focused on him and raised her gun.

He continued as if she posed no threat at all. "I admire your sense of economy. It appears though, Anita Franco, that my butler has killed you. It's a shame really, because I wanted the pleasure of doing that myself ..., eventually."

Anita knew he was right, she was dying. The only thing that was preventing her blood from gushing out was that the knife was acting like a cork. She tried to keep her eyes focused on him, but it was difficult, and the pain was remarkable. The gun suddenly became very heavy forcing her to lower to the floor. Her eyes fluttered and it looked as if she was about to pass out.

Petrus saw that as proof that she was harmless now and an opportunity to make her suffer. "Well perhaps I can still have some fun with his knife." He walked over to her and reached down for it. "Where shall I cut you now?" he said, as his hand came close to the handle.

Anita lifted the gun and fired, hitting him in the gut below the naval. "Woof!" he uttered, staggering back and falling to his knees.

Clutching at the wound with both hands he reeled back on his haunches and yelled obscenities at the ceiling. He looked down at the blood on his hands and the gushing hole. "You fucking-bitch!"

"Oh please, for god-sake will you shut up." She fired again, but she had little control now. That shot hit low on his shoulder and once more he reeled back and gasped for air. "Sounds like I may have nicked your lung that time," she said, letting the gun touch the floor. "Having difficulty breathing now, are you?"

He was, but he managed to say, "You fucking-cunt."

"Oh god, how I hate that word." She took a few deep breaths and lifted the gun up again. "I've nearly killed you. One more should do it. Hold still."

His fear of the inevitable was overwhelming. "No, ..., don't, don't, please!"

"I figured I would die here, but how could you ever think that you were going to survive?" Anita fired again. The effort caused her to close her eyes and she sank down further until she was lying on her side.

When she opened her eyes, he was still kneeling in front of her. The third hole was just to the right of his heart. That one had certainly pierced his lung as he coughed up a stream of frothy blood. "Fucking hell!" she whispered, "Why don't you just-die?"

He made a gurgling sound as he tried to form words she didn't want to hear.

"Oh yeah, that's gotta hurt. I wonder if there is one more in here."

Lifting the gun with a trembling hand she took aim at his head.

"Okay, this one is the kill shot. Are you ready for it?"

She tried, but she couldn't pull the trigger. The little 16-ounce gun was just too heavy now. Her arm hit the floor. She rested for a moment watching him wheeze up pink froth.

Too weak to speak aloud she carried the conversation in her mind.

You don't think I can do it, do you? Well, want to bet?

It didn't matter that he couldn't hear it, it wouldn't have made any sense to him at this point. She lifted the gun again, but she couldn't keep it steady.

"Do me a favor and hold still. Oh fuck! You know ... you may be right. I don't think I can." She put it on the floor beside her again and took a breath.

He tried to say something.

"Wow, I see you struggling there." She swallowed and took a few breaths before she could continue. "I should finish you off, but this little fucker's getting really heavy."

He opened his mouth. He might have said something, but whatever it was she didn't want to hear it. She made one last big effort to lift the gun. Her eyes closed just as she pulled the trigger. The gun jumped out of her hand and hit the floor.

When she opened them again Petrus was on his back with his cheek pressed against the floor in a pool of blood. His eyes were open and staring out over a cavity that used to be his nose.

She closed her eyes again and after letting out a short breath she said very quietly, "There," as if she had just finished a children's bedtime story she whispered, "all done now."

She felt like she was sinking into the floor.

I'm not Anita

She took a short breath,

I'm Kat.

The light through her eyelids grew darker as her world slowly faded to black.

29

WHEN YOU WAKE

Chojna, Poland

The first thing she felt was the warmth of the sun on her face. The song her father used to sing to her at bedtime when she was a little girl was playing in her dream … When you wake you shall have all the pretty little horses.

She struggled to open her eyes, but the room was so bright. She blinked and was back in the dream again … dapples and greys, pintos and bays ... at least she thought she was dreaming.

The man was dark and unfocused. Then, as her focus sharpened, she realized he was dark because his face was covered in black hair. She didn't think she was going to like him. It was like returning to her childhood, she dreaded meeting new men, friends of her uncle.

Her vision cleared enough for more detail. He looked to be fifty-ish with a full beard and long wild and curly black hair flecked with white. He looked evil. She was frightened and pulled away from him.

"Easy now," he said, his voice was soft and deep, but she didn't understand him or recognize the language, which only added to her fear.

He leaned over her and before she could turn away put his thumb on her eyelid and gently pushed it up. He flicked the beam of a pen sized flashlight in her eye, then nodded and made a rumbling sound in his throat. She became less concerned and more curious as he moved his hand to her other eye and repeated the process.

"Where am I?" she asked, reverting automatically to Spanish.

He shook his head. "Shush. You are safe now." he said. She wondered what language he was speaking.

He turned his attention to her chest and gently pulled the top of her gown away from her shoulder. She began to panic but he moved it just enough to see a large bandage taped to her skin. Easing the tape away he lifted the gauze to peek underneath and made another throaty rumbling sound.

She was determined to understand and be understood, so she tried again. "Are you a doctor?"

"It's alright easy now." His rumbling sounded soothing.

"Where am I?"

He put his finger to his lips. He gently pressed the tape back on her skin, replaced the gown, and lifted her wrist, put two fingers on her pulse and looked at his watch.

After a couple of seconds, he made more rumbling sounds and touched her forehead with the back of his hand. It felt surprisingly good, it was cool and soft. She was becoming calmer now, her breathing eased, and she began to remember things.

He nodded, turning to another man who, until now, she hadn't noticed. He had been sitting right beside her the whole time. "Her pulse is strong, there is no infection or fever and the wound is not looking red as it was yesterday."

the doctor said.

The man in the chair smiled. Who was he?

Kat moved her head to see him. She knew him. How did she know him? Then it came to her and everything else rushed in as if a dam had burst.

"Vlad? Is that really you?"

"Shush, I'm sorry my dear kitten, but we cannot use names here. And yes, it is me. The doctor said you are getting better."

"Was there any serious damage inside?"

Vlad translated the question and the answer. "He said there was some muscle damage. You'll have to take it easy for a month or two, but it will heal."

The doctor added, "There was a fair amount of internal bleeding, but we managed to stop that and irrigate the wound. It was very close. If she had been brought in a few minutes later we would not have been able to save her."

"What did he say?"

"That you were very lucky," Vlad said, deciding not to translate that, instead he said, "Thank you, Doctor. May I have a moment alone with my friend?"

The doctor nodded and left the room.

"How are you feeling?"

"Sore, but I guess since I am here, I'm going to live," she said. He smiled though the look of concern remained. "I'm a kitten now? The last time we talked I was a tiger."

"Only an endearment for the sake of the doctor, I assure you. You will always be a tiger. You must have terrorized those men before they died."

"Well, I hurt their feelings I suppose. Where are we?"

"This is Chojna, a village in Poland near the German border. We used it as a staging area for the raid because of that man," he said pointing in the general direction of the door.

"He is an excellent surgeon who owed a friend a debt. I thought it wise to take the precaution in case something happened to you and I am very glad that I did. I almost lost you."

"I guess I'm tougher than I look."

"Indeed, you are," he said.

"What happened?"

"You saw nothing?"

"I heard the helicopter flying away."

"I had hoped that they would be able to proceed without drawing any attention to their presence. I have had my men close to you since you left my house. But they were told not to interfere with your plan unless they saw that you were in immediate danger."

"I was told they were about to intervene when Herbig pulled his gun, but they were quite impressed by the way you dispatched him. Nicely done, it must have been quite a surprise for him."

"He was surprised alright. But how did they know what he was doing? I never saw a sign of them."

"A camera was installed in the dashboard. They saw everything. I was also informed that you have a very fine bosom."

"Gee thanks."

"Did he ever guess why you were there?"

"I didn't take the time to tell him, but I think he figured it out." She moved her hand to her shoulder and touched the spot carefully. "Did you lose anyone?"

"Happily, I did not. The uniforms confused his people. Their bodies were removed by helicopter and disposed of. They had just cleared the area when you went over the gate.

They timed the raid to be over before your ETA. You were quicker than they expected. As you were crossing the cattle field my spotters saw Petrus stopping near Herbig's body. You were nearly at the farmhouse when they drove in through the gate."

Kat said, "I saw two of his guards talking to the farmer."

"We have no idea why they did that."

"They told him to leave me alone. He ignored them, so I was forced to kill him."

"As I said, you are deadly. A small team returned to take you out of there. They were moving into the house as you fired your last shot." He pointed to her wound. "Who did that to you?"

"The butler did it."

"Ah hah," he laughed, "just like in the English murder mysteries."

"Your men saved my life."

"As they were supposed to do. I was told that the four men you killed didn't get off a shot. You are amazing, Katrina."

"He must have ordered them to take me alive. He really had his heart set on killing me himself."

"He was a pompous fool."

"I am in your debt now, Vlad."

"Nonsense, now we are even. It is getting late and I think we have overstayed our welcome. Let's see if you can get out of that bed and walk."

She pushed back the covers and sat up. She reached down with one foot and then the other then shifted her weight so that she was standing. Her ankles felt a bit wobbly so she grabbed the bed to steady herself.

"Careful. Do you need help?"

"No, I'll be alright. She took a few tentative steps. "Yes, I can do this. Where are my clothes?"

"I have placed them on the chair. I bought some things for you in town. I hope they fit."

"Thank you. I will see you outside in a couple of minutes."

"Of course."

She peeled back the bandage and had a peek at the doctor's handywork. The knife had made a clear incision about an inch and a half long.

That doesn't look too bad. Six stiches, neat too. Thanks doc.

She dressed and found Vladimir in the hall talking with the doctor. She approached and thanked the man with a kiss on the cheek.

"If you move, you should have your arm in a sling, otherwise you will tear out the stitches," he said in halting English, "Wait a moment and I will get you one." He fitted her with a simple fabric sling tied behind her neck.

"Thank you," she said, in Russian, kissed his cheek again then thanked him with a smile. He seemed to appreciate the gesture.

"Come now, we have a plane to catch," said Vladimir. A local man sat in a small car outside the clinic and drove them to Chojna's unsupervised airport. Vlad's business jet was waiting on the extended field with its engines powered up and ready to take off. As soon as they were aboard it sped down the runway and lifted into the air.

She sat quietly watching the world get smaller beneath them. When they levelled off Vlad said, "We go to Moscow, though I think you will not wish to remain there. Is there any place you would prefer?"

She thought about it. "The Nest was home, but I can't go back there now, because they think I'm dead. Hmm ... everyone thinks I'm dead. I don't know. I should probably call Devlyn to tell him what happened and see where I stand."

"Of course, you must do what you think is best. Your phone is in your purse." She began to reach for it, but she thought it through and stopped.

"I can't go back can I Vlad?"

"It would be unwise, Katrina."

"I should just let them all think I died." A small involuntary laugh slipped out. "It wouldn't be the first time."

"Just tell me where you would like to go."

"I haven't any idea." She looked out the window at that vast ocean of fluffy white clouds. "Maybe Rome. I lived there for a while."

"Your people would notice you there, Katrina. If I may suggest, what you need is peace and quiet, someplace where you have never been." He sat back, and they shared the view of the clouds. Then an idea came to him. "Of course."

"What is it?"

"Katrina, if you want to vanish then you must go where no one would think to look for you. I have a dacha in the Ukraine, it is peaceful, and the beach is beautiful. You would love it there."

"I couldn't impose on you any further, Vlad. You have done so much for me already."

"My dear, listen to me, you must take it. Having you there looking after the place would be doing me a favor."

"You are such a liar." He shrugged and smiled. She sat and thought about it. "Where is it?"

"On the Sea of Azov, near the town of Berdyans'k. It is a small cottage, but you should be comfortable there."

"What's it like?"

"It is at the end of the road on a sweeping peninsula that reaches far out into sea. Come November though, everyone leaves. If you stayed on you would be virtually alone out there all winter long."

"I don't think I would mind that." She thought about it for a while then smiled and said, "Yes, alright. I truly appreciate everything you have done for me, Vlad."

"It is a pleasure. Excuse me for a moment." He got up and went to the flight deck and spoke to the pilot. Kat felt the plane bank to the right as it changed course.

When Vlad returned, she asked, "We're going there now?"

"It is roughly the same distance to Berdyans'k as it is to Moscow. I will take you there first and get you settled. Your passport and bank cards are in your purse, so you will have no trouble entering the country. There are some nice shops in town. You can buy anything you need there. The house has running water, electricity and it is insulated against the cold.

"Unfortunately, there is only a wood stove for heat and during the winter you will have to keep it lit night and day." She looked dubious. "Don't worry, you will get the hang of it before the snows come, I have stocked plenty of firewood in the shed. Enough to keep you warm for two or three years.

There is also a steel cabinet with a digital lock by the door. It will be useful if you wish to store your valuables."

"Valuables?"

"You may need a weapon. I will supply whatever you want."

"You are a very sweet man Vladimir."

"Honestly, Katrina, I believe that you are the only one in the world who thinks that."

Epilogue

Berdyans'k, Ukraine

Kat fell in love with Vlad's dacha at first sight. The rest of the summer was restful, she made a few casual friends on the beach. She went into town to shop and picked up some comfortable winter clothing and dozens of good books. Then when everyone was gone, she settled into a solitary existence through the winter. She had been thinking about the past too much. There was so much pain there and she knew she had to let it go.

Each day got a little easier and every day she grew a little stronger, physically and mentally. She continued to grieve the loss of Harm and Deacon but at least with Harm she had wonderful memories to keep her company.

She began to think of her future and it didn't include spending the rest of her life as Anita Franco speaking Russian in the Ukraine. There had to be a way to go home again. Perhaps not the home she used to know but one where she could be herself.

That meant reaching out to someone, someone she knew well enough to be able to help her. That excluded Vlad, his world was Russian. She needed someone who had connections to her old life and there was only one person who might understand.

"Hello."

"Jesus Christ, are you fucking kidding me right now? I thought you were dead!"

"I nearly was but Vlad saved me. The thing is I'm trapped here Paul, I don't want to be Anita anymore I want my old life back, to have my real name again."

"I can't do that. I went off the reservation for you setting up that mission, as far as CI knows you were on your own. Hell, I can't even say that name aloud now. You died twice! You can't come back from that."

"But I thought ..."

"What? You think I could just snap my fingers and miraculously turn the clock back?! For Christ's sake, there's a stone in Arlington with your goddamn name on it. No! Whoever you say you are right now that's who you are. Live with it."

"But Paul, I can't live like this."

"Oh, let's get out the violins. You chose that mission. I told you it was suicide and you went right ahead and did it. Okay, you got the bad guy and you survived. I'm happy for you, I really am, but I can't help you now. It sucks being you."

"That's it?"

"Yeah, that's all there is."

"Well, at least you know I'm alive. That's something."

"If you say so. Look, I don't want to be a dick about this. Maybe when things cool off, I can work something out.

But listen to me ... if we go that route there will be strings attached. OK? Don't come to me unless you're prepared for that."

"What strings?"

"When the time comes, we'll let you. That's all I'm going to say"

"But Paul ..."

"Goodbye Anita." He hung up the phone.

"I'm not Anita," she said, "I'm Kat goddamn you, I'm Kat!"

Her life continued in solitude, with infrequent trips to Berdyans'k for groceries, books, and newspapers. On one of those trips in late January she picked up a copy of the International Herald Tribune. While she was getting a gas fill-up, she opened the paper and an article on page four caught her eye.

Canadian scientist Dr. Deacon Loats invents the Loats Fuel Cell

The revolutionary solar charged fuel cell will alter the way industry uses energy worldwide and promises to solve the deepening energy crisis. Already in production in the US, the fuel cell has begun to have a global impact as developing countries are licensed to produce the energy cells for domestic use.

The Cleveland Foundation, a charitable organization run by Dr. Loats, distributes the fuel cell to the population in those countries at no cost.

"Wow. Well, good for you Deacon. You've done an amazing thing for the world." She folded the paper and stuffed it in her shopping bag.

I guess he's going to be a gazillionaire after all. I hope he enjoys it.

When she got back to the dacha, she looked at the article again then dropped the paper into the kindling box and went out for a walk.

****

The End

About the Author

     Hugh Russel lives with his wife Cheryl in the Hills of Mulmur, a beautiful part of the Niagara Escarpment, a hundred kilometers northwest of Toronto. Hugh is and always has been a story teller no matter what the medium. In addition to his writing he is a musician, painter, illustrator, and sculptor. His professional career has spanned over 50 years. Hugh's sculptural works, both monumental and small, are cast in bronze and have been added to several private, academic, and corporate collections around the world, including Vatican City.

Made in the USA
Middletown, DE
27 October 2020